The Woes of Osroes

By Sa'ad Ojeili

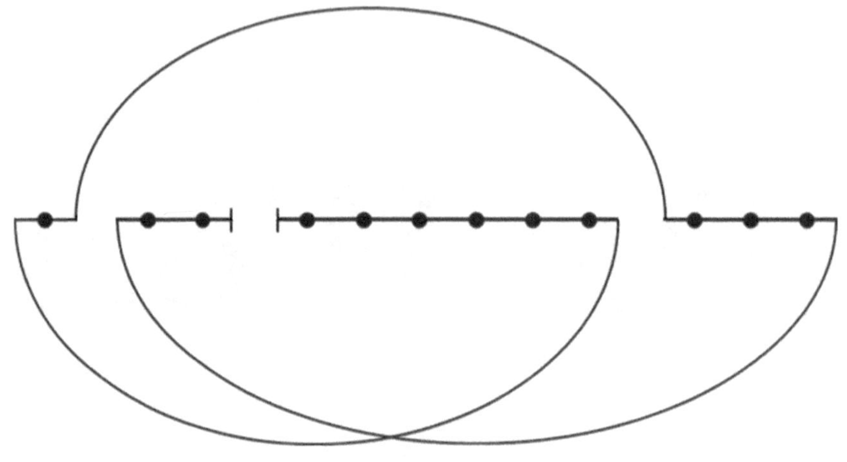

Al Raqqawi

I

Acknowledgment

I acknowledge that the list of peoples mentioned or otherwise below can never do justice to the actual direct or indirect contributions that shaped this book over the many years. I acknowledge that a true list would be as long as the contents of the book itself, if not longer.

I would like to acknowledge first and foremost my ever-supportive family: my brothers, Ibrahim and Omar, my mother, Nada, who is my number one supporter, my father, Madyan, who is the bedrock to everything I do, my stepmother, Hiba, my grandmother, who is a fountain of creativity, Nawal, my grandmother who is a fountain of resilience, Hala. I would like to acknowledge the uncles, the aunts, the cousins and extend my gratitude to a root system that keeps this one tree fed and grounded.

During my formative writing years, there are those who encouraged this form of expression in me. I would like to acknowledge the English teachers who taught me terrific books like The Outsiders, Silas Marner, The Merchant of Venice... and more. I would also like to acknowledge my middle school friends, Mohannad, Marawan, Ahmed, Kapil, Ayeza, Batool... and again plenty more, who read Cirque Du Freak and A Series of Unfortunate Events alongside me.

In high school, I would like to acknowledge my closest friends, Mohammad, Jad, Rowaid, Faris, Rami, Medhat, Alaa, Jad, Abdullah, Obeidat, Abdulghani, Omar, Hazem, and so many more who at various stages encouraged my ability to write both poetry and prose. The list is truly endless and if I did miss any of you wonderful folk, please do forgive me.

At The University of Edinburgh is where I undertook this long and tumultuous journey to arrive at this piece of work. It was not an easy period for me. Nonetheless, I must acknowledge the supportive cast of John, David, Fred, Patrick, Simon, Ali, and more individuals who made an otherwise insufferable section of my life tolerable.

Things changed when I finally made it to London, where most of this book was written. First and foremost, I would like to acknowledge my jubilant flatmates: Boksmati, Emir, and Usman for making Chancery Lane a second home. I would also like to acknowledge the fantastic cast of colourful friends I made during my graduate studies: Rafia, Carmen, Pritam, Adam, Valentina, Celine, Tim, Nicola, Marta... and many that I have undoubtedly missed from this list.

Finally, and if only that were true, I would like to acknowledge all the people that encouraged me over the finish line over these past couple of years. Most importantly, I must acknowledge Asma for tirelessly editing this book and respecting me enough to both give me the time and the constructive feedback that turned all the illegible sentences into coherent ones. I would also like to acknowledge Ammar, Zarina, Wendi, Aditi, Agnes, Norah, and anyone else who spent even a moment reading any words written in this book. Fouz, a special thank you for pushing me towards the finish line and constantly reminding me that I ought to finish this seemingly endless book.

My acknowledgments are meaningless without recognising the love and support that Ala'a has provided me over these years. If a plant requires light to grow, then she shines brightest among all.

Chapters

WRITE WRITE WRITE WRITE WRITE WRITE

Part 1: The Last Spring
Yan Eadful

O how the wind blows, a whistling through the crevices, and reminder of the treachery of my own thoughts, that distil the characteristics of the benign actuality into elements of suffering. A harshness that teases you about past kindness and a coldness that mocks your yearning for warmth. And perhaps I am blessed to be afflicted by the mirage of nostalgia, if it were not for time's reaching hand spanning across and reducing castles to sand. Those structures, their might, a view from great heights, if only history did teach me about the consistency of delight. Why must the fleetingness of joy overshadow suffering's own impermanence? But no, it does not, for suffering is a constant, a shared struggle, an exertion of sorts, to create value from material. And exploitation, which lingers as a parasite, to leech off the value of one's suffering. Here I am, by the entrance, pondering whether I had contributed to escalating the suffering of others, and for my own gain at that.

How silly for a key to betray me and spawn a spiralling from which there is no recovery until I bend down to retrieve it? Unlocking doors it ought not, now it lays still in the deep groves of dilapidated oak tiles inviting more treachery in the form of physical exertion. I bent down to collect it, and there the apparent tile scratches invited my gaze. A stray cat, the likely culprit, but there were none around. Why would there be? A resident or two, the footsteps of a few, are enough to alarm larger creatures.

Metal against metal, the key against the lock, and not once had I considered whether I should enter or not. By then, it was too late, for I was one foot through the doorway. The office, from which I ran the publishing house, also served as my abode – a combination I wholly detested. Not only am I confined to the suffocating space, but I am to dwell in the filth of degrading desire that burdens my working day.

Each time I enter this arena, my eyes are met with towers of cabinets, each overflowing with untold stories. And there, each time, I would whisper to myself, "The tragedy of limited empathy," and then each time I would add to it, "The gift."

Enough stories for a lifetime or a hundred, and I am expected to read through each, not flippantly, but with careful regard to the nuance of common tales. Yet, I enjoy them singularly. Before I do so, I go about my routine setting my suit aside, one of two, and I undress until I am left in nothing but an undergarment. And, as if part of the routine, I collapse onto my bed and stare down at the deflation of my own physicality. The old folks emerge, at the forefront of my mind, and I spend a great deal of time wondering whether they were as oblivious as I am at my age. How did they derive an unquestionable purpose? And if it were questioned, then how were they not enchanted by the sirens that drag you to the depths of the sea?

After I have my session of wallow, I grab my mother's ring from the bedside table, rub it gently between two fingers, and set it aside (I look back at it once more for good measure, fearing I have unconsciously sent it into the abyss). It is an act of solace, which serves to make peace between me and my parents. My nightgown on, I grab a stack of the overflowing, noting the injustice I had committed to the stories at the bottom of the pile, and I raise my feet onto the bed.

Prior to the inwardly transportation, my stomach grumbles, protesting its right to nutrition. But these are the deaf callings of hunger, my appetite outright rejects. When one normally deems it an appropriate hour for lunch, I exit my office and set on a stroll of no destination, navigated left and right by the subconscious; I feel such blissfulness at relinquishing control. Peculiarly, however, in the past many months, Annabelle, the bookkeeper, had tailed my wanderings. To what end? Does she need assurance that I am eating my fill? Perhaps I was naïve to the state of starvation I had subjected myself to, but there I had a belly and full cheeks and ribs hidden. It oppressed me, this spying of hers, and I was made to play the role of an actor pretending to wander whilst taking deliberate and conscious navigational decisions. By the time I had found myself back in the office, she would be there, at her desk, smiling, almost sneering, and she would be ignorant to the state of exhaustion she had put me in. At times, I wished I could release her from those constraints, which her troubled mind had succumbed to. Annabelle appeared lost, immobile, between her life at WRITE and a life after.

The papers in my hand put a stop to the fluttering in my stomach and the butterflies migrated to my mind. Today's story was a short one, 'Mona's Malady,' and it told of a musician in the mid twentieth century navigating the landscape in Syria through music. With every key played on the piano, another coup would be announced. With every pitch she struck on her vocal scale, a promise of reformations and a new beginning would be made. Through the deaths she sang and through the proposals she played. Her brother fell ill to tuberculosis, she played and through a miscarriage she played. The French came, and she played, and they left, and she played.

Thirty pages in, I set the papers down, tears taking hostage of my eyes, yet I did not weep. Instead, I cursed myself for the conviction that such a book would not see the sun's light through a windowpane. And it pained me no less when I flipped the pages to see 'Translated from Arabic.' Words insignificant to me but a jolt to the memory, producing images of a one shunned for his disillusionment. The winds had taken hold again, and I could feel them caressing my bones, whispering "Time abandons us all."

I was forced over to the round window, the only window, no larger than my head, and I pulled at the handle, a futile attempt from the start. I thought, perhaps, that by tugging at the window, I would reassert my dominion and encourage the air's retreat. My eyes glanced over, a couple stories high, and I could see a pile of crumpled notes in the side alley. Mine, ideas of the preposterous kind, I would make a note of upon inspiration and chuck out of the window. It was therapeutic, and a reminder of my own frailty in the battle against ego. But the winds blew some more, and it was I who had retreated onto my bed.

My eyes settled on a notebook, on a table I utilised for a desk, bound in brown leather, and inviting me – nay, guilting me – to scribe in it the tumultuousness of my heart. Next to it, a fine feather, that of a pigeon, a gift from a youngling. I cast her father in the mould of a monster, and I dragged her away from the threat that he was such, but how could she comprehend that? Is the feather symbolic of my own culpability, of plucking the bird's feathers and asking it to fly? Or is it grace, to absolve me, a relief that while I contributed to the bird's plight, I am but one feather of many? Perhaps it was simply a gift from a child, his child. I swept the feather off the table in bitterness, watching it dance its way down till it resided by the bed's leg.

My pen has been kept a distance from my memoirs, lovers across the ocean wide. However, it is not the water that perturbs communication, but a hesitancy of the sailor who carries the letters across. Not since I was approached by a woman and two had I been able to describe the feelings I bear. For fear that the words would reflect harsh truths, and broken oaths I had once sworn to. But when the distance of water is overcome, and the pen and paper embrace as one, the hesitancy dissolves and the words flow, like a dam burst by the pressure of the soul.

*　　*　　*

As I reflect on my life's achievements, I am left disheartened by their magnitude. The concentration of all that my purpose has brought into fruition is contained within those bright eyes. Tales riddled with fibs are not beyond me, yet it would be remiss of me, in this mental memoir, not to accredit both the spark and the fuel (to the flame) to one student. I remember, and perhaps the brush has stroked this painting many times over, a day my words were to the effect of uninspired topography in each student's heart. Rows of them, in a hall grand for its history and name, stared down at me with no dam to the river – no resistance to what I spoke. It flowed freely through them and out. Yet, I place the blame wholly on myself. How could I have expected resistance when I have starved these students of material to resist with?

There were whispers amongst them, fallen heads between them, and winter within them. Nevertheless, there was one, so harrowing were his eyes that I could not spend a second looking into them. Physically, he was average-looking, mediocre to the extreme (you could not pick him out of a crowd). The only feature to remark on was his pitiful attempt at growing a moustache. Someone should have instructed him to be rid of it. Upon memory, that was not me. I would later view it as a mark of distinguishable character – an homage to an identity he struggled to maintain.

He was focused and intently listening to every word I said with a level of scrutiny I was unprepared for. Suddenly, every syllable that left my mouth carried the burden of the entire world. This student would hear, process, and reflect upon every idea I laid out to him. After the lecture, if my memory does not betray me, he would ask for my opinion on a matter I, at the time, could not do the service of commenting on. "A debate between a compatriot and I arose, and we diverged at a fork. Do you think stories are humans' greatest differentiation from other animals? My compatriot argued for love."

Had we both stopped there, our lives would have been for the better. But from his drive, a programme was born, and an influx of similar diamonds, all different cuts, signed up. Variable success, more structured, not successful enough, more rigid, uninspired, creative tasks, Lack of discipline, editors... And so on and so forth until a novel was published regularly and the institution, albeit discreet, invited the pens of many. However, time clawed the drapes of illusion, and revealed the downfall behind every mountain. The higher they were, the harder they fell.

The student showed me the mountain ahead, and so enamoured was I by his brilliance, that my dishonesty was natural. "I could lead you to the top of it." And over the course of years, my barometer skewed, and I could no longer distinguish between ascension and descension. Only when we had reached the edge of a lava pit, and the student was blinded by trust in my guidance, did I abandon him. Now, when I return to present events, I find myself striving to save not the blinded student, for he is too far gone, but many more he might drag along into the fires. How chivalrous of me...

No different was my relationship with a stray student, was my relationship with another. However, the endearment manifested itself unlike before. With Beatrice, C-1 as the other WRITErs knew her, my love transcended ambition and travelled into a realm of the inappropriate and questionable. She bestowed her secrets to me, laid out a set of keys, and trusted me as their guardian. And in a moment of weakness (the shame multiplies with this phrase, believe me), I set out undoing all the locks with those same keys.

And the shame, I alluded to earlier, is founded in three things: the act itself, the plea for understanding following the act, and the inner belief that not a single thing I had with Beatrice was wrong to begin with. O Beatrice... Why did you lose yourself? Curse you and your false morality! She took everything away from me – her love, her life, our life...

She was the first accredited member to sign up to the programme. The student, whose ideas were the roots of WRITE, and I set out interviewing a number of candidates. But much to our dismay, they were characteristic cousins of my lecture attendees. There were components here and there, but all lacked the composition of the well-inked machine necessary to become a writer. Most were oblivious to the power of their hand. And those that succeeded in apprehension, failed by discipline. I look back fondly on days when both of us were on the brink of losing hope. How villainous that hope happened to be.

Then walks in a giant, and our necks strain to behold her in full view. It was not that her stature commanded it, but her aura, which exceeded her, filled the room to its corners. She was direct – "I AM a writer." Oh, how prideful that phrase was. Oh, it bordered on the condescending. The entitlement of it all. But no, her phrase was said both affirmatively and with great humility. Her long locks of black and wavy hair, you could get lost in, like a voyage after dusk through a tumultuous ocean. Her eyes, no less, harboured the same darkness which one could readily sink into. Her skin – words would disgrace its golden shade. Yet, none of those features amounted to a grain of sand when compared with her words. Never did I go to bed without wondering if she recognised her purpose; not that she ever vocalised it, but her actions spoke of a purposefulness hitherto unseen within or outwith.

Much like her friendship with the student, over the years, ours sprouted accordingly. Not only was our passion for literature, of the Dostoyevsky, Mahfouz and otherwise, shared, but conversations around philosophy led us both into passageways of rose bushes. Encompassed by those bushes and sheltered from speculation, we were driven into each other's embrace to avoid the thorns. How could I, a mortal of clay, resist the rhythmic beats, from a heart against mine, of a being that seemed to me, at that moment, from the divine. Curse the devil of desire! Regardless, I offer it my deepest gratitude.

Although her actions alluded to a strive for nurturing her nascent potential, Beatrice was assured in all she did. And it was that pragmatism that drove me to exert pressure on her. "I AM a writer, but how do I convince the masses of it?" I would usually dance around that question, bestowing farcical phrases – "The pen is an extension of yourself, so treat it as such." In essence, I would wrap around her a blanket with holes, like Swiss cheese, and would be taken aback when she would add that she still felt the cold winds. "Do I seem like a child to you?" And I wish I had replied in the affirmative, but instead, her bitter response only served as a motivation to push harder. This giant *had tugged at an insecurity of achievement, and I replied with a show of strength.*

Our sessions were a combination of brutal climbs and intimate descents. We would exercise our minds by adopting an observation of thought. Not that our thoughts were generated by us, but merely random items that materialised in a subliminal space where the necessity to occupy a void dictated the emergence of 'thought.' And as such, in separation from the imperative chaos, we could train our subconscious towards the unattainable limit of original thought.

Afterwards, from the exhaustion of it all, we sought a distraction in each other. It was the kind of physical intimacy that was destructive to the orderly temple we were building for hours prior. Yet, we did it all the same, day after day – building and demolishing. Only one day, she came to me, with evaporating streams running down from her eyes, and she talked of a cluster multiplying within her womb. This divine creature bore a child, our child, a potential, my potential; and suddenly, I understood my purpose in it all. This cluster was the culmination of fifty thousand years of human progression. Beatrice showed no affection for this revelation beyond the scope of 'potential.' She was willing to nurture this creature within her, so long as we both understood that this was a mere extension of her unsurmountable potential.

How could I not shelter them for the world? How could I not fulfil my promise of nurture? They were confined, of their own accord (I swear by it), to a room towards the back of my office at WRITE. There, Beatrice and I continued our writing exercises. She could work on getting her first novel published to the masses and I could hope that the ink would seep through her womb and into the child.

With each passing day, Beatrice grew more joyous and her belly more rotund. She was edging closer to the final draft of her novel, 'The Mountaintop and The River Below.' Her excitement grew almost ravenous by the publishing date, that when the book was finally out of her hands and in that of the masses, Beatrice's deflation was difficult to witness.

Her qualities of the divine waned, and she became an irritable shell of who she once was. She grew skinnier, and yet I persisted in her confinement, hoping that this was a sign of the child's healthy appetite. Some days, I would return to the room to find her in a frenzy scratching away at her abdomen, almost breaking skin. Most other days though, she was calm and reserved. Despite an appearance which had lost all the glow of yesteryears, Beatrice would speak with the same assured tone she once possessed. "The sun is beautiful up here, and yet, I am blinded by it." I would be left dumbfounded at that statement. My only concern during those days was the us within her.

Disgust! Yes, that is the word. What other word could describe my emotions then? This creature had finally escaped its chambers. Glenda was kind enough to deliver the pathetic youngling to us. Beatrice would not look at it, and as soon as the delivery concluded, she retreated to a corner of the room and slept. "I pray for all of you," Glenda commented as she handed the infant to me.

I remember, with regressing memory, staring at the helpless thing for hours wondering how it would ever amount to the greatness I expected of it. Despite that all, there was a part of me, innate and hidden in my depths, which feared for this child, as if it was a fresh wound in me that I needed to bandage. There was an infection, one that weakened me and disregarded any expectations for this child – love. But I had to quell this natural urge within me. This child, son or daughter, I cannot recall, would only climb Everest if its lungs were large enough and its muscles strong enough. As soon as there was any mobility in it, I set the baby down on puddles of ink. Its unbridled freedom in the form of a handprint trail was a language in its own right. Beatrice, indifferent and apathetic at first, eventually became as invested as I was.

Her novel's success expounded her happiness as one of triumph, and a lesson she could teach to the offspring. "With dedication, you will come to see the land beyond, as I do." Beatrice would repeat these words to our child, some days with a victorious tone and others with a tone of defeat. Her eyes, on those other days, would bore through the floor like she could see right through it. Nonetheless, there was a runner's momentum in her which stumbled on despite the pebbles that misbalanced her. Oh, the magnificence of those days, that not even the WRITE programme's deaths, which momentarily shook me, could detract from. Here, in a room, with the simple tools of a mind and ink, we have created worlds beyond our own.

And from WRITE's first great success, rose the fanaticism of many, who joined the programme solely because the value was in the programme's output and not so much its principles. How to weed off such leeches? Well, to begin with, the application processes were rigorous, but with fatigue comes complacency. My plan, had it come to fruition, was to mentor the student, who had struggled in his own regard, to succeed me. If the programme comes to outlive me, then I outlive myself. My fear of death, through name, drove my obsession and chronical occupation for my child. Through the rubble of WRITE, I see the people covered in dust. I rue my neglect for the institution.

Why should I remember that heinous day, but to subject myself and you to the extent of life's suffering? It was a normal day, like any other, navigating the rotting shell to a golden core. WRITE had its cavities where bacteria flourished, yet my belief was that the core remained salvageable. I was wrong about the entire tooth, and now, the entity is speechless. A decade on, and what comes of this 'great' institution? Nothing but the misery of unrealised potential and the disappointment of realised potential – or the illusion thereof.

Where was I? I apologise for the non-linearity of my thoughts. Aha yes, that day... I wish I was gifted with forgetfulness. Excuse the abstraction of the painting, but the detail is too painful to write. There was no sound on the other side of the door. A quietude that alluded to quietus. The room... My pen fails me – or I, it. The room was a canvas of red and black, splattering of blood and ink. A love for two had turned into remorse and abhorrence. In one action, she had destroyed both her potential and mine. Their faces... Were they at peace or relieved from torturous existence? Their eyes were of milky white, a reflection of a ghastly sight. Their jaws were opened and revealed a couple of decaying molars in one and a premature couple of teeth in the other.

A kid, a good kid, of blonde hair, one of the recent editor recruits, was searching for me and happened to walk in during my moment of suffering. He too was distraught, but no more than I, and with little explanation, helped me bury the two in WRITE's own backyard. "It is best you know less," I told him with such grief in my voice that he did not ask for a letter more in explanation. And such was his dutifulness that what he said stuck by me all those years. "Dr. Eadful, in my culture, trust is defined as truth without clarification. I trust you, and if you say so, then it is." The last shovelful of soil was dropped on my beloved. If only the earth would have settled then, but the planting of one soul unearthed a second one.

I lost Beatrice and my child, but I could not lose another. The guilt that succeeded the event, which I had described, led to the eventual retirement of WRITE. Its pillars, once sturdy, had crumbled underneath the pressure of personal responsibility. And as I relayed my decision and Beatrice's demise to my student, I was comforted with the reproach of desperation. To me, that was a mark of a correct decision.

*   *   *

The wooden floor creaked, and my heart rate peaked, for at my vision's periphery I could see darkness in the door's glazed window. But when I finally overcame the irrationality of my fright, I knew it must be another aspiration I would in due course exterminate – not out of desire, but a survival dictated by merciless metrics. I smiled to myself, taking a jibe at my subconscious from assuming a threat when there was none. My pen, which rose and paused akin to a meerkat

12

scanning for a predator, began its descent onto paper, only to be interrupted by a creak once more.

One of my neighbours? I thought to myself. Farida was the nosey type, her nose extensive yet slender, she managed to lodge it into the deepest crevices of the building. Made a widow three years prior, and her only child departing to tread the expanses of the world a year after, most would excuse her intrusiveness. "Poor woman," I would hear them gossip. "If I were a widow neglected by my own, well, the sun would rise but I might not." Vicious words of cruel mouths, and I would pretend to hear none of it when treading the hallways. People here, where the sun sets, kept to themselves generally and attributed an excess of communal interactions as a vulnerability (weakness by their account) or a lack of prestige associated with commoners. But talk was rife, between a few at a time, on matters of material or status. And it bored me to the extreme, this triviality with numbers that ignited the competition within us and jealousy between us.

The shadow beyond the glaze was growing steadily. There was a cautiousness in its approach, skewing left and right as if a tree swaying in the winds. I could eventually put a shape to the darkness, a person, a lionhead? They had the mane of one, a ring that gave the illusion of a grander skull. Not Farida, or if it was then she had finally revealed what hid under the covering. Taut did she wear it, that not a single hair dared escape and the signs of the time were delayed.

Then through my observation, despite its chronological flaws, I saw the shadow warp into a shorter and plumper form. And I would question my limited understanding of biology and morphology, in a vain attempt to put a science to the visuals. In its globularity, the shadow became more prominent and instead of a mass of shade, I could identify markings of a person bending over. Almost simultaneously, I heard paper sliding against wood and I noticed a beige file had forced its way under the door. Repose from the unknown at having the familiarity of paper being teleported from the realm of the creator to the judge, yet this file was starved compared to others before – it could not constitute a short story.

When I stood up to inspect the file, the shadow reacted in franticness, as if it were shocked by a bolt of lightning, mutating and flailing. I could see fingernails, that accumulated dirt, scratching beneath the door, attempting with sordid desperation, to actualise their master's regret. And this fear, it seemed to have for me, made me all the more determined to initiate myself forward. But by the floor's announcement, my foot's location was compromised, and the shadow beyond the glaze took flight. I could hear the fleeting sounds of collisions, the scrambling of the shadow against all obstacles in its path.

If only there was certainty, and not a doubt lingering and murmuring about the person's return, my foot would have extended two steps further seconds earlier. When I, as intended, bent down to grab the file, a sharp pain shot through the lower half of my back. I was made aware then, as I had been on many occasions, of the consequences of carrying my weight and to an extent that of others for as many years as there was breath in me. But, with wilful disregard, I clipped the file's cover between two fingers and collapsed back onto the bed, keeping my back in the same arched position.

What permission had I given for the contents of the folder to be displayed to me? Several photographs and a yellow paper spilled out as if the boundaries of the file evicted them with no due notice. The yellow paper was thick and ripped with little consideration, leaving scraggly edges, unpleasant to the touch. And on it was ink, bold, seemingly written with forceful fingers, with each letter nearly bleeding onto the other so that it formed a block of black. It read...

'Is this confession of mine to the devil that wanders in the woods or an angel that awaits on the mountaintop? Or are these words spoken to a jinni of indifference, a being not coated with hues of good or evil?

To feel what the clouds do when precipitation looms, yet the droplets are interrupted by vision's gloom. This pressure that beset me was a negligible force against the overwhelming terror. The photographs, taken from different angles as if the photographer admired their muse, amounted to words that trampled over the writer's letter. I suspected the author's identity both from handwriting and inference, and if it were on the tip, then the visuals cut at my tongue's base. My mouth wide open, as though I complied with my tongue's executioner, and my breath departed, leaving behind a dryness that ached when I first swallowed.

Sheets of white in the guise of ghosts from decades past, and it would have been comical had it not been for the sunken parts. They revealed orbitals and teeth, ribs and knees, and the frame of an expressionless skeleton that dressed as agony's bride. And to its side was a child, if I were to guess, an infant no less, within the first skeleton's embrace. I paused and I thought, but my mind was fraught with bullets bouncing against my cranium. There was a departure from logic spurred from enough adrenaline to drive a bull mad. "A child?" I asked myself. Vile, this revolution against innocence, this child, who is a representative of humanity, placed in the firing line and rendering us extinct. If there is justice in its death, then let there be justice for all.

The third was exposed to the harshness of the elements, undignified, and left naked, its legs raised to its chest as if it were shielding itself from the wind. It was the most pathetic of the three, deriving the greatest sadness from me. An afterthought, the savagery, of a mediated robbery of two lives followed by the impulsive theft of one. Was it the orbitals? Hollow, yet overflowing with the lived experiences of a creature with no tongue to tell the tale. Never had I seen a skeleton so raw, its bends, the minor cracks that ran through its bones, the teeth protruding giving more significance to the mouth, the body shrivelled in comparison to a skull that carries less of the flesh. And although the truth, which I had known, was that there was no consciousness to this frame, I still ascribed a brain to the skull but no organs to the body. This third skeleton's size was midway between the extremes of the previous two; it was difficult to determine its pre-mortem age.

Little credence lent to my eyes, but must I falter them for mistaking dirt for oblivion when the story was a portrait and the foreground the person? The dirt was speckled with lighter matter, pieces of gravel and otherwise, so that it appeared like the shimmering of stars in the night sky. Staring, almost hypnotically, at the three bodies in a ditch, I was reminded of the author's words. *A madman! And he believes the three there to be Luna and the children? That cannot be. There, walls that shelter from eyes, they lay their nights away – a disservice to the people but protection for them. A madman!* I thought to myself, assuming a hushed tone within.

The hunchback in me rose, energised by adrenaline and a desire for retribution. I sought comfort for my feet to venture onto the street. The breeze had carried a disease, fleeting, and I am to dutifully sieve the human beneath. The seething soul in an unyielding mould needs a breathing hole to relieve its subconscious's toll. A troll, that resides under your bridge, thieving unmeaning thoughts and delivering you the stress of irresolution from otherwise passing concepts. Overwhelming the troubled minds, which find an inclining towards demise, these pondering times. I sighed and set forth.

Heedless of the pain, and with no stretches to attenuate, my back was forced straight and I to my feet. It was all a rush, slowed only by my perspective. I brushed aside this and tossed away that, and the papers rained by my side – words that would ultimately touch ground but not hearts. And when I threw my robe on, items of little consideration flew in a tornado, which appeared as projectiles launched in my direction due to my short-sightedness. A warning, perhaps, of a path rife with thorny bushes and a destination treacherous in its conclusion. But my convictions lay not in fate's signs, they are founded in pride, masquerading as regret, demanding a blemish be erased.

Out of the door, I swivelled my head left and right for no reason – I knew the direction of the shadow's dash. Not towards the unilluminated corner harbouring humidity, but past the bookkeeper's desk, which was made nonparallel by the runner's collision. Cometh the week and I will hear a mouthful from her about the value of organisation, clinical her tidiness was. I scooted past the mess and followed my own footsteps hours earlier. Through a narrow hallway, past Farida's apartment, down a staircase, then past another, it appeared as though I was in a labyrinth of Penrose stairs. And at one corner after the next, I would halt in horror, believing an image of one of the skeletons had appeared ahead of me. This ended with a click, a red button, on a large wooden door with cracked paint.

To anticipate clarity and be delivered a fog, it frightened me momentarily and calmed me soon after. Outside the building, I was welcomed by Earth's own blanket, a shield from precarious visuals. But akin to the glazed window, the blurriness of all aided my imagination. *The lamppost was a person, the garbage bin was a person, the person was a person? The subliminal trusts the eyes, but I do not trust the subliminal.*

There was not one definitively a person; not even an orb to ascribe a mane to. And with no pen to deliver my words, I exclaimed, more at ease with the audible.

"Your request is for deliverance, for which I can grant you," I called out desperately. "If it is certainty that evades you, then let us cast a wider net." When I was met with no reply, I continued. "With honesty that is. Who are those three, Solomon? Have you no honour, Solomon? From ink to blood, Solomon?!" I cried out, but to silence. "My son," I paused, ashamed for having uttered this untruth, "Allow me to aid you as you have aided me. You have deceived yourself, afflicted yourself with the maladies of confusion, harboured the innocence within, for what? To concentrate your innermost suffering into a propulsion, for what? To entertain the masses, for what? I tell you to write, as I always have, not because writing is the realisation of potential, but because if we fail to scribe the truth then we are in danger of being dishonest to ourselves." And my head slumped lower than my shoulders for having told an untruth once more.

Only then, I noticed my feet were misplaced and had wandered out to the middle of the street. So despaired was I by my speech, I was oblivious to my body's manipulation. But the scenery here was no different than there, and not a soul to be found anywhere. *Where have my slippers gone?* I questioned myself, for not only was I barefoot, but there were scratches by my sole. And the scratches reminded me of ones left behind by a cat, that, through rational derivation, I would ascribe the same culprit without scrupulous enquiry.

Amidst a fit of curses that damned the suspected feline, the ground beneath me rumbled and I heard a muffled growl from a distance. *Be it the lion?* I scouted for the ring of hair. The growling grew louder and harsher, that anyone else would have scurried to safety. But I was a distraught man seeking the teeth of the lion, so that I might confirm its existence. Therefore, when gleaming lights shone through the fog, I was gleeful, almost enough to take a step forward.

Teeth of metal, eyes carrying no guilt, and a hairless body. *This is neither a lion nor Solomon,* I thought to myself in preparation for my final departure. And then my thoughts compounded, *if only I had another paragraph in me, I would outlive myself through it. My memoirs will remain unfinished, therefore my spirit incomplete, and I will be remembered in parts: part good, part evil... or wholly either.* However, in rejection of my acceptance and out of the darkness, as if it materialised from within the fog, a hand emerged to pull me out of the engine's trajectory. I had evaded death, a question of 'what after' that yearns for an answer. And as I rotated to make known my saviour from the great unknown, words escaped me, and I am still yet to grasp them back.

*   *   *

An awakening spurred by terror, his body jolted with a desire to meet the ground, but to his dismay, Solomon Osroes was restrained by shackles tightened around his wrists. He was fastened to a chair, of the heavier kind, to limit the erraticism he had begun to display. Motionless before, his eyes flitted left and right, and his eyelids fluttered, all uncertain of where their focus lay. But none of his senses were as acute as touch, for he could feel the contact of four bony fingers, like twigs, on his shoulder. Instinctively, he made his mouth as to bite them, however, he was immediately held back by a uniformed man with kind features. Disgruntled was Osroes, that his aggression did not wane till the grey moustachioed man placed a reaffirming hand on his chest.

Vocal cords, dry and torn, of a nurse that appeared devoid of life herself. Yellow was her skin, an infestation of tobacco, that blood had retreated long ago from her extremities. But pious she seemed, to Solomon anyways, for he could hear whispers of supplications, the humble resignations of outwith control. He could almost hear the mutterings, "Lord be merciful," "Absolve all suffering," "Make accountable those who perform undue harm." Those prayers would

19

be followed by a sequence of coughs to flush out the serenity associated with spiritual escapism. However empathetic she might have been, her voice lent no credence, underlining each sentence with malevolence.

Solomon could hear another, this voice across from him, replying to the supplications dismissively. "The devil has been answering the calls since humanity's conception." A table, white and wide, ahead of him, Osroes's sight ultimately landed on the brown briefcase on top of it. He wanted to broaden his scope of vision further, to see the man across the table, but blinded by the ceiling light above, he refrained.

And the voice, as if it had changed locality, now more intently seemed to address Solomon.

"You delay your confession as if another day will provide you the comfort that yesterday did not. A festering illness, this dishonesty of yours," he addressed Osroes with the impatience of a decade-long interrogation.

Solomon, in turn could only reply glumly, like a child lost in the woods, "Who might you be sir? And where might I be?" And the two, the nurse and the man, the guard less so, could see the swimming irises of a delirious man. So bewildered was Solomon that he could not assume a utilitarian approach for any of the items around. A pencil was wood and belonged to a tree, a tree was cells and belonged to elements, elements were atoms, and so and so forth until every object appeared a part of a whole – a universal concept where air and metal blend as one.

There was silence, a discussion between eyes, before the interrogator ultimately replied. "I am not at my pride's behest; I will indulge you. I am Yan, a mentor and a helper, and you are in a room for the mentees and helped." When he was not met with the desired response, Yan snapped, "How can you bear your own conscience, after all that you have done, when I cannot bear mine?" He slammed his hand on the table, the reverberations travelling through Solomon's hands.

"The bears, beasts of wilderness, driven by their most base instincts, majestic are they not?" Solomon smiled innocently, before adding, "Their inviting embrace, soft fur and tender features, hide their capability to maul you."

There was a cough, unnatural compared to the nurse's previous ones, that was forced in order to capture Yan's attention. "The man is out of his wits. This is not right," she protested, each word a struggle to produce.

"And what is right given the circumstances?" Yan replied with vigour. "To write?" he added sardonically. "To hell with it." He shifted his fangs back towards Solomon and released his venom. "You ask me for my identity, but what is yours? What are the principles for which you live for and are willing to die for?"

Osroes was incapable of responding, his thoughts incoherent and scrambled. To which Yan combatively ordered the nurse, "Administer more."

"That, I shall not. Have we not damaged his mind enough? The man speaks of bears, not as the burdens of life, the weariness we all feel but do not speak of, the innate anxiety we all have with regards to value and purpose, and..." Her voice trailed off into another sequence of coughs, rising towards a crescendo.

Befuddled, Solomon's sight shifted from the cerulean eyes of the man across him to the grey swimmers of the nurse to his right. The despair with which they spoke confounded him. *There you are, alive, able, and in the privileged position of being my oppressors, and yet all you spout are the sorrows I have afflicted? I am shackled,* he thought to himself, attempting to resolve this maze that seemed beginningless to him. *If Luna were to see me in this state, then I fear your worries lie with the wrong devil.* A smirk plastered across his face, which confused the man across. Osroes had been silent, however a dialogue that he was not privy to appeared to ensue. *What is this room? Its brightness burns, welcoming only the sanctimonious to appreciate the purity it assumes*, and while he was scrutinising the room within, Solomon began raising his hand to shield himself from the light.

However, before the sun was eclipsed by his fingers, Solomon's chair, at Yan's request, was tipped backward and dragged away. And as the guard, the essence of jubilance, was forcing him out, Osroes asked one final question. "One request prior to my execution, one last wish for the dying man. May the buffoon drag me to my beloved, the moon and the stars, so that I may bid them farewell?" His voice was trailing, his head halfway outside the door, but he could catch a glimpse of Yan's head as it collapsed into his hands, defeated undoubtedly. And the nurse consoled him, a hand to the shoulder, as though the journey had been arduous.

The screeching of the chair, dragged against the ceramic tiles, would have agonised Osroes had he not been in awe of the setting. Not the dreary hallways or the people, or lack thereof, for his entire surrounding appeared to twist onto itself, exacerbating the dizziness of which he felt. Solomon could have regurgitated, but there was a comforting force settling the turbulence within. This black and white spiral, uncanny from his perspective, was familiar. The odour was that of a grandparent's home, aged and pleasant. His feet were attracted to the flooring, Solomon's toes stretched to feel the tiles underneath. Within all the morphing of shapes and colours, bland as they were, the cell doors stood the forces of perception. They were white-painted doors, tall and uncompromising, with small, barred windows, which reminded the insiders of their lack of freedom and the outsiders of their excess of it. In his restrained position, he was incapable of viewing the cells' insides, however their numbers, C-3, C-4, C-5, C-6, were directly in his line of sight. *What number cages me?* Solomon questioned subconsciously.

All halted by C-12, the symptoms of sickness, the drab diluted into the unnoticeable, the familiarity that obsessed him, and physically, the chair. In the chasm after the screeching and before the creaking, Solomon was drowned by dread. A brightness into darkness into brightness, like the Sun eclipsed by the Moon, and the Moon by the Sun in turn. The light, on and off, shining on a valley with a river and ascending to a mountaintop beside. He could hear the laughter, sinister, followed by laughter, jovial, then followed by the speech of a foreign tongue, nurturing, evolving into yelling, blood curdling, a warning, but Solomon unable to translate. Images of elderly women flashed by; their wrinkles scrutinised and closed on, transforming into dunes of a desert. Camels lay in an oasis forced to travel across tundra to arrive within frost, unknown to them the path back. Solomon, the traveller, an observer in their journey, powerless to curiosity. "Save them Osroes. May you be saved in turn," he could hear a voice calling, language unfamiliar yet words understood. But he thought himself helpless and in need of shelter and food, so he lay by the perishing camels, fed on their meat, and rested inside their carcasses, readying himself for the day's climb towards the mountain peak.

When the guard placed a gentle hand on the nape of his neck, and subsequently brought Solomon's visions to a halt, he felt as if he were sentenced to the wrath of eternal damnation. The edges of his lips were freezing cold while his insides burned with the intensity of magma. "Where does your mind go this early in the morning, friend?" the guard chuckled and rubbed the back of Solomon's neck. "My mother, Lord, may you rest her soul, would always repeat this phrase to me in times of great stress, 'you are blessed by the hands of others, let yours bless theirs.'" And with no further clarification, Osroes was sent into the cell. He pounced on the blanket by the bed and covered his shoulders whilst keeping his chest exposed, hoping to warm the frost and cool the heat.

The door shut and an artificial darkness befell Solomon, perhaps indicative of night-time. Deciding to lay on his left shoulder and prepared for slumber's repose, the visuals returned to him, unbearably loud and graphic. He clenched his teeth and persevered a second more, before his eyes forced open. *Luna, these eyes do not see you. Shams, this nose does not smell you. Amar, these arms do not hold you. Why have I abandoned the Balikh river, its flow that washes away anxieties of the future?* Solomon thought to himself, before attempting to shut his lids once more. To no avail, he would spend the twilight staring above into the darkness, a universe in the ceiling, while swirls appeared, akin to the formations of galaxies, a reminder of his insignificance. And he would tremble trying to reconcile an existence that demanded significant purpose in the face of insignificant consequences.

ماذا هذا يا غلام؟

Part 2: The First of Parched Land

Solomon was caged in a perpetual loop of perspiration and respiration. Had he not been a known patient of the institute, the editors would have been inclined to believe that he simply emptied his bladder's content. Despite the unhygienic state he found himself in, Osroes was no barbarian – though a heathen of sorts perhaps. But in this instance, anxiety bested him. He felt separated from reality by a diaphanous veil. There was a familiarity that lent his estimates of reality credibility, and yet the cloth induced an unavoidable doubt within him.

Sitting on his bed, a couple of deep breaths in, Solomon swiped the trickling droplets off his forehead. "Damn my circumstances," he muttered under his breath. Excuse his foul language; however, all creatures, a monster even, would say no less. And besides, as retribution, he could sense the arid wasteland that was his mouth – sore to the touch. His tongue, like a careless inspector, ran against his gums and teeth. With the little saliva at his disposal, Solomon swished it from cheek to cheek before spitting on the floor. *Sigh* Manners... A colour he did not expect splattered against the concrete below. *No mouthguard once more. Mouth-breathing dimwits!* he thought to himself, much to my disappointment. There is no need for such harsh words, Solomon.

One step, he shivered, his bare foot against the cold floor. Another step, his bloodied spit now on his heel was wiped across the ground. Solomon would not have to witness the spittle each day he woke up. Now at the sink, right next to the toilet, he bore the consequences of his actions. His disdain for the room's interior design resurfaced. More often than not, as was the case now, the consequence was a pungent smell following his excrement's disposal.

His hands were now firmly placed on both sides of the sink. Solomon repeated his saliva trick and spat once more into the bowl. This time, there was less blood (a welcome improvement). Nonetheless, his gums still ached. With his trusty right hand, he turned the singular knob ahead of him. All it controlled was the lame pressure of freezing water. He ran his hands under the water for a few seconds, and that was all it took for his fingers to go numb.

A little in the palm of his hand and slurped into his mouth, Solomon hoped it would numb some of the pain. But no, all it did was aggravate the sensitivities in his mouth of cavities unknown. He swallowed the water before it could do any further damage. Unfortunately, for Solomon, this was no hotel. There was no towel. Therefore, he irrationally decided to raise his hands and wiped the excess water with his untamed beard.

Solomon had only noticed the silence when it was stolen from him. A loud knock was an introduction to a baritone voice. "C-12, leisure hour. Sit on your bed." Had the voice not had the reverb of Zeus, Solomon would have declined. Also, what man in his state of fatigue, was in a position to argue? By the time he obeyed, the editor was no more than a metre away from him.

"Odd! My mouth guard went for a stroll last night. Care to check if you left the door open?"

"If I did, it was only to realise a hope of mine."

"And what might that be?"

"For you to chomp down on your own tongue and finally spare me your words." A re-evaluation of the editor's manner was in order.

In response to Solomon's limp posture, the editor commanded, "A foot ahead of me, now." The words, intended to elicit a mixture of fear and respect common to authoritarianism, did not intimidate. And to Osroes, whose pride was an ever-present beast in the depths of his soul, the command was perceived as compensation for a lack of intelligence.

Yet, the beast would not stand, its joints fatigued. There was a looming sensation of weakness, of the corrosiveness of life, that surfaced sensitivities ought to be sheltered. Although Solomon, in years past, would expose his pride with broad shoulders like a prized ornament, that day he cowered into himself. His sarcasm, a shield to piercing blows, was in limited supply. Nothing he could think of was uttered and if it were, then it would be without conviction.

C-11, C-10... What awful familiarity! An identity he knew so well but was lessened by its equivalent memory. Oh, it was much like seeing an old friend from childhood days who had since undergone drastic physical and mental changes. It is them, but it is not. A WRITE environment that felt a little wrong to Solomon. How could he not remember? Is he spared while I suffer the past decade?

The editor guided my host through a barred door, then another, and then another. A betrayal to its name, they ultimately found themselves in the 'leisure' room. Its walls were dominated by an eggshell colour - one would prefer to be birthed out of a chicken instead. There was a television in the top corner that was both too small to view and unplugged, evoking an aura of leisure but not actuating it. Worn out green couches, a couple of rickety wooden chairs, and an outdated vending machine combined to the effect of lumpy bits swimming in a pool of spew. As a consolation, not that anything could truly console them, the residents were allowed one item from the machine per week. It was not a rule Solomon knew, but one that he felt existed.

A table on the side of the room invited the participation of card or board games. With what? All present games laid out on a shelf had some or most components missing. It appeared deliberate. There were a few WRITErs floating about in their white jumpsuits. None were remarkable enough for a spontaneous hoorah. All sorrowful faces were branded by their cell number. However, some pairs of eyes stood out like the headlights of an incoming van on a foggy night. They stared with such an intent as to weaken Solomon's already frail resolve.

A talker and a listener, one tall and one short, dominant and aloof, two separates that belonged to a whole. They approached Solomon as though they knew him, for they did.

"Gentlemen?" Solomon's inquiry was tethered to the same doubts which balanced the tightrope of the familiar and foreign. Yet, his intonation suggested a scrutiny of their honour.

"Gentlemen, yes, but you seem unconvinced," the Russian (a presumption based on the biases of linguistic analysis) retorted, not yet sure of the ground's construction he stood on.

"Not at all," Solomon replied hastily in fear he had offended them. "Forgive my tone, which is more of a marker of my exhaustion than my approach."

The one man, the talkative one, glanced up at the other man, less talkative, and smiled cynically. "Mr. Osroes," he nervously stuttered before correcting himself, "C-12, do you feel well? Cognitively?"

"There is a fog, but one I can see through." It was a moment of candour that relieved all burdens momentarily before returning them. "Blunt as this is, I perhaps dishonour myself in asking for your names."

What was it that Solomon said to plaster such perplexity on their faces?

Having confronted each other in the battle of the eyes, they turned towards him. "Spud Baikonur," he placed his hand to his chest in greeting. "And my thoughtful brother, Nick." The taller of the two followed suit and placed his hand on his chest too.

"Spud, like the potato?"

Spud chuckled derisively, "A decade on from our encounter and your humour remains as immature as a freshly grown grape." Solomon's confusion was worn on his face; Spud decided to clarify. "We were late entrants to the programme, far too late, if you would remember."

How could Solomon not remember? Truth be told, Spud was, as my host had mentioned, no different than a sack of potatoes. With an abnormally bloated abdomen and a compression that yielded four stringy limbs, how could Solomon think otherwise? Spud's stubby neck was overqualified in supporting his bald and wrinkled head. Like the flavour of truth that needs no salt, the man's skin had both the colour and texture of a potato pulled straight out of the dirt. That beige skin, those irregular blotches on his skin... Spud's age of thirties, forties, fifties was undefined due to his physique.

His socially acceptable counterpart, Nick, was a tall fellow, only a few inches shorter than the nurse. Not only was he lanky, but his legs stretched on for miles; they were disproportionate to his height. His face, much like his body, was long and slim. However, it lacked elasticity and appeared to be melting slowly off its frame. A constant slummed look, that was only accentuated by his jaded eyes. Only his hair, combed to one side, retained any youthful exuberance – a desperate attempt to elevate his attractiveness.

His individuality was more evident in his personality than physicality. A master of silence, a role forced onto him by his muteness, he had captured Solomon's attention. There was a wisdom, unbeknownst to Nick, that Solomon had allocated to him. It was a superficial belief in the superior quality of quiet, for only a fool, much like Spud, would talk to no end. Some would say 'the evolution of thoughts is through conversation.' Therefore, did Nick not think at all? Were his thoughts all primary, unchallenged, unevolved, and fleeting? Only he could answer that, through pen and paper.

"Shall we make haste and execute?" Spud questioned enthusiastically.

Clueless of past and present, Solomon replied accordingly. "Execute? Forgive my ignorance."

There was a tinge of confusion on Nick's face too, but Solomon's predisposition classified it as the mere by-product of a thoughtful mind.

"Execute what indeed? Answer the man," the nurse crept on

from behind Solomon and emphasised. The following coughs were intense and affirmed their radical position as part of Glenda's character. They almost stood to exclaim on her behalf, "Yes, she is sick. Yes, we are a symptom. No, we will not be gone soon."

"A card game! Or a board game even..." Spud's voice trailed off trying to murmur his way out of the apparent sham that was his enthusiasm.

Although there was no indication of the moral designation of either side, Solomon chose to support a façade he deemed worthy of curiosity. "Indeed, a game of berjeece – an olden game that is." The three others appeared disorientated by the name, as if they were lost analysing an abstract painting. Even for Solomon, there was a sourness in his mouth he did not know the origin of. "I see there is none of that here," he added unconvincingly, still deciphering his own reaction.

"Are you feeling well, C-12?" Glenda asked with the tenderness of a grandmother. "That was quite an episode you had yesterday."

Through fleeting time, the events pickled in brine, and a tartness heightened to result in squinting eyes. Solomon dismissed the nurse's concern much like a son does with his mother to alleviate the burdens of his own existence. In doing so, he lets maliciousness brew without the respite of his parents' support. While Nick idled in place, Spud told a tale of the oppressive few and the struggling many. About an escape from the vengeance of another's failure, and how dreadful it was to be asked to WRITE but given no pen to do so. His speech, although rather contrived, made the sourness in Osroes's mouth palatable. And when he finally swallowed it, he was submerged in a fear of a truth unknown to him – the death of three.

His eyes were on a departed nurse, whose fingers latched onto a cigarette as if it were a pacifier. "They mistake death for sleep," Solomon muttered under his breath before vocalising, "How do we unshackle our wings?"

"A vent, a breath of air. There is one in the storage cabinet, to the bottom left." Spud kept a hushed tone and indexed with his eyes. "But how is one to unlock it?" With a gleam in his eyes, he presented Solomon with a tightly wound spring much like someone would hand a rose to their lover. "With this, dawn will break, and our world will be illuminated."

"And am I just to stroll in gaily and proclaim freedom?" retorted Solomon.

After his question was swiped away by the wave of a hand, Solomon was instructed to approach one of the editors in a certain manner to elicit a favourable response. And when he was reassured about the impotence of security, Osroes's vision aligned to this new reality. The institution was indeed sparsely populated compared to the little he remembered of it. Did they disappear just this second? A few editors there, a handful of WRITErs in that corner, it all amounted to a profound emptiness he had just discovered within himself. Through that void, a yearning for the successive would develop – the next, next, next with no tendency to halt and understand current predicaments.

*　　*　　*

Amongst the parted souls I floated, amongst the live ones too, in between the buildings, and past merchants of few. Foraging through the wilderness, the thorns of life, to harvest the fruits of my soul, the very subject of internal strife.

"Have you a life?" I questioned here and there. Desperation is a fragrance that invites their stares.

A merchant, black turban and all, of antiques and pottery, gestured to me to select from their array of crockery. And upon my approach to address the insult to my query, my vision's painter brushed over and altered my scenery. The vastness of the desert, a sea of beige, inspired fear in my heart. A lack of comprehension about its end, and if I, the centre, its start. The merchants, colourful turbans and all, remained, a comforting sight, to ease the symptoms of my momentary fright. Sheds and carpets and free roamers, much like me, wandering, no resolution announced to my inescapable quandary.

"I will make you a deal," a rope to drag me from the abyss, "I will give you life if you take his."

The merchant pointed to an elderly man, so frail he was so frail he could barely walk. There he was, sitting against a wooden pole of a merchant's sheds, singing hymns of better days ahead. Distraught as I was, I succumbed and pondered, is acquiring life worth killing a man of hundred? I was a soul with no vessel, but my heartless heart filled with great guilt. However, these were emotions I could overcome in a life rebuilt.

The devil of desire, I accepted the merchant's proposal, chained by desperation, although I felt remorseful. But upon floating to the elder, I could tell his eyes once cried, for they appeared basins of tears that over the years had dried. I could not carry through with the act. Am I the one to decide who lives? The act executed is not an act worth forgiving. The life I shall receive would not be a life worth living. Glum, his expression spoke of the clueless, his life was spared, for I could have been ruthless.

Hysterical laughter drowned out the elder's singing for my dead soul. And the merchant stated, "How foolish of you to reject a trade of gold for coal."

To be lost, more now than ever, at the merchant's riddle, until the elder fell to his side. His heartful heart had stopped, and the merit of my actions against my desires subsided.

And the riddler stood behind me and patted my back to console. "Have you been blinded by the sea? I am the Merchant of Souls. You can call me Death after all."

*   *   *

"I plead thee Merchant for my life," Solomon repeated in a

manner that could only be mended by a physical reset of the subliminal, which Spud's propensity for violence accomplished in the form of a slap.

"This," he paused, his hand retreating to his side, "is for your benefit, for your dreams of now are to the detriment of your future." The quietest of the three stood ahead of the two, shielding them from the observation of scrutinous editors.

Tempestuous as Osroes was, the calm of his focus, which ignored all external afflictions, transformed into a gaze at the vending machine in front of him. His poor reflection on the glass barrier cast an image of him on the snacks beyond. And what coincidence it was, not that Solomon considered this to be the case, for 'Soul's best bar' to land where his heart ought to be. The eternal mockery of a Merchant who derives pleasure from the growing envy of hindsight. How could Solomon contend with a life that felt equivalent to death?

The brothers looked upon Solomon as they would a mule, occasional pang of pity for overworking it yet content to demand more. They said many things to reel him in, one with his hands and the other with his mouth, but to no avail. Then Spud said to great effect, "Of the Moon, the Sun, the very stars you see in the sky, the principles will propel your work beyond the boundaries of your breath. They will inform extraterrestrial civilisations, of the present and future, who we were. And those principles are this path." Beautiful words had they been received by an attentive listener, yet Solomon's attention halted after 'the Sun.' Luna, Shams, Amar, three names in quick succession and one thought soon after, their embrace. An oddity, the essence of the Merchant's mockery lingered and Osroes felt his remembrance of them was akin to fool's gold, but why? Forgetfulness demanded their existence, and yet, with every memory of them descended the glitter of dream – a persuasive filter to shelter from reality. He would try to strip this amnion membrane, only to retreat at the macabre odour and the Merchant's laughter that penetrated through.

Acclimatisation of the senses, the brain's defence against constant stimuli, was the first step in satiating a morbid curiosity that posed as bravery. Beyond the film, Solomon flitted into the storage closet; he found no abnormality in this – experiencing motion as discrete singularities in space and time. But Solomon stressed to remember, to salvage a decaying memory, the value of a journey that led him here. Alas, to prevent the fractionation of his subconscious into parties of the progressive and conservative, an elastic band wrapped around his head causing him agonising pain.

His senses returned gradually in a show of defeatism against his memory, or perhaps in support. Solomon unwrapped his fingers to reveal the sharp object causing him much discomfort. It was a spring, the one Spud handed to him. "Freedom," he recalled. But the room was dim, and at his behest, the eyes failed to distinguish one storage rack from the next or a vent from the wall. In such limited visibility, each rack appeared an infinite line, a divider of reality. This compartmentalisation reminded Solomon of a graveyard with its many crypts and induced a claustrophobic attack that resulted in a few hushed groans.

As if in response to his discomfort, a vertical line of light appeared, unlike that of the racks, and cut through the morbid illusion. The door had been opened, and now occupying his full attention, Solomon could see a man, plump and joyful, standing at the doorway. His moustache was thick enough, it draped over his top lip; his hair was grey enough, it contrasted his colourful character; his belly was protruding enough, it made space for his heart. Earl was an editor, as indicated by his uniform, but quite unlike the others.

"If only in youth I was afforded an eyesight as good as yours," he chuckled before enquiring, "What forces you into darkness, Sol?"

Positively stunned. No! Bordering on outrage, Solomon could not comprehend the interaction he was forced into. For an editor to speak to him in a manner of benign affability, and not only that, but to shorten his name in a demonstration of presumed camaraderie, was insulting to him. Did Earl know him or of him? Both, yet Solomon's consciousness denied the claim. With all the internal quarrel, his response tended towards the feral. *Within reason*, he tamed the beast subconsciously. And Solomon remained frozen, every muscle across his body tensed purposelessly. A few short breaths escaped him and arose in him a suspicion that he had not been breathing all along.

"None the matter fella," Earl's voice sliced through the tension. "Are you having a hard time locating a towel?" A smile stretched across in rebellion to its curtain.

Solomon felt like a blanket had been thrown at him on a midsummer's day. Unbearable heat and suffocation, but how could anyone deny the benevolence of such a gesture? For if it were any other season, there would be cheers of gratitude. Such is the magnitude of time, that it could turn the good unknowingly malevolent. He could only respond with a meek "Yes," for all other responses his brain could muster would have led to unfavourable escalation.

Earl walked, his gait indicating aid, into the storage cabinet and began his search for the elusive fabric. As his fingers flipped through the first column of racks, the instincts of a weathered taleteller kicked in. "There was a time I was lost in the clouds above. When the skies were full and grey, I would look up and forget all below. I was afraid of what might come crashing down. And when the skies were sparse and blue, I would look down and forget all above. I, too, was afraid of falling and crashing down," a little chuckle escaped him before he continued. "Imagine me, a heavy man, crashing down below. A catastrophe for those surface dwellers." Earl could not restrain a guffaw fermenting in the very belly that dominated his physique. "Where my mind goes at times. Well, one day, one time... It was an embrace by my other half. It was the first cries of a new-born. Its first steps. Yes, but it was also the grip of reassurance on my shoulder by my father. Or was it the odour dancing in the kitchen to the tune of love and culture? It could have been the written words of my mother that urged me to rebel against life's suffering. And yet, it was also the smile I would receive from a stranger upon locking eyes for no other reason than the recognition that we both exist and their existence eases life's burdens on me and vice versa. It was all of them; however, I am chronologically challenged to pinpoint the instance." He paused for a moment, scratched the back of his head, and continued his search. "Look at me rambling on like my grandmother would. I looked straight ahead and all around, neither above nor below, and I was no longer amongst the clouds. No, I realised I was never amongst them. All of it was around, life's suffering and alleviation, its absurdity and purpose." His final pause was intentional, handing Solomon a towel and patting him on his upper back. "You are a good man Sol. Just remember to remove the neck brace and look around."

Rivers of red bifurcated into streams, each protesting against rationale. One flowed into bushes of grey, dyeing them, until a pink basin was reached which archaeologists would claim harboured the truth of our ancestors. Another descended a sloping hill and met the ground below, forming a lake of senseless misery. The nascent river stemmed from a ringed obelisk pierced into the land by an alien civilisation. Communication of assurances via foreign tongues falls onto deaf ears. How could the masters of land expect the aliens to understand them?

But you zoom out, and the rings on the obelisk turn to ridges on a spring. The forest of grey into sprouting hairs. The sloping hill into a neck. The pools of white into eyes. And the lake of misery into blood. Solomon stood there panting like a rabid beast, unconscious of the vile act he had committed.

Incomprehensibly evil, yet reasonable all the same. To him, anyhow, it was a response to aggression of the underlying kind – the caged and the captor. And no matter the demeanour of his allocated oppressor, Solomon merely saw a barrier to freedom. Then, with regards to the manner Earl addressed Solomon, Osroes viewed the final statement as unconscionably merciless; to burden Solomon's existence with the expectations of a 'good man' was brutal, especially when he was battling with both the concepts of what it is to be 'good' and a 'man.' In that moment of speech, he felt ashamed and akin to a child being told about the disappointments of unmet behavioural expectations due to actions (imagine a broken vase).

But when a tear rolled down Earl's cheek and diluted the lake of his blood, Solomon felt the entire gravity of the situation descend upon him. It was a reminder that the tree of blood on the ground was rooted in an organism of water. Yes, Earl was foreign to him, not in memory, but in momentary philosophy, which was shaped by the complete history of his lineage until now. However, once all the nuance was sheared away, their needs, desires, and hopes became both simple and aligned. In this contradiction of convictions, there was a split – an Osroes whose knees met the ground and agonised at the touch of the Merchant's hand, and an Osroes whose feet stood firm and soul unfazed.

"Did you follow the air o-," Spud's sentence was left incomplete, awestruck by the painting he beheld. The brothers, at the cabinet's doorway, stood over a Solomon on his knees, hunched over an editor. With a face like Saturn Devouring His Son, he was hopelessly shovelling blood with his hands back into the wound it had escaped from. Nick was aghast, perhaps to a greater degree than his brother, and had lost appetite for the Soul's chocolate bar he had been consuming. Spud, on the other hand, was resolved in moving past Solomon's mortification, which to him was a minute casualty in the pursuit of the grand.

"Fret not, good friend." Nick's hand placed disapprovingly on his brother's shoulder would not prevent Spud from treading over and consoling Solomon by his back. "Your pen would honour him more than his life did."

Osroes rose but his spirit did not. *What now?* he thought to himself. In the background of his being, Spud had already dropped to the level of Earl's body, seeking to retrieve the key to liberation with minimal mess. His fingers moved around the body meticulously, a scavenger in many ways. The other brother stood tall and observant, like a watch tower, its light flickering, his mind perturbed.

"The greatest of scholars recognised that enlightenment could mean building the dam upstream on occasion," Spud managed the words amidst a panting fit. He had just retrieved the spring and flitted towards some of the detergents on the rack, pouring a few of them on the body in hopes of masking the eventual smell. In the rush of it all, his words came out nervously and had the opposite effect of calming the two others.

Alas, obedient to momentum, Solomon and Nick found themselves at the opening of an air vent, courtesy of Spud's diligent work. There was a hesitancy in both to crawl through, the sort of birth foetuses would endure against. For a man of the Balikh river, the tube represented a further digression into the unknown, and although what he had known thus far was horrid, it was familiar. But for Nick, the reluctance was rooted in the act, more so than the destination. It was a reaffirmation of the cruel principles dictated by Spud.

The rustling sound of editors walking up and down the hallway, perhaps unrelated to their activity, introduced fear in them, nonetheless. Nick, despite his stature, had shrunk behind his brother's shadow for most of his life, and when he eventually crawled behind him into the vent, he found himself in his shadow once more. Solomon was the last of the three to enter, finding no comfort in looking at Earl once more. But his metaphysical apologies would be relegated to the side-lines, for another editor had stomped his foot not too far away from the door – a thunderous roar.

The rhythm of the footsteps aligned with his own heart, and entranced by it, Solomon was transported into the realm of the past. His own toddler-self crawling on a Persian rug to the sound of encouragement. A herd of adults in flowy garments were gathered around him, looking down at him with enchanted eyes. Their ecstasy bordered on the hallucinogenic, and with each step that aligned with the rhythm, the adults would chant uniformly "ماذا هذا يا غلام؟ هل الحياة كثرة آلام؟" He understood none of it, and it caused him insufferable shame, a mockery at his lack of comprehension. And as the rhythm sped up, so did he, his stubby arms lacking the control to pace themselves. He wailed, the way a toddler would, but the beat became more frequent and louder. Three beats in quick succession and one soon after. He managed to escape the encirclement of adults and returned to the rectangular steel tube through which he was crawling.

The last beat was that of an editor who had made his way into the storage cabinet. By then, the escapees had luckily made enough progress for the subsequent yells to reach them as mere murmurs cascading against the steel walls. Only one word, legible to Solomon's ears, he could repeat with some confidence, "Yan."

"Where to now?" The tips of his fingers tugged at the bottom of Nick's jumpsuit.

"How wonderful for us that the damsel has found her voice," Spud snickered at the spear of the involuntary flesh train. "We venture forward until we are struck by light."

Soon enough, the three encountered a fork in the duct's path – right and left, as if the decision bore religious significance. With little to no room for his lengthy limbs, a partially melted, half-eaten chocolate bar was strenuously withdrawn from Nick's pocket. And with that, Spud understood that their procession would rely on a Grimmian approach. Each branch with a bit of the bar would leave smidges of chocolate to retrace to the stem should the other find an exit first. A joke, humourless, was floated by to use bird calls to notify one another and was met with no laughter; concentration was pivotal. With a generic banging signal agreed, Spud and Solomon proceeded right and left Nick to his own accord. There was a recognition in the split. To Spud, Solomon was a prized possession, cherished for his novelty, whereas Nick was an ever presence in his life, his value taken for granted.

A few minutes and the choosers of the right could no longer hear the little clangs of a crawling Nick. "The chocolate, remember the chocolate," Spud would exclaim to the companion right behind him. For the first time in this venture, there was a modicum of concern in his voice. He worried, evidently, for his brother's fate. Lines of perspiration had reached Solomon, a combination of anxiety and heat its contributors. The chocolate marks beneath Osroes were degrading in the process. Each subsequent movement of Spud's knee was more reluctant than the one prior. It spoke in a language Nick was familiar with. *We need to retreat to him, Solomon. The world is treacherous, Solomon. My life is a worthy exchange, Solomon.*

In truth, Osroes was indifferent to the outcome. He yearned for more, of what he was unsure of. Answers, people, inspiration – these are all possibilities to an unknown. Akin to a man lost at sea, he did not concern himself with the topography of the land, its occupants, and its location, only that it is land he desires. Spud and Nick were merely, to Solomon, lost at sea too, and although he was inclined towards their survival so that they may sail these waters together, their demise would not morally burden him. It was a lack of empathy on his behalf but having not come to terms with reality as he currently experienced it, the entire construct had not reinstated itself into his psyche.

"To return now would jeopardise this whole endeavour," Solomon muttered breathlessly to the response of silence. He was not certain the reason why he said, yet a conversation of the unspoken kind compelled him.

The duct seemed to extend endlessly, and although they encountered many a vent, all were a window into a dark space that discouraged freedom. Thus, they persisted despite their aching joints.

They only communicated through pants and grunts. Spud's concern escalated into a form of jitteriness usually ascribed to a caffeine addict. Like a star contracting under its own gravity after it runs out of hydrogen fuel, he was at risk of collapsing onto his own ambition. On the brink of a question that begs, *Have I gone too far?* a piercing light detracted from the self-deprecating quandary.

It was, as the analogy would say, 'a light at the end of a tunnel.' If this were symbolic of Solomon's mental health however, then a finite tunnel, of which reality demanded, would not be applicable. His was an infinite tunnel, a light, at an apparent end of it, flicking on and off, like the passing of day and night, but no matter how far or fast he drove, the end remained as distant as it ever was. Solomon's state was never defined, but perpetually alternating between the journey towards what is known and unknown.

Aching knees and sore elbows, the escapees saw hues of a rainbow. Shown through the metal shutters, the taste of freedom from reality's udders. And before he dived into the sunlight's pool, Spud banged and kicked like a mule. "My brother, hear me. Hear these clangs. Follow the stains of Souls onto eternal light." Spud yelled, despite what his previous composure demanded of him. Solomon, for his part, attempted to calm the lunatic, but to no avail.

"To the detriment of your speech you yell," Solomon grabbed Spud's ankle but quickly retracted his hand when Spud continued his kicking. "This erratic behaviour will only serve in vanity of our progress. Nick," he pondered the name momentarily for assurances of his memory, "Yes Nick will be fine because that is the plan, and our responsibility is to its execution."

In earnest, Solomon believed nothing of what he said, but he had been served an amuse bouche of liberty and had discovered his appetite for the entire meal. In his second attempt to honour the chef's cooking, Solomon brought Spud's foot to a halt. He pinned it down under his elbow to which the man ahead yelled. "Let go, lest you receive a blow from my other leg to the head."

"Yours is one. Theirs are many. I have my preference and I reckon, so do you," Osroes replied cunningly, utilising a rusting tool in his toolbox – manipulation. "Dandy for the tall who crawls ten paces faster than you and I. We acquire our own security, and by the time your voice travels to him, you will find the brother at your heel."

Although Spud believed none of what his trophy claimed, the metallic shutters were the truth. They seduced him with whispers of 'gain' and detracted from worries of potential mishappenings. With a resurgence of hope, the two men crawled faster than they ever have, numb to the aching joints. No leverage to force his way out, Spud shifted onto his back and used the same feet he had kicked Solomon with earlier. And one slam, and another, and the entire sheet of metal gave way. Before any of their other senses were engaged, they were caressed by a breeze that shifted an insufferable heat to an uncomfortable cold – their perspiration into goosebumps.

Birthed from the institution's womb, their perception was heightened. They were blinded by the light initially, and by the time their eyes adjusted to the differential, they understood that one more hurdle remained. A mezzanine, on which they were now located, was a harbour for air conditioning units. Merely a few metres off the ground, and representing a platform to launch their escape, the men saw no challenge in throwing themselves to the ground.

"Mine breaks a bone of one. Theirs are many. I have my preference and I reckon, so do you," referring to the consequences of jumping or being caught, Spud bade a nod to Solomon's earlier remark.

And no sooner had Solomon's feet touched gravel, than an ugly cry escaped him – one of agony and indicative of the injury he sustained. His ankle bent in a manner only tolerable by contortionists. He fell to the ground, his knees pressed against the asphalt.

Falling awkwardly soon after, Spud hurried to Solomon's side. "One broken bone, the price of liberated others." he joked, throwing Solomon's arm over his shoulder and supporting the injured in his rise. Osroes replied with foul words, and although his ankle pained him to no end, he believed that if something hurt then he ought to apply more pressure to mask the pain.

Incessant were Spud's head rotations, glancing one moment and the next to ascertain whether his brother had trailed their prints. So apparent was his distraction that Solomon was almost the victim of slumped shoulders. But Spud's feet wiser than his head, he continued pacing whilst supporting his limping companion. "We the Baikonurs are Siberian survivalists, bear defiant, and Elbrus climbers. Our skin is too thick for the sword, and our hands are too callus for the pen." Solomon could hear the murmurs of his support, as if he were reciting an anthem to himself. And he would dare not interject with snarky remarks, for all that kept Osroes and the ground apart was the wounded man.

From the building, a cacophony of calls merged into a resonant hum. The editors were scrambling, bees in a hive, to find the escapees. Nonetheless, Solomon perceived the sounds as hollow, the building as empty, and the entire escape as a charade performed for the pleasure of a director. It was imprinted within him that the building was brim with writers, their shoulders often caressing others from the occupational density. Spud's urgency, a pulse he could sense quicken, however, alerted Osroes of the dangers forthcoming.

The two trotted past a gate, barbed and black. It was at this moment that Solomon decided to question the particulars of the plan for the very first time. "We are nowhere, nay, worse than nowhere, for in nowhere, we cannot be found. We are somewhere inescapable, only discovered by people contemptible." Osroes's rant was the product of trees, many of them, shrouding sight of the beyond. On the other side of the road from which they stood was a row of impenetrable trees, and to their right and left was an extension of the road, endless to the eyes. "Where to now?"

"Find your composure. Have I not led you this far?" Spud retaliated, his eyes locked ahead, peering at the ocean of trees as if he were attempting to telekinetically part them. Then they widened, and he smiled, "There! Our path is ahead."

Only a colour of grey could prevent the rebuttal of a man whose conviction lay in his demise – a ship steered towards the ice – and it did. Solomon caught sight of Spud's delight, a vehicle expertly hidden behind a few trees, reducing the limitless into an opportunity.

"Blessings upon blessings to you," Spud raised his arm towards the sky and exclaimed.

"Who do you shower with ardent praise?"

"The facilitator of our escape. An angel who follows a lowly man like me," Spud joked in reply before adding, "You will make her acquaintance not too long from now."

His fingers pinched together contorting into the shape of a snake's head, Spud reached into the van's exhaust pipe, desperately searching for the extra lengths the key would provide. Like a mole, his torso plastered to the dirt, he dug further into the pipe until his fingers located the loose metal. And from the vehicle's rear to its front, the two men, entered from adjacent doors and once reclined into their seats, emitted a sigh unbecoming of their current status of escape. Not only were they yet in WRITE's extended reach, but there was no sign of the mute sibling. What could Spud do? With no visual indication, his calls would remain unanswered.

Solomon dusted his jumpsuit, once white but now all shades of filth, and stole a couple deep breaths of the particulate-ridden atmosphere of the van's interior. Immediately after, he was forced to cough, and as his head dropped low during his fit, he noticed swelling around his ankle – the colour did not flatter either. But once his breathing had settled, Solomon had a moment to assess their situation and inquired, "To what do we owe this incaution of ours? Have we been graced with time's mercy?"

"Our time lounging here is a blessing from my brother's sacrifice," Spud shot an eye towards Solomon, cautionary of further indiscretions. "We shall repay his deed by returning some of this gained time back."

Osroes perceived his liberty oppressed at the hands of a tyrant, however, he saw the edge of the axe's blade and retreated to the safety of hushing. If he wished to reach a favourable outcome with the driver, Solomon determined that he must approach the matter tactfully. He spent the following moments weaving a net of manipulation so convoluted that one was liable to mistaking the end for the start. To overthrow the monarch and replace him with another, Solomon began his assassination attempt with a fib, encouraging Spud's anxiety to flare. "There!" he exclaimed, extending his arm across Spud and pointing towards the building.

So flabbergasted was Spud, that all words escaped him as gibberish and incoherent rambling. "Wha- where? Who- what?"

Only then the fib transformed into fact, and Solomon's neck, once threatened by the monarch's axe, was now adorned with a medal. *Did I conjure the man?* he thought to himself. After momentary deliberation about his creational powers and sacrilegious thoughts, Osroes relented. He squinted his eyes and managed to focus on a dot across the road, within WRITE's premises, and at the vent from which they escaped from. It was the head of a man birthed by the building's womb, the arms emerging soon after and flailing as if he was indeed a foetus.

Before Solomon could trap him in his web of lies, Spud cried out, "Bless the lamb that returns after I had threatened it with a knife," and prior to any confused queries, he continued, "My brother has appeared." Not since – well, he could not remember – did Solomon see Spud in such an exuberant state. He, on the other hand, had adopted Spud's nerves and instead of cheering the third of the escapees, Osroes watched silently whilst he scratched the skin by his thumb's nail. It was a habit he had developed at a young age imitating a loved one, and as habits went, the harmful ones were the toughest to quit.

His torso halfway out, his hands now on the mezzanine's gravel, Nick propelled himself forward one arm at a time. Regardless, there seemed to be a force pulling at his legs, and initially it was a mere hindrance, but now the only thing preventing him from being dragged back into WRITE's confines was the strength of his hands pushing against the outlet's frame. And that led to progression, his resistance proving fruitful and his torso touching light once more. On Spud's face hope increased and diminished; it fluctuated like water's ebb and flow. His mouth would open, anticipating a stream of words ready to pour out, and then it would close again. It had the remarkable effect of conjuring a goldfish in Solomon's mind.

The effort, verging on success, was ultimately to no avail. Editors, a couple of them, rushed onto the mezzanine and appeared to slam Nick with the bottom of their boots. With each slam, he sunk deeper back into the vent. The scene was censored for the two by the sheer distance of its occurrence, however they were afflicted with horror all the same. Spud's imagination conjured visceral images, their gore enough to claim the brother's life.

"He cannot speak!" Spud yelled with tears finding their way down to his shirt. "His protests are unheard. Savages! Yan, you claim to guide us towards scribing the truth, but if you are remorseful then where is your guilt in ink?" His voice was deafening and at moments it cracked into a blood curdling shriek, reverberating as if someone had dragged their nails against a chalkboard.

Solomon, although struck into silence, felt compelled to remedy the emerging cracks. "Steady yourself, good man." He placed a firm hand on Spud's shoulder.

"He, a large man, yes. He, a large heart, yes." Spud pointed, his entire arm shaking, towards where his brother had been taken, tears and snot running down his nose indistinguishable from each other. Veins pulsated on his forehead, the blood crowding his mind and fuelling his wrath.

"Our responsibility is to the plan's execution," Solomon reaffirmed and tightened his grip on Spud's shoulder. "My suggestion, within the boundaries of reason, is to secure ourselves so that we might return better equipped and with a well-devised plan to extract your brother." With Spud revealing nothing in way of conviction, Solomon supplemented, "If we rush back in now, we jeopardise our position and Nick's safety. Ponder for a moment, what use have they for him if they have us?"

All words rehearsed in the head from his initial manipulation attempt. Although he pitied the man's loss, this approach was purely pragmatic and an effort to speed the process of acceptance along. Spud, now looking straight ahead, reacted almost robotically, initiating the vehicle's engine and placing the shift stick in the driving gear. Solomon wondered whether the man had heard him at all. And for the remainder of the drive, he would wonder as much, Spud affording him no word along the journey.

Part 3: The Last of Parched Land

I did not bear the suffering of a prisoner's belief, for her accommodation did not instil it in me. Off the gory battlefield and through the muddy grounds, she dragged my body. How she had the physical capability, a woman of her age, I did not know. In my recollection, it was the truth, however marred by dirt, that blurred my vision, and blood that clogged my ears.

Through a burrow and into a warren, like a rabbit she was, living in a hole a few feet under the cursed barrens of Nomad's land. There, the harshest of battles had been fought and the only invasion was a stench of the demised many on the entrenched few. And extinguished was the spirit without a spent cigarette swimming in the shallows of a drunk bottle. Little is spoken of the constant dampness no towel could dry, and one could not distinguish the liquor from the urine from the blood from... the Earth that wept for us to cease, if only to spare us.

"Annabelle, if you cared to name me," she crossed her legs and sat on the ground beside the rug I was lying on.

My energy betrayed me, and I could not respond, only my eyes could, but they chose to observe. A grey scarf, as bleak as her skin tone, was wrapped around a neck that begged for - not its warmth, but structural support. A stout woman she was, however, her frailty was evident by her gait and the wrinkles that persisted despite. Her torso was covered with a floral cardigan, whose blossom might be wilted, for the garment could have been as old as Annabelle.

In her hand, a mug with a warm elixir, forced upon me with the tenderest of insistence. A tea of the mildest kind, served to introduce a warmth in me, which I could feel as its contrasting temperature travelled down my throat and seeped into the interiors of my body. An idle observer, she was watching me intently until unnaturally, almost as if scripted, Annabelle began narrating.

"War warps time. Years, decades, centuries. It started. It continued. When? How? Accounts of conflicting narratives put a sword to the neck for you to believe at their behest. Lest you become the enemy at present or a martyr too late. Falsities of the persuasive nature demand empathy, and who am I, or you, to reject their wonderfully woven stories of glory in the face of oppression? Who am I, or you, to deny their claims to rights of commons – the land, the air, the water? If only history, and historians for that matter, would agree on right and wrong at present and not from the comforts of two hundred years' worth of hindsight. A generational divide worth of comfort, so that the history of those who have suffered is dictated by those who have not. However, who am I, or you, to do without contextualisation of the past? We are merely reactors at present, playing a part in a narrative we know not of. Ideological misalignment, National Alliance for Total Liberty (NAT) and the Democratic National Assembly (DNA), the oppressed versus the oppressors, but which is which?"

It was scripted! It must have been. Annabelle framed the entire monologue like a theatrical performance expounding on a simple phrase to build into an existential climax. A woman of intellect perhaps, but also one with enough time to rehearse her speech.

My body made as to jerk up in revolt to Annabelle's words. Not that I consciously demanded it, but there was an inherent reactionary pathway instilled in me to reject what she said, and even violently oppose it. Her commentary was within reason, yet it felt accusatory as if passing on a baton of guilt. No, no, no, not my party, not the very people who breastfed me.

The last of the tea slid down my chin, a testament to my exhaustion and the physical reluctance to exert myself. My hand rose to wipe away the droplet, but even then, the gentlest of Annabelle's touches were enough to subdue me. Mass depleted, a result of scarce nutrition and an appetite quelled by the frontline, I resigned myself to spectating. Her script half-finished, Annabelle continued her tale under the light of a singular candle.

"The pursuit of power trumps ideological differences and in its wake creates a chasm of uncertainty through which conflict thrives. A farmer dictates the distribution of animal feed and sets off a competition between its cattle to consume the feed. A just farmer ensures the animals are well-fed and with equity. An unjust one, much like a tyrannical leader, sets out to underfeed the animals and create tension between the species. But it is the farmer who is unjust, and not the cattle. The devil is in the uncertainty, and if you were starving, then a conflict with the perception of 'others' is enough to satiate you till the next day, and the next, until you realise your stomach is still empty; but by then, you are already dead. Such is the tyranny of men, who rise as reformers and die by their ego. And such is the pride of men, who rise for their freedom and die by their principles."

Confusion befell me, what started as an exposition about the war and history devolved into barnyard talk. It was not the speech Annabelle had rehearsed. Even her intonations failed her, and her voice had begun to crack. There was a scramble in her speech, an incoherence that alluded to genuineness. The war to her, as it was to me, was personal and Annabelle was trying to extract logic from the irrational. Good and evil, what a beautifully naïve contrast.

Her voice now more aggressive and verging on the hostile, she continued, "The innocence of intentions is eroded by the cruelty of war. An explosive chain reaction that does not discriminate in its nonlinearity. With enough time, the war is caused by past wars and present wars fuel future wars, and the students of history ought to become immortal. Men, women, children and trees, all organisms and their ecosystems, victims of war. People remember and their scars are passed on. The land remembers and its stories are uncovered."

Her tears now in full flow, a waterfall with a limited source, dehydrating its producer gradually. My own wells dry, I understood the process of crying until inability. As if exercising the atrophied muscle of compassion, which decays like the bodies of the fallen, I raised the mug to Annabelle and handed her the last of the tea. Her gulps seemed forced but necessary. And unlike my degraded manners, she managed to wipe the last of chin droplets with her sleeve.

Annabelle exited the room in a worse state than when she entered it. Her statements were a devolution of sound thought and the eroding quality of rationalisation on mental health. However, those big words served nothing but to alienate me from my own empathy, perhaps. I stared up at the ceiling of soil and through its grooves was reminded of the trenches that housed me only yesterday. And one thought to another, a morbid back and forth, I was left wondering whether the decomposition of humans was a nutritious fertiliser for future plants. Will my fellows' tailbones be the seed that sprouts trees? Us, guided by the righteous, we could not be further from evil. Us, fighting for liberty, we could not be further from the oppressors. In that moment of clarity, I was reminded of how misguided Annabelle was. Her paranoia had driven her into disbelief.

And thence, upon the finality of my straying thoughts, Annabelle walked back in. With no will to it, I jolted up in reaction, my torso meeting the line of her barrel's sight. Her eyes were dry, much like my own, in many ways. They harboured a network of scarred sights, etched into her cornea, creating a filter that altered her perception. In me, the wounded soldier across from her, Annabelle saw both the tyrant and the victim. For her, the uncertainty carried outcomes of unequal magnitudes. If I were a tyrant that lived, then the catastrophe would be immeasurable. If I were a victim that died, then the war had done what it always had – claimed yet another grain of sand in the desert.

"Why would you nurture a man only to spill their blood?" I cried in petition for my life. "Do not disregard my attempt to communicate in haste." But it dawned on me, a realisation in hibernation from the moment Annabelle spoke, this was never a dialogue. It was the prologue to a tale that concluded with my death.

Not that it demanded such a conclusion, but that the author insisted on a level of certainty my life could not offer.

Behind me, there was an abstract painted in red. The spherical pellets had travelled through me, the brush to an artist; in their wake I could hear nothing but the ringing – a violent deafness I had become accustomed to. I dropped to the blanket below, the wall behind now in full view. I could finally critique the painting of which I was a constituent as if a portrait had been revealed to me after months of agonising patience. It could only be described, as the painter had prefaced, as 'a cruel act of war.'

Annabelle dragged my limp yet conscious self across the floor with a strength that still confounds me. In my faltering vision, I could see her fold over a couple of rugs to reveal a pit deeper than hers. Its entrance barely the width of a man, I resigned my resting to it.

"My apologies, Shams," she whispered sorrowfully. My breathing elevated and I could feel my heart pump faster; a betrayal to the wound I had sustained. But how did Annabelle know my name? Not a tag, not my comrades, not even my own mouth would have known to inform her. The military had installed a numerical categorisation that stripped many of their individualistic identity. I did not ask her to explain.

"Violence was never the solution to a problem before a problem arose with no solution but violence." To my ears, it was nonsensical babble masquerading as justifications to placate her raging soul. And for some reason, I found comfort in her sensibility. Annabelle did such and such with the conviction of the conflicted.

One kick and there I fell, scraping the walls towards the bottom of the well. The crunching beneath me induced a visceral repugnance that was soon followed by scampering hands. Each finger of mine that searched found an opening between two sticks to lodge itself in. These porous branches yet smooth were familiar to the touch, and their familiarity was only accentuated by the smell of the trenches. The spotlight from the hole above illuminated the pile of skeletons beneath. Annabelle's role in this war was that of a caretaker, not only to maintain the burial place of many fallen but to uproot the seedlings of germinating hatred.

Did she favour those three? I thought to myself, staring across at three skeletons that appeared deliberately positioned. An adult and two children staged in such a way that one, I in this case, would believe Annabelle descended herself and manufactured the dignified placement. Perhaps they meant more to her than misguided bodies. Perhaps they were assigned the role of keeping company to those in the purgatory that was this hole. To kill children after such a speech about the destruction of innocence... Why? Perhaps they were the first and look on vengefully to the tyrants of their demise. Who would fault her in killing a hundred for three? Numbers do not follow mathematical logic when accounting for the human factor.

*　　*　　*

Solomon I, Osroes by family, Balikh by clan, woke up from his hypnotic state in franticness. His eyes flitted from side to side and his lips smacked in contention. His fingers targeted his chest and scratched wildly, scrutinising the arena where the pellets would have been buried. The scratching had become a common occurrence, so much so, that a rash had embedded itself beneath his chest hair.

And no less, his fluids presented themselves like the condensation of morning dew, inviting a chill to run through him. Externally, he was not cold though, and he sensed a warmth that bordered on suffocation.

Solomon could still hear the crunching of bones, just as though he were still laying on a bed of them. The abstraction was gone and so were the wounds.

A room, built outside the classifications of a ditch, with grey brick walls all around contrasted by the hues of orange that caressed one corner more than the next. As his eyes centred on a source, Solomon

55

disregarded the crunching sounds as the mere crackling of wood ignited. The embers sprayed in all directions, creating patterns that enchanted their guest, if only for a moment. But soon, much sooner than anticipated, they represented a bitter reminder of the hydration he lacked.

"Where am I?" Solomon muttered in confusion. "Whose fuel burns to my affliction?"

He had not settled into this construct; therefore, Solomon was susceptible to dissociation. The crackling sound, although conspicuous, heightened his anxiety. He was on a woven chair one second, and on the floor the next, crawling towards the fireplace. His purpose was clear: extinguish the flame. But what to kill the fire with? Nothing in the room presented itself as a viable option for the mission. Water? Yes, water! The antithesis to fire, but where was Solomon to acquire some? And the more he emphasised on ridding of the flame, the more unbearable the sound grew.

Ah hell! Who poured a bucket of its sea in this confinement? An ill attempt at patting away the wood from its base and Solomon retreated to nurse his stinging hand. He grabbed his injured hand with the other as if fearing its independence in action. Never favourable were the odds of confronting hell's fire, he continued blowing gently on the burn.

A young woman, whose wrinkles spoke more of her past suffering than age, advanced through the door. Her hair of blazing red was contrasted by a skin of cracked porcelain, lacking the nutrition to mend its weathered state. Although there was a ferocity in her, perhaps an intensity behind prominent eyes, it was overshadowed by a quality of contrition.

"Shame befalls me. To even look you in the eyes represents an ever-present quarrelling remorse of our past." Solomon, on the floor, hunched over his own hand, was stunned and akin to a mouse having just noticed its predator. "I must set that aside at present, and bid you welcome in this abode should you accept me as a host." She spoke in a manner so pitiful; her voice almost fell with every syllable.

"Who in the tarnation – where is Spud?" Solomon questioned back in hostility, sensing he had an upper hand in a situation he knew not of.

Wary as to not aggravate his paranoia, the woman reassured him, "Spud is two paces away, at a store nearby, purchasing supplies for our benefit." She crouched down to de-escalate any perceived intimidation. "And to answer a question which you have not completed and to which you would not want to know, my name is Annabelle." Overwhelmed by shame, the woman looked away.

"Annabelle?!" Horrific thoughts came crashing forth and his fingers returned to scratch his chest. But there she was, not grey, not aged, not holding the weapon of his demise. Yet, the memory of her name evoked fury. "Annabelle?" There was that thought again; not one wave, but more cascading to amplify their magnitude with each plunge. Tunnel-visioned with a spotlight on her, Solomon felt he was in the ditch again looking up helplessly. The crunching sound returned, now more intense than before, and he could feel the vibrations etch into his cranium.

Like a toad, he sprung from the ground and onto Annabelle. A strength in soul unmatched by her body, she collided onto the brick wall in violent fashion. And off the wall she recoiled and onto the ground she fell, Annabelle bled a few shades darker than her hair. A cry of agony was not enough to stave off the perpetrator, whose knees found their way on either side of her abdomen. Solomon dove deep into her eyes, translating her pleas into an admission of guilt. Vengeful of porcelain, his fingers of adjacent hands met on either side of her neck. A resistance brewed beneath the pleas, and Solomon noticed a defiance that likened her to her fictional predecessor. Not a floral sweater to shelter her torso, yet Solomon was determined to cast her among the deepest roots of flowering plants. *May many more flowers blossom from her nutritious yet treacherous soul,* he thought to himself. And he was reminded of the soldier, the trenches, and the soil once more – a whisper of a false voice.

Her face expressed what words cannot. "Spare me. Spare my soul. Your death was only in vanity if you do not yet understand," her movements spoke. Although the phrases were subject to interpretive bias, certainly Annabelle chose life. A network of vessels in her eyes stretched across her corneas, mapping the beginning of her end.

"Shams? You speak of my son in ill tongue?" He pressed down harder, a testament to an unhealthy rage. "What father would I be..." And the sentence trailed off into nothingness.

Shaded like a ripe nectarine, her face no longer pale, Annabelle scratched away at Solomon's hands. Despite the injuries his hands sustained, the pain only aided his determination. It was a reminder of the ailments the woman had and could subject him to. A final few attempts at taking a breath unrewarded, and Annabelle's spirit was unwelcome in this home of hers. And in its departure, a farewell, as if the spirit were off to war, it looked back to its residence and uttered "Soul's Best Bar." Having heard those words, his fingers involuntarily released and Osroes finally retreated.

The markings of trauma were on her neck, and another day gone, and another was dead. A tragedy to be told by the bricks on the wall of Annabelle's hospitality and her eventual fall. The colour of orange blended with the red, and the flames flickered, a mourning for the dead. A father relieved for his son's future life, then an image formed of a daughter and subsequently a wife. His ear to her chest, searching for the callings to respire; and when none was a breath, his aggression retired.

Standing up, he was finally observing Annabelle from a position of superiority, not morally but physically. Although there was a sense of relief that the struggle had been concluded, Solomon felt it to be bittersweet. Another woe to a list. And the crackling sounds were a sharp reminder of that. More painful than before was the sound that pierced into his core. *Why? The creator of the pit is dead, is she not? Why am I still being punished?* His thoughts were merely background to an ever full and looming sound of crunched bones. *Oh, but the flames do not know her death like I do. An ear to the chest they do not possess.* Osroes rubbed his eyebrow to an extent unrecommended by dermatologists. *They are but vicious consumers. Ah yes, how could the flames understand their redundance to their master? I must send her amongst the fires so they can inspect her like I have.*

The onlookers would have protested the moral degeneration; however, no such sound would condemn a man in isolation; only his own conscience perhaps, which is forever warped by the experiences he is subjected to. And not only that, but the narrative the man creates is born out of the tragedies from a string of his own construction. Therefore, in remembrance, what are discrete unfortunate events are viewed as a tale for the justification of evil.

Annabelle's wrists firmly in his grip, Solomon dragged her across the dusty floor. There was humour in his efficiency, disposing both of what he thought to be 'waste' and cleaning the floor simultaneously. But a trail of blood soon followed, replacing all the progress he thought he had made. Whether out of awe for the patterns produced in red or anxiousness that perturbed his navigation, Solomon's route towards the fireplace was indirect.

Why was it so inhumane? This entire process was systematic and born out of action that justifies the next and the next. Unlike with Earl, not once had Osroes stopped to contemplate the magnitude of his actions. He had just disposed of a life on the basis of a myth, notwithstanding its significance, a myth, nonetheless. And to then feed Annabelle's body to the flames posed a theological conundrum, whereby the creator of the sinner subjects the sinner to punishment for the sin. But he was a mere mortal of vivid imagination, directed by stories and lacking sense of which the doctrine commands. No better than the tyrant he was.

Spirals later and her body was ahead of the roaring flames. To subject her to more humiliation, having pushed her carcass in, Solomon kicked Annabelle's two or three hanging limbs into the blaze. No different than the wood were the crackling sounds, and they subjected the perpetrator to an agony multiple in magnitude than before. It would have driven the man to the verge of insanity had he been confined to the walls. However, the same freedom presented by Annabelle to Solomon had been taken away from her. A door, a slit of ventilation, was a natural path for the crazed man, whose own skin was suffocating. He could not bear the sight of her skin charring, having been subjected to minor burns earlier. *I have angered those very flames. I pardon myself and ask for leave.*

The rustling of feet, the clashing of pottery, and the voices of hagglers, the Merchant was hiding behind one brick or another, laughing as he did at the fool's trade. There was no mercy in the trade – one was a life of guilt and the other an uncertainty with none. The fire's warmth was like the heat of the desert, amplifying a sense of divine scorn.

One bead of sweat rolled into Solomon's eye and from the desert he was transported into a structure masquerading as a house. Most of the rooms were hollow and dingy with a general coldness that disqualified it from being a home. But Osroes's urgency prevented him from scoping the multi-storied flat further. No sooner had he seen the descending stairs than he leapt down, skipping a couple of steps in the process. Spud would return at any moment to discover the chargrilled remains of his friend. And whilst Solomon was too preoccupied with a paranormal entity to consider his escapee partner's sensibilities, he hurried to sprint out of sight. Slam! The door closed a chapter behind him.

A starry night, more so in Galileo's vision than Van Gogh's, however the streetlights did nothing to enhance the constellations above. One, and he did, could reflect for time on matters unrelated to the stars by observing them. Not in an astrological fashion that demands the belief in horoscopes and zodiac signs, but by the imposition of patterns that vary from one set of eyes to another. They could see a fish eluding their capture on a trip from decades ago, or they could see a wife and two children that danced in a garden to the sound of plucked strings. It was the latter for Osroes. In the shimmering celestials, he heard the callings of three.

And there, a vehicle presented itself, both as an opportunity of travel and a reminder to make haste, for Spud was a walking distance away. Door handle after another resisted his pull. The van appeared an impenetrable enclosure. Momentarily, Solomon saw, in the faint reflection of the glass, himself an ape hoping to climb a tree outwith its confines. And were it not for the service of his memory, he would have remained hopeful as such. He remembered Spud's initial key retrieval outside the institution – the exhaust. "What foolery!" Solomon mumbled to himself, internally critical towards the sloppiness of his former dictator. The jangling of keys between his fingers was a chime marking the introduction of an adventure towards the Wandering Woods.

Osroes had not noticed the harshness of the winds until he was within the car's sanctuary. His bones, which endured the brunt of the blows, were grateful to receive the benignity of still air. Once the key was in ignition, he felt the consequences of his burnt hands. Determination beyond the pain, the key scraping against his skin, Solomon had enough in him to get the van to rumble. Although he had identified an objective to his destination, he had not settled on its location.

There was a heavy sigh, and a moment of ponder. *Luna, I find myself in quite a conundrum. And for the first time, perhaps second, or maybe even third... I cannot quite recollect; I do not find you by my side.*

The last he could remember of his beloved wife was an argument about Solomon's facial hair. What started as a shallow tit for tat escalated into an eruption of dormant insecurities. But he had taken a hard-line stance and refused to shave. Therefore, their dispute was mediated with a resulting mutual ceasefire and a de-escalation zone that was destined for a couple of hours. But the hours days, and the days months, and such and such, till one was left to wonder how much time he had been away from the moon. Oh, Solomon yearned for Luna's embrace, which to his mind was a diluent of his problems into an ingestible drink.

I spared the poor man the insufferable logistics of planning a funeral, Solomon thought back to Annabelle's body. It was a twisted perspective on an unjustifiably evil yet understandable act. But he had to live with himself somehow, and having shifted the gear and released the handbrake, he moved on as such.

Bad omens, marked by strong winds and empty roads, plagued the lost man. 22nd Augustus Street – yes, yes, that is precisely where he wanted to be. But where, where was Augustus Street? Navigationally confounded, Solomon was incapable of remembering left from right when it came to his once home. The van's white noise, eerie, was a backdrop that washed away any semblance of compounded thoughts. *Two lefts clockwise around the church's bell tower?* Noise. *No... There?* Noise. *No. Take a right after the medicinal store?* Noise. *No.* Osroes halted his journey by a store, wishing for some answers. Normally, people enter such a store within convenient proximity of their residences to purchase items at a convenient price. He, on the other hand, had entered the store searching for the convenience of geographical clarity.

"You in need of some assistance, fellow?" the shop owner limped from behind the counter. His hair white as snow, contrasted by an olive expression, the man's age was nothing shy of sixty. His wrinkles were minimal for his age and demonstrated a stoicism, perhaps even contentment, in his character. He had a unique accent that filled Osroes with comfort before flooding him with shame – the sort of accent that reminded Solomon of his own uncle.

"It would appear so," Solomon looked down embarrassed, as if he were a child asking his parent for some money. "Have you the directions to Augustus Street?"

Playing his bit part role, the shop owner proceeded to scrutinise Solomon's appearance the way an uncle would. Frail figure, scruffy beard, neglected hygiene – *The youth are misguided these days*, he thought to himself.

"No navigation? Not even a memory to rely on? Your days have been tough, have they not?" the elder chuckled, teasing the young traveller.

"No tougher than yours," Solomon retorted before adding, "What happened to your leg?" Crudely, he enquired about the shop owner's prosthetic limb.

"The world has blunted your blade I see, never mind." the man disregarded his own irritation. "A close friend of once shoved me down a flight of stairs."

"Of once indeed!" exclaimed Solomon with outrage.

"In my death, he sought the confidence of my wife. But here I am with a lost leg, and there he is locked away. I return home to a loving wife, and he observes the men who have done more or less than him." The elder limped back behind the counter, leaning on it for support.

"His thoughts are treacherous," Osroes replied apologetically.

"Nothing of the like. I harbour no resentment for the man." He raised his hand and swiped it across as if he had actually pushed any notion of bitterness away. "He only saw, for a moment, what I had been privileged with for years, and if I were him, then a dagger would have been by my side to finish the job. Lord, have mercy on us all." The final statement brought an air of relief that accompanied a natural conclusion to the story.

Osroes had forgotten his intention behind the stop and was only reminded after the shop owner passed a piece of paper across the counter. "Here you are, fellow. I hope you keep a dagger by your side – for defence, that is."

Farewell bade, and Solomon back on the trail again, he could not shake the curiosity he had about the elder's wife. *To kill a close friend for a companion?* It seemed entirely irrational. *What beauty could do that to someone?* he thought to himself. Solomon patted the right side of his trousers, near his belt, and was left worried by the absence of a dagger.

"Two lefts clockwise around the Church of St. Thecla," he read off the piece of paper. And by the time he shook off imaginary renditions of the shop owner's wife, Osroes found himself in Augustus Street. Hues of yellow from the streetlamps above contrasted against the dark houses; it painted the neighbourhood in grim isolation. Each of the detached cuboids had the juxtaposing qualities of harbouring neither individualistic nor communal characteristics to their exteriors. Neither the odd bike tossed across the lawn, nor the hedges of varying degrees of kempt, nor even the welcome mats or hanging planks to signify the humanity of this block. And further down the road, Solomon found himself in a cul-de-sac of these flawless cages.

In his head, the sounds of other tongues yelling against a backdrop of chirping birds was overwhelming. There was singing too, and the clanging of pots, the flowing of water, the rustling of bushes, the rattling of rolled dice against a wooden board, the bubbling of water, inhales and exhales... Harmonious mess. Then, it was silent again – a terrible loneliness.

22nd Augustus Street, there he was, right ahead of the door. Clean, tidy, uninhabited; those three words rushed in description of the house's exterior. The front yard was immaculate, excessively so, as if the individual grass blades were actively cut or prevented from growth altogether. The driveway was empty, and the footpaths were clear of any debris that would signify normalcy. "Who built you? Who lived in you?" Solomon mumbled under his breath. And as his eyes moved downwards to examine the structure's foundation, he caught sight of his own beard.

"The pyramids of Giza!" Osroes exclaimed fearfully. "Luna shall raise and drop them on my head." Perhaps, in recognition of efficiency, the Pharaoh Khufu would not mind sharing his resting bed with Solomon.

Not a single light, not a single sign of life, no respondent to his knocks. Three knocks in quick succession and one soon after. "Hello? Grace me with your presence O Moon," he yelled. And upon looking high into the sky, he noticed the moon, on this night, was overshadowed by the clouds. Dejected at having been rejected Luna's appearance, Solomon took to the windows to seek his entrance. Twisted and turned, pulled and pushed, but nothing would give way, until out of desperation, he rotated the doorknob. First the van and now the door, it seemed simplicity was an answer first served but last sought. Seemingly a ghost racing with the madman, a gust of wind blew into whatever vacuum had created a negative differential pressure in the residence. The dust danced to the draught, welcoming Solomon back as one of its creators.

A plaintive cry escaped his mouth involuntarily. He had expected the sight of a room with enough clutter to terrify a minimalist: items of great sentiment, paintings average yet core-shaking, rugs worn and stained, uncoordinated furniture with random designs, photos of relatives known and unknown, and the smell of food that invites you to remain for supper, then breakfast, and then forever. But none could be farther from that. Had the room not been occupied by a few functional items, then Solomon would have discounted the tragedy as a case of a mistaken house and one unoccupied yet. No, there they were: a shoe rack, a coat hanger, a cupboard, a coffee table, a couch... all colour coordinated and homogenous, as if picked straight out of a catalogue. Osroes cursed the sign to the doorway's right with carvings of 'Welcome' as an empty gesture designed to provoke a sense of formality that spat, perhaps passively, in the face of his perception of hospitality.

"Where is the purposelessness in this all, Luna? Where is the spirituality that rejects the confines of utility, Luna? Where is my source of light on a starry night, Luna? I am referring to the moon, but only brighter, Luna?" Solomon called for his beloved, directing his voice into the vacuous corners of the house.

And no lonelier did he feel than then, for his body had associated an entrance into this house with copious embraces from his younglings and the warm breath that pre-empted his wife's lips. He trudged around the room with the burden of expectation weighing him down. Searching like a hound dog, through his eyes only, to sniff out the least bit of heart that might be thawing in this refrigerator. At last, he dragged two of his fingers across the coffee table – *Could the dust be a bearer of the unknown?* However, the thought was soon trampled over by another. Rather nauseously, the dust represented more than his own dead skin cells. Luna, Shams, and Amar's cells were all clumped up into this one dust swipe. If only Osroes knew that his feet would bleed and he would eat out of a garbage dump before he received something approximating a hug.

The kitchen, down the end of the hallway, extending an outlook towards the backyard, was no livelier. With just the uncooked memories of yesteryears and half-baked thoughts of broken bread, Solomon was held into submission. On the odd day, he would prepare Luna and the children a service of small dishes, each an element to satisfy a region of the tongue. Orange marmalade, white cheese, pickled aubergine, slices of cucumber and tomato, olive oil, za'atar, eggs of any kind, and bread thick enough to spoon with yet thin enough to complement its passengers; most of those elements required no arduous work and would remain on the tray day and day after if only they were replenished. They were not, but why? It was a simple task, to top up the olive oil, yet he did not – was it out of indolence, or did the man ache at the vulnerability such a task would make him admit to? Anger brewed within Solomon, which he quickly extinguished. The memory, like many others, would remain raw.

Could one stair, or two, or many for that matter, uplift his soul like it did his body? Futile, but at the very least, he could peer into the bedrooms of his loved ones. And into the main bedroom he went, a nail into a coffin buried long ago under mounds of dirt, yet he still dared to hope. Such was the treachery of hope, that it would tease him to no end about the possibility of bringing the dead alive or returning an amputated limb. The hope was many of the devil's tools, yes. If it was not realised then it was a mere tease, and if it was not realised enough times, then it was a failure of the devil having not understood the capacity of its tortured. And if the hope was realised, then it was to remind you that the manifestation of hope is dim in hope's unmanifested light. And thus, the devil realises your hope on occasion only to increase the magnitude of your desire for the next – a cycle of expectation and deflation until despondency arrives. But that was the cynicism of Osroes, viewing both successes and failures as vile outcomes.

The bedroom was empty, and so was the bed that invited Solomon to lay upon it. He paid no attention to the tension in his back until it hit the mattress. Several knots unwound; his spine cracked to the relief of support. There was a twinge in his left foot, a numbness that screamed of nerve damage. Heedless to the pain, Solomon viewed complaints of the body as temporary strife symptomatic of spiritual ailments.

"Welcome me and I will not dare respond unless you desire. Request my leave and I will do so with no desire," he begged her spirit.

Turning to his right, he buried his face in a pillow and he was struck by the initial whiff of jasmine. A smile was threatened by a second odour, more potent and loathsome. It was alcohol, made to disinfect all good, and leave in its aftermath an offensive neutrality. And not only the smell, but Osroes could sense one side of the bed more tender, as a matter of use, than the other. *Did we not rest in each other's arms?* He traced the cavity with his finger.

Now by the window, Osroes stared down onto the backyard. The darkness in its fullness could not hide the disorder. Unlike the house's front, the garden behind was a litany of broken branches, wild growths, patches of broken soil, and leaves which had disintegrated into scatterings of mulch. In the yard's centre, just ahead of a dilapidated shed, was a patch unlike others – larger, with no debris, characterised by human intervention. So dark was the patch that one, at night, could mistake it for a bottomless pit. The shed was sad – but how, you might ask? The wooden structure took on the face of a human, and Solomon could see through its window the neglect it suffered. But there was a consolidatory element to the shed, as would be seen from a patient towards the end of their treatment. Yes, they were on the verge of recovery, but they had sacrificed energy and time to arrive at this possibility. And no one, unfortunately, can recover what was lost. For that, Solomon felt a great guilt that was accompanied by the smell of burning tobacco. His eyes shifted above to the Wandering Woods and the Alienus river beyond.

His two offspring, Shams and Amar, shared a bedroom no larger than the main one. Despite that, it felt more expansive, the walls endless, giving way to the occupiers' trajectory. Perhaps it was the wall paint that lent the room an undeserved spaciousness. Clouds, lacking in artistic quality, were smudged across a pastel blue background. Their little fingers, he could remember them in glimpses, pudgy and disoriented, tips of dry white paint, and an echoing laughter that bordered on haunting. Solomon could see their button noses with paint residue. They had absent-mindedly scratched their itchy noses with their fingers. He licked his thumb and reached out to wipe the mess from Shams's nose first – then they were not there. His wet thumb stood in the middle of the room, caressed by a gentle breeze as a reminder of its existence and nothing else.

"You are the very purpose of my being, and I failed to recognise that." His pitch was inconsistent, and his eyes welled up.

The clouds appeared to float by, but where to? Solomon could scarcely breathe, and he felt the entire weight of the atmosphere in his lungs. Every breath felt dense and nauseating, a dizziness he endured regularly but had not grown accustomed to. He chose to follow the clouds in their journey, but the wall paintings only led him outside the children's bedroom. He looked behind, overtaken by confusion, and found the door closed. Had he entered their bedroom at all?

Not a drop of ink, deliberate or spilt, on paper or otherwise. This was unlike Luna, not to leave a letter disclosing circumstances preceding her disappearance. Her skill with a pen was exceptional and brought much jubilance to postmen who were subjected to her elegant calligraphy. Looped 'L's to end one letter and begin another – none were to be found. Nothing, but the copious dust that appeared to thicken with every glance. It was akin to the house burying itself to bring closure to a chapter of tragedy for the pleasure of future archaeologists.

Down the stairs Solomon descended, more clumsily than in ascension. Rays of light struck his feet first and climbed up his body, illuminating much of the bottom floor. As the first of sun broke through the horizon, Osroes felt he had overstayed his welcome. What was initially hidden by the mercy of night was presented with complete honesty at the dawn of light. He could no longer bear the barrenness of his 'home.' *How could I have let this happen? The degradation of my own soul,* he wiped his nose with the back of his hand. And more spent than when he had entered, Solomon exited the house.

With the gait of a defeated man and the heart of a broken one, Osroes plodded along towards the van. Each step across the yard was meaningful and every blade of grass was made to absorb him in full. He yearned to feel their steps on this grass, their rolling around, their anything... For Solomon, the suffering elicited by memories was most generous. It all appeared novel to him, rarely awarding memories of them as common. And those nascent films rolling in his head only served to compound his love for them; perhaps, even more so than love was desire, which was selfish and obsessive. The sky ahead now clear, the clouds were incomparable to those in his children's bedroom.

His foot on the pedal and his mind elsewhere, Solomon went on to scout for a shaded spot. Although his eyelids had grown heavy, the desire to rest was more for the dreams to ensue. The sun's warmth and the morning embrace, food from his hand into their mouths, laughter and arguments around the dining table, and the late-night tucking into bed, he could experience none of it without the aid of imagery. The moon had gone to rest, and so should he. Yet, the moon could be a wandering entity, lost, calling his name, and residing to a similar defeat during the day.

The vehicle had found itself under a bridge, no different to the many that resided there. Tents upon tents with barrels for heat, the community was relegated to a small segment that brought them much shelter. Solomon could not discern this from that, his vision drunk with lust for a black backdrop. Sounds of tents ruffling, balls being kicked around, and children playfully running about would keep his consciousness occupied for a while longer.

Metal against asphalt, a child had tipped over one of the barrels, spilling a pile of heated coal and burnt plastic near a collection of tents. An elderly man came out screaming and yelling, reprimanding the young girl for her act of wilful negligence. But before he could swipe at her with a branch he had by his side, a group, seemingly belonging to the community, interjected and appeased the old man, mediating the process of crime and punishment. Their language was broken, their clothes filthy, and although he saw elements of anger, joy, and ranges of emotions, it all struck him as feeble and underlined by an incapacity to conduct themselves socially – dignity, honour, pride... How could you maintain any when the world afforded you none? Yet, here they were, protecting one another, settling disputes with one another, and communicating outside the boundaries of archaic limitations with one another. It confused Solomon greatly, and had he been more alert, he would have explored this matter further. But such were the selfish eyes, that afforded him no more time and relegated those thoughts to the subconscious.

An image or two of yellow or blue, Osroes could not distinguish between the painting and its muse. It was a coagulation of colours, forced into existence, to serve the director of the movie. "Merchant?" Solomon whispered under his breath.

"Good morning, my dear. Your face, your eyes, the scruffy beard I dislike, I have missed them all in earnest." The statement was punctuated with a giggle.

"Luna? My dearest! Where are you? I have missed you gravely."

"I am here, Solomon. I am here..."

متى يمكنني العودة الى منزلي

Part 4: Respect

The relativity of time bears no significance to an officer of the law. To use the theory as a justification for unlawful actions is foolish - the man opposite the window knocked three times in quick succession; it served little to endear Solomon. The slumber, in his perspective, had lasted a few minutes, but the officer disagreed. And when the officer knocked once more soon after, Solomon awoke and addressed him. "Is that you, nectar of my soul?" Osroes rolled down the window without the supplementary support of vision.

Burning through his eyelids, the sun's rays turned a backdrop of black into red. The torment he was subjected to in his dreams was climaxed by the hellish red. It forced his arms out as if he were swimming in a pool of hell's lava begging to be saved. And in his forceful arm extension, he nicked the officer's face, escalating a friendly encounter into a hostile one. Had he been given the chance to explain the unrelenting pain he had been put through, the officer surely would have wept by his side and bid him a good day.

"Pardon aside, I request you exit the vehicle instantly." The officer whipped out a truncheon to emphasise his authority.

A nervous tremor appeared in Solomon's body, a symptom of a shaken core. *A voice not as sweet,* he thought to himself. More than the officer's aggression, he was horrified by the prospect of an absent Luna. But when his eyes settled and he could finally put a face to the commander, his aloofness came naturally. Whether the man's threat paled in comparison to his mental anguish, or Osroes had simply grown weary of his own emotions, the entire confrontation was tainted by mockery. Maybe none of those, but the man's stature, short and plump, encouraged Solomon to view his opponent as primitive.

"Sir, afford this interaction cordiality and do not impel me to use force," the officer's face was going red.

"Apologies officer, an erroneous assumption of mine led to a case of mistaken identity." Solomon replied coolly before adding, "If you afford me such time to recount the events preceding this unfortunate outcome, then you would do me a great favour."

A loud bang, the truncheon against the vehicle's door, interrupted Osroes's request. Forced into a façade of humility at the mounting threat, Solomon stepped out of the van. The officer's questions, systematic, were met with mundane answers. Solomon fractured into couplets, one joining the programme of automated query and reply, and the other envisaging the officer as an ape. It was condescending, but Solomon increasingly had come to view the world as a jungle – what was one more ape to it? Law and order seemed trivial matters that were bound to collapse against chaos. Perhaps, in his lack of comprehension, Osroes chose chaos as an all-encompassing answer, finding relief in its certainty. Where were Luna and the children? Chaos. Where was his home? Chaos. Who was he? Chaos. The officer? Chaos.

And therefore, when the officer ultimately demanded to see his driver's license, Solomon found his reaction to the request quite simple – chaos. With the aid of a pencil and paper in the glove compartment, Osroes drew a yellow fruit he thought would appease the lawman. "I would rather test life's limits than be tested on my ability to complete an ape's work. Do you concur, officer?" He handed the paper over.

"What is the meaning of this?" The officer shook the paper in the air, "A banana?"

"Albeit an amateur at the art of bribery, I find my attempt commendable." Solomon replied in a muffled tone, wary that while his insults were tame, life's retaliation was not. The entire interaction bore Osroes, whose sensitivities had waned.

As compliance was mandatory under the boot, Solomon was unsurprised to find himself at the back of the deputy's vehicle. His wrists were sore, an indicator of tightened cuffs, and his knees were constricted by the lack of leg space. But mentally, he was at ease, even delighted to relinquish control over his life for a short while. Solomon had only discovered uneasiness when the car began to move. Motion sickness was a defect passed down his lineage, only experienced as a passenger at the back, and having seen one building then two pass by, his stomach had begun to turn. To stave off any regurgitation of past meals, he distracted himself by conversing with his arrestor.

"Do not humiliate me any further by ignoring my presence. I am not silent cargo being transported for delivery," Osroes began charmingly. "What is your name, lawman?"

There was a pause, slight, marked by thought. "Harold." the officer replied in a matter-of-fact way.

"And is there no family name to this Harold you claim?" If it were his aim to irritate the man, then Solomon was beginning to succeed, however, if it were to elicit a reaction, unfortunately Harold had grown immunity to snark.

"Nothing but Harold."

"Remember that I have afforded you the mercy of not addressing you as 'Nothing but Harold,'" Solomon awaited the man's response to his lame attempt at humour. "What a mouthful of a name, might I add."

"Your silence is the most favourable of companions. Should you choose to disregard its assistance, then your words are a liability holding weight in your prosecution." Harold's face flushed in vexation.

A third building and then a fourth, Solomon exhaled deeply. The diversion from nauseating imagery was necessary, and there were two competing to exit his mouth: a response and partially digested food.

"Very well, 'Nothing but Harold,'" he smirked before continuing, "If my meal of a day or two should find your windshield the 'most favourable of companions,' then you can hold the entire weight of my silence as liable."

*　　*　　*

Who the hell am I? What the hell am I? Where the hell am I? I fear in my repetition of the word 'hell,' I have spoken it into existence. My sentience at best questionable, was I the product of twisted imagination? My perspective was the eyes of this sorrowful man. My memories were accessible at his behest. My timeline was ambiguous. A stalker forced to stalk a man by the name of Harold, whose existence bore no significance to me, or not that I knew of anyhow.

The sun rises and sets, and in between a day is colourless. Why was I watching this man? Not the pleasantry of heaven nor the anguish of hell – a neutrality that epitomises melancholy. Blood, thick, trickling down a throat I did not possess, and yet I felt death in the gasping of air despite the breath I no longer needed. The habit of breathing was difficult to forget. Screams, and silence, in waves echoed into ears, not mine, and yet I could hear. My body non-existent, I could not see my skin, its colour, nor feel its softness.

I wished his death, if only to bring me repose, whether for the better or the worse, repose. Harold's days were like an apple rotting, but slower and more painful. I have attempted to extinguish his existence during slumber in vain, for with each try the man would jolt awake as one would from a nightmare. And to kill him awake, well, that was a suffering I was not prepared to deliver.

Another sip of coffee, strong, Turkish, a sound misophonic people might detest. A sigh, explaining much but offering little in substance. A lit cigarette to compliment the bitterness of his drink. An eye rub, to soothe the irritation from the smoke. "Shalom," words Harold shared with the café owner. The coffee shop inconspicuous, in a narrow alleyway, he had spent the morning, as he did every other, on a stool consuming his chosen substances of spiritual escape. And when the time came to depart, Harold stomped the ground to get rid of any dirt that had lodged itself at the bottom of his boot. He strolled down the alleyway, his mouth dry, as it always was from smoking, swishing saliva from one cheek to another and swallowing. The tobacco's taste on his tongue, he spat down, missing the gutter that ran by the road's side and leaving a blot by the door near it.

Tamar, his junior of twelve years and a companion in enforcement, was at an intersection towards the bottom of the alleyway. She was hounding a young child, one of the others, tan and proud – 'of what?' Harold relayed the thought to me. Proud yet impoverished, that was the tale told by his scrawny frame and garments consisting of a sleeveless shirt, that undoubtedly was once white, and pants with enough holes to render them non-functional. The entire conflict was incomprehensible to Harold: he was here, he was an officer of the law, he was not evil, and therefore they were. Perhaps not evil, he revised, but misguided by the falsities of their power-hungry leaders. I had not been afforded the details behind what conflict Harold thought of, for he had restricted those details and boiled the nuance into the concentrated summary of his choosing.

Tamar had gripped him by the collar of his shirt and was scolding him for the graffiti he had left on the wall, and Harold could see in full view the words in white, "متى يمكنني العودة الى منزلي" Although the language was foreign, they had been taught basic comprehension. But I was overwhelmed, the melancholy flushed away, only to be suppressed by the pinch of Harold's nose bridge.

"You have no home here, you understand?" Tamar violently shook the young boy, no older than ten, ensuring that she physically translated those words for him in spite of the language barrier.

His jaw clenched, and he could almost crack his teeth with the tension. A migraine had set in – he was sure coffee and cigarettes were the cause. But there was an element of guilt and shame that revolted against his idleness. Yes, he viewed 'them' no better than mice, pests, but he did not enjoy hurting mice and could only drive himself to do *so because he was told he was a cat, and that is what cats ought to do.*

"Enough, scurry along and return where you belong," Harold interjected Tamar's lambasting and shoved the child away. The youngling ran away, paying no heed to his direction, yelling words that were rooted in him.

"These rats are popping up left and right, smearing their filth on our walls," Tamar protested her partner's leniency. She was on the cusp of laughter however and bored by the prospect of confrontation. Harold chose to walk side by side with her instead. "This impotence of yours is going to cost us, old man."

Harold was distracted, raising his hand in salutation to the local grocer, who bowed his head down to return the greeting. "Any news on the house?" He yelled, slowing down his pace ever so slightly.

"They have weighed us down with a mound of paper, bureaucracy I tell you." The grocer chuckled and shook his head disagreeably.

"Would you not rather enter after it has been swept and mopped?" Harold smiled back, spelling an end to their chatter.

But Tamar continued, as if Harold had been listening all along, "Every hour, there are three more of them and one of us." He turned and grinned at her, almost derisively. She continued, "The rocks might not scare you, but the rockets will." And she patted Harold on the back mockingly in return.

An amalgamation of music, harmonically confused, and accented by percussions that varied from clanging pots to slapping rugs was the background sound of their day. But occasionally, there was an injection of silence, and Harold could hear his own breathing. It was irregular, fast at times and slower at others, and a hint of wheezing that spoke of difficulties in his bronchioles. Each breath after the other demanded more attention in the arena of silence, and the more attention his breathing drew, the more aggressive it became. Tamar's words... Sharon, peace, Jerusalem, bleed... The silence was better. And it served to further concentrate his attention on his breathing.

Was it the coffee and the cigarettes? he thought to himself again. Harold was on the verge of collapsing, finding himself on the doorstep of one of the more recent settlers in the area. However, he managed, albeit stumbling, with the aid of Tamar's arm to make it through a set of doors and into their station.

"Pull it together. Where has your heart gone?" Tamar nudged him to straighten his posture.

The laughter of men, passing newspapers around, and exchanging flippant remarks about 'pebble throwers.' The heavy sound of a wooden stamp to legitimise this occurrence and the next. The whizzing of fans spanning left and right and the printer machine that seemed to endlessly print one report after the other. The air blown by the fan could almost turn one's stomach against him, and each summer it got warmer, and the offices colder. The walls, all white, their paint shedding and yellow marks in the corners from the moisture. Mould, its stench, underlying but assertive, and yet it was invisible to the eye; or perhaps the filing cabinet and desks had been strategically placed to cover its existence. The sweat, he could see it on everybody's faces, and he could feel it on his own.

The plastic seat absorbed Harold's rear. I could sense his breathing slow amidst a cacophony of distractions, but only one, between his index finger and thumb, mattered. He drew closer to his mouth a cigarette, and I could sense, as soon as its end touched his lips, a relief that bordered on ecstasy travelled through him. But no sooner had he gone to light it than he found his escape between crumpled paper in the trash can.

"This is the very cause of your impotence," Tamar sat on top of the desk across him, her uniform of navy-blue right in his face. "This is a war for our nation's womb, and here you are eroding the remainder of your virility."

The soil to be ploughed and the seed to be sowed, the nation's womb is a place to be sold. Trees uprooted and plants pried, for the concrete they lay mixed with our pride. Brick by brick this wall gets built, to shelter the builders away from their guilt.

Harold pinched the bridge of his nose and there I was relegated away from my throne. Why am I confined to a prison within him, to view the world through a narrow lens of self-preservation? But not mine, his, and even the olive oil, its earthiness and richness, is a bitter taste on his tongue. Something is awfully wrong, and a tension brews – an explosion that dwarfs many supernovas. The nation's wo... Harold pinches the bridge of his nose again. And there is a rejection within me of this apathy that denies suffering because it is convenient, because they enjoy its fruit, because conviction in what was taught is more sanitary than digging through the earth.

Kicking and screaming, a child now, to focus his vision and mine on the events ahead. Four officers held a limb each, forcing a boy, no older than fifteen, to submit like cattle prior to slaughter. Dirt, under his nails, mixed with his sweat, Harold could not restrain thoughts of hygiene. And a baton came slamming down – dirt and blood. The boy, locks greasy and black, shrieked, his knees giving way to torment, and his eyes... Harold could not look into them, and therefore neither could I. Their laughter, the men, louder now, more condescending, each reinforced by the person next to them. Tamar's eyes gleamed; they must have been different from Harold's. And he would grow suspicious of his own, wondering, perhaps even hoping, although he would die before admission, that they saw a cockroach when he did not.

The resistance was futile, yet the resistance persevered. One foot would strike an officer on his shin, and a hand would strike another officer on his face. The child's voice cracked from the yelling, nonetheless his words flowed like great poetry, announcing his pain to deaf ears. The same mouth that sang would bite, if only the enforcers were closer to his teeth. His ribs were apparent through his shirt, each breath visible, expansion and retraction, and his spine akin to miniature peaks and troughs, bending with each convulsion.

It was all an instant, a matter of arrival that spelled departure. Harold would later wonder if the arrested had gone for the bullet to relieve himself or to retaliate, but to what end did it matter? In the grand scheme of numbers, there was a loss. It did matter – he pinched the bridge of his nose. The fingers wrapped around the pistol, and as soon as the gun was in the child's hand, a bullet travelled to eliminate the threat. But what a threat it was, to watch a dog being kicked into a corner, and a naked arm offered to tempt it, yet to further punish it when it growls. A growl, no, the sound of a wild bang that reset everyone's thoughts back onto one thing, the vulnerability of the human soul. The sound of the gun firing triggered a rush of Harold's memories I had no access to before – runners in a race. I could not escape this vision, nor could he, and I found us transported away from the fallen child and onto a narrative that trickled in like dripping water from a tap.

Their lives did matter, but they were accompanied by grey matter splatter. A silence after that shouted in magnitudes. In their uprising, they had planted the seeds from which progress would sprout. Yet, with every germinating seed, its stem would be clipped at the base. And the plant sought the support of trees around, but all they did was exploit it for its nutrients and shade it from the light. Green recognised green, and there was camaraderie against the lumberjacks, but survival, despite each other, prevailed and greed thereafter.

A voice louder than many, Jamal's affinity for literature along with a relentless desire to achieve betterment made him a force to be reckoned with. Although a single drop of water in a wave of people, his was a contribution to the motion. With enough drops, the wave grows until you are eclipsed by a tsunami. One that would wash away the shaky foundation of ill-constructed buildings and return the commons to its people.

Jamal was a young man, his oration fluid and powerful, his metaphors were bountiful, and likened by his peers to Gamal Abdel Nasser naturally. Receiving little yet with much to give, he would arrange scatterings into organised gatherings with clear objectives and strategies to achieve them. But one friend would be killed this month, a family member the next, and the tension to retaliate with force would fractionate the parties into a spectrum – at its extremes: individualistic apathy, collective violence. Although torn at heart, Jamal would reinforce an ideology of political compromise, and one where a peasant negotiates their right to a shed whilst a landowner stays in a manor. He recognised this injustice, internally undermining the principles he espoused, but when the history taught to him talked about dwelling in burrows, the shed appeared a glorious achievement.

His father often, around the breakfast table, with a slice of white cheese wrapped in pita bread in his hand, would restate, "They might have chopped away at the stem, but the water will always be better down in Bethlehem." And Jamal would think none of it but baseless wisdom. He loved his father, Hussein, despite his complacency in matters of honour. Jamal viewed the over-consumption of food and idling on the couch as a resignation towards a lesser right. How could you? When you saw more than I have seen? he would think to himself.

His father's head only left the couch to meet the floor, so much so that he had developed a round mark on his forehead of a darker shade. Jamal's mother, conversely, was active, not in resistance, but in all the matters required to maintain a household. By his father's side during prayer and in every room but the living room, Ruqqayah was a woman of divine empathy. When the news spoke of another death, her tears would flow for the entirety of humankind, and when Jamal suffered the most inconsequential illness, she would be at his side rubbing oil on his chest and whispering supplications for comfort.

And when it came to religion, Jamal found his communication with the Creator dwindling down to singular calls seldom. He would misconstrue faith as hope, and having suffered the disappointment of expectations, he grew frustrated with it all. His parents urged him, "Rekindle your faith, baba. All our labouring now will bear fruit in the afterlife," but to no avail, for how could he focus on the fruits of suffering when the suffering was happening now – the evictions, the bombs, the beatings... the sheer scale of brutality.

"Oh, what a catastrophe!" Ruqayyah exclaimed, having just walked through the main door of the apartment. The two men, Jamal and Hussein, were in the living room, one on the dining table flipping through a newspaper and the other on the couch. After several strained breaths, Jamal's mother continued, "The Nabulsi's, Um Khalil, she lost her son, may God be merciful on his soul." And she wept, her supplications heard from a room over.

"God have mercy on his soul, and may he distance us from all evil," Hussein replied in a tone that revealed no empathy.

"Baba, what mercy? We must demand mercy, not from God but from those accursed that misappropriate angels." The newspaper had found its way to the floor, right by Jamal's feet.

"Patience Jamal, patience baba, this has been the case for seventy years. We have no one to plead to but The Lord."

"And you are resigned for seventy more," Jamal made to storm out. "God curse this ignorance of ours," he yelled as he slammed the apartment's door behind him.

Ruqayyah would later comfort Hussein, who was distraught, despite his stoic exterior. He too loved his son, more than he could show. How could he explain to Jamal that he could not endure watching his son suffer the level of emotional trauma he had to bear during his youth? How could he explain to Jamal that through time he had learnt that justice cannot be demanded from other humans? How could he explain to Jamal that the comfort of a just afterlife is to relieve them all of the burdens of an unjust existence? Hussein could not, for even he had not been driven to this level of introspection, distracted day in and day out by the orchestra of war.

Therefrom, Jamal found comfort on the streets with a can in one hand at first, then a pebble, then a rock. His voice would join the many in protest of the occupation. And the waves, once of water, now of gasoline, erupting in flames with each spark. Every injustice would fuel the fires, and Jamal would sleep each night better having thrown a rock or many. He felt vindicated, the rock of the land revolting against its occupiers. His parents worried for him, reminded themselves of a period of Intifada that resulted in thousands of deaths, but what could they do to quell the flames of dignity? When he was not roaming the streets, they would hear his voice, on occasion, as he entered and exited the apartment.

But the silence would arrive, and his peers would see metal pierce further than any rock could. His contribution, much like Khalil's, was nominal yet crucial – what is the universe if not the sum of its atoms? And Jamal's eyes would shoot for the stars, his faith at its peak when he lay on the ground in a pool of his own blood. He had not realised his fear of death till then, and his faith, better yet hope, was that his parents were correct on matters of the afterlife. All it took for such revelation was a soldier with a gun, an executioner who hid their face from the judgement of reflection. In Jamal, there was a mirror that forced the soldier to stare back at himself, at a child, and in the process of killing, forsake his own humanity. The mirror shatters, and the eyes lose light, and the soldier dwells in darkness, oblivious to the consequences of one finger movement. Not one voice, but many, not Jamal's soul, but his parents, his peers, and humankind as a whole had suffered the loss of life. And in time, years or decades, the injustice flattened and the memory immortalised, predominantly in the soldier's conscience.

Whose remembrance was that? Through Harold's eyes, I could see a *purple sky, the rays of sunlight quelled by its setting. The graduation of colour inspired faith, for even I could not believe the existence of such beauty without an artist. His feet were on a ledge, a rooftop I had no access to prior to this moment. Harold did not pinch the bridge of his nose but observed silently the nation ahead. The network of alleyways, narrow, like blood vessels carrying with complete neutrality nutrition and toxins alike. But unlike those unconscienced carriers, our duty, to the body as a whole, is to assess at each given moment whether we are aiding and abetting harm.*

He could hear the birds chirping in the distance, interrupted by yelling, the sounds of wedding festivities, interrupted by screaming, the sounds of just demands, interrupted by a bang. Harold recognised himself as a thief, of love, of joy, of pain. And beyond the alleyways, he could see a great wall with paintings of resistance, and beyond the wall he could see the sea reflecting the sun's remaining light onto the city. He was the soldier, and I, Jamal.

*   *   **

A particular feeling, one of reawakening, befell Solomon. Unlike his previous exits from the worlds of his making, his eyelids gradually revealed hydrated eyes. Not a grogginess to accompany his rise, but a clarity that dumbfounded him yet further. Had it not been for the general achiness in his right shoulder, Osroes would have believed he were still in a fantastical realm, ungoverned by the consequences of yesterday's actions. But there it was, the metal bench on which he lay on, cold to the touch, that prompted him to exist within reality's construct.

With every crack, back, neck, knuckles, he advanced in levels of comfort and only the metal bars ahead, that limited his mobility, conspired against this illusion. Solomon made as to sit up, however found himself on the floor, imitating a ragdoll. And opposite the hindrances of his freedom, he saw a man, from his viewpoint upside down, in an official capacity. A second attempt at standing would place his hand firmly on the rim of a toilet bowl for support.

"A man of the bottle no less," the constable ahead grinned and then commanded, "Position yourself as to pose no threat to me or yourself."

Neither the ridicule nor the command made Osroes jolt up stiffly and freeze in place. No, it was the memory of a man named Harold, the officer, who resembled no likeness in features or demeanour to the person ahead. His confusion drained what little energy remained, and Solomon could not muster enough to question the imposter. His thoughts, on the other hand, cared not for his physical fatigue and rushed into a mode of assumptions and queries: *Is Harold this Harold that? Am I Jamal, or are you?* he addressed an abstract outwith himself, and finally, *what is Bethlehem?*

But distracted within his own self, Solomon's body went on autopilot and obeyed the commands indiscriminately. Against the wall with his arms behind his back, the officer entered the cell and placed his hands in the shackles of the past day. Out of a cell he was born in, and into a room that, by ambience, represented an identical twin to the white room. There, a man he had seen before, was sitting across, a frown strong enough to push his brows down enough and render eyesight obsolete. However, his presence, perhaps extenuated by the slump of his shoulders, revealed sadness.

It was Yan Eadful, the same man whose vague interrogation had haunted him in the white room. He was wearing a wool suit of earthy green, just a shade lighter than mud, and a red tie against a white shirt, that was washed enough times for the fabric to turn delicate. Solomon shuddered, but his confusion had not been resolved yet, and he was guided by Harold's hand into a seat, by a metallic table and just across from Yan.

"You are here by official capacity Dr. Eadful, and I recommend you respect the guidelines of this room. Should the sir across from you perform actions unbecoming of his current predicament, then I oblige you to exit the room promptly and call for me." Words, from the officer's mouth, nothing more than background noise to Solomon.

Yan bowed his head in response, to appease the constable. Then, as soon as the uninvited guest exited the room, Dr. Eadful let out a heavy sigh that was constricted by the tight opening between his lips; it was as if he were holding two human's worth of air within him. Solomon's expression was blank, and perplexed Yan, who had expected a reaction of either extremes. And when he ultimately settled his hands onto the table, Solomon felt obliged to imitate but was constricted by the cuffs.

If time were infinite, the two contestants would have remained in silence and yielded to their ego. But alas, Yan could not bear the chasm between them a second more and almost snapped under the weight of his own rehearsed thoughts. "Very well, I shall begin then lest the thief returns your tongue. I misunderstand you, perhaps that is my fault, but what is yours?" he asked rhetorically. "You, Mr. Osroes, so that you do not misconstrue the addressed in this claim, have approached me seeking purging of your sins and the reformation of your soul. Am I incorrect?" and again, the question demanded no answer. "There, I approached the matter with the greatest of considerations and empathy as to afford you enough patience to arrive at a resolution gradually. This all despite your horrid actions based on the provided photographs. What are you to say for yourself?" He paused for a mere few seconds before adding, "Nothing. You choose to disregard my hand and cast yourself into the pits of hell," and as if that rant was inadequate, he whispered, "Scoundrel."

"You mistake yourself, guile as your speech was. Your ignorance of me negates your scorn," Solomon yelled in reply, infuriated by the accusations made against him. He stood up, the chair flung to the floor behind him.

"Calm yourself unless you would like to meet the better end of the constable's stick," Yan pointed at Solomon, a demand for obedience.

"I shall recline back to my seat, not out of respect for which your finger demands none, but out of the exhaustion of my own legs," Osroes, with his restricted fingers, struggled but managed to return the chair back into its utilitarian position. "I must reiterate however that I do not know you."

This frustrated Yan to the extreme, but rather than unleashing the fury within a rant, he responded calmly, "Let us set out our agreements so that we may further dissect our disagreements. You do not belong here Solomon, on that we both agree. You want to resolve past errors Solomon, on that we both agree. You want to return home Solomon, on that we both agree. If present in any of these claims, spell your grievances."

"Home?" There was an underlying discomfort and a thoughtfulness that drifted Solomon's eyes down. He could swear the calls of prayer, loud and melodic, were playing in the background, yet all the words were gibberish, to him anyhow. And when he could recentre his focus back onto the present silence, he could only muster a mumbled "Luna?"

Yan was taken aback, his face fell, and the commandeering presence withered into a pathetic raisin. But he rebelled against his own shame and lectured the muttering man across. "Yes, a home. And you have been given the bricks, as God is my witness." He was not a man of faith and was unsure why he would exclaim such hyperbole. "With every brick you lay, you turn around and strike a hammer against it. Then you spend ample time the very next day pondering where your home is and whether it will ever be constructed. And then you claim 'treachery this' and 'treachery that,' but I must assert that the only treachery you have experienced is by your own hands."

By then, Dr. Eadful was pacing back and forth across the room, exercising any shame that threatened to build up. Solomon, in contrast, remained plastered in his seat, a statue of sorts, moulded from the coarsest of clay. Although struck by Yan's words, he assigned more importance to the mindful attempts of restoring the prayer calls. He was unsure of his affinity to it yet felt he had rejected an invitation before comprehending its content. Therefore, the silence between the two ensued until it was broken moments later by Yan again, whose eyes had shifted down to his watch.

"I shall depart. I really must not, but I shall. And my wish is that you return as you did once before, of your own volition. The institution can help you navigate your baser instincts and amend past villainy. And perhaps in doing so, you may begin constructing a home for yourself here and flower into the upstanding citizen I know you can be." He had maintained eye contact with Solomon all throughout his closing statement, up until the last sentence, when his eyes shifted left. "As a former student and a current friend, I plead for you to come forth and confess your misdeeds. To write is to be honest."

The space now empty, apart from Solomon, it no longer resembled the white room. It was much too dark and, unlike the minimalist nature of the white room, clattered with items of redundance. He was left in contemplation, angered by his current predicament, but mostly confused by the haziness of the beginning. There was an element he was missing; he could sense it dampening his spirits and undermining his convictions.

Has my impact been more devastating than what I think I know? he thought to himself. For most of his life, Solomon had been a consumer, of the arts, of knowledge, of luxuries, and yet when it came to contribution, the list was concise. Here he was enjoying the labours of others, his jumpsuit, this cell, the very directions he was provided by the grocer to locate his house, but what did he give back in return? Nothing, and that would leave him wondering for a second whether his existence had relied on the exploitation of others. Solomon was tormented by a book he could not finish, not a family he could not feed, nor by medicine he could not buy. *Were those the misdeeds I ought to confess?* he questioned himself. But he immediately brushed off the notion by convincing himself that the world was unjust, therefore, it is the world's responsibility to resolve such an injustice but not his own.

Returning to his cell by the guidance of Harold's hand, Solomon would spend no more than a quarter of an hour before he was asked to depart it again. However, this time, without shackles, and at the request of the owner of said particular van. Just as he was made to exit the building, Solomon would leave the officer with a scarring question, "Were you forced to kill the child?" Osroes would receive no answer and would content himself with the physical differences that suggested against.

Spud's intentions were masked by the obscurity of distance. Was it vengeance sought for the cremation of a friend? Solomon's perspective on the matter was clear – he rid Spud of a cancerous host. But, with the introduction of nuance, losing someone dear was akin to losing a basket. If the basket holds eggs, then you risk losing those too. And it was difficult to harvest more eggs when they are constantly cracked, and their contents whisked.

There was warmth in the embrace, not enough to suggest recent proximity to fire, however. Solomon was confounded by the hug and no less by the smile that crept into his periphery. Spud was delighted to see him, and when the embrace had concluded, he fixed him in place by the shoulders and admired him, as if he were a prized ornament. "You bastard! Apologies, but I must call you a bastard. You had given me the most intense scare."

Solomon was satisfied in his lack of response, believing that the situation might miraculously resolve itself. More so, he was waiting for the narrative to unfold before he could spin it. His legs twitched, ready to bolt if the conflict turned violent, for not only was he a slave to survival but he felt no affection for the man ahead should he have to face consequences.

"Has Annabelle made your acquaintance? Is she with you? I

wish to see her," Spud added jubilantly to his initial statement.

The words escaped Solomon, almost instinctively, "My memory deceives me, but I do not know any of that name – perhaps only in a dream. For you see, I woke up prior to dusk in a room, on my own. And in a state of bewilderment, as normal of any man who wakes up in a room on his own, I traced my journey down, out of the house, and into the van. And in a state of bewilderment, as normal of any man who wakes up in a room on his own, I drove the van seeking clarity, only to find myself lost and under a bridge of sorts. And in a state of bewilderment, as normal of any man who wakes up in a room on his own, I dozed off to regain my composure only to find myself contemplating my decisions at the back of a cell." Solomon had cunningly latched onto the first question, which introduced doubt around his relationship with Annabelle.

"Settle down fellow, you might strain your throat," Spud replied in a less delighted tone. "This confuses me." and he scratched his head, where a few flecks of dead skin danced their way down to his shoulders. "In my return from the supplementary run, I saw from afar the flat in a blaze, and I would have gone closer for inspection had it not been for the sheer number of spectators and engines around." He paused for a second, certainly in thought, then continued, "And I thought that WRITE had attacked the place, but that you and Annabelle fled before any harm could beset you."

"That certainly could still be the case," Solomon agreed with Spud's presumption, webbing the truth in a matrix of lies. "Anna could have departed at the first signs of smoke."

"Annabelle, but perhaps you have forgotten the name, is not capable of abandonment." And with that, Solomon and Spud's relationship would become a companionship tailed by suspicion. "Very well, let us not dwell on unknowns and make haste of our journey. I know a man who can house us till the sheets reek."

The oven-baked interior took a while to cool down, and the two men, side by side, perspired profusely along their drive. The heat introduced a deliriousness in Solomon, and his longing for the moons and stars only amplified. Unbeknownst to him, Spud had also been driven into a pit of guilt, accentuated by the hellish heat, for abandoning his brother only days prior. And whilst Solomon was comfortable brooding and festering in his own sorrows, Spud found the silence insufferable.

"How does one cope?" and when Solomon turned to him inquisitively, Spud continued, "With the guilt, that not only did you not hinder the loss of a loved one, but you contributed to it." It was difficult to differentiate between the sweat and the tears, but woe needs no physical indicator.

"For you, Nick, and for I, Luna, Shams, and Amar," Solomon replied dejectedly. "I do feel at times, I lie, always, that these fingers," he raised his hands towards his head, "have dug graves for which my beloved are destined to lie in. I remember none of it, and yet I can feel the soil between my fingers and a loneliness of immeasurable distance. And I wonder if their souls have departed the Earth altogether, and I wonder if these hands have denied them entrance back into their home."

In response, Spud wished he had not confided in Solomon altogether. His guilt had amplified but was overshadowed by a resolve that justifies all. The mention of the three made the driver uncomfortable; although for a moment he had displayed a modicum of vulnerability, his inhibitions had returned, and he was wary of every word uttered. Spud's face turned red, but one could easily mistake that as a symptom of the heat. *A writer that writes is a writer that is right,* he thought to himself in constant repetition, attempting to drown his own subconscious.

Past a vast expanse of wheat, endless from Solomon's viewpoint, the van, after an hour or so on the road, had arrived at a gate. More for show, and perhaps to keep the cattle in, Solomon could see beyond the gate, a dirt road that stretched towards a farmhouse. And by the barred entrance stood a man, a behemoth by all measures, whose size ridiculed the gates functionality. Spud's humongous friend pulled on a twine rope tied to the single pivot gate, and it swung open. A hand was raised, both by the man and Spud, in salute, and the van was driven to a halt just by the house. Yellow and brown, two colours that dominated the scenery of a wheat-only blessed land. Had it not been for the little vegetation, the land would have been best described as arid. And the farmhouse was a collection of wooden planks, rotten, and threatened by the softest of winds.

Spud took the keys out of the ignition, a sign of mistrust in his travel companion, and exited the vehicle. His hand in the giant's, Spud appeared a child by comparison. And by his side, Solomon could finally scrutinise the man's appearance. He was tan with an excess of hair on his arms and face, and one could assume the same would be applicable for his torso, but a white sleeveless shirt denied confirmation. The rest of him was garbed in denim overalls, the colour of dirt. His eyes were narrow and perhaps only perceived so because his nose was large. Hair that represented itself more as a mane, for there was a continuity from the long stiff locks of black, that fell towards his shoulders, to a beard of the same colour, that pushed outwards.

Solomon followed suit and shook his hands, full of calluses they were. And when he strained his neck to meet his eyes, he was met with a kind yet merchant-like smile. "They call me Aleabith Aldakhm, and I assume you are none other than Solomon?"

"Solomon Osroes, if you yearned to know."

الطيب الضخم أض
إنتاج الجمهورية العربية ال

Part 5: Scattered

The fiddler's spouse,
the fiddler's daughter,
the fiddler's all had gone.
A life once blazing passion,
smothered to ashes of despair.

Mumble, stumble,
he fell and tumbled.
Fall dealt well by the tall.
On the roof, he sulks, recalls,
that he's only seven feet small.

Ground-bound,
thoughts race and compound.
Visions play of past climbs,
will they surmount his descent?
Hopeful, doubtful, his mind is primed.

Back cracked,
impact bruises him.
But with his soul intact,
he shall return on WRITE's track.
His stomping makes certain of that.

The fiddler climbed atop and whistled,
then he played his fiddle away.
Out of tune, by just a little,
yet played with passion all the same.

Aleabith descended from the low roof and onto dirt, leaving heaps of dust floating in his wake. Much like the citizens of the Kingdom of Saudi Arabia, the tiny organisms around him were subjected to a sandstorm. And in the aftermath of the miniscule natural disaster, the giant man patted his overalls, forcing any of the remaining dirt to flee his monstrous hands.

"Apologies for the nuisance. The past is a litany of pleasant tunes, but not so currently. Do instruments speak to you, Solomon?" His voice, although carrying depth, was soft to the ears and gentle in its enquiry, inviting the addressee to reply.

"If the speech masquerades as wail, then perhaps so," Solomon chuckled in reply. "The incoordination of these digits only subjects them to agony; their potential wasted on torturous sounds. My friend, many people are gifted, many people are cursed, and here I claim, all people are both." Osroes surprised himself with the level of openness with which he addressed his host, but he had found the time spent together thus far replenishing.

A pat on the shoulder followed by a fading guffaw, Aleabith returned, "Indeed, although many more cursed than gifted it seems. How do we spend all our lives bearing these curses?"

"In constant struggle and endless pain, we seek the most suitable painkillers and the path of least resistance. And we resist and we resist until we can no more. That is when the curse ultimately catches up to us and we become less gifted with life and more cursed by it."

"I had loved once – no, twice. Double the gifts – no, double the curse. Have you ever loved Solomon?"

"If you define love as a gift and a curse, then no. I have only known gifts, but tragically for them, I was the curse." A session of reflection between the two, and Solomon found his eyes glued down at the ground. He pondered the whereabouts of his roots, his seeds, and his soil.

"We are much more alike than our appearances would suggest," Aleabith grinned sincerely before adding, "My two thirds had left me after my heart grew too tough and my hands too rough." The giant glanced down at the back of his hands. "How was I to know that the hands that loved you oh so delicately could draw blood? To my wife, I am a dead man, and perhaps all the better. See, my crops are dying because they are unnurtured, and I am dying because what am I to nurture? What is a man as large as I to do in a world so much larger?”

"I believe this is my opportunity to return the apologies. This world is a treache-"

In came the obnoxious interjection of a man unfamiliar with social cues. "O Solomon boy, the fish have returned to shallow waters. I fault myself for setting two individuals of philosophical vanity upon each other. The answer to his question is your question until one is left with a pyramid, its construction endangered by a single block."

Solomon merely responded with a side glance before fixing his gaze back at the host. And with that, Aleabith understood the wavelength at which to communicate. "What crude behaviour, a mouth that operates before the brain instructs it too. Are we alike in observation, Solomon?" The two of them enjoyed a snicker at the outsider. Spud knew the men individually longer than they had known each other, yet they appeared to gel harmoniously.

"There is no strength in using both arms when fighting a man with one." He was irritated and had there been no objective to his initial interjection, Spud would have threatened a squabble. "The Karamazovs must join and use their intellectuality to good effect. Nick, my brother, we need a proposition for his liberation. My heart yields a beat or two for the lanky mute, for not only is he my blood, but he is also our saviour." He gestured towards Solomon, as if to slyly remind him of Nick's contribution to their escape.

"We are no more than The Three Vagabonds by my account," Solomon smirked at Spud's suggestion, likening them to characters of a known Russian novel. "I am lost, so are you, and so is he.," Osroes paused momentarily before continuing, "But we have also lost, I, you, and he. Vagabonds or Losers, I leave the choice to you fine gentlemen."

His collar twisted and there was a sharp pain in his abdomen, Solomon endured the impact of Spud's reaction. Although partially bemused by Spud's barbarianism (I dislike the word's origin), he dreaded the predictable outcome of antagonising a lunatic with a knife. "My admiration for you extends the length of this blade. Should you not extend any appreciation for the effort you are indebted to my brother and I, then a pound of flesh would do." He twisted the blade marginally to emphasise his point.

"I am no thief, and my debt to you shall be repaid in full!" Solomon exclaimed with false confidence.

Retreating into a friendlier stance, Spud lubricated the situation with humour. "To take a pound of flesh off you would be like taking the thumbs off a pigeon." And as though expecting Aleabith to share him in laughter, Spud stared at him amidst his fit. However, Aldakhm only returned an acknowledging smile, fearing that the fellows had wrongly escaped the institution.

"Oh, and in a show of good faith, from a loanee to his loaner, I must in good conscience expound on your statement. As per the Shakespearean literature for which you refer to, you would have to retrieve the pound of flesh without a drop of blood spilt. A task I would venture to call improbable, no less so due to those clumsy hands." Spud itched to reply in a manner vulgar and unbefitting gentry, but the Sun was close to extending its goodnight to the inhabitants of the desolate farm. The three men, fatigued by the battle of the words, made their way into the farmhouse.

A rhythm established, and basic at best. A rhythm he could hear between his two lungs. Two fingers drumming against a wobbly table. A table surrounded by three, more similar than distinct, individuals. Spud was dictating the conversation in a fiery manner, a fire that produces, not consume. A fire unlike the one that had engulfed his dear Annabelle. The two listeners on the opposite end of the spectrum, disinterested and cold to the heat. Aleabith was most curious about Solomon's insights into gifts, curses, and a fire that left nothing but the ashes of what could have been. And on the other side, Solomon longed to find the moon and its moons. Tapping those two fingers, so he could conjure a façade of their heartbeats against his embrace. Staring at a ceiling that blocked his view of the one object that aided his imagination of her.

"Your eyes wander to lust's delight, and the maiden ahead invisible to your sight," Spud extended his arm and placed his hand under the two tapping fingers. He had noticed Osroes's dilated eyes, a sign of a pondering mind, and in a moment of frustration, interjected. The heartbeat was gone, and the disinterested expression, now flushed out, was replaced by a morbid reaction to a loved one's passing. Solomon's eyes shifted towards his two fingers and welled up.

Two taps on a table,
rhythm established, new.
A heart that beats stable,
night, melancholy rue.

A cable snaps, tension,
and zigzag vanished too.
Blank bullets in a brain,
the thoughts collapse to truths.

Eyes fixated nowhere,
visions dancing to muse.
"Do you suffer today?"
and voices ask on cue.

A finger finds home once more,
reverse dilapidation.
Bitterness, treat life's sores,
and sprinkle conversation.

The mind washes back ashore,
calamity evasion.

Upon witnessing the disoriented expression and a tear that travelled
the distance to Solomon's beard, Spud retracted his hand and allowed
the distressed to re-establish a rhythm he had gotten accustomed to.
Two taps. One tap followed by another. A heartbeat – his mother's.
Osroes could hear the soothing sound of her voice. But it was not a
clear voice, spoken from mouth to ear. It was a voice that travelled as
vibrations from her mouth, down through her chest, upon which his
head rested. And try as he might, a force prevented him from raising
his head and drawing a face to the voice.

"If I have done you great harm then excuse this hand, for it
acted on its own accord," Spud addressed Osroes to soothe him. "But
my priorities lie with my brother, and your lack of focus is to his
detriment. You know, and perhaps more so intrinsically, the damage
caused by that ingested medication – you suffer its consequences even
now. For them to dull sharp minds is a travesty they will be answerable
for; and for them to dull one more, that is a travesty we will be
answerable for."

"Your frustration is justified, but I ask you, courteously, to never
lay your hand on me again." Solomon's eyes, both sorrowful yet
threatening, bore into Spud's skull. The little red streaks in the white
of his eyes indicated both an anger and a proclivity towards shedding
anything more than a singular tear. "Have you helped me escape only
to rob me of my agency? What am I of value to you?"

"It is not who you are, Solomon Osroes, whose potential knows
no bounds, that is of great value. It is what you represent, the principles
that reinstate the writer's might back to them. The principles that hold
accountable the promises for which they make. You are promised the
view of the mountaintop and yet are told after hiking for hundreds of
days that no such mountain exists, and the ground below is level. I

protest and so do your principles, that a mountain does exist, and that we are only oppressed from its view by the people at its peak. I protest and so do your principles, that if a mountain did not exist, then the pen's ink would manufacture one for you to climb. I protest and so do your principles, that a writer's obligation is not to the truth but to writing itself, whatever that may be."

It was Aleabith's turn to alleviate the pressure brewing between the two. "A table of three, brothers by limited nature, the Three Vagabonds even – must we not remember our bind?"

Solomon realigned to a reality, dictated first by a penultimate battle between chaos and order, only superseded by the ultimate battle between life and death. He leaned back into his chair, and it creaked in response. The relaxed posture was followed by an equivalently relaxed reply. "No qualms to resolve, but a plan to be told."

Spud, the happier of the two to abate festering resentment, answered diplomatically, "The details scattered, truffles in the woods, and no dogs to hunt for them. My dear Nick deserves an Annabelle and Annabelle deserves a map, and both are more the lost without them." He concluded the statement and his eyes scanned around.

"Is that all there is to it?" Aleabith broke through the intermediate silence.

Solomon, posturing in defence of his recent treaty ally, replied on his behalf, "Spare the man some time, Aleabith," and he gestured to Spud to continue.

His spotty forearm was the victim of rigorous scratching and Spud forced flakes and flakes of skin to fall off. The hesitancy in his demeanour inspired no confidence, and that was exacerbated by a meek, "That is it, and the rest shall organise itself."

"If I am to chip away at an ice block with a wooden stick once more, then it had better be because a well-constructed plan was ill-executed; not vice versa," Solomon criticised.

But as the night drew out, a few drinks were passed around, virgin and otherwise. With how strenuous the past days had been to Solomon and Spud, the inebriation arrived as respite, allowing the two to partially relinquish control over their decisions. Nevertheless, the same worries, the same queries, the same unease, lingered and were only made hazier by the substance. The men partook in social customs and demoted such feelings to their subconscious. A couple of laughs from all directions. A couple of smiles to ease any tension. And a couple of yawns to mark the end of a session. And while the other two retreated to suitable beds, Solomon would wake the next day with his back against the chair and his neck craned over, much to a doctor's displeasure.

The yawns followed by stretches,
crawling from where the chair is.
Then to a room of brushes,
the teeth scratched, also polished.
A desire for the scrumptious,
to replenish as heads first,
into the mundane, endless.

Bowl and a bunch of cereal,
to munch on till feeling full.
Dry, requires a companion,
wet, perfect compounded of.
Craving milk borders intense,
satisfaction to all sense.

Fridge and a carton of milk,
tongue sought sensation of silk.
Grabbed the cap and thus twisted.

Poured contents of wishes for,
waterfall yet more viscous.

Concoction was all in vain,
embrace cereal bowl, dismay.
The milk had gone sour.
The milk had gone sour.

The materials for hygiene, a semi-full toothpaste tube and an adequately tough bristled toothbrush, were present and inconsiderately tested by Solomon. Yet, within Osroes, an infuriation had developed for the lack of an essential dairy item he thought every household was founded upon.

"Show yourself, you disgraceful man. Aleabith, where are you? You ought to be ashamed for offering a breakfast of cereal without the accompaniment of milk." Solomon paced through the farmhouse, yelling through each doorway. "And to hide as well? I had evaluated you wrongly."

He inspected a spoonful of cereal and lumpy milk within a few inches of his right eye. The milk was neither a delightful yoghurt nor a breeding hub for cultures not yet as developed as our own (also yoghurt). And finalising his inspection, Solomon dropped the spoon back into the bowl heedless of the splatter that rained onto the table. He would wonder if this particular group of dots was of any interest to the up-and-coming blood splatter analysts of his day. Or whether, amusing himself with hypotheticals, aspiring analysts of a younger age would begin with the milk and graduate later to the advanced and gory courses.

Minutes and some more, yet no sign of life in the farmhouse to distress over the mess Solomon had made. "The vagabonds live truly by their name. Where must they be?" he muttered under his breath. His body still reeling from the effects of last night's uncomfortable slumber, Osroes desired the bliss of a few more hours of shut eye, or better yet, for a butcher to tenderise the stiffness in his neck.

But neither remedies would resolve the movies of suffering he was subjected to every night, and helpless he felt, in his own mind, watching the closest and ultimately the furthest of humanity perish to the falling debris of material annihilation. The skies of red, the ghouls that devoured all, the collapse of buildings, and the water that boiled into magma – akin, by his limited knowledge, to descriptions in religious texts. However, he could not let himself be consumed by those visions and chose instead to laugh at them as mere projections of insanity. And most absurd of all, whilst all but a minor segment of humanity is made extinct, he survives the trials and tribulations, only to find himself on board a schooner that slowly rises towards the heavens. Him?! Solomon? No better than his neighbour, more sinful than his children, Solomon? Therefore, the entire scenario, to him, was egotistical imagination.

Without any further hesitation, and perhaps to distract himself from where his mind had wandered, Solomon exited the farmhouse onto the porch. How disrespectful for the host and his friend to abandon him without notice. He extended his vision as far as he could, strained by the ability of his short-sighted eyes. A sea of gold, spiritless and dry crop, hid the landscape beyond, but for a scarecrow that swam in its midst. Solomon wanted to approach the strawman to scrutinise its function closely. Yet, the hassle of going through the wall of wheat rendered the journey intolerable.

"Do me the pleasure of returning this greeting," he called out, hoping the scarecrow would bestow guidance.

And undoubtedly real was the muffled sound that shouted back, only moments later, "The sun has arrived, and so should you. Come here."

He was perplexed and had someone told Solomon he had ingested a hallucinogen; he would not have thought twice about the matter. The sound's source was geometrically ambiguous; therefore, within the margin of reason with which Solomon was afforded, he placed his focus solely on the scarecrow. And sprint did he, careless, pushing aside the wheat which offered little resistance to the man parting the sea. And lunged did he, fearless, tackling the crafted project to the ground.

A burlap sack full of wheat straw, a woven corn straw hat, two black buttons, and a stitched smile with black thread that mocked Solomon for his assumption. Despite the manufactured state of the scarecrow, his convictions had led him thus far and damned by his curiosity, he sought assurances. Solomon grabbed the head and fiercely interrogated it. A few shakes later, the head detached from the rest of the body, sending a mixture of signals down his spine from shock and partial pleasure at having decapitated a potential man. This split-second reaction was immediately quelled by the realisation that the scarecrow never could speak, no matter how much he yearned to.

The heat in full effect and bearing down on him, Solomon picked up the straw hat and placed it on his own head. Drawn through inspiration by the simplicity of a scarecrow's life, an idea sparked. From the red flannel to the jeans tied at the bottom for a lack of any feet, he undressed it. Afterwards, he did just the same to himself, untying the jumpsuit he had been wearing ever since the escape from around his waist. And beyond it went, chucked a fair distance into the wheat abyss, a sign of his incarceration, C-12, clearly visible mid-flight. Overcome by shame at the prospect of being seen in his undergarments, Solomon hastily threw on the scarecrow's garments. They were a tad loose and perhaps originally Aleabith's expendable clothes. Solomon thought about placing the burlap sack on his head too, but it had no eye holes, and the fabric was too dense to breathe through.

Irrational was his desire to imitate the scarecrow, but he found delight in the prospect of a singular purpose, uncontested by a free will that rendered him feeling prisoned. Solomon stretched his arms as far perpendicularly to his torso as he could, and remained as still as a column with the inherent dynamism of life could. Embodying the scarecrow carried more nuances than standing still – an exhaustive awareness of one's surroundings and the elevation of one objective above all thoughts, *SCARE THE CROWS.* While apparently effortless from the stick-based man, Solomon's maybe more delightful appearance made the task all the more difficult. And focus much did he, that his vision began to blur all the unessential background.

An opportunistic eater swept down, not long since the assumption of his new role, and landed on one of the wheat stalks. The crow, a pest by Solomon's eyes, was the sole determination of his; and he wished to fulfil an objective of scaring it away without the movements or sounds the laws of a scarecrow prohibits. Osroes concentrated. The bird remained. Osroes concentrated further. The bird remained. A collection of veins bulged on his forehead. Yet, the bird remained. No more than a few minutes later, the crow flew away, having had its fill of the wheat. Whether he had frightened the crow or not, Solomon felt accomplished, understanding that although it was a simple task, the responsibility it bore made it important. "What a travesty," he remarked to himself. Nothing he had ever written or produced, projects of months or better yet years, had moved him in such a manner. Muscles tensed in his face for as long as they had been now relaxed and he could feel a tightness within him ease. Had it not been for the principles he had just instilled, Solomon would have collapsed to his knees. Not a single thing could distract him from this one task, until...

Scratching, though minor, at an itch that had formed near his thigh. It was probably the rough jeans or the excess wheat straw rubbing against his skin.

"The wheat had consumed the boy in the distant past. Odes to the day we see the man emerge at last."

"Blame the wheat and not the man, for it misguides. Should we not listen well to the lost that cry?"

Osroes could hear the calls of Spud and Aleabith, loud and omnidirectional they were. With no compass to guide him north, he ventured directionless thereafter. The wheat as high as him, his only refuge was the sky. Not a star in the blue, not the blessings of the moon, not even the sun now for it was overshadowed, the clouds travelled, and he did too. And with his eyes to the sky, every step brought him closer in proximity, but the ground was not blessed with his departure.

Scratching, turned major, at the once itch-become-rash, he ripped off article after article. Although the undergarments would have sufficed, guarded by the discretion of wheat, Solomon favoured radical solutions and found little wrong with removing the remainder of his clothing. Now, an exposed man strolling around a field of wheat; that ought to scare the crows.

Ought to scare the crows,
Duty to the role.
But abandoned the job,
In search of what was lost.

Ought to scare the crows,
To distract from woes.
But the silence, it speaks,
Of a corner that reeks.

Ought to scare the crows,
What meaning to all?
Death graces the fallen,
And the crows come calling.

Mother Nature begot Osroes, and much like a childbirth under normal conditions, he was naked, devoid of purpose, and left to the moulding fingers of his environment. Out of the womb of wheat, Solomon emerged in search of carers. And not only could he not locate his fellow vagabonds, which had morphed into the image of interim parents, he could no longer see the farmhouse. Of a dairy item

– milk, milk, milk – he was reminded, and now, more than all, Solomon desired milk. The obsession, logical in infancy, over milk had led him astray, yet it stemmed from an innate want for nutrition, a hollowness that begged to be filled.

He would wait no longer, and to his dismay he would discover, for with the conclusion of the search comes the realisation, the necessity of another. In the distance, neither far nor close, Solomon observed a human exploiting a cow. Driven by curiosity and forces of wanderlust, he had no option but to approach the person. And upon the multiplication of his steps, features now more defined, Solomon discovered her to be a woman. In her kneeling, her stature was ill-defined, however it was clear she was middle-aged. Strands of gold, akin to the wheat, and brown, mixed to form a head of hair that shied little from manual work. That, combined with glimpses of erratic movement, brought out a youthfulness in her. But the more one scrutinised, the rings of darkness around her hazel eyes and the callus formations on her knuckles, the more conflicted they became in their initial assessment. This was a woman of many stories.

"May the Lord bless your yield, Madam," Solomon greeted the woman, whose concentration lied either solely on the task or far outwith her head. He raised his right arm to his chest and bowed his head slightly as a mark of courtesy.

The woman, having raised her head, gasped in disbelief. "You despicable shell of a man. Have you no shame for your crudeness? Oh, how the cows are more dignified than you." She was furious, her hands leaving the cow's udders and flailing in reprimand. And Solomon was baffled by it all, lacking comprehension for such a hostile response.

But he had forgotten his outfit consisted of none, and made aware, he hid what he could with as much of his hands he could offer. Now on either side of the cow, Osroes apologetically replied, "An unfortunate situation, for which I do apologise. Let me clarify should you choose to afford me some of my dignity back. My friend and our host had abandoned me upon early rise, and I found myself lost in a field of wheat in search of them. But you must laugh, for I had gone looking for them because the milk had gone sour. Then, awfully ridiculous as well, in the middle of the field, a scarecrow appeared to reply to my calls. Apparently, this was not the case, but how humorous it would have been if it was. Nevertheless, I was intrigued by the prospect of embodying a scare-"

"Your tale dulls me, and I refuse to hear the end of it, vile man," the woman raised a pair of sheers by her side and pointed them towards Solomon. "Now leave, lest I make a eunuch of you."

"But to cut a story short before the bes-"

"The best part appeals to your narcissism." She stared out into the golden sea. "You are not the first cruel man to emerge from those fields, and not the last. The sea washes ashore treasures, debris, and pirates alike."

"To live is to suffer, be blessed, yet suffer nonethe-"

"Here I am the fool to have believed love to be the greatest of suffering. And can I be blamed when my husband's hand taught me no other kind? No, no, I will tell you, the greatest suffering is the confliction I have every moment that perhaps I had not suffered at all. And perhaps, that was love. And perhaps, I am the fool indeed."

Solomon empathised to no end with the woman, and yet despite that, the sensation of irritation brewed within – at something petty no less. Why did she have to interrupt him at every turn?

"My apologies offer nothing but could you te-"

She bulldozed midsentence, "He came to me a sower and he left me a reaper."

"What justification is th-"

"Can there be a just-"

And Solomon's vexation boiled over, leaving his empathy in tatters. "As a matter of justification, your interruptive nature offers one explanation."

"A pest among the wheats; by your very nature," the woman replied with venom in her voice. "All you know is to infest and consume. You came here and sought help. Could you not have spared a few moments to listen rather than impose yourself? Oh, you speak of spoilt milk, but I reckon it is none other than you."

Left bewildered, and with regret for his harsh words, Solomon realised this was no time for his tale. "I have apologised plenty but one more I will. My actions, inexcu-"

The woman calmed and her face softened, "It is understandable, for we yearn to share our burden than to share theirs. And more so, we pretend no such burden exists at all. Do we not burden others because we wish to not burden them or because we do not want to admit our own fallibility?" And when Solomon paused, not knowing how to respond to the question, she added, "I have not caught your name."

He replied meekly, "Solomon Os-"

"Ah Solomon, a common man's name. Is there nothing else you men do not share?" She smirked, and for the first time, he saw the dimples in her cheeks.

Solomon's forearm tensed, enticed by the thought of relieving his irritation upon her head. But instead, he nominated sensibility and responded sarcastically, "your expertise in the matter outweighs mine. Do share if you may." He was buoyed by the prospect of her having outgrown her interruptive habit.

"On a sunnier day, Mr. Os." She stood up, so that now her eyes were level with his. "In search of two people and a fine glass of milk. And no finer one than straight from a cow's udder."

"On this, I cann-" But his optimism was unfounded, and the interruptive habit ensued.

"The two people, describe their appearances."

"One, like a tuber, short and stout. Do not mistake my pronunciation for a tumour that tears a family apart. I speak of a tuber that brings them together round a dinner table. The second like the botched offspring of a caveman who had intercourse with a mam-"

Much like a swing in its momentum, she returned to scolding ways. "That villain ought to keep his waste on the other side of the field."

"Pardon me, but am I mistaken-"

"Are his hands rougher than his heart?"

And Solomon, prepared to answer a question for which he did not understand the context of, began, "A-," only to be interrupted by her once more.

"Never mind, no answer of yours would suffice. A host and his spoilt milk, I should have known it was the beast," her voice soft again, "He never could keep the milk fresh."

How could a giant, feet as wide as tombstones, be afforded the trait of sneakiness? By this incident, it was not so. The rustle of wheat heard loud by the conversers, not even the wind could be suspected. Momentarily, struck by paranoia, Solomon would fear the crows had figured out his ruse and returned in vengeance for a lost meal. However, evident by the woman's facial expression, a mixture of fear and defiance, Osroes relegated himself to witness. And no sooner had the giant's head emerged from among the gold, that her pose strained.

"Solomon? Good friend, Solomon?" He stared in shock at Osroes, before shifting his eyes towards the woman. "What is he doing here exposed to the elements, Thakiah?" Although mild-mannered, Aleabith's question had an undertone of fury.

"We leave you a morning and you yield to the cravings of the night?" Spud, who had emerged just after Aleabith, added derisively.

Glumly, and afforded no doubt for his guilt, Solomon replied in his defence, "If you would hear the sequence of luckless happenings, then you would do more than pit-"

Aleabith had attended Thakiah's Academy for Social Ethics, for he also could not resist interrupting Osroes.

"Will you leave behind this shameful life you lead and return with me?" Aleabith extended a hand forward laying out its palm in an inviting yet condescending manner. This entire ordeal had positioned Solomon as an infant and Thakiah as a nurse, being reprimanded by his father.

Aleabith allowed enough time for the first question to simmer before compounding with another. "Has enough time not passed to venture past the past? Are we to die by death or remain alive?"

Although not experts on social cues, Solomon and Spud understood that the personal quarrel fared better without their injection.

"Shameful? The shameless man ought to be full of shame. You question everything but your own actions. The fiddle is not the only thing tormented by the touch of the fiddler." A slight pause after a string of jabs. "I am away because of you!" Thakiah's roar of a statement induced fear. "Tahira is gone because of you." Thakiah's whisper of a statement reduced to tears. "I need more than a field of wheat. I need a scarecrow to keep away the beast."

And so, the beast clomped away. Through the field of wheat, its body gradually disappeared. However, credit to its height, the beast's head remained in sight.

Succumbing to the burdens of her mouth, Thakiah crumbled back down to her knees. But what comfort could her knees afford her, and moments later she resumed her fall, embracing the earth. Initially, she lay on her abdomen, arms stretched as far as they would allow. Her soul, after expending much of its energy, yearned for a warm embrace to replenish it; Earth would refuse to deliver. And when she understood that to be the case, Thakiah rolled over, her eyes now towards the sky. There, she remained, gazing at the clouds, wispy and dense, pleading her case to the trains of above.

Part 6: Burning Heat

It was all but a cloudy affair.

A cluster of gas and droplets bound by forces, their advancement beyond my comprehension. Perhaps my existence was driven by necessity; yet my responsibilities remained unclear. Much like a bathroom mirror after a steamy shower, I could reflect on myself but rather faintly.

Whether an hour or so or a full nine months, my gestation period was over - humans for long, trees longer, but us the least of all. Despite the hefty realisation of a life that was merely a short story in an otherwise long novel, the sky's joy detracts its impact. We have climbed the ladder away from a precarious foundation. The herd was tranquil, finding contentment in its ride in the windy train.

Wiser by much, older by a little, Wispy formed a few sunbeams prior to me. It was quiet, and beyond reason at times. A distant whistle, at distant intervals, would bring my distant mind back the distance it travelled.

A colourful scenery tending towards the monochromatic on occasion, developing a gradient. The spectrum was wider the lower the herd descended. Visuals were but a partial component of the colours. The essence of interactions between all geographically lower organisms was a beautiful complexity – The hues of whos. Our herd, in contrast, was shepherded by the laws of the azure.

My sight was fixated downwards, but not in defeat, only in awe.

"Do not stray, for your obsession will only lead you far away."
Wispy floating as the neighbour, brushing its wisdom against an unsuspecting me.

"Apologies, I cannot restrain what I cannot perceive. I find simplicity in familiarity, but I am left perplexed by this view."

Wispy snickered, "Cumulus, you are delightfully dense."

A long pause ensued, interrupted only by the whistles of wind, hither and yon, to detract from the ubiquitous silence.

Cough

Cough

Cough

A brief pause...

Cough

"You cough akin to a greyer cloud. Why so, when your appearance is that of the young and white?"

"Your humour distracts me from what hurts, these toxins. You have my gratitude, Cumulus." And Wispy's coughing fit continued.

"Find patience within," I rebutted, slightly combative in tone. "You talk of toxins high up here?"

"I fear so, fellow traveller," Wispy replied, unfazed by brashness. "The wind does not discriminate; toxins and clouds alike."

"Your words border on the blasphemous. The winds have been kind."

"The winds persist as they are, winds, and the earth dwellers persist as they are, earth dwellers. Their waste we breathe and their harm we reap. We descend amongst them, and they rise amongst us. My intention is not to drown, and theirs is not to burn. But such are the circumstances of our existence, which favours the self. My hope is with the travelling sun we might bathe in nothing but cyclical peace. I suspect my hopes will wither with me. And yet, I hope you hope my hopes into existence." With that, Wispy went quiet, neither coughing nor talking.

"The herd travels less than your words do," I tried, with

humour, to lessen the blow to my beliefs, but Wispy was unamused.

"With time, you will come to realise, Cumulus, and perhaps you might wish me ill for not sparing you your ignorance."

The solace of false belief I could not attain with its equivalent truth. Why was I eager, despite the horror, to understand? To plague myself with a life of equivalent outcome? To travel to yonder side of the river without a bridge but through the treacherous waters?

Of coughs, there was plentiful more amidst the herd. My fellow clouds sang the tune of the sick and weary. Gradually, my fear of the outcome exceeded my fear of the unknown.

"To what purpose do the earth dwellers harm us?" I was made to wait for the termination of a sequence of coughs before I received Wispy's reply.

"Possibly, they are dissatisfied by the lack of rains. Possibly, they are dissatisfied by the excess of rains. With purpose and intention, even the winds are blind." Before I could address its hyperbole, Wispy continued, "The clouds do as they do, wishing no harm to those below; but it is long overdue for their negligent fires to water down on them." Wispy's vocals turned scratchy. The rough coughs had damaged its smooth voice.

"Water down? By the laws of the wind, do tell," I requested in a tone angrier than I had intended for. Its justification, if asked I would have provided, was that most of the treachery of the world I had only just come to know.

"My journey's end is nigh. Hence, I will take all that is with me through time and space to drop or dissipate. A choice I lack both the wisdom to comprehend and the ability to make."

"Pardon my oblivious nature, but you speak of death?"

"Aye-"

"And is death all there is to conquer?"

"Death then rebirth then death then rebirth then death then rebirth then-"

"Wispy, your repetition unnerves me." My tone progressed into agitation.

"Truth is mundane and repetitive. Or I am led to believe it the truth by legends passed down to me by the elders."

"So, cyclical death, that is to be our purpose?"

"Or cyclical life. I have not the answers, but if it eases your suffering, then let me inform you that you have no need for them. We do as the laws of the azure command and carry all we can, painful or not, until the hour arrives."

"What hour?"

"The hour of great depression." Wispy smiled reassuringly. It was content with a statement as vague as my responsibilities. And this indomitable outlook Wispy attained with its smile imprinted on me. I was only informed of a life where I live, and I die, and I carry, and I release. Before then, my knowledge was limited to cyclical peace. But perplexed by Wispy's words, an internal conflict brewed, stretching and compressing me. Should I loathe or empathise with the earth dwellers? They hurt with no intention to hurt. I carry and drop their harm with no intention to harm. If the laws would sanction my actions, then I would have done no less than relay a message to communicate my intent. Thereafter, I would joyously carry and guiltlessly release. Nevertheless, our languages dance on different grounds.

The herd depressed and the view below was shaded into obscurity.

Wispy had grown wispier, and I was made to ponder if it had not borne enough. *"Is this our descent?"*

"It is yours, my honourable companion, not mine, for I have not carried enough. The laws will scatter me thin until I concentrate again sometime somewhere. Let it be known, to the youth of our herd,

*that I could not have requested- *cough* -fo- *COUGH* -better companionship than yours." Wispy's voice softened with this final declaration of gratitude. It was becoming more difficult to envisage it.*

"By the mercy of the winds and the azure, I beseech you, stay, for a great depression would not honour the name without you," one last cry for a companion lost. But it was all futile for a companion to be found.

Its body spread further and thinner till one could not tell the difference between the cloud and the blue. No longer the wispiness and its immeasurable lightness, but the weight of a vacuum within.

The herd depressed further disregarding the dissipation of many.

"Am I to become a victim of time's indifference?" An empty question that fills no void, comforts no soul, and qualms no woes.

"Our progression is into the great depression," replied a squeaky voice drifting close behind me.

"Partaken no great, forsaken my mate."

"Its companionship endures to be shared, yet it is fiction for its companionship I miss," the cloud gradually floated by me.

Despite my sorrow's carcass, curiosity is a vulture awaiting its feed. "And who are you to it?"

"Wispy had been a reserved mass," chortled the seemingly elder cloud. "Nimbus is the name, but its utility perishes with our descent.

Nimbus occupied a larger portion of the sky and was far greyer, its expansiveness a sight to behold. Therefore, I subconsciously fell in time's trap and was focused on outlining the cluster from one droplet to another at either extreme.

"Your manners trail behind you," Nimbus commented but my eyes would not let. "It is rather rude for your vision to fixate on me."

The brightest streak of white shot down like a crack in the azure, and it was followed by a deafening sound that was akin to an argument in the heavens. It did little to frighten me however, for it was common for clouds to collide in lighting and thunderous fashion. What rattled me was the precipitous alteration of its mood. Nimbus was quick to laugh it off, leaving the polarity of its behaviour in question.

Moreover, the herd depressed even further.

'Delightfully dense' bore a different connotation at this phase of existence. My shoulders managed weight my back could not handle. Besides, the low pressure was a seductress, inviting me into its fold. It whispered to me, breezes from the east, in the pleasantest nature, to release – all the beneficial, harmful, or neutral.

"Your tension is unfounded. Let the laws guide you as they have done thus far," Nimbus consoled me, its voice soft, matching the gentleness of the low pressure.

"But I am light in contrast to the world's density. Is it not just for me to carry least what my heart, not my back, can bear?"

"Release!" Nimbus roared thunderously, more so than before, and with a level of vexation not derived from the playful. "For the fools think they know more and the wise less."

After the sun had travelled a short distance, I surmised cyclical peace was a reality rather than a desired concept. Nimbus was right; how could I know what weight I could bear? The tragedies of the commons were lessons taught to me by Wispy. It would talk about how those tragedies were a tragedy for all, how neglect here is death there, and how the responsibilities of one were a consequence to all. If not to honour the laws, and not to honour the lessons, then to honour the companion. Release Cumulus, release. Hence, I released.

A breeze caressed me, and my inhibitions unfettered. All that constitutes me began to condense into droplets carrying the history of what you had done and the future of what would be. Like messages from the azure of words I could not speak, the droplets were a form of communication unrecognised by the senses but endured by the soul – far too foreign, yet most common – the tragedies and the fortunes.

Three splats in quick succession and one soon after to mark the transition from end to beginning.

Of shades green and brown rejoiced as the first of me dropped onto parched soil. The plants cheered, drinking and replenishing themselves in the process. They paid their gratitude and drank till they could no longer. Oh, so full they were, and more of me did drop. The plants begged, "enough of you," and more of me did drop. If only I was the conductor to give you what you beseeched for, but the laws had ordered and more of me did drop. I could bring forth life and death; I sought the former, however more of me did drop.

On earth dwellers I fell, their tearful and merry faces. The tears and I raced down their faces. I was oblivious whether they originated of joy or suffering.

"God, Most Merciful and Exalted, bless us with more," prayed one of the local farmers whose crops had lacked rain.

Subsequently, my attention shifted to another, younger, with naïve jubilance plastered across her face.

"Nada, get inside now," commanded a middle-aged woman from her front porch to her unsuspecting daughter sitting on a tire swing by a large tree. "It has begun to pour heavily, and I am afraid this is only the start."

"Patience mumsy, what are ten more minutes to a day?" The daughter replied, her tone audibly disappointed.

"By the second hand on the clock, not a second more," the mother responded assertively.

Her shoes sloshing in the mud, Nada stomped her way towards the house. And in an attempt to comfort her with an explanation, her *mother added when she was only a few paces away. "Hastily, before you catch a cold, or Lord knows what else." As the mother closed the front door behind Nada, I could hear her conclude, "The clouds are no longer water, and the rain no longer a blessing."*

In turmoil once more, for the daughter wanted to take advantage of my descent, however, I am capable of inflicting damage to this child. Perhaps it was an incident marked by its specificity rather than a generality of the earth dwellers. It was the case that many of those same dwellers gave no notice to my precipitation. Sheets were raised to protect them from my inconvenience. Otherwise, everyone persisted walking on puddle- riddled sidewalks, waiting under wet banners, running to the next destination, or calling for a car because they ended up late for an appointment too important to miss. All had their own priorities they cared for, but none did mine. I was an annoyance to some, a blessing to others, and unnoticed by many.

"Oh, Wispy, I hope these dwellers are made aware of me soon, for I do not desire harm for any."

*   *   *

Exhaustion to the extreme, the fumes of the vehicle's exhaust danced around an exhausted Solomon, whose body was slouched on an exhausted rubber tyre. Droplets from the heavens tapped the slumbering man on the face. Initially a nuisance to Solomon, the matter was resolved with a slight head movement. Another droplet fell an inch beyond his lips, but before it could roll out of reach, his tongue snaked its way onto the droplet. And as if calibrating a receiver, Solomon shifted his head a little more, relieving himself of the chaser's duty.

Drop after drop, they collected in the dry well that was Solomon's oral orifice. Like the arid soil that rejects the water initially, the water did nothing to moisturise his mouth. With each rising level, his teeth ached, sensitive to the foreign invaders. There was enough liquid in his mouth; any more would have trickled down the chapped sides where the side of his lips met. With one courageous gulp, he downed what he had collected.

A grimace followed by lip smacking followed by a few spittle swallows. What was that odd taste? Was it the taste of the rust seeping into the water from a bullet hole above? Was it all the air pollutants mingling with the rain after years of unidentified particulates rising among the clouds? Was it the sour taste of Solomon's own mouth after hours of keeping his mouth open? Or was it the culmination of all the bacteria building cities on his tongue following his lumpy milk ingestion? ORRR perhaps it was - okay I will halt this assault of probabilities.

Osroes' body rose, rejecting gravity for a few moments, and then plunged violently.

"The worms were snatched, and the owls are well-fed, your meal of today had flown to the next," sang a familiar voice. There was a chuckle battle happening between the occupiers of the other seats.

"What was it that killed his slumber: the rain, the bump, or your tiresome voice?" Another familiar voice struggled to string those questions together amidst their laughing fit.

"I reckon it was your lousy driving. With feet as big as yours, the pedals might as well be one." The unusually witty reply was enough to snuff the asker's laughter.

Solomon groaned and shuffled around in his uncomfortable disposition. "Wispy and Nimbus! Is it you, my depression's greatest companions? Does the next cycle reunite us?"

"A reunion with your wits would remedy this," replied sardonically the potato-shaped man. "And who might those two be?"

"Better companions than you," Solomon replied glumly, his awareness returning from its voyage ashore. He muscled his way out of the tyre, crawled on the van's floor, one uncomfortable spot to the next, then shuffled about until his head was poking between Spud's and Aleabith's seats.

"What happened to Tha-," Solomon remembered the weight of her name and held his tongue.

"The tongue disobeys its master – the what?" Aleabith wondered what the end of the question was.

"The... The milk! Did one of you, thoughtless individuals, ponder replacing the lumpy drink?"

"What time is there for a beverage, Solomon?" Aleabith raised his hand, brushing away Osroes's question. "Saving Nick from his enclosure is not enough to quench your soul?"

"My thoughts are treacherous, so I will spare you the truth," Solomon muttered in reply.

Mechanically, Spud rotated his head and scowled at Solomon. He had viewed the man with great admiration from afar, however now, in close quarters, a disdain for Osroes was festering within. Although, to Spud, Solomon was symbolic of a multiplicity of principles, he had also ascribed onto him communal values. But with many obstacles behind, Solomon had set a precedent of individualistic favouritism, acting in instances with complete disregard for the others around and only with auspicious outcomes to his end in mind.

The rain had departed and there were no more trickling drops to awaken the sleepers and the tranced. Beyond the clouds, the sun emerged with confident intensity. The bullet holes in the vans roof were now spotlights creating a polka dot pattern below. And the piercing light travelling through the windscreen blinded Solomon, bringing a question out of the shadows and to the forefront of his mind.

"How long had I been subdued by the mistress of my dreams? It was but a few minutes ago that the first drops had settled."

"A few minutes by your measure perhaps. Is your clock wound accurately?" The crooked-nose behemoth asked. Why would Osroes scrutinise the curvature of his nose, its provenance, its purpose, and ultimately its fate? To begin in one direction and end up in another; that was a journey Solomon was all too familiar with. But it was neither the beginning nor the end that amplified Solomon's interest. It was the infliction point, where the destiny of yesterday differs from the next. And, more than its mere existence, the why intrigues him; did the sudden change occur naturally, a characteristic defined by his lineage, or forcefully, yet still naturally, through perhaps a physical altercation or otherwise?

Following Solomon's prolonged silence, which had turned into a matter of concern for his companions, Spud added, "Friend, you have been out of this realm since yesterday. Yes, Aleabith can attest to that." He looked over to his driving partner, as though he was garnering support, before continuing, "Your eyes had not seen light since the incident with the misses." And although Spud would have delighted in teasing his friend about marital problems, he was wary of the size of Aleabith's hands.

He had forgotten the purpose of a conversation, that is to exchange knowledge, and pursued his narration. "To think you would have woken up in an hour or a couple, but there we left you near the fields only to find you locationally chained to the same spot; naked and all, as natured intended." A cough limited his chuckle, and Spud persisted despite his throat's resistance, "But Lady Luck smiles upon you, for she instructed us, quite kindly, to fetch you from the harshness, dress you in the jumpsuit which the winds had incidentally blown our way, and to toss you into the comforts of this van."

"Us?! One brother mute and the other deaf. If you had heard the Lady's instructions then I can only conclude that you outright rejected them, for you refused to lay a finger on our exposed companion." With a smile wide enough to reveal his molars and a meaty hand on Spud's shoulders, Aleabith jeeringly queried, "Are you terrified of the natural form?"

"Our effort, although unequal, was equitable."

Solomon had heard enough of both their jibber jabber, and he had travelled worlds whilst they retold past events. "Your companionship is shielded from any piercing blow," he commented dismissively. *I am rather baffled by time's slippery tail. I chase it, yet at every corner, when its tail is in prime view, my hands react slower than I intend.* And as was customary of a man with his scraggly beard, he scratched at it in thought. Wheat straw and flakes of dead skin descended from his wild mane, and his pondering gaze shifted down onto his own clothing. C-12, there on his jumpsuit, taunting him, and although he was tortured by it, he could not avert his eyes.

The vibration caused by the coarse asphalt and the lack of adequate suspension in the vehicle caused Osroes's knees to begin to ache. He threw himself back onto the rubber tyre at the back of the van, seeking the respite of a seat. With his bottom hugged, in the least assuring manner, and amidst a conversation between the two ahead too meaningless to recall, Solomon peered through the windshield at the oncoming onslaught of trees. Although he was not positioned for an ideal view of the screening, the flood of horror upon rooting out the destination of their inevitable halt felt all too cinematic. But he remained seated, perhaps out of sheer indolence or an embrace of the wilderness; for he, despite his appearance, was accustomed to a life amongst concrete and metal, yet then, he thought to himself, "If nature intends for the wild man to die then tant pis pour nous."

And though the sun had started to emerge between the clouds, it was once again shadowed by families of oak. "Keep your wits about you, for the road ahead is dark and treacherous."

.

.

.

"Have we been smote for past blasphemies?" Solomon asked,

befuddled by the violent impact he and his comrades were privy to.

"Fur of the wild, but a dent in this van. Would you venture a guess?" A heavy sigh escaping him, Aleabith raised the vehicle's handbrake and threw open his door.

"What filth the wilderness brings, only for a life of destitution to end at capital's desire." Spud snickered, prompting an impulsive scowl from Solomon, not too dissimilar to the one he had received earlier.

Osroes knew a dog once, and although his memory was shrouded with dark blotches, Rugrub was a spot of joy. Shades of brown to black, like the bark of a nourished tree, he was a sizable beast. Rugrub could not be restrained by anything other than his love for the family. Amar would ride him like a gladiator into battle, Shams would scurry away to avoid being trampled over, Luna would stare ever so joyously at the children fooling around in the garden, and Solomon would look ever so contently at his wife. But the memory would be interrupted by a singular bark, and Solomon would be forced to settle for the momentary bliss.

A cigarette expended between the two fingers of the man that had just yelled, "What more is there to it than a nudge to either side of the road?" Three puffs in quick succession and one drawn out soon after, the smoke from the cancerous stick danced in the breeze and was enhanced by light's stroke. And in this illustration of lines, Solomon could see Rugrub's eyes, pleading, in the manner a dog would, to prevent the maltreatment of his likeness.

"Heed your legs lest you lose them," Spud warned Solomon, who had pushed past Spud, into the driver's seat, and out of the van.

If this were a musical then Osroes stumbled upon a song's crescendo – a visual that screamed at the highest pitch, a moral moulding moment, an impasse, which historians can refer to as evidence of a character's ethical degradation or its improvement. "Lower your foot!" shouted Solomon.

At the back of the van, there Aleabith was with his elephant-sized foot raised above a pile of flesh and fur. "You ought to choose your words more carefully," he muttered with a gentle smile. "It is in unimaginable pain, Solomon. Perhaps we ought to expedite its deliverance, yet I wonder whether I would be relieving it of its pain or mine?" He smiled no longer and his voice had evolved into a mixture of pity and fury.

Solomon rushed to the side of the whimpering animal, rejecting the notion of a coup de grace and defiantly sheltering the animal's body with his own. And he spoke softly to the wounded creature, assuring it of his intentions, supplemented by patting its dirty grey fur. "Other than matters of the heart, what ails you, little beast?"

A warm sensation engulfed his hand, and when he raised it for further inspection, Solomon deduced the cause – blood, and the crimson fluid oozed from the animal's hind leg. He wiped his against his thigh leaving an artistic smear on his jumpsuit. With no further hesitation, irrationally so, akin to a mother entering a burning building for her offspring, he cradled the creature and carried it towards the van's trunk.

"Their reputation announces them with hostility. Are you certain it is wise to drag a beast among friends?" Aleabith stared inquisitively over his shoulder at Solomon, who paid no heed to the caution that feigned being a question and continued his petting of the injured animal.

"If you wish to rendezvous with death, then do so solo, but do not force us into the coyote's jaw," Spud slammed the armrest in frustration. And with the same vigour of his previous call, he yelled, "Set me free of your self-annihilating tendences."

Solomon's cognitive ability was put to the question, for his silence - although often - combined with his paternal coddling of the coyote, according to Aleabith and Spud, was evidence of mania. However, with the limitations of obvious choices, the two shrugged the entire matter off and filed it under the antics of an imaginative fellow. But nothing is without consequence. Day after day, the oppressive heat bore down on them, turning their skin redder; the sun was becoming difficult to ignore. They were victims of momentum, and when the sound of an overburdened engine was cued in, a partition was placed in the timeline of their experiences, and they ventured ahead.

With the heat setting in, Solomon saw no use for two sleeves on his jumpsuit. He ripped one off at the seams and repurposed it into a makeshift tourniquet. This precise and idle focus of his, combined with the vehicle's reverberations as a matter of velocity, induced bouts of nausea in Osroes. Despite that, he lifted the coyote's hind leg with care, placing the sleeve under it. As though instinctively, he mumbled a tune, akin to a children's rhyme, as he was tying the cloth around the animal's leg. "He circled around the mountain hill. She circled around the mountain hill. They met at the valley below and jumped into the river to see where it flowed. Be it an ocean or be it a lake, their fingers intertwined as they awaited their fat-

"أطلب من الكلب الصبر!"

Solomon's furious call was unrecognised by all, but most significantly himself. It rose from his stomach and was carried with vehemence by his throat before being moulded by his lips, like a potter with clay, only to be defined by ears as the erratic drivel of a suffering man. The two sets of eyes, shocked, shot back at Osroes as if to say, *Look at him, this most illogical man. No! A mockery to the species with this excess of hair such that one cannot differentiate him from the creature he tends for. Look at him, flailing his arms about. This is a man driven only by base instincts, his heart, his skin, and his loins. Let us proclaim that this, his being, is wholly unbecoming of a writer.* Although no words were exchanged, Solomon was ashamed by his own behaviour, and those thoughts which he ascribed to them, he also thought himself.

"Other than matters of the heart, what ails you?" Words were finally exchanged, and the first of them was a sardonic enquiry by Aleabith. Spud, adversely, added nothing to the conversation besides an endorsing nod towards his parallel, awaiting to view the comment's outcome.

"May God curse this beast and its teeth; it bit me." And with determination to unleash his wrath on its neck, Solomon lunged forward with both palms exposed. He retreated swiftly, however, when the coyote threatened to bite again.

"Put this van to rest, so that I might do the same to the coyote," commanded Osroes.

"Is it wise for a vehicle of motion to be motionless often?" Aleabith packaged his form of nonsensical philosophy within a humourless question.

"Is it wise for a man to expose his neck often?" Solomon's threatening approach prompted the driver to oblige with little hesitation. Yet it was not the threat that evoked such a response, for Aleabith determined to halt the vehicle from the initial command. He merely found the prospect of trading words entertaining.

Solomon rose, supported his bleeding arm, opened the door, and booted the coyote's rubber tyre nest. Three toe pokes in rapid succession and one great kick shortly after were enough to drive the coyote and its temporary housing out. The biter whimpered but attempts at gaining the sympathy of the bitten were fruitless. "You are no Rugrub," Solomon yelled with whatever force his lungs could muster. "You are no Rugrub," he muttered once more with a hefty sigh, perhaps for dramatic effect, or perhaps because he recognised the villainy in his expectations - the error of assigning the qualities of one onto another.

As per his questionable judgement, put to the sword of his companion's scrutiny, the ever so conflicted Osroes leapt down and squatted next to the coyote. "The fault lies with the bitten, for how could I ask a toddler to tend for itself? You are a coyote, nameless - ah yes, Nameless - and indeed I shall attempt and respect you as such." With the tips of his fingers, wary as to not expose much to its teeth, he reassuringly traced Nameless's back, informing it that the broken trust could be mended.

Ripping off the other sleeve, Solomon fashioned another one of his renowned tourniquets; however, this one was not meant to care for wounds but to prevent them. He laid his body gently onto Nameless, ensuring that the wilderness was quelled before swiftly placing the restraint around its mouth, tightening it in the process.

"The vagabonds have a fourth, but only for now," he addressed the animal. Struggling for breath, Osroes dragged Nameless' nest back into the van.

With a raspiness that betrayed him and a woebegone appearance on his face, Spud exclaimed, "I question your lucidity, for it is all darkness where your conscious lies. You cannot be serious!"

"Am I to leave this helpless creature among the thoughtless?" Solomon retorted with an air of dignity, as if his morality had finally found its footing.

"If I am to be done with you piece by piece, the coyote can consume you for all I care. When it gets to your core, perhaps then I could see the man I once held a modicum of respect for. A man held back by nothing except his ability to exert. A man whose drive terrified him because he might soon discover his feet are off the ground. Not this man, no! Not you." Spud's rant was concluded by a less than subtle nudge by the large man.

"We should not allow a vulture to make a vulture of us all, agreed?" Aleabith made no attempt to hide his discontentment with Spud.

Silence settled upon them, setting the mood for the remainder of the journey and leaving the van's settlers feeling rather unsettled. The linearity of the road made it appear infinite, and the passengers were left with a sense of neither beginning nor end. The front passengers glanced at each other occasionally, while the back passengers stared at each other continuously. Nameless's drool was escaping its mouth guard, possibly at the thought of completing its lunch. Solomon, on the contrary, was not staring at the coyote but through it, reflecting on his own journey momentarily.

The eyes of the broken man were awoken by unspoken words labelling an oak-fenced structure. One would hope to forget the title of a past chapter, but alas it was forbidden. It was the house of trapped minds, the –

Wellness and Recreational Institute for Therapeutic Exploration.

The chorus of a familiar jingle began playing in Osroes's head:

'We are here to WRITE your wrongs,

So, we can help you right your wrongs.'

A drought requires the assistance of time unlike a flash flood that annihilates the land through its suddenness. The former is felt to be a symptom of permanence, whereas the latter a catastrophe through impermanence. Yet, defying the constraints set by the environment, the words of the jingle alone were enough to leave Solomon's mouth feeling like an arid landscape, more so than he could remember. And as the image of a sun-baked desert formed in his mind, he could see the mud cracks, patches of land with lines in between them like a network. His vision zoomed out thereafter and Solomon saw the cracks minimised into the wrinkles on the skin of a palm of a hand. The hand was cupped in a manner as if it were pleading for sustenance, and he could hear the echoed shouts behind him, "Balikh, Balikh! Al-Furat, Al-Furat!" And he could hear the gushing of water, and then he saw a flow of water rushing against the hand, its abundance escaping between the finger slits. Then, as though his vision was an elastic band retracting back to its pre-tensed state, he could see once more how the cracks in the desert refused the water and the river's water accumulated at the top, killing whatever wildlife remained sheltered between the mud cracks.

The settled silence was disturbed by Aleabith's hushed voice, "How could many benevolent adjectives and nouns lead to villainous verbs?" There was no reply to the question where no reply would suffice. They all gazed at their past place of residence as brick by brick emerged in their scope of sight.

After guiding the driver to a spot like where Annabelle had left the vehicle for him to escape, Spud dove into an investigative state marked by a focused intensity that left him disoriented. Neither the coyote nor the two companions had been the primary cause of his agitation, yet he felt a screeching at the back of his head akin to a violin's string being abused by its bow. The tinnitus was drowned out and soon Spud could only hear the high-pitched noise and the sound of cardboard being crumpled in his subconscious, unassailable by his fingers, rendering all attempts at muffling the abominable band of noises useless. But outwardly he appeared as he had been for the journey's length except for his neck that craned down to accentuate his nape and his mouth which remained open during his momentary gaze. *My brother, if I have lost you eternally then I conceivably failed you and if I find you shortly then I have certainly failed you and all doubt to my own selfish relief's gain is to be cast into the exiles of my own conscience. In your drift, you might be idling in paradises or conquering forts, but to be found then the narrative is definitive, and you are on level ground with me, hell's resident.* The internal monologue was battling for the spotlight against the cacophony of noises, a symptom of which manifested itself physically in the gradual scrunching of Spud's face.

He was assuaged from his anguish when the words of Aleabith imitated a conductor's cut-off gesture of Spud's internal orchestra. "We wait till when?"

"We wait till then," Spud replied automatically, almost oblivious to the words he had uttered.

"Then has arrived, made our acquaintance, and departed on

amiable terms." Solomon retorted. "But I understand how time escapes you," he muttered, pity plastered all over his face.

Spud, having reclaimed cognitive awareness, scanned the area around, scrutinised it even, and realised the image ahead of him. "Not a whisper but from the wind that meanders brick corners. Where are the souls that tormented their kin for wishing to grow outwith their skin?" The words were hushed and carried a sinister undertone that leaked from his depths. The sentences were like daggers hidden under a cloak waiting for the exposure of Yan's neck to draw blood. And you could see frothing at the corner of Spud's lips, an unsettling desire that could force him rabid. Not too dissimilar from a desire he had fully unleashed on Ulla; it was the same innate instinct that drove him to pursue a writer, to abandon his brother, and to reconnect with the fiddler. "Where are the pigs that have ventured beyond the pigsty?" An apropos question for the vengeful hatred he harboured within. It was a speck within his being, so minor that if you could extract it with tweezers, it would be no larger than a particulate of dust, yet when called upon, it dominated him entirely that even his unquenchable well of ambition appeared an effortlessly fillable bucket.

Aleabith exited the vehicle, followed promptly by Solomon, who scooted past the stagnant Spud and slammed the door behind him, leaving a half-cracked open window for Nameless's respiratory needs. The violent departure brought awareness back to the Baikonur, whose ears had only caught Solomon's trailing voice as he strolled off. "The magazines have been depleted, and the blood has been shed. Fine men, let us set forth and explore the trenches."

The Three Vagabonds, who had thus far been lost at sea, became bored of the boat's swaying and instead gripped the helm, sailing ahead with the conviction of locating a destination undefined. The waters roared as the main entrance of the WRITE facility squeaked open and the waves of nostalgia came crashing through. What joy can be derived from past suffering and what suffering can be derived from past joy – an inseparable couple. Creatures from deep and dark floated by the sailors' boat, that no longer was capsizing their worst nightmare but their most probable reality. Aleabith's heavy footsteps reminded the two other men to take heaps of breath before diving into the depths of explored yet abandoned waters.

It was more lifeless than Solomon could remember, not that his remembrance was a primary source of past actuality, but rather supplementary. There was a lack of physical vessels to carry the life consuming yet contradictorily lifeless souls that Osroes attributed to the editors. He struggled to identify the cause of his disdain for the people, yet he speculated, nonetheless. Perhaps they stood as a reminder of his modest output as an aspiring writer (his writing was plenty, but his paragraphs were empty); better yet, it possibly was the restrictions they had placed upon him in exploring the landscape of his invention; it could have even been hatred through association, for they were one aspect of WRITE that applied during its glory and denied at its decline. Not even the lack of lighting could shed light on the obscurities.

Despite the reminiscence, or lack thereof, Solomon found himself in a space he had never been in before, the reception room. One could excuse the unhospitable atmosphere of the institute given its lack of occupancy. However, one could also be doubtful about whether occupants would make any difference. Meanwhile, on the less thoughtful end of the spectrum, Spud chose to yell into the hollowness, "HELLOOO?" (a cliché of calling out when no one is within visible vicinity). No less banal was his walk over to the empty reception desk and tapping on the call bell. Three taps in quick succession and one soon after, only then did the reality of the situation dawn on him.

"Where are the writers whose heads slump in shame when they are asked about what they have written? Where are the editors whose torturous remarks deliver them great pleasure? Where is Yan whose promises have gone unfulfilled? Where is Glenda whose touch chills my spine? Where is Nick, my brother, whose love I do not deserve?" He cried out and would have fallen to his knees had he not supported himself against the reception counter.

Solomon shifted his attention towards his distressed compatriot and attempted disingenuously to comfort him. "Answers to all your questions lie beneath this very crust," and he pointed ahead of him before adding, "An organisation held together by disorganised individuals is bound to leave meaningful clutter in the debris."

And what prompted the demented man to join Spud at the counter, swipe two of his fingers against the dust-laden surface, and compare the texture to that of Luna's abode? You might say, "the derangement you speak of is dangerously palpable. The dust reminds Solomon of an unfortunate period in his journey; one where he had to reconcile with the consolidation of his loneliness and the ideation of unbearable outcomes – all of which are true until one is." But would you hold this same conviction if I added that Solomon Osroes proceeded to place the two fingers in his mouth, ingesting the dust as if it were salvation's medication? You might then ask, "What was the lunatic trying to taste, the amalgamation of skin leftovers?" However, as I am not afforded absolute oversight over his thoughts, you will have to tolerate the unknowable, even if Solomon himself were present to retell the tale.

Solomon progressed through the double doors with a swagger that compelled parliament to issue a vote of confidence and reluctantly follow its misguided prime minister. The three men were delighted to see that the courteous abandoners had left the door to the recreation room open behind. Yet, for Solomon, the delight was short-lived, for to his right was a familiar closet. He hoped the skeleton it harboured had been removed, but when the door swung open, the malodorous stench swimming in a sea of pungent caustic chemicals and acidity dragged him back into a macabre embrace.

*　　*　　*

"Rising sun, gentle sir. A good morning and a blessed day to you," grinned a moustachioed ray of sunshine.

"On you alone. The sun does not shine on buried men," I replied with an air of cynicism.

"Even the shortest plants are entitled to the sun," Earl rebutted, his face almost unrecognisable behind a bright beam of light.

"I renounce this privilege if only to attain the admiration of the Moon."

"Luna? Is that the Moon of whom you speak?" Earl chuckled warmly before adding, *"She was, as my eyes and ears have recalled, a wonderful woman."*

"Was?! Is. She is!" My voice was almost lost in its magnitude.

*   *   *

"I meant no offence," Spud shook Solomon by the shoulder, worried by his companion's idleness. "I was merely reminiscing about your heroic sacrifice, with a spring no less."

Solomon mumbled incoherently in reply, "What do you speak of?" His mouth and mind did not align, for one questioned what was stated and the latter what was seen. Everything Solomon remembered was offset by a degree enough for him to doubt their present falsities. But he was only afforded a few moments to scrutinise the quality of his remembrance before external elements interjected and rendered his progress null.

"Of Earl!" Spud cried out emphatically. "Oh, they should be singing ballads of your heroics. Oh, if none will then rest assured you will be hearing my children chant from the rooftops at twilight." An unwelcomed grin and a heavy-handed pat on the back were elements of Spud's supporting tools.

"Do not taint my act with your tasteless tongue," Solomon

rebutted scornfully, shame plastered across his face. "Earl was a fine man, a palette of many colours. The floor was my canvas, his soul the acrylics, and the painting... Well, the painting should speak of the casualties in the pursuit of liberty. Yet, I suspect that no keen eye would see a vision as mine, for no two pairs of eyes are exactly alike." And he said the last sentence with such a hushed tone that none other than those with ears at his lips could hear him.

There was perpetual torment in Solomon's words. He admired Earl for all his kindness, his short-lived magnanimity, and a moustache which he had long sought to emulate in its thickness and pride. The moustache, although insignificant in its tangibleness, was seen by Osroes as outstanding in three parts: the hairs reaffirm a confidence in one's cultural background (the way past men had adorned a fez on their head), its weight on one's lips reminds the bearer of the might of his words, and it also acts as a shield to filter the air travelling towards one's nose from all the smells that might remind one that they have been carried far west by the current. There was no scientific basis for Solomon's assumption of a thick moustache's attributes, yet perhaps because he lacked a sufficient one, he placed the facial hair among royalty. His admiration of the man amounted to no more than disturbed soil, the moustache hairs finding their home amongst planted roots.

Alas, he was alleviated of his torment when the vagabonds proceeded ahead as if in heedless demonstration against his internal strife. Solomon instinctively shut the closet door behind and treaded sluggishly behind the two seemingly carefree individuals; unbeknownst to him was their many mental anguishes. They all, perhaps collectively but certainly separately, were dreading the prospect of further revisitations.

Directed by the familiar floorplan, the fellows stumbled into the leisure room soon after. Much of their perilous escape plan had been devised in this room, and only one would suffer the consequences of its haphazardness. A heaping cloud of dust rose from the green couch, as Spud found residence in the recognisable piece of furniture. Flick went his lighter and the smoke from his cigarette mingled with the floating dust particulates.

"Our time apart had never exceeded this," Spud said dejectedly, exhaling another plume of the spent tobacco. Then he smiled in remembrance, as if a thought had just emerged in his head, and he scratched gently at his arm, as if he were aiding the thought's development. "We had thought of developing an autobiographical film in our youth – THE ADVENTURES OF THE BAIKONURS." He waved his hands up in the air envisioning the title in bold letters and bright lights. "It was Nickel's idea. I am merely the mouth that relays them."

"Your fine brother's name was Nickel?" Aleabith beat Solomon to the question on both their minds.

"A product of Mother's humour," Spud burst into a coarse laughter that was promptly followed by a series of smoking-induced coughs. To suppress his throat's ailment, he took another puff before adding, "The Tatarian matriarch (not by choice mind you), she did not courtesy Nick with a name till several years after he had popped out. When asked for an explanation, mother Minana would always reply that a name must be earned. However, in all honesty, either the woman's demons made the choice an impossibility to evaluate or, better yet, she was a little lazy."

Spud's last sentence ended so abruptly that both Solomon and Aleabith wondered whether there was more to tell. And Osroes, left unsatisfied by a lack of clarification about Nickel's name, queried simply, "Nickel's name?"

"Ah, yes! Well, I hope you see the humour in the story as I do," Spud chuckled lightly. "One day - Nick was no older than four or five – we were strolling down the street. It was not long after we had immigrated from my father's land. Where was I? Ah, yes! Well, we pass by a candy shop, heh heh, and the little sucker notices a sucker in the display window (how sharp his eyes were). As any child would, my younger brother begins to point at the candy and to tug at mother's pants (persistent rascal, heh heh). She was having none of it, and his nagging only drove her towards fury. My mother, God rest her soul, she was a short-tempered woman, and no sooner does Nick begin to cry does she shoot him a side eye and slap him silent with the back of her hand (we would joke many years later that at that moment, my brother had officially become a mute). Ah, yes! Forgive me gentlemen, the name. Well, when mother slaps him, she says, almost yells, 'If you are not worth a nickel, then you sure as hell are not worth a dime.'"

By the tale's end, Solomon had already lost interest and departed before its conclusion. His attention eluded him, and he sensed unintentionally that he had been chasing curiosity's cat, if only to bring the creature to a halt. But in the cat's stroll, it was predestined to find respite by a vending machine that bore great significance for Osroes's past. It was there, if his memories were to be trusted, where he had initially made the Merchant's acquaintance. And surprisingly, as if the Merchant himself had engaged in mischief, one item had remained unselected and stocked amidst an already underwhelming array of snacks. Seemingly, 'Soul's Best Bar' remained everyone's favourite last choice.

Inadvertently callous, yet on topic all the same, Solomon enquired, "Do any of you hold a dime?"

"That is awfully harsh," Spud retaliated. "Mockery of my brother is best left to me."

Aleabith reached into his pocket and flicked over a dime with two of his fingers. "Do you claim, with certainty, Solomon's intention?"

If only the world was rendered faultlessly and flicks and tosses would execute seamlessly, from one hand and into another. But it was not, and the dime fell a couple tiles short. What an unfortunate time for Solomon to have kempt nails, for he effortfully slid the coin across the flooring until a groove in the tiles finally assisted its uprising. "I label thee a fidus Achates!" Osroes exclaimed delightfully as he held the coin between two fingers.

*   *   *

"*Hello fellow, you appear a little mellow for a bitter drifter searching through the litter.*"

"*Ridiculous how meticulous your synthesis of fiction. Perhaps with time elapsed, but what forces you to say that?*"

"*A familiarity of commonality.*" There was a brief pause. "*In actuality, I know you and you know me.*"

"*You make no sense, but I must confess, my memory has been the cause of much distress.*"

"*I waved to you to save you from this cave; a bridge I crave to remain built.*"

"*I don't follow your hollow tale of sorrowful happenstance.*"

"*I digress for I too must confess; I am the Merchant of Souls, and you took my deal after all.*"

"*I?! Not I! The elder man died at the hands of clocks, not I.*"

"*Aye, not I. Definitely not I, me Lord. Or shall I refer to you as Earl?*"

"*Earl... Well, Earl died for the restitution of my basic liberties. His contribution to this institution led to his execution.*"

"*I can tell by your remorseful shell. Oh, but tell me more about Annabelle.*"

"*Annabelle... Well, Annabelle died to avenge a death in me. That wench threw me in the trench and upon my descent I decided to defend the soldier within.*"

"*By earth you have buried your mind and by skies your heart. I wish to ask you one more. What about-* ”

*   *   *

With the taste of stale coconut cream still prancing about his tongue, Solomon stretched the orange wrapper with his hands in preparation of its inspection. In lieu of a discovery that would send him downstream the river, he was distracted by a sharp pain in his bottom right molar. Some of the textural coconut shavings within the bar were hiding from his tongue. *Cavities,* Osroes thought to himself before sighing heavily.

Where did the two other vagabonds go? A minute or so ago, Spud was retelling a story better told to organisations for the protection of children. A minute or so ago, Aleabith was tossing a dime treacherously too far from a friend. A minute or so ago, Solomon's mouth was clear of any wreckage from the calamitous journey of Soul's Best Bar through the treacherous waters of his digestive tract. Was a minute or so ago by his recollection, a minute or so ago?

But who was he to disobey the road that coaxed him ahead? As if fate was dragging him by the arm, Solomon disregarded his present loneliness and proceeded ahead. At the sight of familiar bars, he remembered the laughter they induced as a matter of juxtaposition – encouragement of therapeutic exploration yet a prisoner's door right ahead. Lacking any of the appropriate hesitation someone in his current precarious setting ought to have, Osroes slammed the door right behind him and ventured further into the depths of his past.

C-1, C-2, C-3, C-4, C-5, C-6... “C-6?” Yes Solomon, and what of it? It was the cell's number; no more. He carried on. C-7, C-8, C-9, C-10, C-11. “Have I found my destination or my very beginning?” He mumbled the question under his own breath (he was worried a stranger might attempt to answer it), and with the monotony of a machine. We have programmed machines to mimic us, and we have been programmed by the machines to mimic them. In the quasi-

142

symbiotic relationship, one is left to wonder how the materials around shape ideation, and if we have shaped the materials through these ideas to construct novel materials. Is it an infinitely iterative process that approaches an outcome of universality between all humans and materials? Are materials and ideas bound to become one and the same, forever intertwined, rendering creativity and love relics of a past that was rife with naivety?

Solomon scoured in his pockets for keys he knew he did not have, for a door that did not require them. C-12, C-12, C-12.

Part 7: Forbidden
Solomon Osroes

"C-12, C-12. C-12? C-12!"

"Will you keep quiet?"

Rubbing heavy eyes with calloused knuckles, I could discern an intense metallic odour coming off my fingertips. In the gloom of an unlit room, my eyes found adjustment manageable. With my lenses finally coming into focus, I could see aged blood flaking off my nails. Artistically inclined, one could assume this was the result of another creative enterprise.

In this confine of mine, my bed hugged the wall, not out of affection, but out of fear of what lay beyond. And as I had routinely done every morning (or at the time when I had awoken), I tilted my head left and right and scouted a room with which I had become wholly accustomed. Coordination between my curiosity and memory was non-existent: *What might that be? Oh, that is the sink. And what might that be? Oh, that is a wall.*

As my eyes settled onto recognisable walls, I deduced that my excessive nail filing had not been squandered. Clouds at dusk were far too light, and clouds at twilight were far too dark; my crimson clouds were a perfect medium of self-expression. But this discovery begs the question, what had I been attempting to express? Ever so tenderly, my fingers glided across the wall, tracing the outline of a makeshift sky. Past cells may decide to communicate their frontline tales to present soldiers, or they might be harbouring resentment for their unsung demise.

An adequately sized rectangular window separating my grey from theirs swiped open.

"Good morning." There was a twinge of pre-emptive joy in the tone of their voice.

"Good morning?" There was a twinge of calamitous uncertainty in the tone of my voice.

"Good morning!" There was a wave of sadistic ecstasy in the tone of their voice.

Of the universe's finite states of matter, solid would defeat liquid in the battle of direction. We do not mention gas in this conversation, the most directionless of all. Unlike Brownian motion would suggest, my suspension in liquid was purposeful.

Remnants of clouds perspired less than I, and I could hear the spattering sound that would ultimately conduct the rhythm of my panting. On my knees, I appeared to submit to the will of my oppressor. Whilst rising, momentarily, my two eyes paralleled its one – or was it a mouth? Was I staring at a hose? Nevertheless, the hosing down was an overlooked consequence of my misdemeanour.

The hose retreated and my hands succeeded. "You make the mundane a little more bearable," my chaperone laughed theatrically from the opposite side of the door. Unlike wedding rings, which signified lifelong imprisonment, these metallic ones were placed on my wrists to convey temporary reform. "The lengths I would go to have a peek at your face," added the editor with a sardonic tone.

"Oh, how charming of you," I replied, my face almost meeting the door. "Is this a marriage proposition? If so, then I do. I do! A million times, I do!"

"Not one thing will ever be as humorous as your submission."

Attempts at cajoling my escort were all in vain. Often, I strove to learn their name, therefore establishing grounds for a lasting relationship. Gradually, I would erode their principled core, integrate my own convictions, and apply a healthy coat of sugar to make it all a bit more palatable. To my disappointment, capital was an imperishable coat to a decaying core. Ergo, my focus marched on to different prospects.

Indoor balconies were an architectural anomaly. There were twelve cells upwards mirroring the twelve on the ground floor. Wooden balconies appeared accessible from the rooms and the rooms from the balconies; both appeared inaccessible otherwise. Were other writers in those rooms, high above? If so, I had not received the pleasure of encountering any of them since my arrival at the institution. Perhaps, most plausibly, people of luxury remained in the company of luxury. Alas, we forgo our quandary and continue wandering.

And as though I had through happenstance stumbled upon this most unfortunate, and yet imperative hurdle, I was onto my first task of the day.

"Your persistence in using obsolete material is painful," I groaned, out of sheer habit, and perhaps out of condescension for the accompanying editor. Here I was, the creator of worlds, the inducer of emotions, the inciter of rebellions, and the messenger of knowledge; there they were, the constraints upon my worlds, the rationale behind my heart, the strategy behind the revolution, and the moderator of knowledge. Perversely, I had initially suggested the installation of such units, for despite their many misgivings, the editors were the structural integrity of the buildings. The 'grout between the bricks' as Yan would say. And yet, at that given moment, I could not help but jab at the guardian of my creativity. "Are you an Iron Age denialist?"

Intermediate schooling was a far stretch away, both locationally and temporally, but momentarily my surroundings evoked a childish disdain exclusive to the first class of the day. Being physically instructed to sit in an awkwardly small chair and desk, I was to be left alone in the middle of a chilled room.

Although the guard refused to reply to my rhetorical question, he unsurprisingly presented me with a cuboid alongside six wooden sticks. They resembled chopsticks geometrically; however, these carving tools were far too primitive. The cuboid was a block of ice wide enough to match my torso, and heavy enough to make that same torso collapse under its weight.

"If you await time's succour, then death shall arrive prior," the editor commented at my idleness.

Urged to transition back from the Iron Age to the Ice Age, I instinctively grabbed one of the sticks. Every time, I would stare blankly at the task ahead, oblivious of how to commence it. Do I chip at the corners, knowing that the corners are a vulnerability of the structure? Better yet, should I drive at the heart of the block, create a chasm and allow the room's heat to dissipate all through the cube?

The crimson red ran thin. Haem was merely a drop of pigment swimming in an ocean. The more I persevered, the more the haem concentrated; the more I persevered, the more the haem diluted. It was a race between the quantity of ice I could transmute into water and the quantity of blood that could steadily depart my body.

Hours on and there was a mound of crushed ice swimming in a pool of its own blood and mine. Not a feather pillow by any means, but my head did not care the least. A fainting conclusion seemed imminent yet distant like a pendulum swinging to and fro reality's bounds. The following scenes played like discrete events rather than one continuous story.

A shadow descended upon me as if the greyest of clouds floated above; a thunderous cough distracted me from the sharp pain in my fingertips and the numbness in my closing eyelids. "Your productivity astounds machines." Glenda circled around the desk, noting the answers to my faux examination. "It is a shame you have tainted this batch with your blood, for with less pain and more patience, the result would have been finer," she added, a mixture of pity and pragmatism battling for the tone of her voice.

Foolish patience, I thought to myself. It demands me exercise my hope in time and externalities. Am I to wait until these micro progressions coalesce into output of great magnitude? Or does patience wish I would realise the significance of the micro in time's compounding effect? Oh, this all bores me greatly, for my curiosity commands future results presently. And perhaps that is why I struggle to labour, that is, today's stride is tomorrow's view – my ambition is undercut by my impatience.

Nevertheless, I was in no shape to reply, yet the vulture, as I viewed her, with her craned neck and all, continued nibbling at my carcass. "And you broke all six sticks too?" Glenda sighed rather dramatically, before adding, "Nobody appreciates a messy cook." The sounds of her tutting echoed through the hallways as she departed my crime scene.

As if cued in by Mother Nature, one vulture replaced another. Oddly, however, there was a lack of biting, therefore the bird metamorphosed into a humanoid creature. And this humanoid wrapped a figurative blanket around me. "Fellow, see the hurt you have caused yourself," he berated me parentally. Aiming to comfort me in my dishevelled state, he added, "Let us get you speckless and scented." I felt immense relief, which was not solely due to my slush pillow. It compelled me to look up in admiration of my comforter.

"My favourite type of tea," I replied in a hushed tone that only served to emphasise my delirium.

The editor, Earl, had wounded his foot before the starting pistol was fired. To any other person, my statement would have been a kind and approachable method of greeting. However, to a person mocked in their youth for bearing the name Earl Grey, my words simply carried baggage most airlines would deem too heavy. And as I stared at his moustache drape ever so slightly over his top lip, I understood the severity of my words. My awareness of his past trauma made the mocking even more terrible. But before I could reconcile with the editor, I had developed a friendship with –

Swoosh, the ice was swept down the drain. Splosh, my fingers were bloodless again. Housekeeping duty was done and thereafter proceeded the fun: onto my second task of the day.

Three gentle pats on the shoulder followed by one reassuring grip.

"The boy has got his fingers a little short of mangled," Earl informed another editor across. I was in another room, its ambience more hospitable and its editors more caring. Thematically oak, the space was clustered with desks and bookshelves fabricated from the bright wood. The books' arrangement was haphazard, lacking classifications in terms of genre, age, or even language.

The other editor was a blonde teenager with the pompousness of a struggling merchant. Fata haughtily strolled by, claiming the title of *minimus militum*. His parents doubtlessly thought summer employment at the recreational facility would develop him into a fine young man. I thought his stint caused the erosion of his character. In perfect contrast to a well-nourished Earl, Fata had a gaunt figure that complimented the dark rings around his periorbitals.

"The nurse is displeased with your inconsistency." Fata tossed one of the many hardcover books arranged on the top shelf. "She claims you have heart palpitations."

Time to WRITE: Vol. 7

My fingers travelled along the indentations on the leather-cased volume. It was as if we were apes – the book was my master, and I was its subject. Out of sheer mercy, the book had laid out its palm for me to trace with my fingers. The tribe of apes around would view this as a gesture of reconciliation, up until my next transgression.

"You are a little beyond a thousand words into volume seven," he added before handing me a pen over my shoulder.

"To write is to inscribe inspiration. Frankly, of late, I have not been inspired."

Lacking the lexicon to describe a gratifying melodic rip, Fata approached me with some duct tape in hand. He grabbed my hand swiftly and indelicately, disregarding any affliction caused to my bruised and tumefied fingers.

I yelled in agony, but sarcastically, carefully avoiding the exposure of my vulnerabilities. "Ach- careful here! You would not handle a saloon vehicle so boorishly."

"If they are what you claim, I would have chopped and sold them for parts." Fata rolled and rolled till my hand and the pen were married by the ordained tape. "It is my hope that you feel a little more inspired now."

"Your inspiration borders on abuse," I addressed him with a side-eye.

"Not in our culture," shrugged Fata in response. "But you might have forgotten this."

As we danced aimlessly around the subject, there was one inevitability: me writing. My fingers fought through the pain like a candle on a window frame. Fuelled by thoughts, treacherous and otherwise, they would flicker with every passing breeze. Certainly, it was not a question of if the flame would die but what would kill the flame. It was either me being taken away from the fuel or it being taken away from me.

"...Mmm pecan, a treasured occurence," I said, *knowingly contributing to a trope that draws the main character into a scene. Pecan pie was a delicacy in my household. Although a rarity to begin with, my family had given up on it immaturely. I, on the other hand, longed for the pastry.*

Guilt subsiding, my fingers dug deep into it. Mouthful to a mouth full, as soon as a spoonful entered my mouth, I was preparing the next bite. What flavour I tasted was short-lived for the process of consumption was more gratifying than the pie itself.

My eyes panned down onto sticky fingers. "I'll never do that again."

It was but a few moments subjectively.

"Mmm apple, a delight indeed," I said, prancing towards the

My tingling hand had given in to one of two foes: the bleeding wounds or the tightly wrapped tape. The flickering flame finally succumbed to the wind.

"A few hundred words, is that it? And about pie? Not about jasmine, not about marmalade, not even about the breeze," Fata scrutinised my work. "Give my niece some crayons and she would write with more heart on walls." After failing to see the desired reaction on my face, the blond editor tucked his hands under my armpits, attempting pitifully to lift me from the writing station.

"Is that all? My daughter could carry more with the tiniest hands of all," I guffawed in turn.

"A daughter of yours?" He bellowed with laughter right in my ear. "What lunatic would-"

But before he could finish his ill words, I interrupted his impertinence. "You have made a mockery of your strength, and your hands now reek of sweat."

After ample back and forth, Fata decided that enough of my lunch break had been wasted and that nutrition was paramount before my next task of the day. He would reiterate, as he dragged me along, that his parents, like mine, would raise the earth and drop it onto him if he were to miss a meal. The cafeteria was a little over half the size of the leisure room. Breathing space was a conditional element determined by the room's occupancy. However, due to blundered schedules or malevolent minds, the room found itself at maximum capacity every lunch.

A colourful palette for a distinguished palate; a vibrant assortment was tossed in front of me across the metal surface. Perhaps appealing to some eyes but not mine, for I was not colour blind. The distinct and emetic colours of each food item disoriented my guts. The pita was blue, the mushy peas were green, the lamb was yellow, and worst of all, the tabbouleh salad was charcoal black. I viewed the cuisine with the naivety of a foreigner, finding the colours as unappetising as the lack of familiarity. But I knew each one of these foods. "Foods by the river," I thought to myself. I felt a strangeness in my gut, the kind you would feel when drinking coffee on an empty stomach. A jitteriness overtook me, and the very tips of my fingers turned frosty in a moment.

Nevertheless, I swiped my finger across the green spread in hopes of making sense of the nonsense.

"You might as well lick your fingers," a woman sitting next to me said. "You will get a full scope of the germs you have introduced."

"What is a germ or two to the mould that has grown through this spread?" I lifted my finger dramatically and in one swift motion, sucked the rest of the persistent peas off. "No, not mushy peas... Hummus! Delightfully confusing." My momentary smile collapsed into dejection.

"You have mistaken this period for respite, C-12."

"I despise your lack of respiration."

"I breathe to live, not to survive. Consume what you have and set forth to your demise." What a loaded reply. It was theatrical and absurd – who would ever say such a thing? And yet, what irked me most was that she stood up and dispensed her tray away, passively refusing to grant me the opportunity for rebuttal.

That vexation dissipated in a moment, for if I was compelled to provide a description of her face, I could not. I would dispel this forgetfulness of mine because, were they not all minute details in the grandness of my life? However, it is also in these small, insignificant, and barely visible specks of life where I sensed the greatest value would lie. Years on, I would sporadically remember these moments of insignificance and feel an overwhelming regret; paradoxically, I would believe these instances were the stresses that moulded my inevitability.

After consuming two well-constructed heaps of hummus using the blue bread, someone interjected before the third. "C-12, C-12. C-12? C-12!" I glanced up, licked the remnants of the chickpea spread off the corners of my mouth, and scanned across the room for the recognisable caller. I was sickened by the sore sight of a strawberry-haired woman. Annabelle, the same editor that had tortured me that morning, was now calling for me as if nothing had transpired.

"Where do they find these colourful rodents?" I muttered looking back down at my plate only to realise how well she would fit amongst this colourful array.

"Aha! There you are." she walked over to me with a pep in her step, which due to my misanthropic nature, was subliminally interpreted as taunting. I sneered at her in return. "Dr. Eadful has requested your attendance in his chambers."

And there we were, standing stationary at the doorway of his office waiting for his inevitable yet required admission. "Solomon, to what do I owe this encounter?"

Seemingly, our lunch menu was inspired by him today. The initially warm and emetic odour that had smacked me in the face had settled into a characteristically familiar one.

Under his desk, Yan swung his leg about trying to shift the chair across into an inviting orientation. I understood it as a signal to sit and I politely replied.

"This ginger wen-

He waved his hand across my face dismissingly and guffawed. "I am fooling around with you, Sol. Watch your tongue lest my attitude changes."

Right on cue, Annabelle curled her lips and exited the parameter. We had not met eye to eye – literally and figuratively – for every occasion our gaze would have locked, I purposely avoided it. There was an intimidating level of conviction in her stare. Where I questioned everything from conception to annihilation, Annabelle seemed certain in whatever she did. Alas, I did not need to dwell on her for too long; her next victim awaited her.

Concealed by the untrained eye, Yan's office might be mistaken for an inadequate living space leased by a graduate student attempting to kickstart the next stage of life – the nerve-wracking and wearisome days of adulthood. It is a façade of freedom masking an unwieldy mountain of utility bills and medical appointments. But Yan was a senior by all accounts, and to my eye, this room had an unsettling characteristic. Was it the lack of any penetrating natural light? Was it the lack of walkable space because piles of paper formed a cluster of miniature skyscrapers? Perhaps it was the inconspicuous door at the back of the room that for no reason, other than its plainness and closure, made me uneasy at the possibilities it hid.

My focus made its way back to Yan, and I asked a question of little significance. "I hear there are fresh chickens in the coup?"

He pulled his chair marginally closer to the desk. "You mean the twins?" He pinches his eyebrow as if he were in thought. And I could tell (well, not really) that he suspected the line of questioning was meaningless filler.

"No, no, no. I hear them talking about a face," I reply nonchalantly. "A moon among gloom."

"You should put that poetry of yours to good use."

"Always the preacher and never the sinner," I simpered suggestively.

There was a shift in Dr. Eadful's face. His eyebrows fell far enough to cover his eyes. Could I hear his teeth crack? The abrupt silence caused me to hallucinate, and I had somehow translated the tension in his jaw into the sounds of destruction. His cheeks were strained as if they were the facial dams holding his tears at bay. With a sombre tone, Yan decided to bypass the remaining pleasantries and address the principal matter.

"We had two commits this past month alone." He did not look up and instead gazed down at his finger which he was rhythmically tapping against the table. "There was word circulating around last month about a big fellow. He, his wife, their daughter, and a terrible fire. Three enter and two emerge. And when the blaze settled, all he would do was write and sing." Yan paused, and his voice fell a couple of levels lower. "These are methods of madness, Sol. How dare we claim to help others navigate waters we have not sailed?"

I glanced downwards, taking a mental photograph of the identification tag on my jumpsuit. Not only had I associated this number with my identity, but I had ascribed to it the entire purpose of my being. I was a writer, I would write a novel, and that work would earn me great renown, I would write another novel, and the novel would fall victim to the surpassed expectation of its predecessor, I would write a third novel, it would have an even greater fall – not because it was of any literary regression or the lack of an engaging plot, but because by then, I would have grown large enough to attract greater criticism, criticism defeats acclaim, I become convinced that no peak is even grander than the first, I collapse in a fit of despair, and I bury myself before nature intends. But this was all categorically my purpose – to be the grandest of dying stars.

He heaved a sigh of submission and continued, "Retirement is imminent."

"This language is inspired," I rebutted.

"Our mistakes linger thus tragedy looms."

"Our mistakes blossom thus words bloom."

"Hardly the scent of beauty."

"Reality masked by a façade of beauty."

He was almost choked up by the end of the exchange, however, Yan found his resolve and steadied himself. "Regardless, I am signing all WRITErs off this programme within the next few months. We will slowly deescalate the intensity of the tasks and hopefully give you a solid foundation from which to take off."

With my own set conviction, I replied, "I would like to remain an essential contributor to the refinement of the programme."

Dr. Eadful slammed the table with enough force to shake the entire room. "I presume you misconstrued what I said. Retirement, not refinement."

An insult was thrown or withheld, but alas the conversation had arrived at its end. As the sound of the metal cabinet, that I kicked on my way out, reverberated throughout the adjacent hallway, I deliberated over my time at WRITE. Six chapters were written here, albeit subject to comprehensive editing. The 'what' had been predetermined, truthfully, however, all other questions of the interrogative adverb nature were left unanswered.

While time seemed to be a construct difficult to comprehend at times, the duration of my stay I could estimate was more than a year but less than two. The first few months, I suspect, were particularly difficult acclimatising to the brilliance-manifesting loneliness. Companionship here was discouraged yet accrued. After the interview, C-1 and I kept our conversations to a minimum, for originality was a focal point of the programme. Inspiration, on the other hand, was suspended indefinitely between novelty and plagiarism. Therefore, C-1 and I inspired each other, more with our eyes than with our tongues. Her eyes danced frantically here and there exploring details in a setting lacking much of it.

Perhaps weeks drifted, but our vision intersected frequently. Our need for further connection was insatiable. Our lips would quiver like a starter motor trying to ignite an engine running on an empty battery. Our conversations gradually transcended salutations and generalities becoming increasingly purposeful while still retaining an appropriate level of ambiguity. Both wielders of pen, our purpose was a Trojan horse used to veil the underlying desperation rumbling within our beastly selves. We, I assumed, wanted to share with the world a slice of our hearts. But unbeknownst to us, we both required pacemakers.

Although C-1 and I started the marathon upon dawn's early light, her stride was greater than mine. And by nightfall, my thousands were dwarfed by her hundreds of thousands. WRITE had its first successful candidate. C-1's words spread till a hunger in her was fed. One day I would walk into the leisure room at the scheduled time slot to find my eyes wandering more aimlessly than before. "Who was C-1?"

C-1 was a moment in time. Anyhow, here we are in the present, a gift I seem incapable of unwrapping. From the silent falls of identical droplets to the inevitable sound they made splatting against the metal basin, my mind felt enough relief to initiate the shutdown sequence.

Woke up. Hosed down. Ice block. Blood gown. Write task. Lunchtime. Coloured food.

"Where are we headed?" I asked dejectedly, knowing the woeful conclusion of the programme.

"Room climb." Fata guided me away from the maladroit meal.

Presumably, given my affluent experience in this programme, I ought to know what task to expect. Consistency was half the battle and that was covered by the pre-lunch assignments. However, the after-lunch assignment was designed with frequent rotation in mind. When asked about the rationale, Yan would reply "I trust the pen to carry ink and the pen trusts me to not betray its utility." His bombast impressed me the least but stuck with me the most.

The door slammed shut behind me and I was left inside of a room where the only travelling direction was up. The posthaste construction of the room was evident by the rickety wooden ramp. Forcefully, I could break through the wooden flooring. But my belief in the programme exceeded my desire for non-conformity.

"What is the meaning of this?" I asked though I knew the answer to my question.

A buzzing sound was soon followed by a loud announcement.

"Simply put for the simple man, climb the ramp and retrieve the key to the door," Yan replied matter-of-factly, his voice distorted by the amplifier's quality.

Arguing with Dr. Eadful was a futile pursuit because none of the exchanges assumed a dialectic purpose. Therefore, I shifted my energy to the assignment and placed my hands on the flimsy ramp. My arachnidian fingers explored the wooden surface attempting to claim some leverage ahead of the climb. However, with nothing to grip on and a few splinters embedded, the bookmakers were not kind to my odds.

My interphalangeal joints were aching to be cracked. With my fingers releasing the pent-up gas, my lungs followed suit. Amidst heaves and pants, I wiped whatever sweat my eyebrows could no longer carry. This was an impossible task by my estimation. Not only did it require considerable effort, but it also demanded an endurance that denied rest. I could not sit halfway up the ramp – I would slide down.

A common theme I would come to discover throughout my adventure at WRITE was the slipperiness of time. No matter how much I exerted to stabilise time's speed, its acceleration seemed forever variable. Hours to days, days to nights, and months to years. Perhaps I was exaggerating the narrative (lunch and sleep were routine activities), but it was all for the sake of an interesting tale. And in this story, the task took on a relatively extortionate amount of time.

"What is this all for? If I climb, I get out and if I do not then what? I lay isolated from human connection, then water, and then food?" I yelled in between my continuous burst of short breaths. Inwardly, I relished the challenge. It was both a distraction from the retirement of the programme and a reminder of why I was fond of the institution, to begin with.

Like bees to a beekeeper, the buzzing sound made another cameo. "Have you forgotten the fundamental principles of writing?"

With no answer to an asinine question, silence elicited contemplation. I was knowledgeable about the principles of writing, but possibly struggled to apply them. Conviction in the outcome had debilitated my consistency. Where does a climber go after the mountain peak? Practically downwards, which is in itself an upsetting realisation. But more upsetting perhaps is assuming that no summit would ever be higher. Therefore, there is comfort in leaving the mountain unclimbed. The climber lays in bed all day long dreaming of summits they will never climb and thereupon having nightmares about them.

A climber is instructed to avoid looking downwards. Nevertheless, I am compelled to glance occasionally to remind myself of the beginning. Where I am and where I was are but a couple of points on a timeline. Where I will be is an extrapolation based on assumptions that I am too ignorant to apply. Albeit counterintuitive, perhaps walking backwards up the hill could serve as a prompt; today's summit is yesterday's climb. And no matter how many peaks I conquer, there will always be another hill and another trough.

With the psychological gymnastics out of the way, my head was upward, both figuratively and literally. Unusually, I laid down to exert effort. My legs were my propulsion, my eyes glanced downwards at my progression, and my hands fell victim to abrasion. I ought to moisturise extensively in the following days.

The back of my head bumped against a sharp corner. As fuzzy as my mind was, I managed to strain my neck sideways and catch a glimpse of the award. "Where to now?" I murmured to myself. "Practically downwards," I sighed, staring down at my point of origin. With my scraped hands ultimately proving handy, I snatched the keys off the shelf and carelessly descended.

Overwhelmed at the lack of emotion despite succeeding at the task, an apathetic I was escorted through one doorway and another. I was discarded back into my cell. As I settled down, I noticed there was a trace of blood left on one of my fingers that could have originated from any of the earlier tasks. Being that I was enveloped by the room's darkness, I was in no quandary about wiping my finger against the wall. After which (following a logical trail), I raised my finger for a quick olfactory examination. There was a lack of iron in the scent, but I could not discount the aid of my continually congested nose.

Many mornings later, I sat up to find a fresh C-12 jumpsuit awaiting to embrace me. Although bedsheets were customarily changed out bimonthly, we were offered fresh uniforms biweekly. Some of the WRITErs would tease about the editors being 'cursed with clear nasal canals' and that the editors were shielding themselves from our festering must.

"Time for a change," called an unrecognisable voice after a bout of persistent knocking on the cell door.

Dr. Eadful had introduced needless cautionary measures after the 'one or two gone too blue' cases. A lack of surveillance cameras magnified the perverseness of these practices. It was ironic how Yan's desire for the practical could yield such impractical outcomes. Through the door slots, editors had been instructed to peep at the programme's participants whilst changing their clothes – perhaps out of fear that the entire cloth might find its way around a WRITErs neck. Whatever diminishing confidence I had over the dominion of my own abode departed entirely, and in lieu was an ever-dilated pupil scouring the shadows for truth. No longer was it the eye of a hose, but that of a human.

"You might assume the appearance of one, but you are very much unhuman," I said whilst retaining a posture of nonchalance. The pupil drifted downwards momentarily – possibly chagrined by my comment – before returning to its original position. I was made to wonder who the guardian was.

A flurry of snaps snapped me back from pondering. "Are you all there?" I had been chronologically transported from the morning in my cell to the afternoon in the recreation room.

There she was once more, the moon I had mentioned to Yan. My infatuation with the moon, however, was dulled by the sun preceding her, for she was a mere reflection of the light's origin.

"I am where fate had intended for me to be," I replied sardonically.

"Does fate excuse you from accountability?" she countered.

A waft carrying a fetid stench interrupted my exchange with this newcomer. Kusai, as I had come to know from others who did not respect the sanctity of the principles, was a young man best spoken to at a distance. Although indeterminate in age, his unfettered spirit and heedless exterior secured him the title of 'WRITE Child' – WC for short. Some, and I share this opinion, believe that WC was spread as a means to mock his hygienic shortcomings.

Little was known about his background, but stories had claimed him as the unwelcomed offspring of a Japanese nobleman. When the aristocrat learned of Kusai's undesirable birth, he sent for his head. But instead of providing the mercy of instantaneous death, the nobleman had placed him into a wooden crate and tasked a sailor with the shipment's disposal discreetly into the ocean. Despite Kusai's mother's destitution, her supplications to a Deity proved valuable. The assigned sailor fell ill with scurvy and with time succumbed to death. And when the other boat dwellers finally discovered the wailing infant, they adopted him as one of their own. His journeys with them would be many until he ventured astray, landing on the shores of WRITE one day.

"You C-1, you see them all," teased Kusai.

"C-1? You are not C-1", I involuntarily furrowed my brows at her.

"If they are ranking us based on capabilities, then C-1 is about right for me," she smirked unconvincingly. "But if you are the competitive sort, you can call me Luna."

More weary than irate, I disregarded Luna's remarks and rose to leave. My infatuation with her was premature and just then, I decided to nip the flowering bud. As I strolled away from the brief exchange, I could hear Kusai relay advice discreetly.

"The name, keep it to yourself," he paused briefly before adding, "Do not tie your ankle to an albatross. It might soar today, but it will surely die tomorrow."

Distracted by what I construed as hypocrisy, I bumped into two contrasting figures: one stumpy and the other lanky.

"Do all drivers look backward here?" Why was he so loud? Did he assume I could not comprehend him a head's distance apart?

"Pardon me, I will be on my way," I responded flippantly, placing an apologetic hand on my chest.

With a twinkle in his eye, as if he had noticed a spark to ignite the flame within, he halted my departure with a firm hand on my shoulder. "I apologise for my brashness." He scratched the back of his head. "Not under ideal circumstances, but I am glad to have finally met you. I am Spud and this is my tight-lipped brother Nick." He made it as if to shake my hand. "Yan had spoken so grac-"

"Akin to the satellite or the vaccine?" I interjected.

And as readily as he offered his hand, he retracted it. His eyes spoke fluent wrath, while Nick stood aside basking in aloofness. A few seconds later, when no word had been spoken, I shrugged my way out of the conversation and made my way towards the exit. Thirty minutes of recreation time remained. Despite that, I had come to find solace amongst my cell's walls. Their presence was a hug demanding no welcome or farewell. I would learn to slot myself between their inviting arms each night.

Time elapsed and it was the hour to write. Today's ice block had melted due to the incompetence of a saucier. In their attempt to prepare this evening's jute stew yesternight, one of the leaf bags had initiated its great escape only to be lodged between the industrial freezer's door and the wall. What a waste of foreseeably mediocre mulukhiya. Because of the culinary mishap, my stomach was discontented; my fingers, on both hands, were grateful to be spared the pain of being whacked into an uncompromising obstacle.

My fingers pressed against a familiar pen, twitching ever so slightly at the anticipation of cascading ink with what my heart but also my head could realise. I felt discouraged by my internal dilution of concentrated feelings and thoughts. To my productivity's downfall, I tried to understand whether the dilution was an inevitable consequence of my limited aptitude, either literary or inwardly, or a cowardly filtration system I had applied on myself to avoid the condemnation of the outside upon sharing my crude perceptions. Regardless, if "the pen is mightier than the sword" as many remark, then I ought to be careful where I swing. Write... Write. What rhymes with write? Kite. Blight?

...The blight of many kite flyers is their perpetual fight against the wind: too light and the kite goes quiet, too heavy and the kite is out of sight. To wait till the wind is right only to realise the certitude of night

Ultimately, my thoughts trampled over each other leaving a bleeding blot of ink like a pile of bodies, each trying to climb over only to add to its height. My pen was transfixed on that period. In a clear attempt to exude frustration, I progressively perforated the paper until the pen was uncertain whether it was to note on this sheet or the next.

Footsteps interrupted my silent fit of vexation, which was occurring within the boundaries of my crossed arms. I raised my head from the confines I had established and peered over my left shoulder to see a paternal face. Yan's fine brown hair was casually combed over on most days, yet today it appeared formally constructed, highlighting a contrast with his sprouting stubble. Greyness crept from within him as if the roots had grown wearisome from pledging colour to his life. While his face had begun to show signs of the time too, nothing could distract from his prominent brow ridge and droopy eyebrows which seemingly attempted, with little success, to conceal his cerulean eyes. Was his vision curtained or did his brain omit the obscurity as it had done previously with the nose?

"I have provided you with room, tools, and most importantly I have provided you with seclusion. So, confess your mind, what ails you, my friend?"

I took a deep breath worthy of the lengthy monologue I was ready to declare. "Why are you retiring the programme if not for its failure? And if so, then without question the failure is a reflection of me, the inspirator." Yan's lips parted with an eagerness to interject, but I forged ahead. "I promise you the actualisation was the fault of my hand and my tongue but not my head. If storytellers of past and future could substantiate their literary brilliance then why can I not provide one piece of evidence to be read to the jurors, that my heart but not my head could visualise, defending the fraudulence claims presented forward by a prosecution team led by my head."

Yan rotated around my left side until he was no longer in my peripheral, but central vision. While my head was still subservient to shame, my domineering eyes were fixed on his. There was an unspoken quarrel for the next spoken word. My eyes gave way after a few moments and Yan pounced on the opportunity to address my self-accusations.

"A programme inspired by you is evidence of brilliance." Yan exhaled, lowered his gaze as I did, and continued. "I believe I pushed too firmly at times and in doing so cracked the egg instead of providing it warmth." His wrinkles yielded to the sadness brewing beneath his face. It was immense and would have derived empathy had it not been for the resentment I harboured. He had inadvertently forced my arms to rotate a wall-facing mirror and reflect upon the undefined ugliness, which provoked me to focus further, hoping I would find a vision beyond the murk. Only I had come to discover the ugliness was the undefined, and enraged by my findings, I would throw the mirror onto the wall it had previously faced.

Distraught and desperate for guidance, I would scram to the floor, grab one of the many mirror shards, and raise it in demonstration. However, by then, upon reflection, I would appear to be no more than an apoplectic man with a weapon. That image switched to black in an instant.

When was she? A moment in time bombarded by opposite yet formidable forces. My admiration bordered on inspiration and therefore conjured detestation. She was a gazelle thrown in the wilderness amongst predators and she would outpace hunters, manoeuvre amongst vehicles, and leap over fallen trees; yet when there were no threats to her but herself, she forfeited. My hands would tense, stifling a manifestation of her, but I could not. I would not, for if I did, I am a threat.

"Beatrice is dead." A statement which would have borne little to no impact if not for what followed, "C-1." Before I could muster a response, Yan placed a consoling hand on my shoulder and departed – I could feel it trembling. It felt rushed akin to walking up centre stage in a cap and gown to be handed your graduation diploma from Being University. Perhaps my reaction to his announcement was agonisingly gradual. While mentally I was firing on all cylinders trying to process information that inflicted mostly confusion, physically I remained apathetic.

I was a runner-up in a race with no first place. Before I had the chance to cross the finish line, she denounced the contest. But I had begun sprinting and my momentum was only restrained by my legs and heart. After the denouncement of the race, time had urged me to slow down but how could I? Thereafter, I attempted to keep up with myself the way trainers would when their camels were galloping.

Over the next month, time became hitched to me. I would go through the motions like pages in a chapter. At times, I would pay attention to the finer details allowing myself to be momentarily involved in a scene that did not involve me. But most times, I would skim through the pages, seeing the cloth of the story yet disregarding its fabric. The new interwoven with the old and the seams disappeared. Conversation was a needle guiding a string. A man to a man to a woman to a man to a woman to a woman to a man to a Nick to a – no one because Nick was a mute. The needle would become directionless by orders of the fingers. Nick would provide me with a brief respite.

Mediocrity loomed, for what was once a boundless expedition had transitioned into a porting cruise. Yet all passengers performed their parts unhindered. There were murmurs from some, who had not seen the vastness of the ocean, but alas their complaints were drowned out by the white noise of unremarkable exchanges.

My headspace was treacherous following one of the 'remedial' tasks. It was the thirteenth iteration of a self-portrait. A mirror sat across from me during my first sketch, and then my first sketch during my second, and then my second sketch during my third, and then... There I was, sitting across myself. The drawing looked exactly like me, yet not at all. It was devoid of details and colour, emphasised by shadows, my orbitals appeared endlessly deep, and my eyes could not help but sink. Across the iterations, my artistic quality regressed but my self-perception progressed. And I would perceive a dialogue as such. "Hello, I, a fellow guy, why cannot I classify you? Are you my conception or expiration? The artist's charcoal would suggest the latter; however, I see life in you. I wish you could reply." I sighed. "But why would it matter? My ignorance is yours and your enlightenment is mine." My ears betrayed me, and another unremarkable exchange suspended my conversation. "Now, a celebration of one would bring my rumination's demise."

"Felicitations Kusai!" I was uncertain whether the statement was made in a hushed tone, or the distance travelled made it sound as such. My eyes rolled away from the ceiling and onto the source.

Luna beamed and rubbed Kusai's greasy hair regretfully until an approaching Yan put a halt to the best wishes. A tut was followed by "0.3% of your lifetime is your birthdays. Why do we not focus on the 99.7%?" Yan asked rhetorically.

Other than Kusai's unwavering respect for Yan, he could not contend because Luna offered an apology forthwith. "Kusai is a child and in a moment of ill-judgement, I decided to congratulate him to alleviate his superficial despondency," she replied robotically while she wiped the grease off her hand and onto her jumpsuit.

This would become a recurring pattern with Ms. Dakin. She would cross WRITE-dictated boundaries, but instead of dragging the line with her when caught, Luna would douse herself in innocence at the expense of others. She hung off a cliff with the strength of a helping hand and when her grip began to fail her, she pulled herself up by pulling another down. Yan set the lines and loosened her grips.

Stop! No, the clock rolls down the slope. Time had caught up to me only to continue ahead. Six volumes away from the deafening music of a crowd that could be heard from underneath the dirt. Or so I hoped, of a rope I could hold onto my home, this world, or a house too dear to move away from. I worry, because cowardice prevents me from admitting my fears, that the six volumes away could be six volumes away; that with every word I pen, I cut a fibre of hemp. And I end up further away from home than I ever was before. Alas, I fled the dread in my head through vicarious living.

Yan and Luna had gone from generalities to pleasantries, Spud and Nick had gone from abstraction to action, Kusai had gone from traveller to passenger, Fata had gone from wicked to insipid, Annabelle had gone from vivacious to anxious, the person missing their pinkie on one hand but compensated with an extra thumb on the other had gone from tragedy to irony, and Earl had gone for tea – HAH! And I had just gone, with no lazy rhymes to escape the time.

"Twenty-four hours or so and the bricks I laid are no more."

"O Solomon, the bricks are there. You must lay them elsewhere."

"They are too heavy to carry around from one hill to another."

"Only if you insist on carrying the bricks on your own. You isolate yourself from companionship worrying of consequential tremors to your foundation. But what are bricks if not for the cement that keeps them together? And what are ladders if not steadied by loyal hands?"

A crumbling home and a bricklayer's night terrors? I thought to myself sardonically, for a moment, however my thoughts soon turned scornful. *Why had I cast you in this role that wields enormous influence over me? It was you, a dreadful man! Your treacherous ideas instilled in me a belief in bricks. If it were otherwise, I would have thought you to be the wolf. No, you are worse. You are the pig that tricked me into building his house with the promise of shelter. I have found more warmth in a wolf's belly than under a pig's arm.*

Yan dusted my sleeve with the back of his hand and a proud smile on his face, akin to a father dropping off their child on their first day of college. After adjusting my jumpsuit collar, he grabbed my face with both hands assuredly as though he feared my head would fly off into the stratosphere whilst searching for a tabula rasa. "Do not mistake my advice for an excuse to step off the ladder. I merely do not want to watch you fall off it. You must persevere and share your perseverance so others would use your perseverance as a reason for theirs, just as a climber would share the story of their hike and their perspective of the peak." My face dropped off a little, but his hands assured my head of their presence. He added, "C-1 could not see what one could see at the very top of the climb."

"And what might that be?" I asked glumly.

"The sunrise before others."

*   *   *

The furry little creature jumping above one steel bar and squeezing under another was camouflaged by the colour of the train track and the shadows it cast upon the floor. I watched it intently. Part of me feared for its safety, for the train would arrive at any moment. The other more governing part was driven by amusement towards apathy. Whatever fate lay for the mouse was of no concern to me, so long as I could witness it.

At the screeching sound of the train's arrival, the mouse scurried deeper under the tracks, never to be seen again. I was disappointed, but only briefly, because I was quickly distracted by my need to depart. I stood up from one seat outside to sit on another one inside. A long breath escaped me as an indication of my deflation. I felt I had had a long week; however, all weeks since my time at WRITE had felt long. Therefore, it was awkward to discern which of the following reasons was honest: my threshold for arduous weeks had dropped, life handed me more responsibilities without consulting my capacity, or my perception of strenuous work had deceived me.

My propensity to read increased while I took a hiatus from writing. Perhaps, one skill drained from the other like a muscle demanding most of the body's energy during a localised exercise. I made a great deal of acquaintances through books, whose effects on me were short-lived but impactful. I looked down at the open book in my palms; the page rustled as my thumb dragged it across others.

I was reminded of an inscribed character, described as a college

170

student in Syria trying her best to ignore the falling droplets that threatened to shatter her bubble. Noor had an exam coming up on Wednesday. *'The Syrian regime claims rising insurgency motivated by foreign actors.'* Studying required energy, consequently, she decided her famous late-night macaroni with garlicky Greek yoghurt was in order. *'With their blood and their souls, the Syrian people have spoken.'* "That's the night then," Noor told herself. The electricity had given out, and recognising her clumsiness, she decided against boiling water in the dark. *'The United Nations has condemned Bashar's use of chemical weapons.'* Instead, she picked up a candle from her late grandmother's nightstand and resolved to revise 'Chapter 6: Introduction to Cardiovascular Systems'. *'ISIS – a quick guide to the terrorist organisation's origin and its role in destabilising Syria.'* "May God bless you and keep you safe. Is it not better for you to study on the dining table? You will hurt your back like that," Noor's mother remarked standing by the doorway. Her mother, still wearing the prayer dress after concluding Isha (night) prayer, watched her cross-legged daughter sitting on her bed studying with the limited illumination of a candle. *'Syrian War 10th anniversary – What once were red hands are now crimson pants – Where do we go now?'* Noor looked up at her mother and smiled gently in disagreement, "I hope you wake up to goodness, Mama." "I hope you wake up to light, Noor," replied her mother.

Announcement after announcement of destinations I was not destined for. Although I was familiar with the sequence of stations and had no reason to anticipate my arrival, I involuntarily glanced at the track map. My eyes shifted from one station to the next until they landed on a...

Moth on the ride,
doth it want to escape?
Cloth shelters me from rain.
Soft the sounds of wheel on rail.

Views afar so lovely,
who am I to complain?
Cue a brick or two or many,
hues of brown dull colours of plenty.

A cool breeze drifted through the open mechanical doors reminding me of yet another stop which was not mine. I watched a few people enter and a few leave as if different areas were trying to balance the numbers towards absolute neutrality. Or maybe it is a cruel metaphor for the abundance of puzzle pieces adaptable enough to replace missing ones. Then there was the moth. It had finally escaped or arrived; whichever was vital to its existence.

Levity, albeit vexatious, arrived in the form of a nudge. A hip bumping into my shoulder was not surprising given the crowded state of the train. My eyes refused to budge and remained glued to a book I had not been attentive to. Are not the ailments of Noor's environment greater than mine? Why should one minor tap divest my peace when the whole world collapsing does nothing to hers? My suspicions were confirmed when another, more deliberate, nudge compelled me to investigate.

Before my vision rose to the occasion, a voice vaguely familiar - it was attempting to mimic another vaguely familiar voice - remarked.

"You C-1, you see them all."

In my heart of hearts, I wished to see a face belonging to a dark-haired woman whom I still admired. She either felt too lonely at the height of her climb or the peak was close to the sun. Despite my yearning for Beatrice, I knew the truth was disillusioning. The eyes behind my eyes only hardened the ugliness beyond beauty. It banished the latter to an unmaintained grave, forgotten by many, to lay with its owner. Hidden by rising blades of grass, 'The Best of Authors' was etched beneath her name. A legacy that lasted a week before being displaced by a sci-fi trilogy about a divided society with a brewing rebellion led by a character with a love interest or two. My visits to Beatrice were regular the first couple of months after WRITE, but alas time and distance erode frequency.

"Have I mistaken a stranger for a friend? Your silence is either a blissful moment of reminiscence and an inability to put words to feelings or a consequence of the confusion following my harassment." She smiled down at me mischievously assuring me of her indifference to my response.

I smiled in return but with less confidence than hers. Yan's hands were absent and consequently, my head flew off my shoulders. First evading trees, then floating amidst the clouds, and finally soaring beyond the Kármán line. Whether it was the breathtaking views of where my head was and where it would be or the lack of oxygen, I remained breathless. It was months before my journey turned from nomadic to settled. My head fell onto the side of the moon unbeknownst to many. It was dark, not for lack of sunlight, but the relative scarcity of enlightenment surrounding its surface. My head rolled around the lunar soil in deafening silence. In space, I was a passenger on an expedition ship but now on the moon I was a captain with decisions to make regarding my direction, my destination, and the overall survival of this vessel under tumultuous conditions.

When the sun shone on my head, my hair melted, and my skin would burn and blister. When night fell, the extreme cold would turn me numb and my skin itchy. I surrendered myself to the pain, forcing my brain to receive it positively. Pain was just my physical form warning me of the dangers I was to face. However, given pain's inescapable nature, I had to welcome it as a flawed system attempting its best to keep me safe like a mother scolding her child and grabbing their wrist firmly after the child's enthusiastic chase after an ice cream truck.

Something hindered my constant. It was an obstacle I could not roll over. A slab of rock reminded me of the pain I endured. Could this be the slate I had been searching for since my terrestrial departure? In a moment of relinquished distraction and hopeful delusion, I saw a glow radiating from the slab. My teeth had decayed, and I lost all but one of my incisors clung desperately to its roots. But in this toolless world, that tooth appeared to me the perfect chisel. It was daytime when I had begun and nighttime when I was done. There it was, etched on the tabula rasa, my first sentence. "Salve, Luna."

Part 8: Raised

Solomon rubbed Nameless' scruff in the back of the mobile van. His other, unoccupied, hand reached into his left pocket to pull out a chocolate bar wrapper. He cautiously scrutinised the piece of orange polypropylene, front and back, to avoid engaging the pilots' attention. His prudence was unwarranted, however, for the vehicle was an ensemble of unpleasant noises. Notwithstanding the van's own orchestra, the distorted Russian ballad playing through the blown speaker was authoritatively elected lead singer.

"What foreign wisdom is the woman teaching?" Solomon faintly heard Aleabith's bass voice query. His eyes peered upwards anticipating a response from the driver.

"Music, but if only I could translate her Tatar tongue." Spud began mumbling along with the musician lending himself some of her wisdom through attempted repetition.

"Tatar? What brings a Muscovite to the East?" the giant asked inquisitively.

Spud shot Aleabith a puzzled look as if to say, *you seem to know too much for someone who asks so much.* He replied, "My mama was from Kazan and Dyeda Bulat used to play her this music when she was an infant to calm her cries."

Their voices gradually migrated from the fore to the background, blending seamlessly with the inharmonious. That was a consequence of Solomon's rejuvenated focus on the wrapper. 'If your soul aches, have a coconutty break.' Painfully reminded of the toothache he suffered earlier, Solomon fled from the words pasted on the front and instead inspected the nutritional information and ingredients list on the back, aiming to name the culprits responsible for his ailment. '90 Mayfield Rd', an ingredient obscure to him by taste but not locality. The Food Standards Agency would never stand for such a blatant lack of transparency from Yunohu Ltd., the manufacturers, towards its consumers. What next – they will claim that the calories per 100g is 'Rawda St.'? Curses upon curses on the wicked men who line their pockets with cash while they fill stomachs with trash.

Solomon only had to scour a few remembrances to pin the phrase to a memory. It was a cottage near the banks of the Balikh River, which was long enough to split a city in two and wide enough to support a few towheads. The cottage, however, lay closer to the river source, Ain al-Arous Spring, where the flowing water was narrow enough to be called a stream. Solomon recalled that in his late teenage years he would walk along the river till the soles of his feet began to ache. He was searching for the river's source or sink, not because it would extinguish a burning question inside him, but because everything demands an answer when a man is lost.

Why does the river I see appear alien to me? Solomon thought to himself. The Balikh River was nothing like the river in his proximity – not in its flow, shade, width, or depth. The water here was stagnant to the ears, grey to the eyes, and odourless to the nose. It inspired nothing more in Solomon than remembrance of the vibrant Balikh River.

Spare yourself and ask nothing for a day, so – *A location by the law of randomness or purpose? And for me or us or none?* Solomon asked himself, heedlessly interrupting me and concurrently ignoring my advice. For now, he concealed the discovery from the folks up north to content rising suspicions that the message was destined for him only. It was a near equal blend of narcissism and belief, making it difficult to deduce which element dominated the concoction.

*   *   *

"Hey! Sorry, before you leave, I found this log from the Eye of Odin program. It was never logged into the archive. What should I do with it?"

"Eye of Odin? Isn't that a discontinued program?" Frederick,

177

the Director, continued packing his bag, shoving all the papers that remained on his desk.

Nahid replied enthusiastically. "Yes, it briefly ran four decades ago. It got shut down by the ESA after public backlash prompted the DBEIS to investigate."

"And who's written this entry log?"

"The programme's only volunteer, Juri Al-Aaliyah."

The director paused his packing and sat on the edge of his desk. "What does it say?"

[Log 378 – March 17, 2131]

Entry 1 - Spaghettified! How could a verb so delicious be so horrific? I pray, if it even matters, that I grow a few inches before I perish. Then perhaps, when the explorers of future generations discover a string for a body, they will update entries about my height on their virtual encyclopaedias. My biography could be written like so: Juri Al-Aaliyah (born April 17, 2082 – disappeared March 15, 2125) was a Syrian-born astronaut and engineer. She was the first volunteer as part of the controversial 'Eye of Odin' space program aiming to study 'The Unicorn'. Al-Aaliyah also set the record for the furthest distance ever travelled by a human and became the 11th astronaut to travel outside the solar system.

Entry 2 - It was humbling to hear crowds cheer as announcers called me 'The Heir to Earheart'. At a time when my boots were clanging against the metallic bridge that connected the umbilical tower to the space rocket, I felt undeserving of the title. Amelia, rest her soul, had earned her legacy through decades of shattered ceilings and dedicated servitude. I, on the other hand, had a decade of desk work and a few years of planned and concentrated training. Her disappearance was an unfortunate mishap in the pursuit of greatness. My eventual disappearance will be a deliberate effort to cower from reality. I want to take a shortcut to greatness, and if not afforded to me, then exit the path altogether.

Entry 3 *- Oh, I hope my father does not blame his hands. They did not push me. Oh, I hope my mother's face is dry. Her tenderness did not harden me. And oh, I hope my younger siblings understand. I did not mean for them to look up to me beyond what eyes could see. If only pride from my promoted achievements could glue together the shattered pieces I left behind. If only it were like kintsugi, but I fear my achievements are different to gold.*

Entry 4 *- Thankfully, the heart's woes last only as long as it beats. Or so I hope. The only protection I have from the extreme weather of space is a suit designed by engineers who have experienced none of it. If only they had designed for my pod to contain more oxygen than it did. When I was warned about the depleted oxygen, I had to relinquish my seat and rely on the little conserved oxygen that remained in my suit. My actions, however, only serve to delay the inevitable. Am I to die like a mortal suffocating, no better under dirt or in space? Or am I to pass by the flames of an immortal? Better yet, I will die, not because of my physical limitations, but by the action of my hand.*

Entry 5 *- Why am I delaying it? Truthfully, I am scared. From a distance, it appears as a dot, like a period after a sentence. Now, I cannot tell where the sentence begins, only where it ends. No matter how hard I try, I cannot start the sentence after. Everything appears unmoving: I, the celestials, and everything in between. Yet the big It, so big that my vocabulary betrays me, appears to be expanding.*

Entry 6 *- I am laughing, why? Why have I dismissed the action of my hand? I had left the injection behind on the pod. The needle I was provided by my supervisors, in order to have some control over my death, is not on my person. Who knows if I would have gone through with it either way? I ran away every chance I could, not because it was right, but because commitment to a path would introduce expectations. If I remained on my desk, then a career was expected. If I remained at home, then marriage was expected. And if I had the injection on me then death would be expected.*

Entry 7 *- Numb is feeling nothing, yet nothing feels exuberant. The silence, broken by my long breaths, complements the ambience. I wish I had the courage to scream till my lungs collapsed to escape this loneliness. No, every breath counts. No, I need a distraction. I need a story through which I can live vicariously.*

Entry 8 *- I could think of nothing other than of a giant sucking a healthy portion of the universe through a straw as if we are pulp in its juice - little bits of concentrated texture and flavour that are more or less disregarded by the drinker. If my fate is landing in a giant's belly, so be it, for its stomach is another universe altogether. Would I then be destined for excretion through another black hole? What an unromantic view of the universe: a cycle of consumption and excretion.*

Entry 9 *- I write this for no one or for many. Either way, it does not matter; the outcome remains the same, and my legacy outlives me. Time repeatedly warns us that titles are written in ink while the essays are written in lead. So, bear witness, people of the future, how my life is reduced to dichotomous nouns: heroism or villainy, greatness or failure, bravery or cowardice. If you do come across the headline 'Juri Al-Aaliyah: The Heir to Earheart', I plead with you to ignore it and* *digest the entirety of my essay. I promise you I am better than how their words betray me, and I promise you I am worse than how their words portray me.*

__Entry 10__ - When will my life flash before my eyes? My vision is destitute of souvenirs, but replete with alternative prospects. Some are zealous, some are saturated with maladies, but most are unremarkable and comfortable. I latch onto the miserable ones, for what fool will I be to renounce a vibrant future for this moment. With luck, I will be noticed by the beyond like a grain of sand between two fingertips. There is liberty with imminent death; my breaths have become short and wasteful. Oh God, it is close. I can feel it. I wish to pause this moment so that I can find closure within myself. Why did I do this? If suffocation is a deprived sleep, then this is a nightmare from which one wakes only to realise their nightmare is a dream and that sleep is mercy. Oh God, I wish to wake up. I can feel the suction reaching my toes as I lay on this comically small bed. Oh God, I wish to escape death if only to meet it again shortly. Whatever light remaining departs as the giant places its finger against the peephole. Oh God,

__[End of Log]__

*   *   *

There was no light coming through the other side. His eye, which he had just regained function of, was pressed against the wrong end of a peephole. As a matter of fact, his entire face was pressed against the door with much of his body weight relying on the door for its integrity. This compromising position granted him the ability to hear a hoarse grumble, "Sell your soul elsewhere,". Despite the resident's complaint, several clicks and moving bolts later, the door swung open with more force than intended. With no support, Solomon's body collapsed, and he fell face-first towards the ground. Instinctively his arms realigned

181

into a protective position and shielded his face from the brunt of the fall.

Although disoriented, Solomon was finally awake. His face was glued to the floor, his chest felt off like there was a hair in his heart, and his right kidney was being prodded by the end of a coat rack, but he was awake. "Get out, you pesky bum!" a voice said as the prodding continued. In his momentary exhaustion, Solomon ignored all demands. But when the poking stopped and silence ensued, curiosity pushed aside the mental fatigue. Before he could fully rotate his head and get a full view of the cottage's interior, a blunt object struck him on his right ear. If tinnitus was a solo singer, then the ringing in his ear, for the next minute or so, was a vocal group. "iiiiiiiwhyiiareiiiiiyouiihereiiiiSol?"

As the fuzz relented, he could make out webs of purple on a fleshy canvas. "Glenda...?" Solomon asked the owner of the varicose veins.

"I must have struck you real hard," Glenda laughed in an unusually phlegmy manner and then continued. "My sister did advise me against underestimating my own strength." When she found the owner of the jumpsuit unresponsive to her wit, she added "In my day, men could take a few hits. But maybe the inebriation dulled their senses."

Partly to escape the dreary history lesson, Solomon forced himself up, aided by a shoe rack halfway up. The other, less obvious, part of him was a parliament of emotions with different schools of thought. Why did one of the elected ministers represent relief in seeing depravity personified? This woman wearing a beige cardigan had nursed him towards forgetfulness. However, in his inner depths, he viewed her as a grandmother that, despite her scorn and conservative ways, cared for him. "If I were not haunted by reckless abandon, I would not assign superiority to a warm slap over a cold hug," I could hear Solomon's thoughts reverberating through the parliament building. I contended that the woman's fingers were bony and therefore lacked adequate circulation for warmth. There were murmurs amongst the ministers however they amounted to no concessions.

Solomon dusted the stained jumpsuit in a meaningless gesture of sanitation. He had masterfully tied his uniform around his waist, leaving his white undershirt exposed. Although his undergarments were regularly replaced, more out of habit than hygiene, ever since his flit from WRITE, the jumpsuit had become a staple piece. His clothing underlined a clash of desires: reformation and preservation.

Glenda, unthreatened by his appearance, retreated with her back to him. Despite her hunch exaggerating with age, her height remained enviable. Due to her stature, her hands navigated her surroundings both horizontally and vertically, warning the crone about potential obstacles. With an apparent loss of vigour, she waddled her way towards the sitting room, her feet barely leaving the floor.

Solomon followed his host leisurely, taking in his surroundings. He craved to understand her so he could sympathise with her heavy-handedness. Ignoring the fine craftsmanship of a wooden chest drawer, Solomon's eyes were drawn to the framed photograph on top of it. The picture, albeit dated in quality, displayed a concentrated essence of Glenda without the discolouration of age. Her hair, now wisps of white failing to mask her scalp, was once thick coal-black curls travelling in all directions like the serpents on Medusa's head. Stood next to her was a comically short-statured man with brown skin, thick eyeglasses, a plumpness indicative of a healthy appetite, and a tuft of hair combed over to combat claims against his baldness. Despite lacking in many desirable attributes, Solomon envied the man's bushy moustache that draped over his top lip. His lineage was crowded with moustached men, all the way back to his fez-wearing ancestors. However, he was not blessed with sufficient insulation to shield his philtrum from harsh winter winds. Or perhaps his complaint was premature, for he had not yet entered his third decade.

"In days of black and white, coloured ones like that cost a

week's worth of food." Slightly agitated by his excessive investigation of the picture, Glenda thought to herself, *I worry if you stare a moment longer your vision might pierce through it.*

Continuing his scrutiny of the photograph, that was captured in the tropics, Solomon asked derisively, "And is this one of those inebriated men?"

"Mr. Mulaj?" Glenda shot back, losing her composure for a moment. "Drinking is for men unaccountable for their happiness or the sorrows they cause."

"And eating? Who accounts for that?" he continued with his sardonic tone.

Her imminent reply was preceded by one deep cough. "Eating leads to a full belly but drinking only yields an empty soul. Many start with one in their early years, only to find themselves at the bottom of the barrel hiding from love and responsibility. For one leads you to the edge of the cliff and the other restrains you from jumping."

"Cliffs and peaks and hills and troughs – your metaphors are unimaginative. My landscape is flat. I start there," Solomon pointed outside the doorway towards an absolute left, "and I end there." His arm shifted to point towards an absolute right. "The cliff is merely a line when you observe from far enough."

His theatrical outburst prompted Glenda to guffaw. "Solomon's skin has grown thin. One more syllable out of these lips and the prodigy's condition becomes critical." Before he could respond, the host continued, "Now come in and settle down before you say something that lands you at the sharp end of my coat rack."

Between the sips of cardamom-infused tea, Solomon glanced down at his cup and was reminded of a recurring episode he experienced. *Why did I find myself abandoned with a barrel of ink? I gave no notice to its scent and sight, but I could not escape the muffled screams I heard coming from its depths. With my indexes, I dug to clear out the outskirts of my ear canal in hope I could make out the words being screamed, but to no avail. Yet, I was overwhelmed with this urge to save whoever was drowning, if only to satisfy my ego. I got on my knees and dragged my hands through the ink, trying with all my might to sieve out the victims. With every few sways of my hands, I pulled them up and rubbed my fingertips together. Maybe I could sense particulates as evidence of their presence, like searching for diamonds in a sea of quartz. This routine persisted until I was deterred by the fumes. But the screaming and my inability to help overwhelmed me. I needed to help them. I needed to, but how? If they could scream for me then, perhaps, I could scream for someone else. They needed me and I needed a phone. How had I not noticed? The room was empty and dark at its extremities with only a stack of loose papers and a pen near it. What choice did I have but to write a letter pleading for help? I crawled to the stack as if I were a parched wanderer who had just discovered an oasis in the desert. Panicking, I picked up the pen and wrote 'To whom it may co-' Splat! An ink droplet escapes my right hand onto the paper, covering the first words of the imploration. How was I foolish enough to forget my ink-drenched hands? I dragged them across the carpet, ignoring what friction burns I received, to remove as much of the ink as I could. Afterwards, I scrapped the first draft and started with a new letter, 'If you come acro-' Blot! I wiped my hands against the carpet once more and started my letter afresh, 'Please, there are peo-' Drop! Where was this other drop coming from? Again, I rubbed, and I wrote, 'HEL-' Nope! Before I could finish my 'P', another droplet denied me. This time it was my nose bleeding with ink. I looked down at my hands, and ink. And I rubbed my hands, and ink. And I rubbed my nose and ink. It was endless...* "And that is how the episode ends."

"What episode?" Mrs. Mulaj asked inquisitively.

Solomon realised that his last thought had escaped its intended confines. And to avoid sharing his inner depths to a woman who indubitably would use them as a tool to torture him, he lied. "On TV, they were re-running the finale episode of my favourite show: Lies in Libya." Why he felt compelled to elaborate on this lie, I could not tell. "The main character acquired closure, through killing his culpable parents, following the revelation that his sister had died while being trafficked in a truck across North Africa."

Glenda, noting Solomon twist a clump of his beard into a string and remembering it as a tell-tale sign for his dishonesty, grinned and moved the conversation along. "How did you find me?" Pleasantries were foregone.

"Truthfully, I was uncertain I was looking for you to begin with." He pulled out the wrapper from deep within his pocket and passed it across the coffee table.

Without much scrutiny through her now milky eyes, she shared, "Yan views the ill as creative, the tormented as passionate, and a candy wrapper as a trail to truth." Glenda sighed, while maintaining an expression of neutrality. Had age hardened her heart, caging in her true feelings? Or had it atrophied her facial muscles and provided her feelings with a cloak of wrinkles to conceal her sensitivities? It may well be that elders feel the fire that youth do and are assisted or betrayed in hiding their griefs or passions by their symptomatic physicality.

"If the tormenter sees no passion in the cause, then why does she contribute to it?" Solomon ignored the totality of her argument in pursuit of ointments to soothe his past wounds.

"You are like a friend's son to me. The existence of our relationship ceases with his disappearance. What am I, a paediatrician, to do when a friend presents their ill child?"

With no apparent intent to release the escalating pressure in the pot, Solomon retorted, "You are a nurse, and as such, I await your diagnosis."

"I am a doctor," she replied sternly and continued, "Blighted by your thoughts and a lack of accountability for your actions, to escape prosecution from your own conscience, you have inebriated yourself with fantasy."

"If sobriety is my possession, then you have robbed me of it. How could I be accountable for what I remember nothing of?" A fuse was alight. "Have you no qualms with the pills? You have given me enough to neutralise a whale. And now that you want to address the elephant in the room, you wonder why it lies dead?"

Her unyielding eyes revealed no depth to the piercing blow, but their subtle shifts indicated discomfort. "You were supposed to ingest only one benzco a week."

"Benzco?"

Mrs. Mulaj's eyes stopped shifting and homed in on Solomon. "It started off with one benzodiazepine pill a week, but you would just become drowsy. So, Dr. Eadful, against my advice, laced your supplement with ample amounts of caffeine." Her tone was not sympathetic. She sounded as frank as a doctor suggesting a Do Not Resuscitate order to a patient's family. "Despite paying hefty deposits, you still would not let us into your home. Soon one turned to two and we had no choice but to barge in, for the home is where the heart is." She took her coat off to unveil a poet.

Unlike with Yan, Mr. Osroes did not harbour the same resentment towards Glenda. *Her objectiveness inclines me to absolve her of guilt. Still, she shook hands with the red-handed Yan, leaving her an offender by association. What if she were wearing gloves? She is a nurse, better yet a doctor. Do not most doctors find their hands red after treating a patient only to dispose of their gloves? Perhaps my analysis only extends to surgeons who get their hands bloody in order to save a patient from illness or death.* The thoughts were intrusive and caused a prolonged silence, which both parties welcomed.

But silence is defined by the noise that precedes or succeeds it,

Solomon finally replied, "What was all this vandalism for?"

"For accountability. For an adult who bore responsibility for others. For two children who were promised they would grow old to witness the blessings and afflictions of freedom. For three people who would die for a vandalised home because theirs was seized never to be returned."

*   *   *

"This is not the way to care for a camel, O Sa'ad", my Jedo (grandfather) would repeat this Arabic proverb to me while I sat on his lap.

Here I am, years later, kneeling beneath a palm tree in a situation written by the authors of foreshadowing. "What did he mean, Ibil?"

He looked down at me with his golden-brown orbs which were protected by long hairs. Despite looking like majestic suns, the aloofness of his eyes, which I mistook for confusion, prompted me to add, "my grandfather."

Ibil smacked his lips, revealing the bottom set of his large yellow teeth. Was he trying to reassure me about the meaninglessness of Jedo's advice or grinding his teeth to break down some of the leftover cactus he had consumed along our journey? "Akh," I sighed, conveying a frustration behind an unanswered question, and admitting defeat in its pursuit.

The kufiya I had wrapped around my head did little to protect me from the merciless conditions of the desert. Why I decided to venture into the Rub' al Khali is beyond me, but now that I am lost in the Empty Quarter, I implore God for groundwater to rise as a river from beneath me and carry me to the Red Sea.

Despite my persistence, the scarce greenery prevented me from being fully immersed in the illusive haven. Water, shelter, and food in that order were permanent occupants of my mind. And then there was Ibil, an occupant of my heart, who I volunteered to take care of in my youth when he was deemed unfit to be a racing camel. But now, older than me in human years, Ibil's mannerisms were synonymous with a child refusing to eat their vegetables. "My friend, how have you survived the world with a weak knee and a fear of water?" I rubbed the side of his belly assuring him of the sympathy behind my words.

His leash would not budge. I pulled, it was taut, and Ibil refused to surrender. "Fourteen suns have passed, and the sun does not lie." I stood up, wrapped my arms around his neck, and urged him by way of force. "Would you drink for me?" But my grunts were only met with a nasal exhale. "Two deaths are yet to visit me: the death of my heart and the death of my mind. I fear that in your refusal, I might find both at once."

Unlike Ibil, the water had obeyed me and now flew in all directions but into his stubborn mouth. In pulling too hard, I found myself hugged by the waters of the oasis. It was a weighted blanket wrapped around my weightless self, comforting me from the treachery that I had and would come across. If only the blanket had not been wrapped around my head too, then I would enjoy the serenity without the objection of my lungs. I looked up, and there he was, Ibil, staring down at me through the transparent barrier. Momentarily, we lived in two different media: him in the land of life and suffering, and I in the sea of death and bliss.

Composure found me and my flailing legs settled on solid floor. The depth of water embarrassed me, moments ago my limbs panicked in an attempt to grab hold of any support the elements offered. With my lungs pleading for the anticipated visit of air, my legs disobeyed my true desires and propelled me upwards. I wished to relieve myself of these worldly duties, but what would Jedo think of me?

*   *   *

189

Solomon raised his head from the stream, colloquially known by locals as Sha'ari, and gasped for air. After coughing up the remainder of the water that had settled in his lungs, he found himself at the bank of the Balikh waters across from Glenda's cottage. *This is not the Balikh. This is the Alienus*, Solomon assured himself. From being on his knees moments ago to sitting cross-legged, he ran his hand across his face wiping away most of the excess water. His fingers traced the soil back into the stream and continued with annular movements. "How have I gone from sips of cardamom tea to gulps of spring water? From there... to here." Solomon looked back at Glenda's abode, which had its front door peculiarly open, and pondered the circumstances of his exit. However, despite its status, the entryway of the cottage felt unwelcoming. "The answers I seek live in a chest that reeks." Perhaps it was Solomon's chest, but it felt partially comforting to attribute the discomfort towards something else.

A day's travel later, Aleabith's farm travelled from the horizon into full view. This was only after the streams merged into a river and Solomon walked half a day from the river inland. Silent footsteps evolved into loud crunches as his feet made their way from asphalt onto gravel and dirt.

Beyond the unguarded metal gates, his eyes fixated on a grey van parked in the driveway, but he was soon distracted by the sight of a coyote. "Nameless!" exclaimed Solomon, forgetting the animal's tendency to bite. Luckily for him, a leash and a wooden pole spared him from the coyote's teeth.

Unfortunately, there was another set of sharp teeth that Solomon needed to be wary of: Spud's teeth. The wooden door of the dilapidated farmhouse swung open to reveal a threatening man with an unthreatening stature. He bounced around like a potato in a boiling pot of water before rushing towards the visitor.

"How dare you approach me like Columbus approached King Ferdinand with news of the Indies?"

Solomon would have guffawed had he not been exhausted after his expedition. He could only reply with a sneer, passing Spud on the way to the door.

Spud was quick in grabbing him by the shoulder, spinning him around aggressively, and yelling "But like Columbus, your voyage is misguided, and your information flawed." He calmed down a little before adding, "Where have you been for the past four days?"

It could have been delirium from the lack of food and water that motivated him to reply with "The nurse before the hearse, Glenda." nonchalantly. Silenced by shock, Spud could not prevent Solomon from continuing his way.

"Did you lose your path navigating the sea of wheat?" Aleabith approached the matter with a jolly tone. His eyes departed the newspaper, glanced over his absurdly small spectacles at Solomon, then made their way back towards the general politics section of the paper.

Again, Solomon replied with a meagre smile matching his overall demeanour. His movement was driven by a subconscious focus to replenish his thirst and hunger, and what better way to serve his needs simultaneously than a glass of fresh milk? But much to his disappointment, Mr. Aldakhm proved to be an unreliable supplier of milk once more. With lumps visible in the milk, Solomon slammed the glass on the dining table and sent some of the expired drink in all directions.

"What is the meaning of this?" Aleabith questioned, his tone no longer jolly.

"Of cows there are plenty, but of fresh milk there is none."

An argument ensued about the logistics of storing raw unpasteurised milk for prolonged periods. Although the two could not reach common ground with Aleabith asking all the questions and Solomon answering none, the round was concluded upon another's entrance.

Behind him, the orange hues of sunset through the open door portrayed Spud in glorious light.

However, the glory was short-lived. A tint of blue flushed out what little colours Spud had on his face. Like a volcano erupting beneath the snow, his disheartened eyes hid a growing rage. Solomon, unaware of the imminent eruption, attempted to bulldoze over Spud's grand entrance, but Aleabith, who had been burnt once, approached him cautiously.

"Why don't you have a seat with us and convince this wandering son that the Ayran yoghurt is made of purpose, not of negligence?"

Spud hobbled, perhaps because of a herniated disk in his spine, towards the dining table. He ripped a handful of the pita bread laying on the countertop, swiped a clump of yoghurt on the table, and forcefully stuffed the quick snack into his mouth.

"Is the bread I baked from the wheat I milled to your liking?"

The half-Tatar man hooked his foot on the leg of a stool hidden under the shadows of the table and dragged it closer to Aleabith. Ignoring the large man's enquiry, Spud sat next to him and wrapped his arm around his shoulder, but kept his layered eyes fixed on Solomon.

"This dog! This son of a dog visited a friend of ours. A friend that writes to write and not to right." Spud spoke with a mouthful that muffled his blows.

"Yan?!" Aleabith's eye grew wider than his spectacles.

"What is it to you both? Am I not free to pursue the truth at the start of the Balikh?"

Gradually, their individuality subsided, and they merged into a homogenous blob of ravenous rage. "You say you seek right but then travel left." A little piece of mechanically digested bread left Spud's mouth.

Aleabith, now pledging allegiance to Spud, added, "What truth might you find in a fibster's handbook?"

"Any news of Nick?" Spud more whispered than asked, giving Solomon an excuse to push it aside.

"Accountability, for perhaps you both have none."

"Any news of Nick?" and again, the question was trampled over.

Aleabith threw his arms in the air, generating a momentary gust. "HAH! And if you do not wash your jumpsuit, you unaccountable twit, will the pneumonia get to you before my fist?"

"Here comes the beast, out of his field of wheat." Osroes rushed his due diligence of thought before spouting the next statement, "Tahira was too pure for his threats, and yet she lays eternally in her bed."

Before the giant could land his fatal blow, Spud slammed the table and asked more deliberately this time around, "Any news of my beloved brother, Nick?" Beloved, a word Spud scarcely uttered with respect to his brother. How distance and time makes us long for what we once repelled.

"No news of your brother, just of depravity."

"More depraved than a man who took three others in hopes of writing seven more? Either your mathematics is unfounded or the shame in their eyes was more than you could bear." The triad of companions took turns playing either aggressor or mitigator, and now Aleabith, who moments earlier was aiming to strike Solomon's head clean off his shoulders, nudged Spud's knee.

With the bread consumed, he reached behind him for some more, but his fingertips only met the cold steel of a butterknife. Spud resigned himself to scooping up orange marmalade from an open jar across him, and added, "Two weeks late and Mr. Osroes would have met an executioner in hell. But instead, here he is, the ungrateful son, meeting with a nurse at the start of the river."

"Glenda?! He went to meet the nurse who brings you ever closer to death?"

"Aye fellow, he went to meet the woman whom our blood, sweat, and tears were sacrificed to distance him from."

Solomon could not bear the onslaught on his character any longer. "She was not the intent of my travel. But even if she was, then where I travel is my decision. If it is into the depths of hell, then I shall bear the brunt of the burns. However, I found her residence far too cool for hell and her words far too sincere for Iblis."

"Mrs. Mulaj is insincere, for she is well-acquainted with escapism." Whilst Spud presented evidence portraying the defendant's bad character, Aleabith stood up and ambled around the room. "She was a paediatrician who suffered two miscarriages: the first could not be avoided, but the second was a choice."

Another scoop of marmalade, "Her geneticist husband ran a screening and discovered that the child would develop Huntington's disease. In Glenda's case, responsibility is easier spoken of than upheld."

Decibels rose and Solomon bellowed in protest, "You are no writer! No writer would condense the intensity of such a decision into a few apathetic words." His eyes shifted here and there, the table and the door, before he continued calmly, "This room suddenly feels a little too warm. Perhaps I have ventured too far."

Like lightning before thunder, he felt a gust of wind caress the back of his neck before receiving a blow square to his jaw. *Déjà vu, what are you?* It was a familiar feeling, the cold wooden tiles against his warm flushed face, where cells were rushing to repair the damage. Solomon's vision left him behind for a few seconds in a world that was darker despite its sun and without its moon. The last of his senses to depart was his hearing, which delivered its final parcel: a clang of metal against wood.

I see more than your eyes, but I see nothing without them. I hear more than your ears, but I hear nothing without them. I am more than you are, but I am nothing without you. Wake up Solomon... If not for you, then for me.

And the first of his senses to arrive was his hearing. The whispers of plotters tapped against his ear drum.

"He has retreated into his cage. I am not sure we will be able to drag him out again."

A heavy sigh was followed by, "How long before he eats from the zookeeper's palm?"

Solomon's sight returned, and although it was aided by a singular yellow bulb suspended from the ceiling, it remained too blurry for him to put definite boundaries to colours.

"The programme can run without him, but what a shame – the stories are less without him." The smaller of the two shapes became larger and more distinct. It was Spud and he was approaching a dazed Solomon with a pitying demeanour but was abruptly interrupted by Aleabith's question.

"What do we do with him?"

A pause, a sigh, and a spin – what followed was the admission of a man who knew least of the leadership responsibilities thrust upon him. "Like the unpainted canvases of tormented artists, I am drawing a blank." What did leaders, of past and present, do? "The concoction!"

"The concoction?"

"Yeah, the pills the nurse and the doctor prescribed to him."

Aleabith awaited Spud's elaboration on the matter. But silence ensued, and his curiosity grew. Spud had diverted his attention to some of the kitchen cabinets, hoping to find the answer in one of them.

"What were they – the pills?"

"My memory betrays me, but it was the stuff of dreams and

nightmares."

"Are your words alluding to benzos?"

Although Solomon could hear the faint sound of a kiss followed by the exclamation, "You beautiful giant!" his ears twitched at the sound of a drug that bent his principles, forgave his inhibitions, and repressed his memories. The very twitch sent a jolt through his system like a defibrillator on a dying heart. The once rounded shapes around him were now sharp, assuming polygonal structures and sending his alertness into overdrive. He was prey scouting the predatory landscape of Aleabith's farmhouse.

It was instinctual – a butterknife, an exposed thigh, a piercing cry, a fleeing guy from the evil eyes into fleeting light, not a scarecrow in sight, and Solomon wondered "Left, or right?" He was panting, not because he had run an exorbitant distance, but because his heart knew that after the scream died down the hunt would begin.

Left! he exclaimed internally at the sight of the camouflaged van. The twilight sky, bar its aesthetic, offered little assistance in illumination and navigation. Solomon jolted towards the vehicle forgetting to ask himself crucial questions about the steps after the next. However, the next steps caught up to him and he was left empty-handed after looking near the ignition and rummaging through the glovebox.

The van's exhaust pipe was his last resort to find the keys. Leaving heaps of dirt behind him, Solomon sprinted towards the back of the van but was met with a collision of hard heads. Letter after letter floated downwards carrying the wretched beast's name 'Aleabith' – some hand-written and others printed. There was no time for concussions, just the repercussions of passing time. Solomon scurried around grabbing the dirt-covered letters and apologised to the victim for his recklessness, "Apologies but you were the obstacle of a fleeing pre-"

"The dim-witted nudist enthusiast makes a return," interrupted Thakiah, brushing the dirt from her blonde streaks.

"I have little time for your jib-jabs. Please refra-"

In the spirit of time preservation, Thakiah interrupted him once more. "The perpetrator cannot protest the reaction to his offence," she replied aggressively but her inquisitive nature calmed her, "Plus, what hurries you away from the beast of the east?"

"To summarise, my life is in disarray: my journey's companions are anchors to my ship, my family is a destination I cannot find, my memories are a map scribbled in parts, and the pirates might be sailors saving me drifting away from homely shores."

Solomon's shoulders felt a little lighter; Thakiah had not interrupted him. He looked up into her eyes, fearing someone might have slit her throat preventing her from vocalising harmful opinions. Instead, he was met with sympathetic tearful eyes. "For once, I hoped she would speak," he thought to himself.

She stood up, patted her farming gown clean, and extended her hand to Solomon. "Stand up captain, I will help you unload some of the weight off your ship." He rose, with energy unlocked, and she bent down to grab the knife he had dropped during their collision. His hopeful attitude was slashed by the sounds of two vengeful dogs shouting insults from the farmhouse's doorway.

"You vermin! You belong under my shoe. You son of a who-"

Thakiah's command overlayed the distant shouts, "Run Solomon! May your legs carry you till you bleed and some more." She nudged him forward, like an owner commanding its horse to gallop away. On the other hand, she used the bloody butterknife and drove it straight between the tyres and the rims. At the sound of air escaping, Solomon was off to the races.

But his legs carried him the opposite way, following the gentle whining of Nameless. Solomon would have been wary of the coyote's teeth, however there was a natural accord between the two animals to cooperate in their escape. Or was it the cries of Nameless setting off memories of Rugrub, who provided him much warmth on the coldest nights? Before Amar was born and just after Shams was, Rugrub was the honorary middle child, whose familial presence was often overlooked, but his role in mending domestic fractures could not be overstated.

Notwithstanding, the leash was off, and the prey was stumbling through the treacherous wilderness. They ran side by side through the path of least resistance on the dirt road away from perilous conditions. The last thing Solomon heard was Spud's yelling, almost sardonically, "Remember Solomon, a writer that writes is a writer that's right." Nothing after that – he was an astronaut floating in absolute darkness and complete silence. Every couple of paces or so, he would snap out of his astronomical trance and his senses would be overloaded by the sounds of Nameless's panting, his bare feet against the dirt, and the feeling of his own overburdened heart travelling up his throat.

Although his running degraded to walking, mentally his momentum was no different. Soon, the darkness was revived by hues of orange and Solomon would think, hours later, whether it was dusk or dawn. "Does it even matter?" he thought to himself. "Three hours or twenty-four, I have the luxury of time but no place to go." His eyes then shifted to Nameless, who despite the imminent hunger and the definite thirst, has not shown any signs of hostility thus far. "Would you eat me if I collapsed here and died?"

Solomon collapsed next to the wheatfield, which ran parallel to the dirt road. Even then, mentally, he was still running. It was not his mind, heart, or even legs that gave up but the soles of his feet, which would have been dirt black had it not been for the blood. He sat up and carefully began removing some of the smaller gravel and shards that have lodged their way into his feet. There was no pain for him to wince, for the nerves in his feet had given up on trying to warn their host.

After getting the last of the pieces out, he laid back against the wheat stalks and ran his hands through the grains. His eyelids were on the brink of meeting each other, but he could faintly feel something rubbing against the bottom of his feet. He looked down to find Nameless licking the blood off his soles. Before he could ponder the implications of such an omen, Solomon found himself drifting away to the land of unaccountability.

رحلة إلى الشرق

Part 9: The One of Truce

What if my confession leads to no love, but an eternal pause and my shattered heart?

My mother, my father, I apologise for being distant. I ought to involve you in my life more, the way you have invested much of yours in mine.

I wake up every day unsure of whether I will get out of bed, whether I will take a shower, whether the neighbour will catch me leaving my flat, whether pedestrians will notice my weight gain, whether the person sitting next to me on the tube will feel uncomfortable, whether my colleague will be happy to see me, and whether my boss will finally notice the rock amongst the eggs.

Is this home or is that home? Is my birthplace home or is where I grew up home? Is my father's home my home and is my mother's home my home too? Are they all my homes or are none of them my home at all? And if your heart is my home, then who are you?

Faith requires practice, and it is a bridge from here to there. The planks are wearing down, but where am I to repair?

I write so I can hide because my readers have no face. Their reaction to the absurdities of my mind is quickly erased. They read the whole passage and come out with a summary of two lines or three, but I continue to hide my treachery in the lines in between.

*   *   *

"Stop! I beg you all to stop," Solomon's voice left him before his eyes could even open. Then, they did and what he saw and heard were not the anxious bystanders spilling their weight onto him. There was a bridge and buildings on either side separated by a sheet of heavy rain. The sound, like static from a broken television, was the perfect antithesis to the voices that crowded his head moments ago. One neon

"

sign penetrated through the barrier of visibility declaring '24/7 In Hell you find Heaven' with a conspicuous arrow pointing down a stairwell into an alleyway. Around him was a colony of tents, their amount exaggerated by the congestion. His fingers no longer felt the grains of wheat but the plastic of the tarp he laid on. Ash-filled barrels were distributed amongst the tents and one of those barrels were close enough to Solomon that he could feel the heat of a past fire radiate against him.

A putrid smell guided him towards his next observation: a man sitting cross-legged across from him. His grease riddled locks of black covered most of his dirty face. His clothes were a culmination of dull-coloured rags layered over each other. He was hunched over dissecting the red meat off a bone with his overgrown nails. Chewing, chewing, chewing and then before his mouth was done mechanically grinding down the meat, he spoke up "Eat."

Solomon found a small pile of meat, which was courteously separated from the bones, on the corner of his tarp. "Where am I?"

"Away from the anxious bodies. Now eat before you consume yourself." The man pushed the meat closer to Solomon with his foot.

His appetite was bridled by the podiatric contamination, so he felt comfortable continuing his line of questioning. "What do you know of the anxious bodies?"

"I know that you write, and I know that you live what you write. I know you had been to WRITE for the right reasons, and I know you went back to right your treasons." The words leaving the man's thin lips made Solomon's heart strain. With every pump, his heart would pause for a second too long.

He stood up to bolt away as he had before when confronted with truth. With no time to map his route out of the compound of singularities, he fell over one of the more pristine tents, breaking his fall on the resident occupying it.

No sooner had he recollected his composure than he found himself at the end of the resident's toes. Solomon groaned in pain as his kidney received blow after blow. His host, who graciously had set up the tarp and meal for him, had interjected passively by raising his hand and calling, "Nakama, leave the man alone. He has not eaten yet."

The victim of rashness grunted and mumbled under his breath as he moved away from Solomon. "I will help you set up your tent later," added the man on the tarp to dampen any further hostility. Solomon rose onto his elbows and knees moaning and regaining some of his lost breath. Again, but forcefully, the man on the tarp pushed the red meat towards him with his foot. "Eat."

With the cold, the blows, and the general exhaustion all finally catching up to him, Solomon ate a sliver of the barely warm meat. "What is this?" The taste did not bother him as much, but there was a general faultiness, perhaps the blandness, that founded his curiosity.

"Do not name what you eat," replied the man nonchalantly in between mouthfuls.

"And why is that?"

"For fear of assigning it value more than your life." Solomon fell silent but his eyes continued their investigation. Soon, the wispy moustache, the low nasal bridge, the round face, and the smell, the SMELL, all aligned themselves to form a facial composite akin to a police sketch artist's rendition.

"Is this you, Kusai?"

"No Mr. Osroes, no longer. I only knew Kusai in my early years, but I have come to learn of its cruel origin at the mercy of the sailors who have taken me far from home's shores. I am a man now, so please call me Otoko."

Solomon lunged forward to hug the man on the other side of the tarp. "Otoko, I shall call you then." Although he never shared the deepest sentiment for Kus- Otoko in the past, their embrace was full.

Back to the corner of his tarp again, Solomon chuckled, "I see through the years you have lost your belly."

But Otoko was quick to retort, "And I see through the years you have gained a beard, and your fashion has regressed."

The comment about his beard reminded Solomon of Luna and his promise to get rid of it. "Why have I not?" he thought to himself. "There is fear in me, but I cannot quite pinpoint it." However, he could: it was the uncertainty of the outcome or the certainty of an unfavourable one. Perhaps if he distracted himself to the very end then he would never have to shave his beard and find out.

"Where have you gone?"

Solomon raised his head and straightened his slumped posture. "I am here now. Where have you been?"

Otoko explained to him how unkind the years have been. After the WRITE programme was officially resigned, he was left to roam the streets of the city. Madam Ferazia, a well-respected woman three decades his senior, took pity on his lost soul and steered him away from the hostile architecture of modern bridges. Unlike the cold and dampness of the Japanese boat, inside the cells at the WRITE facility, or under the bridges during winter, the Madam's house had the warmth of a fireplace and the pleasantness of pastel colours. Their relationship was founded on nourishment: she would encourage him to write his heart and he would cook her food for the soul. Under her nurturing atmosphere, Otoko was able to combine a series of short stories into a collection of sheets titled 'Journey from the East'. Before his words could turn to quotes, his relationship with Madam Ferazia turned vituperative. She exploited his youth, stole his truth, and made him believe his nightmares were more skewed dreams. The words began like the singing of birds in the morning and turned to the yelling of foxes at night. The maternal love he had developed for her had turned incestuous. Where could Otoko go but to the sewers amongst the excreted? With choices unworthy of the name, he picked the former and persevered with the Madam. As the days wore, he would think to himself, "Has it always been so yellow?" Her teeth had turned yellow, her eyes had turned yellow, and the walls had turned yellow like the symptoms of a habitual smoker. Part of Otoko still felt his heart bleed for Madam Ferazia. Perhaps love was taught to her differently and she was a victim of her past abuse. However, an excuse is a taut string held over a candle. And one day when the Madam intentionally threw some scorching hot soup at Otoko þecause it was "too spicy for her delicate buds", he snapped – not at that moment, but hours later when he saw the blisters that had formed as a reminder of the abuse. The next morning, he snuck out. He could hear the wailing of Madam Ferazia, like a mother who had lost her child right in front of her eyes. Otoko would think to himself, as he ventured away with nothing in his possession but the unsorted words of his heart, how Ferazia was a woman who was taught that love was a violent pursuit requiring the taming of brutes. He would look down at his blisters and burnt skin thinking, 'She must have loved me to the moon.' He found himself with nowhere to go but the hostile architecture he was steered away from. A day goes by, and the hunger grows. His face becomes dirty, and his soul erodes. "Is this rain or is this spit?" The bystander watches from the top of the pit.

"What would you eat?"

"Never a feast but at least I have pages of my 'Journey from the East'."

*　*　*

It was the forty-seventh day of Istiraha, or whatever the natives called it. King Zaki had decreed fifty days of relaxation following the end of the 'Maarakit Feroza' or the Battle of Turquoise. There was widespread debate about why it was named after the valuable rock: some speculated it was because the Ghaloon tribe found a turquoise mine on the border of the Satari territory, while others associated it with a spiritual conflict to appease The One.

205

King Zaki, the ruler of the peninsula, had invited me and Dofo, in exchange for riches, to bring forth concessions between the two tribes. Word had spread far east to these primitive men of our negotiation skills. All it took was a couple of hours and promises of companionship and the Ghaloon tribesmen were claiming arbitration victory. Oh, simple men, my gratitude is only exceeded by your ignorance, I thought to myself.

The turquoise pebbles rolled across my fingers and down into the palm of my hands. This? It is but a pebble to the blind. And there one and then another flew from my hand and onto the slumbering Dofo's rotund belly. We were basking in the Satari's definition of pinnacle luxury: I in my deck chair and Dofo in his under the mercy of palm trees. Two tables across from us were packed to the brim with fruits harvested from months ago. However, under the scorching sun of the peninsula, all of life's splendour melted away into puddles of reflection.

I shifted my chair, as I had done every hour or so, to relieve my exposed skin of the blistering sun that, because of the palm tree leaves, threatened to leave me looking like a zebra. Appease The One for what? For the lack of rain or the lack of crops? Or better yet, for the lack of sense that requires a western man's interference? A smirk instinctively drew itself across my face.

O what blessed cloud brought this shade? Was this all but a cloudy affair? The tremors suggested otherwise, but they were insignificant – until they were not. The vibrations grew and so did my attention. Oh, the blissful shade! Oh, the tremors grew. Oh, should I stay, or should I go? The marching of feet grew, and they were many as if the collective tribes, united in their shared disdain for me, have come to the fruit-filled tables for retribution. And I looked to the clouds only to find my shade falling on me. A foot of a giant, so gigantic that my neck stretched from side to side to get a glimpse of its heel to its toes. Do I look ahead to the marching men or above to the stepping giant? The rate of my heartbeat increased and aligned with the tribe's march *until I could no longer distinguish between their rhythm and mine.*

*   *   *

Solomon could sense a shadow move across his shut eyes and he reacted with a scream.

"Wake up Osroes," Otoko shook him by the shoulder.

With enough force, Solomon woke up from his slumber, his eyes bleeding red. "What- what?" he asked confusedly.

"The clouds are parted, and the night has been dry. We better hurry up and search for our meals before the rot beats us to it."

A few hours or later, Otoko handed Solomon an empty tuna can with little chunks stuck to its rim. Expecting enthusiasm at the great acquisition, he was instead met with a deflated response. Could it be the miasma of 'garbage stew' – a name adopted to describe the concoction of concentrated waste? No, over the last months where their acquaintanceship had manifested itself into a fellowship, Solomon has not shown repugnance towards Otoko's tools for survival.

"What a pity it is that you should frown in the face of luxury." Otoko looked over at Numa, the young child of seven, who pranced around joyfully having found a ripped sock at the bottom of one of the bags. Numa was the daughter of the victim of Solomon's tumble when he first met Otoko. Although her father was a grouch and avoided conversing with his circumstantial neighbours, he pleaded with Otoko to care for his daughter before he passed away with lung cancer lest she end up in a negligent system. Still in the earlier part of two decades, his journey and the responsibilities bestowed upon him inclined Solomon to think him his senior.

"It is not that, Otoko." Solomon replied, his slump was inconsolable even with Numa's infectious joy circulating.

Otoko knew from the moment Solomon woke up what it was but chose to play the fool until now hoping the treacherous part of his friend's mind would relinquish control. "I know," answered Otoko, while he pinched Numa's cheek to show admiration for her discovery. "What say your dreams this time?"

"I dream of a giant foot stamping on me; and the marching men, Otoko, you should hear them. Oh God, they are so loud," Solomon paused in respite. "Despite being crushed, I persist in clutching the bottom of the foot as it travels along. Again, it rises slowly and drops quickly; and I can feel the pressure so much that my eyes threaten to leave their orbitals to view a world beyond the gaps between its toes."

Numa tugged on Solomon's pinkie, distracting him from his friend's uncomfortable silence. Anger succeeded his sorrow, and he jerked his hand away from her. He saw in her the playfulness of Amar but on the surface, they were nothing alike. Where were the beautiful brown curls, the eyes of hazel, the field of freckles dotted across her face, and the button nose that she would always twitch in a sniffle? As she hugged his arm in protest, he could feel droplets manoeuvring down his hairs. *The world offers no hand, yet you cry for a pinkie,* Solomon thought to himself envying the purity of her soul.

Sympathetic to his friend's woes, Otoko handed Solomon his prized possession: a cigarette butt with a little less than a centimetre of tobacco left at its end. "I was saving this for a better occasion, but a birthday cake is appreciated more when all else is asleep." The cigarette made its way between his dry lips without the accompaniment of a lighter. Solomon would inhale through his mouth attempting to taste the life of another person's spent tobacco. *What lips have touched you? What words did they speak?* His lips spoke none, just the exhale of an addict feeling the rush at having tasted something he had not for a long time.

"Numa-chan, come along," Otoko gestured with his hand for the little girl to come to him. "Come along! We need to start dinner before sundown." She was on the verge of agreeing but needed a

nudge. "The chef decided on tuna casserole for tonight's main meal."
She went to him.

The weeks of spring rain mixed with a spoonful of graphite powder
had inspired him to put pen, or a toothpick he was gifted by a man
leaving an Afghani restaurant, to paper after a lengthy hiatus. Otoko
and Numa were yards across playing football with an empty can of
beans, while Solomon was hunched over a piece of discarded
cardboard. Words, but which ones? There were many but few at the
disposal of his rusty mind, yet he was determined to produce a
sentence of brilliance that would astound its own creator.

*'Plenty upon a time, it was a common tale of a cat roaming the
alleyways for a private and favourably dry space to lay down. Kita, as
her owner of four years past would call her, was plump and due for
labour after two months of gestation. Consumed at the cost of her
kitten's survival, Kita was collapsing every few strides or so due to the
weight.*

*By the fourth kitten, she was depleted, panting and unable to
differentiate between resting and fainting. Therefore, in fear of losing
the remainder of her lives, Kita fought desperately to stay awake. Also,
as wicked as nature was, there were a couple more kittens awaiting
their queue. Her fourth, unnamed and hairless, had stolen by wasting
much of its mother's scant energy on a delicate body.*

*From eradicating illness to replenishing energy, Kita had plenty to
justify eating her fourth. Oh, how she fought with every fibre of her
being to keep her teeth clean of her own blood. But the fifth pushed
on, and with the sixth to come, the cat had no choice. If she did, it was
to die and perhaps not long after the offspring to follow. However
selfishly or selflessly, out of fear or love, momentary or premeditated,
the act, which transcends the horrors of a human parent losing their
child, was done.'*

Solomon shuddered at the last sentence he wrote. *A parent killing their child, and for what, a life for them or their other children?* His spine stiffened and he rotated his head to look over at the gleeful Numa dejectedly. It had been months since he wrote, yet he wished he had not written. Solomon would give up every poorly transcribed letter, like Kita with her fourth, to see Shams and Amar once more. And Numa, he softened for her, but like the ray of sunshine she was, he could not gaze at her for long. It tortured him; she, an orphan, and he, a word used to describe a parent who had lost it all.

"Sickening! This is all?" Otoko scooped another spoonful of the tuna gratin, casserole, or whatever name appropriate for the culinary abomination, onto Numa's plate. The cardboard piece with the cat's tale was illuminated by the barrel fire situated far enough to prevent the toxic fumes from making a home of the diners' lungs.

"Unworthy of even a draft. How treacherous yet true your words are..."

"I meant the topic of your writing," Otoko grinned, which quickly transformed itself into an expression of pitiful concern. "There might be truth in your interpretation though," he added quietly. For the month preceding this tragedy of literature, he had coaxed Solomon in therapizing himself with pen and paper. There was no news of Spud and Aleabith since his escape, and as his nerves had settled, he elected to practise the only form of self-care he had ever known. But what horrible results this exercise had yielded. Perhaps it was a muscle he had not exercised for a long while; nonetheless, the practice had left Solomon discouraged.

Here was Solomon, a disparaged man, eating the combination of tuna, cabbage, and cheese with no sign of his usual hesitation or snarky remarks. The dejected attitude left a sour taste in Otoko's mouth that did not complement the bitterness of the disposed coffee-ground drink he was sipping. Against his better judgement, Otoko suggested "I know of a place," he hesitated a little before continuing, "for people of our literary inclination. It could do you well to find some inspiration."

"What use is there? Where are they and where am I?" Solomon replied, his mouth still full. He gulped the rest of the bite, while attempting his best to avoid it from settling on his taste buds. "I need to wash the blood from these hands."

Otoko tapped his senior on the knee. "You have the seeds, my friend, but you have been using the wrong fertiliser." It had become common for him to ignore some of Solomon's outrageous comments, despite how horrified they left him internally. *Blood?! Of his hard work or of his crimes?* he thought to himself. Realising the vacuum in dialogue he had left, he hastily added "Not now, maybe a week from now when the spring rains have returned. We need to capitalise on these dry days." Solomon nodded politely, while Otoko moved on to persuade Numa to finish the last of the casserole on her newspaper plate.

Nights after then, Mr. Osroes would huddle up under his jumpsuit in the tent to avoid the moonlight. Days would go by, and he would stretch his feet out of the tent's opening to get what little sunlight he could. Otoko understood his plight and afforded him the space to resolve his depressive episode. On the other hand, Numa often suspended his cognitive dissonance masquerading as inner peace. She would rush into his tent at night, exposing his face briefly to the lunar effulgence, and come out a few moments later with tears rolling down her cheeks. Otoko would comfort her and repeat, "Leave Uncle Sol to rest." But did the young girl listen? No, she was there night after night receiving a cold shoulder often and a scolding seldom.

Time passed, marked by Solomon's ever declining hygiene and the slovenliness of his beard. Yet who could address him? He first came as an outsider and now they considered him a native. Such is the way of the nomads, whose clocks run quicker. Yesterday their roof was made of bricks and today they would be lucky if it were polyester. Then perhaps he was not a native at all, but the next in line to wake up and find their roof was gone. And while at first, they would enjoy the sunlight, the clouds were soon to come.

Lungs depleted,
they put coals and repeat it.
Insightful talk superseded,
by smoke, mouths have excreted.

Visually pleasing,
his mind has been appeased,
by visions of dancing steam in a dying breeze.
Cease his thoughts as he tries to seize these thoughts.

Fading stories,
his hands could not grab their glory.
Blank air now looks so boring.
Hands could not express, and his eyes had turned so sorry.

Ink drying,
slumping posture and excessive sighing.
Blotched ink and botched writing,
could not create what once inspired him.

The rising smoke from several mouths made it difficult to distinguish any of the faces sitting at the tables, and generally gave the establishment a murky ambience. Visually, the place could be described in inexactitudes. The yellow lights were too dim, and the accompanying red lights provided no support. Teeth emerged amidst fleeting laughter. Hands waved in the air, swiping away at the clouds of steam, and called over the bringer of coals. Although eyes were hidden in shadows, the shapes of lips told truths, or at least partial ones. The waiters, bringers of coal, and other administrative figures, who wore fezzes and traditional levant attire, bore downward smiles. The seated ones, the ones who sourced the brunt of the laughter, had upward smiles that appeared carelessly disingenuous.

"Otoko, why are we here?" asked Solomon. However, due to the volume of chatter, his question was relegated to an internal thought.

Otoko, whose demeanour was incredibly reserved, covered most of his face with his hair. He grabbed Solomon's hand and guided him between the tables to a booth situated at the very back of the café. Once at the destined booth, Solomon could see a singular man of scrawny stature, despite the kaftan and oversized blazer he wore. His blonde hair was combed meticulously to the right. His eyes of fading brown were accentuated by the dark circles around them. He also had a razor thin moustache, which was fighting a battle for recognition against his full lips.

Otoko patted Solomon forward whilst addressing the man, who had his nose buried in pen and paper. "Mr. Abdulfattah, I bring to you a friend in need."

The seated man raised his head only to grab the shisha pipe placed on the table and inhaled deeply from it. After releasing a plume of grape-flavoured smoke, Abdulfattah gestured for the two men to take a seat. As Solomon sat across from him, their eyes locked, and a shudder travelled down his spine akin to being struck by lightning. Before he could utter the name, Abdulfattah slammed the table and roared in laughter. "May God destroy your house! Is this really the prodigy – Suleiman? It has been night and day since I have seen you, good friend."

Solomon was in utter disbelief, only capable of returning a nervous smile. Here, sat across from him, was the boy, now man, he once knew by the name Fata. Despite being a young adult, the mischievous twinkle in his eyes had not been scrubbed away. Otoko chuckled along and replied on Solomon's behalf, "Excuse him. He is out of practice."

Abdulfattah played the part of host and asked the two men to join him in smoking from the argila, which after a brief enquiry he explained that he meant shisha. The brief back and forth of invitation and polite refusal gave Solomon the opportunity to reclaim some of his wandering thoughts. With a heavy grip on his sarcasm, he looked over at Otoko with piercing eyes, "Why have you hidden this delight from me?"

And Otoko, perhaps misunderstanding the underlying derision, answered genuinely. "I am unwelcome here," his pause alluding to the great pain he felt. "This is a place for writers within striking distance of a viper."

"Melancholy has struck the poet!" Abdulfattah chuckled with more vigour than before.

Coals were exchanged and tobacco burnt, the three men sang and reminisced. Suleiman, by Abdulfattah's tongue, was full of contempt for the man when the first of many smokes rose; but by the third or fourth hour, stories of past torture were met with laughter as if he were inebriated by life itself. "Show me your fingers." And Solomon obliged, laying his feelers out, which were calloused and crooked after a long period of frozen labour. Talk continued and the contempt returned, not at the past, but at his present situation. Fata, by Solomon's tongue, has published a trilogy of books 'Streets I have Passed', which ended up gaining local and even national renown. And yet, his senior of several years, the 'prodigy' as previously acclaimed, the one before C-1, could not get past Volume 7. "Pathetic!" he criticised himself internally, but he was quick to excuse his nonfulfillment "How could I write with no wife or children in sight?" Abdulfattah and Otoko rolled on with the conversation, while Solomon was stuck in his internal monologue – until the phrase "Writers Write Right " dragged him back in.

"Writers Write... Right..." Where had he heard that before?

"Evangelists of the writing faith," scoffed Abdulfattah when he mentioned the WWR, an acronym he said was commonly used to describe the 'fanatics.'

"WWR – who are they?" asked Solomon with innocent inquisitiveness.

Fata raised an eyebrow to accentuate his puzzled expression. "The founder's son himself does not know of the WWR? You are their prophet in unwritten words." Otoko kept a solemn expression while Fata snickered and continued, "After WRITE was disbanded by Yan, a decision that was unpopular with few as you might well know, several of the ambitious members, perhaps to the point of delusion, decided to follow a sect with one core belief..."

Before Abdulfattah could conclude his narration, Solomon interrupted theatrically, "A writer that writes is a writer that's right."

"A prophet after all!" exclaimed Abdulfattah sarcastically with arms raised to the ceiling. "And what other profundity do you have to bestow?"

Ignoring the rhetorical question, and moving on to an answerable one, "Might you know the Tatar brothers – of the Baikonurs? Spud and Nick? A potato man and a tall mute." Solomon gave every description of the Russian brothers he could think of before adding, "And a behemoth of a man – Aleabith." Fata waved his hand to stop the spontaneous ramblings. "I know of the brothers, from afar, like a stalker who is new to his habit. I suspect Kusai does too," Otoko's expression turned nervous. "But the programme was made redundant shortly after they enlisted."

There was silence, in a bubble; while all around them, the tables roared with laughter, songs, and insults. Within their immediate vicinity, all those sounds blended into a homogenous mixture to constitute the new baseline of noise. And then there was the sound of bubbling from the water of Abdulfattah's shisha. And then Solomon's eyes shifted over to look at Otoko, a friend who had hardly spoken since the conversation of WRITE began. Was he silent because the mention of the institution reminded him of his own failures – 'Journey from the East'? That was certainly the case for Solomon, whose every train of thoughts would eventually stop at its destination – the unwritten chapters.

"You must, and I stress, must, as a person who sees you as a man wandering the forest with no map; you must see Yan. I see you have pulled back at the mention of his name, but... look, he understands you better than your parents – your ambitions, your desires, the causes of your instability. I apologise for mentioning your parents. You are in control here Suleiman, and the people, the people are cheering for you, but you are being misguided by evangelists, whose lies have muddied your waters. They lie that a writer that writes is a writer that's right. How?! A writer, like you or I, are liars by the admission of the words we write. Whether fiction or not, we lie and if we think we don't then readers will tell us otherwise. What narcissistic creatures are we to believe that what we write is inherently right?"

A victim to his own rashness, Solomon slammed the table and rose, no words spoken after. Only after pacing half the distance away between the table and the exit did he realise that Otoko lagged behind. He looked back, like a child nagging their parents to come along, and found the two men standing and conversing in a hushed tone. Fata had a hand on Otoko's shoulder and appeared to be instructing him sternly to do something.

"What was the prolonged farewell for?" asked Solomon with apparent irritation as his friend rejoined the ranks.

"Nothing of concern." Only to relieve some of the pressure in Solomon's head, he added. "He was urging me to drive you to reconsider your decision."

And that short exchange marked the beginning of the degradation of their relationship. The early summer lessened their shackling appetites, which eased the burden of harvesting food. The dehydration accompanying days of scorching heat, on the other hand, reminded them of the bliss of spring's rain. Numa was oblivious to both the dynamics of her foster parents' relationship and the climate around her. She kept with her merry ways, finding joy in the darkest of days. But the community of tents around her saw what Numa could not when mirrors were scarce. Her cheeks were sunken, her eyes bulged from their sockets, and her olive skin had lost its definition. Yet, Solomon was as blinded as she was and all he could see was her radiant smile and the endearing maniacal laughter as she tossed the cowry shells on the asphalt.

"One benj... Two benj... Three in a row! Show me your hands," Solomon grabbed Numa's hands and examined them palm-side up. "Hmm, the thief manages to escape again."

Accompanied by a childish laugh, Numa chose to respond by moving her pawn along the woven cloth. A metallic clang could be heard as she knocked Solomon's frontrunner forcefully off the playing field. He grabbed his pawn and rubbed it between his fingers.

How could a life of loss at the bottom of a pit find room to prance around in the dirt? The community of 'tenters' often understood this; not by the tongues they spoke with, but by the eyes by which they looked at Numa. They, or some of them, knew her father, Barakah, a man who was the subject of Solomon's inconsideration. Barakah, who had nothing to his name, wished he were tall enough to throw his daughter out of the pit himself, but fear of the fall kept Numa firmly against his chest. Although the community, an unfitting name for the group of ailed individuals, had moments of unity to help fulfil Barakah's wish, the ones who managed to crawl out of the pit usually kicked behind. They saw it all the same, as did Otoko, the world was consuming more of her than her of it.

While the thought did dance in Solomon's head a few times, outwardly he gave no further consideration to Abdulfattah's suggestion. Fata Abdulfattah for all intents and purposes, to Solomon, was the same cruel boy with the wicked twinkle in his eyes from the days of WRITE. Why would he trust anything his former torturer said? He did not, but the visit did as Otoko had hoped and inspired

Solomon to regain his lost love for the pen. But obliquely, he redirected this newfound energy to Numa.

On some of the hottest nights, Numa would huddle up between Solomon's legs in the tent and put graphite to whatever empty space there was left on whichever new piece of cardboard they were able to pick up on one of their harvest runs. He would scrutinise every one of her written words, and while in his head he criticised her vocabulary, spelling, and grammar severely, his pride in her came out the victor and prevented him from delivering anything but praise.

'ther was a girl caled nora and she liked her family alot, she had one brother and one sister and they all lived very happyly on a mountin in a very big house. they also had alot of food and they could eat tuna caserol every nite becuz they were rich...'

What a heap of gibberish! Solomon thought to himself as he oversaw Numa writing her tale, *But I love it more than anything I ever wrote.* With every written piece, his youthful passion for the literary arts would return a little. Although he was significantly better with the laws of the language at her age than she was, her words had an ingenuous feeling unspoiled by promises of adulation.

Every now and then, Solomon and Numa would go on a 'dry walk' – they called it that because there was no direction for the walk, no conversation to accompany the walk, and no objective to the walk. It was something Yan and him had done during lunch breaks at the 'university of mediocrity', Solomon smiled in remembrance of his professor's joke. They would hike up the nearby hill behind the campus, wander into the woods with trees higher than they cared to see and sit on an oddly placed bench to enjoy their lunch in silence.

Upon returning from one of their infrequent dry walks, the pair were met with an oddity in their community. The young girl rushed over first to inspect and satiate her ravenous curiosity, while Solomon, who was hungry all the same, trailed behind and exercised patience. Approaching the scene of surrounding people, he found a feeble elderly man laying down at the centre of it. The man was covered with nothing but greyish green towels to mask regions unwelcome to the eye. Seemingly attempting to groan in pain, the sounds he emitted were close to silent except for the few abrupt exhales, which expended all his might. His eyes searching for the wandering girl, Solomon found her standing next to Otoko amongst the audience. Otoko had knelt over to comfort the injured man and there on his face Solomon saw an expression of guilt. Solomon pushed himself sloppily through the crowd, bothered least about his standing with these people. Murmurs here and there, yet, in action, none seemed to care. The bystanders appeared content to watch over and whisper to each other about the tragedy they are witnessing as if a screen separated them from reality.

"What happened here?"

Although his question was directed for Otoko, the answer came from one of the women behind him. "Two men, nuff said. Okay well if you insist... I saw them, oh yes, I saw them – with my two eyes that is. My doctor says one of them is no good – 'wonky' he said. I tell you I saw them, no double vision either. And I don't drink, you can smell me," As Solomon looked behind, she pulled her shirt towards him urging him to take a whiff. "What say you? No liquor for me, no, too expensive and bad for my health – unless someone can spare a little," a short burst of laughter and then she continued, "Where was I? Oh yes, two men, one large and the other shorter... Or normal, I'm not so sure – my right eye is no good. The large one, oh yes large, he must've drunk a cow dry with bones that thick. He was hairy too! His eyebrows were too thick. Couldn't tell if he had honest eyes. I was also too far to see. Did I tell you my eyes are no good?" More of a chuckle than a burst this time. "He pushed the poor fellow over. That one," she pointed at the victim, "You can see him on the ground, can't you? They were having an argument of sorts. Couldn't hear them either. Is the weather cold? It's not winter but my earwax claims otherwise." She stuck a finger in her ear and waggled it up and down.

Why is he glaring at me in such a manner? Solomon thought to himself. Like the eyes of the starving towards a bakery for the elites, Otoko stared at Solomon spitefully. In a manner which seemed to portray the look as unintentional, he went on to add, "It was your friends." Once perhaps involuntary, but twice struck Solomon as if a nail had finally been hammered all the way through; Otoko had stressed on the word 'your.' "Spud, Aleabith, they have made an appearance, and showmen that they are, left a few memories as souvenirs."

Dumbfounded by the revelation of his seekers, Solomon's eyes widened as he stared forward at nothing and no one. The stress of being caught by his former companions had withered away gradually over the last few months. However, akin to a futile attempt to suppress retching a poisonous meal, Solomon's past fear surfaced all at once. Otoko's features softened as he saw the conspicuous fear painted on a face he admired in the past and pitied in the present. And all the while, Numa was playfully poking Otoko, oblivious of what is or what could have been.

If their relationship was once a twine rope, it was now a few threads. But as respectable parents before an imminent divorce, they kept their frustrations bottled within for the sake of Numa. If the luxury were afforded to them, they would sleep in separate tents. Solomon was passive. He did not push Otoko away but received the push like a sailor distancing their boat from the dock. Beneath the apathetic surface, Solomon's scarred tissue was being torn again. *I am at peace here. We are at peace here.* He would repeat those thoughts over and over to convince himself and the unknowing world around him. However, every time he saw Otoko's brooding eyes, a crashing wave would come forth. "Why were they here? Why am I here?" But then the more he looked at Otoko and Numa, the more serene he became. It was just another hill and another trough. A heartbeat's systole and diastole. *Oh yes, that is what they are,* he thought to himself. Numa gathered all the blood back into his heart, when there was fear of him bleeding out, and Otoko pumped it to the rest of his body parts, when there was fear of him losing his breath. That morbid thought calmed Solomon because, in his own twisted manner, he had surrendered control. Not to me, but to them.

It was morning. Solomon could hear something, but it was not the sounds of birds chirping or the pitter patter of rain. It was not the sounds of rascals running about or plastic tarps flailing about. After his mind scanned through a catalogue of morning sounds, trying to put an image to a sensation, he could now feel it too. Squeak squeak followed by the movement of distinct paws across his face. In one swift motion, he rose into a seated position and flung the mouse from his face against the side of the tent. Hardly translucent was the tent but light still shone through. Or was it the marginal slit at the tent's flap that was inviting the sun in? Solomon, scratching his beard, did not know. His heart had settled after the rodent scare – a cruel reminder of his current habitat. Never mind that, for he was ready to start the day with a bowl of bird seed cereal and a gruelling session of raising Numa to the peak of writer-dom.

There were clanging pots, words thrown, the engine of passing vehicles, the flapping tarp, the whistling wind, and the ringing in his own ear. Yet it was silent. A hefty realisation dawned on him: for the first time in months, he was left to his own devices. A smile that stretched across his face was quickly replaced by an expression of neutrality, as if the waves of the sea had washed a drawing off the shore. Any feeling that betrayed a lack of neutrality was sidelined by Solomon's facial muscles. Panic had set in. He was looking around more frantically than he had seconds ago. In his WRITE jumpsuit, he appeared to be an escapee patient of a psych ward. If he were, his life would require no more than a simple summary to describe who he was and why he was. "Oto- Otoko... Numa, have you seen any of them?" by the shoulder, he shook a woman, then a man, and then a child without sight.

The buildings on both sides of the bridge were creeping closer. The sunlight, albeit indirect, was now blinding. Why were people screaming at him? He shouted back in return, "Otoko! Numa!" His eyes were darting left and right. To cower from the world, he collapsed into a ball. "Numa! Numa!" Did he think for a moment that they might have been off on a harvesting expedition? Perhaps not, for he irresponsibly abandoned but feared abandonment.

In barrels, between tents, from one person to another, and the shadows of all, he could not find a trace of a family that he had only realised were as much after they were gone. Although shielded by the bridge, the sun was unmistakably high at noon. In the corner of the tent, where a stack of loose cardboards was placed, Solomon grabbed one of them and read.

'why did nora hav to leeve?'

He held back the tears but much like he, Spud, and Nick were when they had attempted to flee the WRITE facility, two droplets ran down his cheek and a third threatened to escape. Solomon rushed out of the tent, almost crushing a pigeon that had managed to escape on his way out. He found himself fixated on the only sign providing him a sense of direction: '24/7 In Hell you find Heaven.' The alley, the green door on the side of the building, the corridor, the staircase to the basement, the music seeping outside a wooden door, the face of a wicked man – it all came back to him one domino piece after another.

A total contrast to the brightness and silence he woke up to, the room he found himself in was dark and loud. It was precisely the same, the atmosphere, the customers, as it was when Otoko and he had first entered the establishment. However, it felt like an entirely different experience for Solomon, particularly because his focus lent him a shield from the overwhelming music, laughter, smoke, and other sensory stimulants.

"Where are they?" He rushed to the back of the room, bumping along the way one of the shisha stands and knocking over the coals that lay on top of it. "I beg you! If there was a shred of decency in you, you would spare me further inquisition."

There were yells, mostly incoherent to Solomon, coming from behind him. But for a few words like "coals" and "blind", it was in a Middle Eastern dialect. Abdelfattah, who at first appeared to anticipate his appearance only to be shell-shocked moments later by his tantrum, stood quickly to defend Solomon. "Exercise patience Hajjeh! You are right and that right is on my head." He then placed his hand on his head in a show of respect that silenced the irate woman and resumed the laughter and conversations. In defiance to her own surrender, the woman standing behind the bar's countertop continued, "We are letting in filth now? Give him a few coins and send him on his way." She bore a smirk, however, which announced the playful tone of the comment. And thus, Abdulfattah, took it upon himself to laugh along and stroke his chin in one final plea. That was enough to satisfy the Hajjeh and she quickly returned her focus to one of the patrons leaning against the bar.

As a shepherd would to sheep, he stood up, placed his hand on Solomon's back, and guided him towards a chair opposite him. "You have lit up this room, both positively and negatively," Abdelfattah chortled. Solomon was recovering from his outburst which had left him drained of any response. "You have made quite an impression on the madam."

"Who is that?" asked Solomon with an air of lethargy.

"The owner of this establishment and a couple more – Madam Ferazia. I am surprised Otoko had not mentioned her to you. He had made her acquaintance in the past... And between you and I, there were rumours of the unkind type."

Damnation on your existence, you vile woman! Solomon thought to himself with a renewed passion. Or perhaps it was his longing for

Otoko and Numa manifesting itself in enragement towards the woman who had caused his friend to love despite the poison. *Yellow eyes, yellow teeth... Has the smoke all around her diffused into her?* He shrugged the trail of questions that were sure to follow and reminded himself of the intention behind his visit.

Before Solomon could restart his rant, Abdelfattah asked almost knowingly, "Would you like to drink something?"

"Please tell me wher-"

"A cup of tea it is, Suleiman. I promise you, I will tell you all that you yearn to know." As he walked towards the maître d', he glanced back at the visitor and added haughtily, "I assure you that a drink will push you no further from the answers you seek."

Abdelfattah returned to the table and patted Solomon on the shoulder before taking a seat. It felt condescending for no reason in particular other than it was Fata doing it. *He knows something. He must know. I can feel it through the fingers on my shoulders. Tell a lie, so I can show the world that the mischievous twinkle in your eye is not what I see but what I know.* Was it a minute or a few seconds? He redirected his lost focus on his host. *Why is he looking at me in silence? Observing me like a hawk would a rabbit. He is toying with me. Look. Look! He is smiling at me so deviously. But his eyes look miserable, and his smile is of pity?* Was it an hour or a few minutes?

The tea arrived with an exchange of pleasantries between the waiter and Abdelfattah. Following a smirk, he enquired, "Sweet as you are, would you like some sugar?"

"Thank you, but I take mine bitter."

"Aha! Why does no one speak of this problem in our everyday? Enjoying the bitterness and pain and the stress and... What else? Oh, the awful weather. Yes, there are those that enjoy the unenjoyable; I misspoke, fear the enjoyable. One might ponder why – especially if they were as rash as you. Bear with me, for this hypothesis is a draft of the unwritten kind: we are afraid of removing all the causes for unhappiness we thought we knew, only to find ourselves unhappy with causes unknown. I cannot think, perhaps from all the smoke, of a misery worse than a misery with nothing to blame. But you could say 'I blame myself' and to that I would say 'if you do, then you might as well have some sugar with your tea.' What do you say to that, Suleiman?"

Solomon pushed the teacup towards Fata, "I will have one cube." Abdelfattah's smile fell at the request and the overall smug features that once occupied his face were replaced by disappointment. Nonetheless, he obliged and dropped one sugar cube from the saucer in front of him into Solomon's cup. Without much hesitation and in a show of confidence, Solomon dragged the cup back towards himself and took a sip, which left his tongue scorched. The floral notes penetrated through despite the temperature of the drink, and he was able to recognise the tea. However, he found himself unable to name it, either because he forgot its name or because he associated its name with someone whose memory brought him chest pains.

Abdelfattah pulled a piece of paper folded over twice out of the inner pocket of the vest he was wearing over his kaftan. He placed the paper in front of Solomon and stood up to leave. "You have been courteous despite the strain on your patience. At Kusai's request, I have not read a word of this. But I say this, no matter the contents of the letter, you need guidance. And with that, I will leave you be. Drink to your health and farewell, brother."

He was growing anxious with every sip, and though his courage was waning, he unfolded the letter and read:

'Until my Journey to the West Mr. Osroes,

I begin my letter as such to remind you that it is least my intention to forsake our friendship. Read this through to the end and do not subject the entirety of this passage to the injustice of a few sentences. Another request, the very last if I may, is that you drink your tea ever so gingerly that you may have a sip at the end of this passage. I shall relay the events as they happened, and before judgement is passed, my purpose will be made clear.

In the region of a fortnight ago, in your presence at the establishment you find yourself in, I was approached by Mr. Abdelfattah with a proposal. For months beforehand, Dr. Eadful had learnt of your diversion from the Right Writers fanatics (henceforth called WWR). Upon knowing, he requested whoever harboured him to deliver him over, in good faith. Because you may knowingly disregard it, I choose to stress the final phrase: in good faith. Despite my belief in the practices of inscribed Therapeutic Exploration, I had a gut feeling, which could have been the hunger, that you may find quietude under the bridge. Was I right? You were struck with grief. And not by the death of your wife and children, which you refuse to admit to, but by a death long preceding theirs.

Out to the sea for one,
The waves see you back to shore,

The crewmen on my journey to the east would chant the above – it signifies little to me, but I suspect your unorthodoxy might ascribe to it a meaning.

'Then why did you and Numa abandon me?' I hear you asking the question at this moment. How? I ask myself that very same question. Before I attempt to answer a question I had not answered myself, I must thank you for treating me more than less. From the top, you saw me at the bed of the pit; you had no strength to haul me up, and yet, you tried. But my gratitude is notwithstanding this show of common nobility – a façade by most. You dropped to the bottom of the pit and called me Otoko...'

There were a few words written after 'Otoko' but the ink had run dry. Solomon's eyes remained glued to the passage, whilst he made a conscious effort to respect Otoko's request. With another sip, he continued reading where the ink had found a new lease of life.

'I am at sea now and we are sailing away. I shall not look back for fear that we are drifting astray. I wish I could look back, Solomon. But with all the love I have for you, at the sight of a few blisters, I knew I must take her away. Numa deserves a love that does not blister. It is unfortunate that all the boiling liquid flows to the depths of the pit. I remembered that to be fact when the two, of whom you knew, paid a visit on behalf of the WWR to stake claim to your mind. In that moment, I was reminded of Madam Ferazia too. I despised myself and more so when I saw her, the little girl, prancing around jovially. And although all my ambitions had festered into self-loathe, I could grant Barakah's wish. Not Numa's, for she did not want to leave; all because of you. See, excuse my harshness, you write because your heart is void and you hope to shade in the emptiness, but she, my dear friend... She writes because her heart is full and in excess and that excess spills onto paper and the ink dances, unlike my pen and yours. This is my solemn promise that I shall nurture that in her.

Excuse my digression. Now you know that my heart remains in the pit, but if nothing else, Numa is halfway out. For that reason, when an offer of three thousand notes and a crew to sail us east was relayed to me, I refused at the outset. I thought I could revive your love for writing. But as the events spoken of transpired, I found myself already loosening the dock line. I could wait no longer; death occurs in an instance.

I lied. I have one more request, although my right to one is speculative at best. Take care of yourself friend (ashamed as I am to be called that). I hope you find warmth on winter days. I hope your thoughts remain loyal. But most of all, I hope to see you again with Numa, whose cheeks shall fill up with a smile and, if the ingredients permit me, hundreds of tuna casseroles.

His reaction was meek and not a single tear threatened to expose him. To him, it was odd, because simultaneously his insides burned with fervour and were slowly being consumed by a heterogenous mixture of rage and hatred. Not onto the interim family that left him in the pit, but towards himself. His regrets felt insurmountable, yet incomprehensible all the same – he regretted past actions and inactions, but also abstracts which presented him as the devil incarnated in these narratives. *I should never have made Otoko feel resentment towards himself... I should never have taught Numa a dark art such as writing... I should never have embodied the person that I am at this moment, for without me the bergamot would set, the bells would ring, the moon would shine, the man would find contentment, and the blessing would return.* Amidst all these explosive feelings, Solomon could only muster a yawn. With one last sip of his tea, as promised, and an outstretched hand creeping closer towards his face, he found his heavy eyelids dragging him down into the abyss.

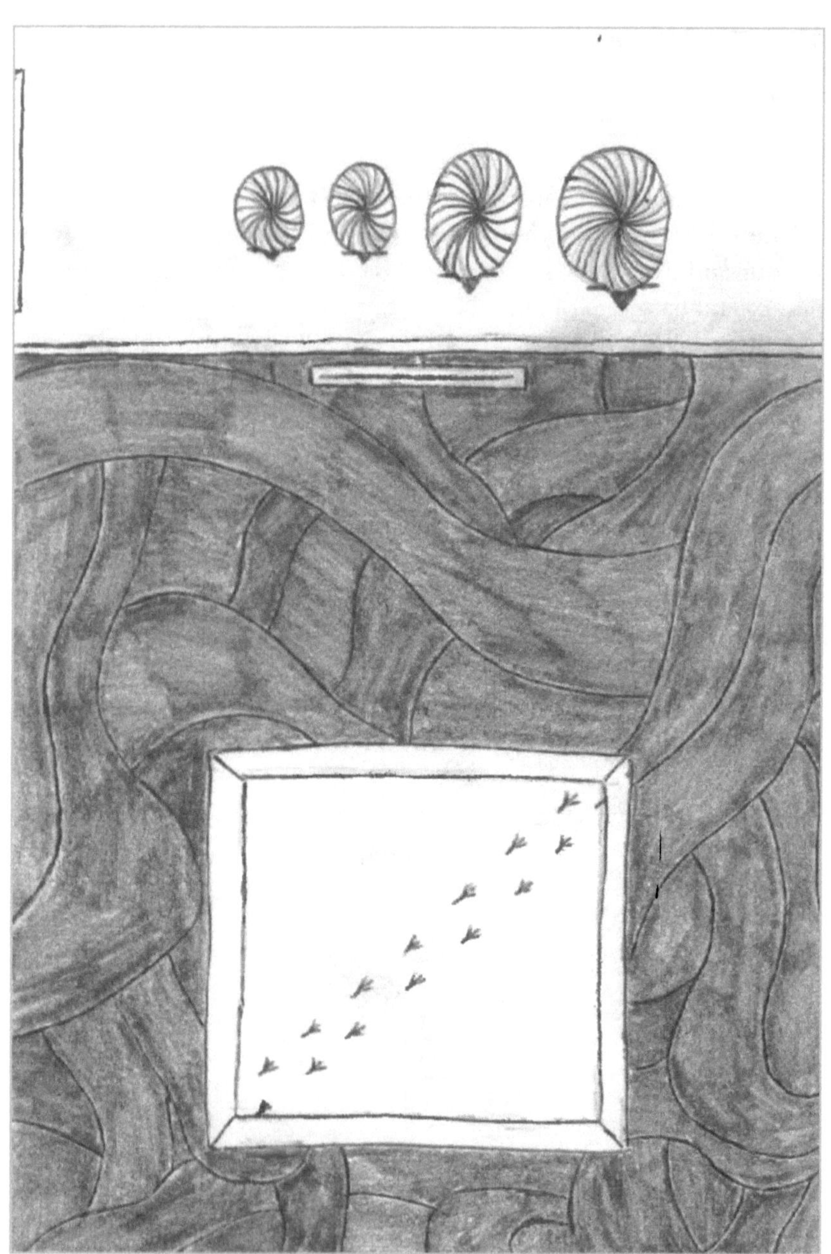

Part 10: The One of Pilgrimage

If I am forgotten by all then who am I? The elder at the bus station, a recurring listener of my daily rants, finally succumbed to the tragedy of my existence. "Do I know you?" And the more I insisted he did, the more agitated he became. Why should I argue for my existence? The only proof of it is my perception of my physical being, and once that decays then there it ceases – my entire being. The gradual decay began a few years ago, when at first the forgetfulness of others within my vicinity appeared to be a lame comedy by design, but after the life nested in my parents' eyes flew away and my mother's warmth escaped, I collapsed into a fit of crying. So much so, that although my eyes grew sore and my tear ducts dried, I still cried some more.

The further down I dig for hope to sustain me, the darker it gets. And although there are people offering momentary hope, they end up forgetting me all the same. If only just one thought of me circulated in someone's head after my death, then I might find an afterlife. I sought the relief of the end by stealing an unattended sedan at a petrol station and driving it full speed into a tree. In those brief moments prior to impact, I dreaded the absoluteness of my decision. I chose to eradicate any hope of ever being remembered ever again, even for a minute.

Freedom is awful.

Freedom is better.

...The freedom came to haunt me again when the absolute manifested itself in the form of an infant. There I was, with the taste of blood still fresh in my mouth, in a new-born's body. It was horrific and a relief and I cried from the lack of comprehension. As an arm swung past the door frame in my line of sight, I anticipated it to be my parents and for my entire pre-existence to have been one prolonged nightmare. No, it was two strangers, a couple, who approached me with the attentiveness of recent parents. As the man picked me up and swaddled me, I should have maintained a state of agitation, but I found

myself selfishly warm and in complete surrender to the intimacy.

Years on and I grew accustomed to my newfound body. I grew up, I made friends, I loved, I hated, I- no, the people around me shared memories with me. Despite no longer being starved, I found myself at times obsessing over the formation of memories – and I forgot to live. Who could blame me? The warmth of my parents, the struggle of calling them such faded over the years, made it impossible for a smile to depart my face.

One fateful morning, as I concluded my routine and descended the flight of stairs, ready to add to my long list of memories, I was met with a familiar scene. My mother's eyes were unusually beady and filled with terror. I did not yet understand the significance of her expression, however my mind, in autopilot mode initiated the following phrase in my head. Please do not say those three words. But before the thought's completion, my mother unfortunately asked, "Who are you?" As if the foundations of the rebuilt structure had been constructed on loose soil, the ground beneath me gave way. There I was, back in the abyss, which I had ironically forgotten about. At that, I ran directionless, but away at the very least – the feeling of the oak tiles under my feet and the sound of my soles slapping against them with every stride.

*   *   *

The slapping sound was replaced seamlessly by banging on a glass window – one could not tell when one sound ended and the other began. Despite his conscious efforts to breathe through his nose, Solomon woke up to find his mouth dry. He would have given it no further consideration years prior, but now that his tongue could feel the effect of his receding gums, he was struck with trepidation that his teeth might fall out. What were a few missing teeth to an unkempt man? Again, he was not particularly keen on maintaining a socially acceptable level of hygiene – as made apparent by his unintentionally multi-coloured jumpsuit. It was the permanence that caused him great paranoia. He could no longer deceive himself with ideals of a rectified

231

tomorrow. Whilst he swished saliva around his mouth to ease the symptoms, he finally acknowledged his other afflictions: his sore eyes, the ringing in his ears, the itchiness of his dry scalp, the dandruff that fell when he scratched it, and the stabbing sensation that terrorised his guts.

He felt naked. Not that he was, but Solomon had not felt this light since he pranced around in a wheat field. *Where is my jumpsuit?* he thought to himself. He felt his physical identity had been tampered with; he was wearing socks now? None of it was particularly unusual fashion-wise, however the sensation of cotton on his feet and off his body was, to him, a leap from one extreme to another. And yet, his feet still felt cold to the very bone. And he forgot how hairy he was – a 'beast' as Thakiah would call her past husband. From the armpit hairs that protruded from his vest to the jungles of strands on his chest and legs... It all overwhelmed him for no reason other than their abundance. Solomon clenched his fists to the extreme – a technique which would calm him at times. As he saw the bulging veins on his hand, he was reminded how, like the blood that travelled to his extremities, he had come a long way.

The room was dingy and there were no windows, but there was a skylight that provided a direct view of the grey clouds above on the precipice of precipitation. The walls around him were discoloured and of a faint beige that made its origins questionable. In front of him was a desk, much like the one he was provided during his mandatory task at WRITE. It was wooden with metal supports, straight out of a middle school. And in his direct line of sight, was a large glass plane that spanned almost the full extent of the wall. There were handprints plastered across it, however in a manner that made it difficult to distinguish whether their originators were standing on his side or the opposite. The wooden frame surrounding the window was in dire need of refurbishment, for there were various chips that appeared purposeful, as if someone had driven a pointed tool through the frame in attempts to dislodge it. To its left was a wooden door of an unremarkable nature, except for the brass knob that was either recently installed or intentionally polished. He could almost see his reflection in it, although he refrained from trying.

Three knocks in quick succession and one soon after. So loud was the sound, yet no echo around, but it rang and bounced through his head until he obliged and directed his eyes ahead. Of stature and body, a tale of the meek and dreary, for he wore his shoulders closer to his chest and his hands clasped as if providing assurance to each other. However, his head could have been the size of the entire windowpane. And it had to be since it carried those large cerulean eyes that were only a quarter of the way masked by his drooping eyebrows, their appearance exacerbated by either the sorrowful expression on his face or the deterioration of his facial muscles. His head was shaved, leaving white remnants of past hair like a field of dandelions on the cusp of being blown away; and his beard was more of the same, albeit slightly longer.

Through a ring of perforations above the glass pane, a voice could be heard. "Your sentences have run on, and it is time to introduce a full stop." So hushed was this spoken that Solomon could have easily mistaken one word for another. Alas, he was struck by the sentence enough to leave him quaking and on the verge of spilling tears – not by the content of what was said, but by who spoke it.

His voice trembled and he swallowed his heart at least three times before he could muster, "Yan?" Then, his entire body collapsed to the floor in complete servitude to the request he was about to make. "I suspect myself, at the risk of being called deranged, of acts worthy of a sinner and perhaps a scoundrel and possibly the senseless." Solomon rose up back to his seat revealing an aggrieved smile, which bordered on the ironic. One minute had passed, with which Solomon utilised to gain the necessary courage to continue. "I plead you for help; a request from a pauper to the prosperous."

Yan, whose stance was tentative and listened keenly, appeared to receive the plea with some insult. Never was he a man accused of kneeling to his own wrath, yet, at that moment, the professor's eyes were red to the rim and if he were to open his mouth, then one would be foolish not to expect a little fire to materialise. Sensibility dominated the seconds after, but with undertones of internalised rage, Yan replied, "What use is there when a horse is placed in a field with hay and the hay is sought outwith?"

The two men, on opposite sides of the wall, remained in complete silence, partially to retain leverage through their stoicism and partially because they had little else to say. The sound of the pigeon's talons against the skylight broke Solomon's composure and he inspected its source above. Once he lowered his gaze to meet Yan's, he saw in the background a door and then another to his opponent's right side; however, the majority of it was shielded from his sight. *Should I escape?* The question repeated in his head, as it had done previously in various moments of discomfort. Unlike the plethora of times where he would succumb to his initial instinct, he firmly held his jittery knees down and composed himself.

Ultimately, the prisoner, by means of assumption, realised there was no leverage to be had and spoke, or more accurately stammered along. "Yan, why am I here? And why do I feel a terrible drowsiness at the head and an alertness at the heart? And one more question, if you would permit me, why am I here? I have asked it before, but we often remember the last statement first, so in fear of burying it in my ramblings, I will ask once again. Why am I here?!"

"Confession for your vile actions, of which I am partially guilty of." Dejected, Yan momentarily looked away before continuing, "I had not imagined, despite pressing you harder than any before, that you would crack in such a fashion and leave behind you a trail of misery. What base actions... I-I instilled a belief in you that your parents, for their simple nature, could not." And yet again, he could not bear the sight of Solomon, for its weight would crush his conscience. "But what are you if not the product of thousands, or better yet tens of thousands of years of bricks laid on top of each other? What am I to expect of a building with cracks in its foundation?" The questions came out as the regurgitation of Yan's mind.

Amidst the silence, Yan wiped the sweat from his forehead with a cloth. There was a knock on the door from Solomon's side of the wall. He jerked his head towards the source, guided by paranoia, meanwhile Yan's actions were driven by expectancy, only looking sideways with a solemn expression. The doorknob rotated and a tall man entered, whose height owed gratitude to his abnormally long legs. Despite the length of his limbs, he was quiet. No sooner had his back turned away from him, did Solomon realise the elongated face belonged to...

"You must help me, and in turn, I shall return you to the warmth of your brother." Solomon found himself, having stood up abruptly, with his hands on either shoulder of the apathetic man. "Nick. Nickel?" He paused for a second in reflection before continuing, "Oh, I apologise for spouting a name for the cruelty of mothers."

Solomon, at his adrenaline's behest, received as he had given, a hand on his shoulder; only this one did not grip in plea but shepherded him back into his seat. It had a calming effect on him and reminded him to exclaim his jubilance. "You are alive and well, from what my eyes can tell." Yet it was not jubilance that drove him to say that, but the guilt of having evicted all thought of the man ever since the day they attempted their escape from WRITE.

In his other hand, the one not pre-occupied with Solomon's shoulder, was a stack of papers and a fountain pen on top. Nick, paying no heed to Solomon's remark and maintaining an expression of resilience, set the items down on the desk. No sooner had the machinery of literature presented itself to Solomon did he jolt up again – a secondary wave of plea. "You must help me, as you did once before, for I am a boat and Yan the storm and this room the ocean. My family awaits at shore, and so do yours." His hands were tightened around the mute man's collars, whose response was to, yet again, guide Solomon back into his seat. His expression again unchanged, however this instance, Nick grabbed the pen and wrote in large letters on the first of many papers 'Write your Wrongs.' And, on that que, he departed the room as he had entered it, quietly. Solomon was left staring at a paper, which to him seemed unfathomable and only managed to reduce him to tears.

"You chose a path of literature, of writing, of creating a writing programme, of being a novelist. All that is being asked of you is to remain loyal to your choices, as they have done to you, and to write about those from which you robbed choices." Yan's voice, much clearer now, delivered the parental scolding.

Solomon was on the verge of hysteria and divided by the freedom of choices: to believe or otherwise, to follow or otherwise, to write or otherwise, to escape or otherwise. To him, the only honest answer was no choice at all. He recalled narrating the dream of being stamped by a giant foot to Otoko, but what he omitted, at the time, was the comfort he felt under that same foot. The warmth, the pressure, the direction, all, at one point in the dream, were suppressants from letting his soul spread itself too thin and within finite time across the vastness; and concurrently, discouraging the void in his chest from becoming hollower.

At the top of his lungs, and to interrupt Solomon's inner conflict, Yan bellowed, "Write! Write write write write, or my right will leave another canvas black and blue, none of which will be ink." A playful smirk plastered across his face as he remembered the mental jousting between Solomon and him in yesteryears.

There was an air of uncertainty surrounding the pupil, for now that an action, as a result of coercion, had been presented to him, he had the least idea how to start. Nevertheless, he found comfort in the command itself.

*　　*　　*

236

"What about the three?" the Merchant of Souls questioned once more.

"Why am I here? A question I have repeated so much I fear it might be the death of my vocabulary."

"I am giving you another chance though my patience wears thin," the merchant, wearing a black cloak and a turban of beige, pointed with their bony finger towards a mud house with a collapsed roof. "In there is an infant of no more than a couple of months," The wailing of a baby, as if orchestrated, began. "Defenceless and death bound as a result of its parents' disappearance and its grandfather's death, with whom you are familiar." The merchant smiled cynically as if to mock Solomon for his past choice. "The choice, simple for the wise and torturous for the fool, is either to end the infant's life prematurely or to relinquish it to the wild." Again, on que, the sound of howling wolves filled the skies. "If you choose to end its life, then I will save you from the imprisonment of choices and responsibility."

Before the merchant's conclusion, which I had become accustomed to, I ran towards the mud house. Its doorway of loose straw would have been a nuisance to get through had it not been for the adrenaline, which manifested itself as a yelling in my head – save the child! There, on a wooden table of amateur constitution, in the middle of the hut, lay a baby. The cries had stopped, or had they ever begun? The infant resisted my support by pushing on my arms when I attempted to carry it. Ultimately, I was able to force my arm under the bare baby and scooped it up towards my chest.

No sooner had the baby's head rested on my chest, an excruciating pain shot through my ribs akin to molten lava flowing between the bars of a cage. How agonising it was that a physical pain should overcome me and force me to return a purpose of mine to the table, helpless. Two or three times, with the merchant's laugh in the background, I tried but to no avail. I returned to the dealer, dejected as I was, ready to plead mercy for the young one's soul. But my body was redirected towards the hut, which a window had collapsed within, to allow me full view of it.

"Why must you forsake it, and in turn, forsake me?" My voice quivered and my eyes grew wet.

"Watch and you might learn from this theatre I have erected," the merchant replied. And although I could not see his face, I could sense his wicked smile boring through my back.

Bones cracking – a sound, had I been asked its source my reply would have been none other than my skull. Yet my eyes perceived what my ears could not, and there it was, the infant, squirming and twisting on the table of its origin. Its limbs were contorting and growing irregularly as if its bones were being broken and reassembled. For whatever reason, I could not look away. And moments later, I wished more than ever that I could. Born from the innocence of the infant, a humanoid in my resemblance grew into its natural form. It was a mirror image of me, and that made it all the more revolting.

"And in turn, me..." My voice trailed off. The wolves, who were scoping their prey from its infancy, realised the potential of their patience, and returned to collect their dividends. Why was I, I mean it, subjected to wolves' teeth? I saw myself, I mean it, being ripped shred by shred into the bare constituents of its being. The agonising screams, which resembled mine, reverberated through the hut until one the wolves surgically removed the humanoid's larynx. As I witnessed the bones exposed to the elements, an itching sensation spread under the entirety of my skin. It was not loudly pronounced; only enough to trigger a desire in me. The urge to peel my skin off and return to a state of infancy. For what are wolves to a newborn if not family?

*   *   *

Solomon's eyes snapped open, and his eyelids appeared locked at the extremity. His head had fallen onto the paper ahead of him, and when

238

he raised it, at the sound of three consecutive knocks and one soon after, the paper rose along. Glued by sweat to his forehead, the sheet obstructed his view. Trances and knocks – a combination turned to routine. With his past experiences laying the groundwork, Solomon was quick to awake. Upon removing the paper, its contents became recognisable. Was it him who had written this declaration of absentmindedness? Before he could scrutinise it, with both excitement for its literary potential and fear for what it might uncover, Yan interrupted him.

"Heed the sands and hand it over," he knocked on the window again to alert the awoken.

Meekly, the writer, who unknowingly wrote, traipsed towards his former lecturer. Under the pane was a metallic slot akin to a letter box, which Solomon used to slide the paper through to the other side. Yan, whose eyebrow ridge was permanently fixed into a frown, snatched the paper as soon as it partially emerged. He inspected it with great concentration whilst his eyes spoke in theatrics. It left none to the imagination and allowed Solomon to decipher his encrypted reaction. *Is that disbelief? And now disappointment? And now misery? And finally, fury? Are those all emotions his or mine?* The pupil's mind was plagued with agonising questions feeding his self-doubt.

To quell the mental civil war, Solomon tossed a lit match towards the centre of the room. "I have confessed – have I not? Now release me if you may and I will relieve you of future dismay."

But unbeknownst to him, the room, at its centre, held barrels of ink, none of it water based. Therefore, at his toss, he was met with a scorching blaze. Yan chose to put his question to one side and let the words, by Solomon's own hand, constitute a reply. He orated:

"To you, my Confessor,

Guilt had been tied to my ankle by a thin string which I am able to cut.

Yet I cannot, for I find myself in a dessert of fine sand and the same string camouflaged within. I could expend energy searching for it amidst the sea, and perhaps if I found it and cut it, then I could travel further. Or I could drag it along with me, slower in pace, and travel further. I must find water in this heat so I can travel further.

You ask me to confess, but my sins outnumber these pages. And of what? Death? Two of which I am guilty – a traitor and a saviour. The merchant, who offers to assuage the weight I drag, was standing in a town with no water. I should travel further. His proposition was to end the life of two: one at its end and another at its beginning. For what? To relieve my burdens. What was I to do? Nothing. I could not execute. But why? With Earl, his death came seamlessly by my hands. And Annabelle... Well with her, death came desirably by those same hands. Therefore, why could I not execute the infant and the elder? HAH! Simply, the merchant presented a series of tests and I passed. Absolution achieved, for if a life was taken then another was spared. I should travel further..."

I will spare you the ramblings of the man, although Yan spared himself and Solomon none. He read the confession to the last word. Yan's face contorted despite his best attempts to retain composure. – "And with this, I have expunged myself of any wrongdoing and the sands parted to reveal the string." As he read the last sentence, his hand, with which he carried the paper, and his general demeanour both dropped.

"Annabelle and Earl..." He let out a dramatic sigh, before continuing, "I figured as much to be true and yet I chose not to believe." He paused, allowing enough time for his tone to change and his tempo to pick up. "Solomon, how could you?" Solemn Yan anticipated an answer Solomon could not provide. Nevertheless, for time turns wounds into scar tissue, he contented himself with the marginal victory over Solomon's soul. Those deaths, to him, were the realisation of occupational hazards. Yes, he was in grief as he was with the death of WRITE members and staff before, but a professional guard prevented him from burrowing into his own chest, ripping his heart out, and relieving himself from the corrosive woe he would otherwise endure.

However, he ached to rip his heart out for three others to whom the skeletons belonged. Images of the decayed flashed in his head – one large figure and two small ones. Yan retreated a couple steps back as if the memory had knocked him off balance. He regained his footing, but less so his thoughts, which were stumbling along the winding path. "Who were they?" They were unaccounted victims; not because of the pursuit of more or the occupational risks of supporting the climber in their rise. But rather, they were unsuspecting bystanders with no vision of the mountain they stood beside. "How could they account for the avalanche?"

Bewildered at Yan's behaviour, Solomon could not help but state, "There is a confession – a burden I no longer carry." In response to an ensuing silence, he asked nervously, "May I leave now?"

"Leave?! You despicable waste of potential." Yan burst into a furious rage and regained the steps he had lost towards the partitioning window. Solomon saw in him what he himself was accused of many times, an emotional explosion. The pigeon had returned and its taps against the skylight once again distracted Solomon from the confrontation.

In a moment, Yan retreated, his shoulders slumped, and he sighed. "I apologise. I should not succumb to hyperboles of the heart. My desire, as it must be yours, is to be an author of your truth. When you write, fiction or otherwise, your entirety is transcribed within the sentences; strike that, within the letters." Yan approached the window again, now with sympathy by his side. "For this same reason, you have not been able to write. Every time your pen touches paper, you are revolted by your own dishonesty. You are not the same writer who approached me with such raw ambition that inspired a programme focused on the realisation of oneself and maximising the output of one's potential."

Despite being addressed with an impassioned speech, the bird had retained most of his attention. The pigeon had a lame foot. Its lameness was a result of limp talons that dragged behind its ankle. Solomon was fascinated by the pigeon's ability to maintain its mobility despite its physical impediment. *Why walk when you can fly?* he thought to himself.

"Are you aware of yourself?" Yan roared. "You have escaped once again... Why do you choose to escape from accountability like the pigeon above?" He slapped his hand against the window to gain authority over Solomon's attention. "This is not a cage. On the contrary, this is the bolt cutter to your chains." He paused, contemplating the tangential course this session has strayed along, before pulling it back. "To the two before, you have inadequately taken responsibility. But there is more to be written: a confession of three, whose lives were stolen and their names unacknowledged."

If a jury were present, then they would have seen an accused man with a perplexed expression. The clinical psychologist would not be able to discern whether the man on the stand was truthfully oblivious or merely feigning it. Although every fibre of his being urged him to escape with the pigeon, Solomon kept his eyes fixed on the accuser ahead. But he could not deny temptation, and his neck snapped up again. The bird had flown away. "Traitor," Solomon muttered.

He looked forward again. The panic had finally set in and the matter at hand, which he had previously been able to outrun had finally caught up to him. His shoulders tensed as if the Merchant himself had laid his fingers upon him. In protest to the internal flashes of his own memory, he stood up abruptly. Solomon clenched his fists again and again, hoping to force the blood away from his heart. It was racing, unlike his thoughts which had settled on one – 'a confession of three'.

"Here, here, here. Stay with me. Stay with me!" The former professor knocked on the window with his knuckles. "Or else your friend of the past will unwillingly glue your eyes towards me."

"There aren't three others. There cannot be." He rubbed his
fingers together, assessing their callousness. And then he rotated his
wrist and laid his right palm open towards the sky; it felt heavy.

To hold a breath of air,
Fluids travel beyond reach,
But with determination to prevail,
To the hands he does beseech.

Unclenching one fist,
To appear an inviting plate,
To feel a strain on the wrist,
Oh, he can feel its weight.

To clench again swiftly,
And feel nothing yet ponder,
How the elements outwit him,
To the chances he had squandered.

Perhaps he is afraid of death,
To the air, his hand is a prison,
To try and hold his breath,
And bring forward his submission.

Time had fled, yet Solomon was none the wiser. Before preoccupying
himself with chronicles, he collapsed back into his seat under the
overbearing eyes of Yan. Without further coaxing from his mandated
therapist, he put pen to paper.

*I have stolen you and therefore I have stolen from the world. You
trusted me to be the guardian of your light, and now the moon and the
stars are all the dimmer. I hear four knocks and I am left to ponder*

where you and the kids have gone to wander. For if I am the sun, which I thought I was, then your day is dictated by mine. However, upon reflection, you are all suns, and I am the dimmest of all. I would have threatened to collapse if I had not mistaken your brightness for mine.

The false confidence as a result of your presence was, to me, a hollow mountain of paper mâché disguising itself as the grand obstacle. And I stepped on it, attempting to climb it, without realising that the structure was stuffed with your own ambitions – a sacrifice to support my weight. As I reached the top of this mountain, I saw no sunrise at all. There were shadows cast upon me of greater heights. I could hear from the top of another mountain the yells of Beatrice calling "Solomon! Solomon! Join me, Solomon. The sun shines brighter up here." I could not get to her; how could I? And, in that moment, I cursed the very ground that raised me only halfway high. I jumped and I stomped, and I roared and I – and before I knew it, the hollow mountain collapsed below me. Lower than I ever was, and I came to know moments ago, I was higher than I ever was.

Could he be writing of the three? Yan thought to himself while he attempted to glance a peak at the written words. All he could see was the exuded agony on Solomon's face which, like the mountains, cast a shadow on the canvas ahead. Having taken liberty with his assumptions, he determined the 'three' that were forced into early departure were random. If so, why was Osroes's hand twitching like an actuator lagging behind its controller? His fingers struggled to keep up with his heart, and the one page risked becoming two. Following along the train of thought, Yan was now on his tiptoes. *How could he write so much on those he barely knew?*

"I apologise for interrupting this breakthrough, but I must ask of whom you write."

Solomon looked up puzzled, perhaps even offended by the insensitive question. Of the tears that had streamed down his face, lines of clarity sat vertically across his dirt covered face.

The question was coarse and rubbed off on him like a grater. Despite being betrothed to anguish, Solomon could muster a few words. "The three bestowed upon the unworthy: Luna, Shams, and Amar." He inhaled in deeply and wiped his face across with the back of his hand, leaving a smudge where the tear trails once were. "You have not abandoned your cruel ways," he continued with more vigour. "But who am I to complain?" And Solomon glanced down at his hands, which appeared to him crimson.

"Hand me the paper this instance," Yan yelled loud enough to designate the perforations above the window redundant.

Initially, Solomon hesitated; a resistance was growing within. *Why would I subject my truth to the scrutiny of a liar?* he thought to himself. His lips, which pursed, were in disapproval to the protest of his mind. He could not find it within him to dissent in such a manner. Perhaps, as earlier, Solomon found direction in the commandeering nature of his former mentor and, in turn, solace from freedom.

He stumbled across his half of the room and slid the paper through the slot. This time, the man on the other side would let the paper fall to the floor before bending down to retrieve it. Yan had felt partial reprieve from his own guilt when Solomon began to scribe his confession of the 'three'. Yet the guilt that was floating away came crashing down all the same. Those were not his 'three'. He was depleted and had expended all his energy on a race with an incorrect finish line. Nonetheless, he skimmed through the letters and gave no attention to the words. With blatant disregard to his once friend, Yan crumpled the paper and tossed it to his side.

Fingers attacked Yan's side of the paper slot as Solomon rushed across the room to retrieve his prized confession off the floor. Not only were the words honest, but he viewed the entire piece as an example of literary brilliance. Not in a long time, dating back to prior the degradation of quality post Volume 6, had he felt proud of what he wrote. Internally, it was a dance of pain and pride. His fingers, despite their twists and turns, could not locate the paper. And all the sulking man was left with, his back now resting against the wall under the window, was the demarcation of desire on his knuckles.

"What else is there for me to do?" His voice was desperate yet gentle. "You asked and all of me did drop. Have I not quenched your fire and drained away my water?" His chest rose and depressed with every breath.

Empathy rode in waves and Yan felt pity for the writer across the partition. To him, Solomon had denied accountability, and edged towards delusion. *No, no, there was a sense of accountability in him. He had confessed to what he thought he had known.* He paused momentarily, contemplating the next question of his internal monologue. *Could he not know of 'three' others?* There was a sense that the pendulum might swing the other way. But Yan stopped it midway. *Not a chance! That decrepit creature, whose spine rejected him, had taken two innocents before that. What would three more be to him?* Amidst the tumultuous thoughts, he let out a concentrated statement. "I speak of three others."

"Three others... How could there be three others when the only three that matter to me are gone?" Solomon had stood up and was now pacing around the room. "You are speaking in riddles to persuade me that lunacy is reality."

"Solomon, I plead you to refrain from denial. This is no game and I am no jester." Yan had grown visibly exhausted.

"Not a game, but a therapy." His arms flailed about theatrically. "A hypocrite stands before me. He enforces therapies but denies an institute for therapeutic exploration. He pushes you to the edge of the cliff and urges you not to give into temptation. Well sir, unlike subjects of past, this subject knows how to fly." And he pointed upwards towards the skylight, knowing fully that no visual aid was present.

He had been patient thus far, but the limits he had set when he commenced this journey had been exceeded multiple times over. It was his own fault. To think he could have realised his prodigy's potential by subjecting him to external stimuli. How foolish was he? And yet, how could he have done otherwise? Solomon had become consumptive. Not only had he consumed the explorer within, but he left his family malnourished too. *Nonetheless, we have arrived here all the same,* he thought. The salvation of three and one other for the death of three and one other.

"Nick!" Yan awaited a reply. A knock could be heard from the door behind him, to which Yan returned a similar knock. "Would you please let them in?"

The letters on the slab erased gradually and the rock disintegrated into a mound of dust. His teeth crawled back on their roots like a colony of spiders in search of a nest. Onto his face and into his mouth, each tooth lodged itself back into its designated area in the gum. Scabs of burnt skin flaked away and were carried off by the wind. He felt the sensation of clay spreading across his face, covering every crevice. It hardened initially and then softened with the tears streaming down. The top of his head tickled. He could feel individual fibres growing through his scalp until he once again supported a mane. The sensation of lunar soil beneath him was gone as he floated away. With no anchor, the ship returned him home, Earth. His head descended gently onto familiar shoulders, yet his surroundings were foreign. How long had he been gone? Holographic displays and fluidised machinery were technologies alien to him. There were many more, but his brain lagged in comprehension. The only intelligible thing, other than his own shoulders, was the beaconing signal that presumably called for his return. It was displayed on a screen large enough to challenge one's peripheral vision. "Salve, Sol", says the woman tenderly.

"Where are you?" He was hysterical, justifiably, at the sight of ghosts. "Merchant, where are you? For now, I choose death."

The irregularities of the window's surface made the three appear as a mirage in the desert. The woman cowering behind Yan's shoulder was pale in her entirety except for the concentric darkness revolving around her hazel eyes. Aura-wise, she resembled Thakiah, not due to any specific markers but the distress she emitted. At hip level were two children, a boy and a girl, standing with their heads fixated on their toes. Second to the initial shock of seeing them reborn, he was astonished at how frightened they seemed. The two children took alternate turns to look up at him; it seemed they could only bear the sight of him briefly before reverting to their toes.

Solomon fell to his knees and begged, "If what I see is real then I was once condemned to hell, out of mercy shown heaven, and am now stuck in purgatory."

The man in front of them was devoid of Sol. Luna, whose fright was divorced into two, was contemplating his reaction as much as hers. How could she ever explain her act as one of love and not loathing? She herself was undecided. This was the man she chose despite the abundance of suitors. This was the man that infected her with ambition and inseminated her with potential. This was the man that showed her, from afar, how high mountains could go. This was the man that promised his hand if she sacrificed her back. This was the man that stepped on her back to rise, and when the rise was not high enough, he stomped till she broke. This was the man that slapped her with the same hand he promised. This was the man she cried for till she could cry no more, both out of love and loathing.

He scraped his knees across the floor, scooting closer to the audience of his horror. Amar was terrified of him and kept clasping at her mother's leg. Shams was too, but he was predisposed to the role of the protector, as his maternal grandfather would often instruct him. "When your father is away, you must protect my two moons." The eldest Dakin would grab Shams by the arm and dig his index into his chest as he repeated "you are the man" over and over again. Solomon could tell the boy was scared, but Shams wore a valiant mask.

His fingers, now on the glass, traced the outline of the three invitees. "You know me, right?" He covered his beard with one hand and revealed a set of deteriorating teeth with a smile. It was the desperate attempt of a man fanning embers into flames. "I am Solomon Osroes. Your father." He said, pointing at his offspring. "Your husband," he said, shifting his finger towards his wife. He then lodged the finger between his teeth and bit down – not enough to break skin, but enough to cause considerable pain.

The ocean of emotion Yan had voyaged across a while ago was subject to another expedition – the slump of pity and the rise of wrath. Beside him were sailors of novice experience, while he was a veteran weathered by these waters. Nevertheless, this was Solomon, his prized pupil - a building he could see the schematics of but thus far had not been constructed.

"Do not scorn her for my steering," Yan waved his arm to grab Solomon's attention before continuing, "I decided rightly for them, but wrongly for you."

Luna interjected, "You look unwell, Sol." Her eyes bore into Yan's skull before she snapped, "You gave your word that he would be safe and well."

The host did not level with her eyes but calmly replied, "A promise I honoured until his escape forced me into dishonour."

Despite an argument resting on the tip of her tongue, Luna reverted her attention to her husband – only by legalities. "Wha- what," she stuttered, then took a deep breath readying for combat. "I have thought about this decision for all twenty-four hours of a day and all days of your absence. Even in sleep, I cannot escape you. I worried for you and for the debasement of my own morals. What partner does what I did to you?" The almonds in her eyes glistened and her voice remained shaken. "My love for you was unsurmountable. That hand of yours would write for me beautiful poetry. Why did it curl up onto itself as a spider would in its death? An ever after fist, neither yielding nor receiving. And your palm, soft and inviting, only onto me as an expression of hurt." Her hands were unsure of themselves and periodically executed different actions: pulling her earlobe, scratching her forearm, rubbing her nose... "My conscience left me ill and bed-ridden and incapable of mothering our children. It was as if my own body rejected the guilt I had. My decision to leave filled me with many regrets, and yet I regret none of it. I shall not return, even now."

Clouded by the ecstasy of their appearance, he had thus far disregarded their sickly appearance. All three, four if he were to include himself, had lost considerable weight. And at that thought, his heart sunk. "Three others" - the voice of Yan rang through Solomon's head.

Was his heart the king and his mind the jester? He suddenly felt light-headed and the people in front of him warped into others. Solomon squinted his eyes hoping to alleviate the dizziness and recalibrate the visuals. When that achieved nothing but a headache, he rubbed his knuckle against his temple.

Luna into Beatrice, Shams into Otoko, and Amar into Numa. A horrific scene, but one that brought an unconscious joy to him. To Beatrice, he wanted to exclaim his desire for her. Oh, how he had hoped to amble through gardens with her. He wished to erect a mountain too high for her to climb, but she sprinted to the finish line. To Otoko, he wanted to wish his friend a fruitful journey to the east, away from written words. He desired to dine with him on more than unpublished novels and tuna casseroles. To Numa, he wanted to tell her if she wrote a word then the whole world would bow to it and if she did not, then the world would be worse for it. In his eyes, she unknowingly ruled it.

Before he could utter any of their names, their skin, their muscular tissues, their organs melted into a puddle at their feet. "Three others" The skeletons stood across him, expressionless by nature. Dirt began to spill from the hollowness of their eye sockets. His own eyes zoomed in on their own accord and he could discern a population of maggots exiting their last meal. Their jaws dislocated wide and although no audible sound was uttered, Solomon could hear a resonance within, "Who am I?"

As timely as they had dropped, the congregation of internal organs raced one another to re-establish themselves on the human stems. While each organ scrambled and pushed against another, everything flowed upwards like an engulfing lava. And suddenly, as if the conductor of this orchestra had raised their baton, the organs came alive as contractions and expansions. The skins, blankets tossed to the floor, unfolded themselves and by the glove-like hands grabbed each respective ankle and began their climb. Limb by limb, the three characters were dressed until each finger was at the extremities and the covering was as taut as before.

Numa sailed away once more with no farewell; Solomon was left distraught by the thought. A reflection of the position he occupied before; his back was against the wall opposite the spectators. He was panting akin to a dog in the heat of the summers in the south. The mortified expression of the four others left him further bewildered. However, in their defence, they had seen their once beloved scurry back on all four limbs like a cat encountering that same dog.

"Baba, stop this behaviour." Shams stomped ahead of the two, "Can you not see how scared you have made them?" He felt emboldened by his patriarch's retreat. His grandfather's words resonated to a grander extent having turned eight years old recently.

"Please Baba," Amar cried, keeping a hold of her brother's arm.

The crying only exacerbated his longing for Numa. Only a vile parent would despise their own kids, which Solomon was not. He was more of a father to Numa in those months than to Shams and Amar for years preceding. His indifference towards Shams and Amar had caused him great anguish. He detested himself for presenting them with declining care and stifling their potential in the process. Moreover, realisation of potential was a core component to his ethos, yet in that respect, he had failed at its implementation worse than Dr. Eadful. The negligence of Solomon, unnoticed at first, festered into black mould; it spread with the moisture of his children's eyes. From great love stemmed the great hatred Shams had for his father, whereas Amar held on dearly to the dying branch.

Yan slammed his hand against the glass forcefully and tremors left the room at mercy to thunder. Luna flinched, while the two young ones returned to their cowering positions. "Who are the other three?" A roar that would certainly strain his vocal cords.

The skeletons reappeared, only fleetingly, like a misplaced frame in a film. Solomon could not retreat any further. Alternatively, his eyes widened, his teeth gritted, and his muscles clenched. If it was not for the palliative voice of Luna, he would have embedded himself into the wall's constitution. She was beseeching Yan, but other than the odd word "benzco", the dialogue to him was drivel.

"I plead with you to meet my eyes." She squatted down until her head was level with his. Her soothing voice and her youthful face, which only contrasted with aged eyes, disarmed him. He wanted no less than to be embosomed by her; for her arms and legs to wrap around him and shield him with her wholeness. To feel her heartbeat through her chest against his and to guide his rhythm until synchronous. A human ball he let half of wither and die.

"Sol, who are the other three?" And once more the skeletons flashed before his eyes. He could not fathom a concept more sinister – a ghost asking about another. He had hitherto dismissed the presence of his deceased family as either an illusion of the mind or a punishment from the Omnipotent. His skin screamed ice, his heart yelled fire, and the rest of his internal organs cried escape. Although his brain urged him to run, even if it were only around the room, his body's weight felt insuperable. Tufts of hair on their feather-like descent from Solomon pulling at his beard because he could not cope otherwise. What could he do but answer the question?

He could sense something rising through his gullet. It was pulling itself up by the soft tissue, although the mucus hindered the climb. Ultimately, it grabbed onto the uvula and as it readied to launch itself out, a banging interrupted. Solomon shut his mouth instantaneously and the opportunity was lost.

Either the person banging the door on his side of the partition did so with both arms arrhythmically, or it was more than one individual. "Osroes, you incredulous dog, do not let them in." The door with the brass knob shook with every bang. The tone of the yelling and 'incredulous dog' struck Solomon as oddly familiar.

On the other side, the four were joined by a fifth. Unlike the loudness of his counterpart, Nick, despite his tall frame, entered with minimal disturbance. Yan's attention turned to the mute, who proceeded to sign his exclamation. First, he scribed on the palm of his hand with an invisible pen and then he followed it up by pointing right aggressively. "Writers write right... The WWRA are here," Yan's eyebrows rose imperceptibly, and he let out a sigh of annoyance.

"A writer that writes is a writer that's right. A WRITER THAT WRITES IS A WRITER THAT'S RIGHT." Repeatedly, Spud and Aleabith exchanged turns trying to drill the mantra into Solomon's head. However, on Aleabith's part, each statement would assume the form of a question. "A writer that writes is a writer that's right?"

None of it registered with Solomon, whose mind had paused since the ghost's question. The spaces where his beard had once occupied were filled with specks of blood. *Luna, where art thou? I have rid myself of the loathsome hair,* he thought to himself. He was reduced to a wild animal, on all fours, with his ears perking up to all sounds. His beliefs had been undermined and his faith had collapsed. The truth was far enough across the river to appear a blur to his unassisted eyes. Was it taunting him or begging him to chase after it?

"Stay with me, stay with us, Sol. The WWRA led you astray," Luna called for him.

Yan tapped with his finger against the glass, "I led you to water when there was a drought. And now that I ask you to drink, you are filled with doubt?"

The door slams slowed down; however, their loudness was only replaced by Spud's voice. "Liars! And bastards at that. They asked you to write, then claimed it wrong." His stamina betrayed him, and he inhaled before adding, "We have been through the trenches, and it is THEM who were firing."

With time, Solomon had expected for clouds to part and reveal an azure approaching the cerulean of Yan's eyes. The skylight above was masquerading as a barrel of ink, if he fixated long enough the mutiny of gravity would drop him in. The room would have been no less dark had it not been for the hues of tinted orange, sourced from the lit side across the window. Those who once were part of the audience had turned into actors on the main stage, their different expressions were a nod to melodramatic plays. He returned to his seat and assumed the dignified posture of a theatre-attending gentleman. As a man with an upset stomach but social etiquette, he internalised his anxiety until the curtains closed.

The pen glided with no hesitation across the paper – a sign of an author writing their final draft. With clarity, Solomon was writing about the movie playing right in front of his eyes. These were not the ramblings of an unseeing man. He had built the bridge across, and the truth was a mere few metres away. His conviction had caused the actors to pause their theatrics. *Finally, in darkness truth comes to light,* Yan thought to himself. But the unveiling of the truth had to wait.

The minutes rolled on and the children collapsed to the floor, out of view from the stoic writer. The three adults across, of graduating heights, had their concentrations strained on the paper. His once fellow vagabonds were audibly exhausted.

"Who are the three others?" Yan cried once more desperately; his head rested on the glass ahead.

"Only Earl, only-", Spud's voice trailed off. But bordering on screeching, his strained voice returned. "The three that should have been dead are across from him, but the three that are dead are from the garden of WRITE."

Dr. Eadful underwent temporary rigor mortis. The light was not dim enough to mask the colour flushing out of his body. Although it suffered a deviation in the pattern, he was a heartbeat away from a corpse. He was cold to the touch. And if it were not for the fuse he had lit under this structure, he would have remained frozen for longer. Yet he had given the statement inadequate processing time and thawed under the heat of the burning building.

"Sea won," Spud's voice cracked.

Solomon envisaged the mighty waves of the west capsizing Otoko's vessel. The storm would bring debris back to shore, but in his head, Otoko and Numa would never surface. It was like the asphalt to sailors of streets to the sea.

None would distract him, and he would find himself refocused on his essay akin to a bent spring swinging sideways only to settle back to its initial position. Even the return of the lame-footed pigeon and its taps could not rob him of his momentum. At this pace, he could have written the entirety of the seven volumes in a month. The man he was had discarded two volumes from his initial outline to ease the task, citing the decision as a creative one. For all the justifications and licence he allowed himself, he could not finish a single volume in the seven years succeeding the WRITE programme. But that Solomon was not this.

Alas, the pen paused and so did everyone around it. Solomon was skimming through the words in review, The adults across the partition were too curious to speak, the children found comfort sulking near the floor, and Spud and Aleabith somehow understood to be silent too.

And when the pen rose from the paper, its subjects averted their gazes downwards; some would exclaim out of respect, but many knew it to be fear.

The author's posture relapsed into a hunch. The pen, held up by three fingers at eyeline like a rose being admired, was the latest object of his scrutiny. He angled the sharp tool towards his face, whose ink had dripped periodically. His face was disfigured and bordered on the unrecognisable. The confidence he exuded amidst his writing stint had dried up and introduced a vacancy. The emptiness within had left him feeling light, and in turn insatiably hungry. Solomon, in Tarrare fashion, would devour everything and everyone in the room and outwith if only to fill himself enough until he ached and forgot.

"With this last ounce of freedom, I choose to join the Merchant." Solomon paused momentarily before adding, "I leave you with this: my thoughts are treacherous but so are yours."

An ensemble of expletives and heartful pleas rained down on him. From "tarnation" of Spud to "my Sun" of Luna, the cacophony of phrases fueled his drive. Had their response been tranquil, then the treachery of his thoughts would have swayed him back and forth till the pen lay still once more. *Freedom is better*, Solomon afforded himself this one last thought.

He drove the pen with force through the left side of his neck, hoping to expel the bookkeeper of his sins along the way. Cries of anguish reverberated through the rooms. Aleabith and Spud yelled questions for clarification. Yan was left in disbelief, yet the production of the ultimate confession softened the blow. And Luna, despite her strength giving in, managed to resist Amar's urge to stand and witness. Shams reacted in his mother's aid and grabbed Amar down, hugging her closely as she wailed.

Solomon's torso collapsed ahead onto the desk, a mixture of blood and ink spilling onto the paper pile. In this forever slumber, he could discern between his trances and reality – a comfort he could not attain before.

With most of the credit going to Aldakhm's broad shoulders, his two former companions ultimately managed to bring the door down. Spud and Aleabith stood in front of Solomon's still body. Their farewells were silent, kept within, and served to escalate their anger. Luna wasted no time either. She pushed through Yan and Nick, who had not yet considered their response, and walked through the door on the right and then another before pushing through two others. She collapsed on her knees, her head resting on Solomon's feet, and mourned; her fall appeared like a soldier who was fatally struck by a sword.

"Your selfishness," her voice croaked. "It knows no bounds." Droplets of blood made their way onto her hair, giving her streaks of red.

Spud glanced down at her and then back up at Solomon. "You always had an eye for the theatrics," he wanted to say but could not muster authority over his throat.

The viscous red, having travelled far enough, reached the tips of the two men's feet. "Was he cursed by life, or are we?" Aleabith mumbled a prayer to himself and then ran a hand across his face.

Yan, followed by the languid strides of Nick, were the last to enter Solomon's tomb. Shams prevented Amar from chasing after her mother by guarding the door with his outstretched limbs. Hereupon, Spud took a couple of limbering steps to lunge at the, in his viewpoint, de facto dictator of his associate's demise. "For your base actions, a writer ought to write your obituary."

The room's dimness and the cries of a grieving wife were enough to mask Nick's meek presence. However, when Spud's vision adjusted appropriately and his brother came into sight, he relinquished his offensive stance.

"Nickel?"

He nodded and Spud would have seen the shame on his brother's face had it not been masked by the shadow cast upon. The siblings spoke no further and embraced each other in silence. Questions of betrayal, that lingered in the back of Spud's mind, were in a queue preceded by the pain of longing and the warmth of affection.

On the other hand, Yan, whose reaction to the dastardly words was absent, was focused on the top of Solomon's head. *If only I could reach through his thick skull and salvage the brilliance from the torment*, he thought. This feeling of loss was a sequel to Beatrice's, and it carried no less impact the second time around. In pushing Beatrice to the pinnacle of the mountain, he had neglected her descent altogether. Whereas with Solomon, he pulled the mountain range from under him and forgot to leave the ground. Had the decades slipped past him? He felt feeble and his stature far exceeded his age.

Dr. Eadful ran his fingers through the pool of blood on Solomon's resting desk. He nudged the deceased's head to grab hold of the epilogue. The bottom half of the thick paper was drenched, and he shook it a few times to get rid of any excess. His hand, which was just as crimson, he wiped against his pants. Oblivious to his current threshold, Yan chose to read the passage aloud – for himself and others, but mostly for Solomon.

'I shall spare you the introduction, for whoever reads this is either present or recognises the appropriate salutations from the contents of this confession.

If guilt is a demon, then pride the devil. And in pride, I have learnt to hide my own failures. The purpose to which I ascribed my life was seven parts away. Yet, I believe that latently I chose to keep the pen away because otherwise my happiness, or a manifestation of contentment, would be my liability. Therefore, I admire the pen. However, I also despise it. I understand that internal hyperboles, such as insanity, might be charging through your subconscious, but allow me to clarify.

Early on, prior to the completion of the seventh volume, the pen served as an outlet for my discontentment. Therein, I could use an array of literary tools to describe my appetite for the flavour on my grandma's fingertips. I could describe the waters of the south that flow downwards to water the jasmine bushes. And most of all, I could describe the words out of my parent's mouth – a dying language from a weathered soul. For others, who have started halfway up the mountain, the harsh winds are but a breeze and the peak is a view of the sun. But for me, the start is at the riverbank and the peak is a view of that same river below. I would break and kick down rubble from the mountaintop if it brought us level some more. And here enters pride, which whispers to stare to the sun. And here enters guilt, which prevents me from looking back to the river.

Finally, cometh fear, which halts my ascension altogether – the completion of the seventh volume. The pen is despised now because there is no outlet for my dissatisfaction. And you would ask me to talk? To that I answer: I did, to Beatrice. And then you ask me to talk to another? To that I answer: I cannot. Out here, halfway up the mountain, the residents speak a foreign tongue. They approach me with warmth and point me to another river within view, however it all remains alien to me.

But occasionally, a climber native to the Balikh waters would pass. I would warn them about the climb ahead and share all my apprehensions; nonetheless, they would persevere. In reply, they would say, "Our people are starving. The river's fish are overharvested upstream, and the trees have grown too high. I will send some rocks down south and perhaps they can reach heights to bear their fruits." In turn I would ask, "Why not cut them down?" They would finally explain, "The trees provide them with shade." At every encounter, I would be left with compounding frustration. They remind me of the river and of the peak, yet here I am, once more, halfway up.

The snow around me would melt and the halfway residents would cry out, "Why?" But my frustration exuded was an explosion of delusion and everyone around would suffer. Why should innocents be collateral to a battle within? As a result, I would isolate myself from them in a hut somewhere on the other side. However, the people halfway up are forgiving. Oh, why are they so forgiving?'

Yan had no choice but to ponder that question briefly. The blood had soaked into the rest of the paper, and it would take him a moment to decipher the rest of the text. The letters stood out by the grooves and the darker shade of ink against the blood. He collected himself before continuing.

'Who are the three others? Rather unsatisfactorily, I do not know. My fires do not discriminate and while I recognised some of my victims and miscategorised others, perhaps there were many in the vicinity whom I could not see. And since my family is alive and I am to be condemned to this purgatory of conflicting emotions, I have finally chosen absoluteness. Either I am to suffer a punishment for inflicting harm on the people halfway up or I am to be subjected to the mountain's mercy; or neither, and in that case, it is absolute all the same.'

Part 11: Void

"What is with the racket?" He yelled from two rooms across.

There was a knock, a click, followed by a slam, and finally the familiar sound of two hard rubber shoe soles dropping on the hardwood floor. She rushed, without running, across the entry hallway and into the dimly lit living room. "Oh, how dreadful the news is!"

The man, although unconventional in appearance, replied with less vigour. "Then gift me a better day and spare me."

*   *   *

His pupils were dilated, and to her, it was an openness within – a vulnerability she ached for. Luna awoke an hour before Solomon, yet she remained in bed, as she had done ever since she felt the splintering of their bridge. For a brief period, every morning, her partner would wake up with a smile and a radiance that fuelled her till the next day. After that brief period, her partner's face would collapse into sorrow. Her hand would caress his cheek, feeling every bit of growing hair from his premature beard. *Perhaps I can restore it,* she wondered.

"Your hairs have overstayed their welcome," she would smirk. But to no avail, Luna would have to wait till the next day for a repeat. *Sol can only see one,* she would remind herself.

Solomon would reply with a soft smile, indicative of disengagement. The jovial, albeit irksome, noises of the children downstairs served as an ideal excuse to postpone any confrontation between the heads. The blatant disregard of Shams and Amar for their parents' rest was subject to a unified scolding. But Solomon, whose uneasiness exacerbated in Luna's singular presence, secretly found relief in the distractions.

*   *   *

At the groan of a Tatar man and a whistle, Spud was soon joined by his brother, who knelt before the fireplace, alongside Madame Ferazia and Kusai. Abdelfattah, a current visitor of the Madame's first leisure establishment, also convened, sipping a glass of Moroccan tea by the archway. Stood in the darkness beyond the room's entrance was Ulla - the once temporary housemaid who had evolved into a fringe member of the group.

Annabelle felt a tinge of pressure at being the focal point, but under those circumstances she became emboldened; and this was no different. "A conspiracy is afoot as I speak and a once great representative for the principles of this delegation is at risk of interminable suffering."

Nick's eyes shifted from the flames ahead to the woman speaking just above him. At the announcement, Ulla's face crept forward into the light. Like a fly plucked from the air, Annabelle's masterful words had captured the attendants' attention.

"And who might that be?" the Madame asked with blasé comportment. Her lips were holding a thin cigarette, and her eyes were red, irritated by the hovering smoke in the still air.

"Solomon Osroes, C-12, a WRITE debutant."

At this, Spud perked up and Kusai was no less excited. "In as little detail as required, what suffering do you speak of?"

She took a moment to recollect the events of hours before. "As any other day, I was filling administrative papers-"

"There's a mute," he gestured to his brother. "And now here's a deaf woman. In as little detail-"

"As spoken before the impertinent interruption, I was filling administrative papers for Dr. Eadful when I overheard, in his office, a woman cry of a man mistreating her."

"What of it?" Ferazia guffawed and raised her chin. "A century-old story."

Annabelle bore an irritated face, enough to silence the Madame, before continuing, "I could not hear the the dialogue in its entirety because Yan had shut the door midway through. However, I heard 'Sol' and a plan to 'alleviate her of him and him of her'."

"I beg you to carry on," pleaded the anxious Kusai.

"That is all."

"The great suffering?" His anxiety was replaced by puzzlement.

"It is there. I beseech you all to act with me." And when she noticed the hesitation curtain over them, her speech became impassioned. "For you were not there to hear their tones and you were not there to bear witness to their faces. You were not there when that gut-wrenching feeling struck like a bolt and my intestines felt like they would unravel and rip out of my abdomen."

There was a general aura of shame around the room, with a few prideful individuals attempting their best to mask it. Ulla quickened to the floor, finding it more comfortable brushing cigarette ash off the carpet than highlighting her individuality within the group. Spud and Nick had invested in the cause's urgency from the moment "Solomon Osroes" was uttered. Abdelfattah, on the other hand, resumed his tea-sipping and found the matter wholly uninteresting. The last two were opposed. Kusai respected Solomon and would have liked to aid the man he would have called a friend at WRITE. But doubts emerged around his response when Madame Ferazia urged him to distance himself from such a matter. After all, Kusai had been writing a book and if he were to interfere in Yan's affair then his dream of publishing would be hindered.

*   *   *

Sol was huddled in his shed, with his shoulders slouched inwards like they were trying to embrace him. His feet were raised onto the chair and his thighs rested against his abdomen. From Luna's perspective, having walked in from behind him, he appeared to be a hunched pigeon that had recently broken out of its eggshell. He was trying to preserve as much warmth as he could whilst click-clacking away on his typewriter. 'Vol. 7' she could see written on the header of the page.

She wrapped a fleece blanket around the shivering creative. "Your body aches for the land which your mother called 'the beauty mark upon this earth'. How long has it been since you visited home, Sol?"

"We do not belong down there amidst the broken, the misguided, and the caged." He turned around to shoo her away with his hand. How could he progress with his magnum opus when he was distracted at every breakthrough?

"You have turned hateful. The land and its parents are more than just flavors." Luna paused, assessing the impact of her words on the quarter of Sol's face that was visible to her. "Like Yan would say, what we think, what we know, and what we are is only the product of thousands or hundreds of thousands of years that precede us. Neglecting your foundation will only cause your building to collapse."

"Do not mention that spineless hypocrite to me. Had he believed a word he spouted, then the institution would be operational."

Luna sighed, feeling that if she pulled any further the taut rope would snap. "What about your parents? How long has it been since you have spoken to your mother?" She assumed a parental tone, knowing that her partner would not respond otherwise.

Against perceived limitations, his shoulders slumped further. His face, as if at a total loss of motor function and weighed down by years of earth's gravity, sagged. The bags under his eyes drooped lower, his eyebrows almost slid down his face, his cheeks formed flaps on either side, and his lips collapsed towards his jaw. His fingers contorted as he lifted them and pinched the bridge of his nose.

"There is nothing I have to say. They sent me here with coal and fire. I will only return with gold acquired."

*   *   *

Two months on from the gathering of delegates and Annabelle had little fuel to stoke the fire. The Baikonur brothers encouraged her to obtain more evidence of the alleged scheme, but with the resumption of her mundane hours at Yan's publishing house 'Better than Honey', Annabelle, despite her paranoia, could not find any substance worth relaying.

Why was she obsessed with aiding a man she had not seen in over seven years? Yes, Annabelle had in her past days at WRITE tortured the poor Solomon, however that was on the account of her admiration for the programme and its principles. If she were to assume the role of the tormenter, as instructed by Yan, then she would do it justice. But, like Spud and Nick, there was a part of her that felt betrayal after Yan's termination of WRITE, and Mr. Osroes represented the antithesis of that decision.

Those thoughts, which transpired as the currency of recent events led to diminishing returns, were impeded by the oddities of following events. She was squatting down by the filing cabinet outside of Yan's office searching for the title Dr. Eadful had asked for earlier, 'Zealous Zero', when her employer rushed out.

"Oh Annabelle, yes, there you are, busy as a bee, as always," he rambled. "How inconsiderate of me to disturb your momentum. Anyhow, I shall see to a matter and return shortly."

As she stared up, Annabelle was reminded of how rarely she had seen Yan flustered. His philosophy, as she understood, frowned against reactionary measures, and encouraged a measured response guided by decorum. She replied with an obedient smile and a nod.

266

With a coat, despite the ensuing summer heat, in one hand and the door handle in another, the head of the publishing house asked, "Has my guidance misled you before?"

Annabelle had pondered the question internally before, at various times, yet she had not anticipated being the subject of someone else's query. To her, any answer would betray the question and she simply did not have enough time to explain the spectrum on which her reply would exist and its current position. A yes or no would not do it justice. During the time she was eliminating unnecessary detail from her drafted response, Annabelle heard the door slam shut and glanced up to find the room empty.

A mixture of dread and excitement flooded her body. *What am I to stalk him like a madwoman?* She challenged her own legs, which assumed a mind of their own. Moments later, as if she had blacked out and another assumed control, Annabelle found herself stood in front of the door with her scarlet hair tied into a clumsy bun and a dark shawl fashioned into a hooded cloak around her.

And soon she was out in the streets rotating her head frantically left and right, trying to locate her object of observation. This was Annabelle's first chase, and if there were any rules formulated for it, she did not know any. Her eyes ultimately honed onto Yan, the man in the distance wearing a beige coat. He was pacing towards the end of the road, at mercy to the oncoming intersection.

"If I place you under oath-"

"I will swear by it!"

"Very well..." Spud scratched his bald head and flakes skin of dead skin danced downwards towards his lap. "If the wicked nurse is supplying him with the benzos, then the plan is indeed nefarious."

"Yes, and we must act on it swiftly or risk losing Mr. Osroes to the depths of valleys." At that, Ulla, whose ear had chased the conversation thus far, chose to dust the cabinet instead - the word 'action' struck terror in her. The short housemaid tiptoed from one piece of furniture to the next till she could find relief in oblivion.

After Spud had enough time to rub his lower eyelids, he calmly replied, "No, we cannot act-

"But we must!" Anabelle interjected with fervour.

"Listen vixen!" he yelled before settling back down into his seat. "I apologise for my outburst, dear friend, but your passion is misplaced on occasion. We cannot act yet, for there is little to act on. Let us suggest the following scenario: you intervene before any of the plan has been set in motion. If you go to Solomon, then his wife would deny it and you would be cast as a schizophrenic at best. Then let us assume you confront Yan instead. Well, then he would deny your eyes. And if he does not, then he would deny your presumption behind the purpose of the pills' prescription. If neither, then at the very least, you would have lost the trust you do not desire but gravely require."

*　　*　　*

Amar ran down the back garden towards her father's dilapidated shed. Overgrown through negligence, the plants succumbed to the surrounding weeds and wild bushes. Due to her clumsy nature and short stubby legs, she found herself on the ground. There was mud on her hands and an abrasion on her knee, yet, with the irrational fearlessness of youth, she picked herself up and sprinted once more towards her father.

There he was, several heads above her, a statue of a Roman emperor, carved from fine marble with a laurel wreath made of gold delicately placed on his head. The light piercing through the dusty window complimented the carver's detail by highlighting the shadows around every crevice. And yet, there he was, several heads above her, with the dulled hues of blue against skin loose to the bone and eyes that bulge from the socket. There was no crown, but a blanket wrapped around him, despite the summer heat, as if all warmth had escaped him.

"Baba," she tried to capture the attention of the man who stared at nothing, or the contents of the paper loaded into the typewriter. And when he finally looked down, after a few tugs, she exclaimed, "The food is ready, but the table is empty."

Solomon, unkempt in all categories, bent down. "You ought to be more careful running in the fields." He squatted down next to his daughter, licked his thumb, and rubbed it gently against the hurt knee.

Amar winced in pain, but she prioritised the aim of her mission. "Would you join us for dinner please?" Perhaps intentionally, the cunning little devil, she pulled a face that would force a robot to empathise.

"Scurry along little moon," he replied with a smile, that caused soreness to spread across his face. He realised, by his own volition, those muscles had been expendable for some duration. "There is a spark in my work today and I could not forgive myself if I lose it." He gave her a gentle bite on the cheek and sent her on her merry way.

And yet, merry her way was not, for she stomped through the back garden with the heaviness of disappointment. Amar had left behind a father, whose spark existed everyday yet whose shed remained cold.

He lit a cigarette after her departure. "Oh tobacco, spare them of me, for in death I could not possibly disappoint." And with three consecutive drags, he scraped the butt against his desk, an unpolished wooden one with enough imperfections to age it a few decades, then he brushed off a pile of ash leaving behind a black mark on the back of his hand. A day like many preceding it with a blank paper across from him, taunting him, "Write, write, write. What do you fear? Write!" He would click a button then bin the paper, then click another and bin it too, till what was left to his left at the day's end was a pile of quenched sparks.

Hours on, Solomon could hear from the top window of their house the cries of his wife, who agonised at his lies. From waking up to narrow eyes to waking up to no eyes of any kind, Luna could not imagine an emptiness more consuming until she awoke day after day to an unexploited half of their bed. Her husband chose to abode in the shed, while she would look from above down at him, wishing a letter would make its way onto his final draft. Solomon's insecurity gnawed at hers until she was left a hollow shell of the woman she once was.

"My forbearance punishes me," Luna lamented to herself in the mirror. She was using her hands to stretch out the crow's feet and the wrinkles on her forehead, which to the naked eye bordered on invisible. "Is it these – or these?" She pinched different parts of her body through her kaftan, exaggerating the excess of fat at her disposal. Upon the streets, uninvited flattery showered her, but she cared only for the words of Solomon Osroes. She looked down on him once more and wondered, *what beauty does he see when ahead of him is only paper and trees?* And then she would search within, for if beauty, to her husband, did not lie on the surface but in the content then what were once rocky waters on the horizon were now crashing waves come forth.

"The tortured genius he is, look at him," she said spitefully. "What does he have to show for it? A covetous mind and a neglected family." Luna, driven to resentment, hoped Sol would hear her, if only to extract honesty from him. "I could write a novel of your failures and a little less than an abstract of your triumphs." Although she raised her voice gradually, she could see, from the corner of her eyes, that the man down below either did not hear or chose not to. The war drums sounded, and she was not about to retreat. The window, which was open by just a few inches, was pushed wide open. It was night-time and the darkness was only contrasted by three sources of luminescence: the moonlight, the yellow bulb? emanating from Luna's room, and the dim white light doing little to illuminate the shed. "You are a scoundrel, Solomon!" she yelled but again was met with no response. This infuriated her, for how could he, even in hatred, neglect her?

The children, laying on parallel beds, could hear their mother's yells. "Why is mama yelling?" Amar whispered across to her brother with youthful fear penetrating her voice.

Shams shushed her reproachingly, "Go to sleep Amar. She is just calling Baba to bed."

"But she sounds angry," Amar persisted.

"Go to sleep," Shams reiterated, this time in a quieter manner.

Both knew, however, that this was no extraordinary outburst but a volcanic eruption following a few tremors. Over the past weeks, their mother had been displaying similar behaviour, shouting at Amar over a few drops of spilt water on the bathroom floor. However, they could not attribute her anger to a particular causation. Therefore, they were left to ponder, in their beds with eyes wide open, why their mother was yelling like a wolf howling to the moon.

With no restraint or fear of repercussions, Luna bellowed out, "Your parents sent you with coal, and what have you now? Less of it."

Through the obscured vision of night, Luna had a sharp pair of eyes looking like those of a nocturnal animal out to hunt prey. His head rotated quickly, and his glare burrowed into her eyes. Her spine stiffened and she could not utter another word, not with a knife being held to her throat. Despite that, part of her was relieved to discover that her distant husband cared to some extent.

Although her teeth chattered and she hastened to switch the light off and head to bed, the spiteful embrace would not last past the morning when the cycle would repeat. But determined to bring abroad a man who seemingly swam towards the roaring storm, Luna jolted awake at dawn to the sound of rustling downstairs. There she found Solomon, in the kitchen, with a singular piece of pita bread in one hand and a bowl of oil and za'atar mix in the other. He was barefoot and had a large blanket wrapped around him. Solomon appeared ashamed and, like a mouse at the sight of a cat, attempted to scurry off onto the patio and back to his shed.

Luna, her hope revitalised from yester night's interaction, called to him, "Sol, I plead you wait. For the sake of the sun and the moon, wait. Courtesy to this good morning, wait."

With Solomon's marginal reluctance to disregard her calls, Luna opportunistically and perhaps rather desperately continued, "Let me prepare you a meal, some fuel worthy of the work you are to accomplish." Even though the conversation was one-sided, she would not lay this moment to waste. "I reckon great writers were men of full stomachs."

I wonder if she is mocking me, fitting, he thought to himself. *I wonder if he thinks I am mocking him, for I am not,* Luna thought to herself. Her face contorted, cringing at her encroachment of his conversational boundary.

Solomon, whose eyes were fixed on the floor a few steps ahead of Luna, returned his sight to the shed and his legs began to follow. "Do not leave," Luna cried out. She lunged across the room and grabbed him by the forearm, forcing him to drop the bread.

While Solomon, day by day, had developed a tolerance for silence and even found comfort in it, Luna dreaded it. She would be ambushed by a barrage of questions to which there were no answers. And, therefore, when she was threatened with another silent response from Solomon, she had no choice but to act aggressively.

"Let me be," commanded Solomon softly. He did not want to look Luna in the eyes and was embarrassed to address her at all. He pried his forearm away and attempted to carry on with his journey.

Again, Luna grabbed his forearm forcefully and spun him around. "Shame on you for condemning me to the clichés of a hysterical woman." Tears dropped to the floor and one or two of the droplets struck Solomon's foot, thawing a little of his heart.

"Let me be," he replied once more sternly. What else could he say? Being distant had become a habit to him. At first, he normalised the lack of communication with his parents out of both negligence and shame, and now it was all the same with Luna. The difference lay in the repercussions. With his parents, their faces were too far to see, but with his own wife and children, he could not escape further than the shed.

"Why do you reduce me to this?" Luna grabbed Solomon by the blanket, ensuring he could not depart. "Almost a decade later and you no longer love me, that is if you ever did. You shall not leave lest you look me in the eyes and impart overdue honesty." And when her plea was met with silence, she continued, "You would rather stomp on me and break my back then receive my hand, and why? Because you are a proud man no less. How dare you force me, force us, into a descent you choose for yourself?" Wrath had overcome her sorrow, and she could not restrain herself any further. "If a writer is to write then you are not a writer at all, and if your parents were to see you then they would wonder what it was all for."

His hands were on her shoulders and her back was slammed against the wall. Luna's words had the effect of dragging Solomon back from the shed and into reality, where he was on high alert like a hare amidst the wild grass. But cornered by pseudo predators, he chose aggression to frighten them away. His partner's eyes had widened, and her cries progressed into sniffles. Solomon, no less, was shocked too by this violent act, yet he did not release his grip on her. Within him, a crack and a few droplets evolved into the collapse of a dam and the depletion of a lake.

"Have you gone mad?" Luna stammered through her enquiry. Her tone was at odds between anger and fear.

Osroes shook her against the wall once more. "Have I gone mad?" he replied loudly in a manner such that an objective listener could not discern whether it was a statement or a question. "Let me be and you would not. You are the settler on the mountain, the erosion of my being, your cries torture me, and your very existence demands completion from me. I cannot rest, for a moment with you is but a test."

The beast, of black and brown fur, aroused by the audible wrestling chose to mediate between the two. Rugrub's barks, along with his nudges, caught the attention of his owners momentarily. He was patted away roughly by Solomon, who did not appreciate the spatial invasion. "Leave, you will be fed," scolded Solomon. Rugrub, however, whilst respecting their space by dropping back a few, lapped next to the two and incessantly whimpered.

And when he saw Luna's lips quiver, a signal of an incoming reply, Solomon threatened, "Spare me or I will drag us all to the bottom of the Balikh." He pointed outside with one of his hands.

"Balikh?! Do you hear yourself?" There was worry in her voice, more for him than herself. "The Balikh is where your roots are. Those rotten roots with growing mould that you abandoned, not because of distance but because you had grown distant. This river, the Alienus, is where you reside, where you planted your seeds." If it were not for the contrasting visuals, one could assume it was a teacher lecturing their mentee.

And as Solomon departed back to his cave, he heard his wife's fury, a fading scream followed by:

"All I see is a broken shell, a hermit sneaking away. He might relish in isolation... or maybe he is just afraid."

The bruising on her shoulders and her back resembled ink blotches. Had it not been for the force of her beloved, the force from her accursed would have left a red mark on the back of her head. The percussion of Rugrub's barks, the sweet harmonics of Amar's cries, and the rough bass of Shams's yells forced Solomon to surrender his hold and retreat to his habitat. 'Baba' – a word that was repeated in plea to him, the aggressor, had become forever interlinked with an abundance of strong emotions: guilt, shame, disgust...

Luna scrutinised her body in the mirror with such ignorance as to disregard its suppleness and beauty, rather she focused on its temporary marks of violence. Her finger traced her collarbone before finding itself at one of the blotches. *What do they say, these foreign characters?* she questioned within.

The sound of glass clinking and juvenile laughter brought the mother to her knees with only her eyes and the top of her head visible in the dresser mirror. She had no strength to throw on her robe and silence the reminders of her agony.

Whether it was the internal patches of ink, the kohl running down her cheeks, or an obscurity unbeknownst to us, Luna was reminded of an idol of her past, Yan. Over the years, having spent ample time with Solomon, her perception of Yan devolved into a muddied form of unfulfilled promises and lawless practices. Yet, in an epiphanic moment, the dirt build-up that layered on her former mentor shed off in parts. While she kneeled, he appeared beyond her eyes as a saviour figure.

*   *   *

Report after report of inactivity at the Osroes' would send Spud into a spiral of inexplicable conclusions. "It cannot be that after all these months, the man is no better off than he was." He was set off, this time, by the muted words of his brother's hands. Following the disappearance of Solomon's family, Nickel and Ulla had alternated scoping his vitals from afar, hidden in the congregation of trees. The Baikonur, sunk into an armchair unsuitably large for his frame, assumed leadership over the members of the disjointed fellowship.

"A light switched on and then off?" the seated man asked with overenthusiasm unwarranted by the question.

And when Nickel nodded, Spud raised himself in attentiveness. "That is all there is to report?"

Silence, both because of his brother's muteness and the implied affirmation, forced Spud back into his chair. He scoured the room of grey and crimson for inspiration. An emptiness remained from the once lively room. The fire was dead as a consequence of a humid summer. Annabelle was away, having retained her role as Yan's reliable bookkeeper and avid stalker. Where he went, so did she, but over the months, he left much less and so did she. Kusai and the Madame, lovers from different generations, chose, perhaps coaxed with respect to the young man, to part ways with the enterprise to tread a faltering line between companionship and success. News of the two was sparse and seldom believable. Fata, or Abdelfattah as he was called in maturity, was a boy and an observer, ever present but never involved. He remained as such during these recent months. Spud viewed Nickel and Ulla, one mute and the other a coward, with contempt and therefore undervalued their contributions, reserving them for trifling tasks.

Nick, towering over his counterpart, tapped Spud on his shoulder. With the different gestures, Spud was able to interpret his brother's communication as a query regarding Spud's predisposition to aid Solomon instead of focusing on the group's initial aim of continuing the writing legacy of **WRITE** by facilitating writers to 'write right'. To add, Nick pointed to his heart. The paraphrasing continued; Nick spanned his arms across the room, like a waiter presenting a platter, and signified the death of the once thriving room.

Spud flailed his hand as if he was swatting a fly away. "How can we write when a representation of our cause stands to fall?"

Seemingly unconvinced and bordering on the facetious, Nick was expounded to by his unpleasing twin. "If Solomon falls then another column of **WRITE** does too."

The brother's argumentative nature led to an hour-long debate on the direction of this informal succession to WRITE. Alas, his inexplicable conclusion forced Spud off his seat, much to his dissatisfaction, and out the door to a house by the Wander Woods at 22nd Augustus Rd, for a confrontation with a man, who to him was a writer worthy of the name but caked in pity. How could Spud trust any of his minions to inspire the dead back to life?

The knocks were assertive, but the response less so. The white wooden door gave little away with respect to the occupants of the household. The squalid state of the amuse-bouche, that is the porch and front yard, lessened the appetite of the inquisitor. An eye peered through a convenient curtain slit beyond the unmaintained window and found, amidst the shadows of an unoccupied room, particulates of dust dancing in the rays of sunlight piercing through.

"The neighbours, they stare," Spud knocked a few times more with greater aggression. "Please heed my embarrassment."

Eerily there was no one around and the yards, although kempt to a degree of communistic severity meaning all the hedges and grass were aligned in shape, length, and colour; they lent themselves no character in the form of lawn decorations or the support of parked cars in adjacent driveways.

The neighbourhood was awake with the sound of none; the bell did ring, but no one did come. The deafening sound of the church bell drowned the detective in Spud and instead reduced him to a panicked rodent with a swivelling head. His eyes widened with every rotation – a dramatic response to the absence of a visual explanation. After minutes, though it felt like hours, of the directionless clanging, tranquillity returned, and his anxiety dissipated.

He would not wait a moment longer for its second coming. Spud found himself with one foot in and another out of the back garden, which blended seamlessly with the woods around due to the overgrowth. Had it not rained the night prior, he would have found himself already at the infamous shed. However, here he was sloshing about in the mud taking twice as long on his journey. His shoes were unsalvageable, but at the very least, the harmonious smells of vegetation and mud put his mind at ease.

Several metres away, a voice called out, "Your approach is rather conspicuous. Who is this?" A head, supporting a mane and a full beard, a jungle hiding a pond in its own respect, poked outside the shed's entrance.

"A friend from past years," Spud responded hesitantly, dropping the hat he wore on the sunny day to his chest.

"And who might that be?" The shed-dweller scowled at the intrusion of his peace.

"A fellow WRITE-er, one whose admiration for you was evident," Spud flattered before adding as an assurance, "My name is Spud and... and I have come to pay respects in consideration of your passing family."

Solomon grumbled under his breath, "A friend? That you are not. A jester perhaps." Then, in contention to the visitor, he loudly added, "The family has not passed, but are merely on a hiatus from life. Now, if you may, out of the respect that you wish to pay, leave me be."

Spud was infuriated by Solomon's remark, but he maintained a flattering façade to avoid a breakdown in the ongoing negotiations. "Had I not left you be all these months?" Spud chuckled to soften the mood. "And on the matter of your family, the semantics matter the least for my respects are due nonetheless."

Not out of wallow, but the unwillingness to engage any further in a futile argument, Solomon retreated to the shadows. To which, Spud responded, "Is that it? The chief principle of your remaining days is to indulge in recounting your woes? And not to others so that you might gain insight beyond within, or better yet, recognition on the account of your tragedies?"

Accounts differ regarding Solomon's response. Spud claims, as he did that fateful night when a scheme of treachery compounded upon an already nefarious plan to produce a tangled web wrapped around a lost head, that Mr. Osroes begged him for aid. However, we are also led to believe, on the account of Solomon's character and his wife's and other associates' contrary opinions of him, that Solomon was likely to agonise in despair and succumb to the stubbornness of a defeatist, inaction being his greatest weapon. Nevertheless, the Tatar man would return that same day to a question that would set the cogs in motion.

"What shall we do?" asked Annabelle after Spud retold his encounter with Solomon only minutes after her recount of a mundane day at the publishing house.

The man, who was panting despite being seated for quarter the hour, replied, "We are at a fork in our path, and we must choose one of the following: either we let Solomon wither due to our cowardly patience at the improbability of his family's return or we subject ourselves to discomfort by relieving our comrade of the unknown."

Nick rolled his eyes at the expense of his brother's conviction, while Abdelfattah who passed by for a customary cup of Moroccan tea listened intently half-masked by the shadow of the archway. Annabelle dropped to her knees next to the armchair like an eager dog; she was a woman of action having grown amongst the languid rich. Coming just behind the unassuming Abdelfattah, Ulla dropped gingerly down the staircase to not alert anyone of her presence.

"And how do we eliminate the unknown?" Annabelle rushed into her queries without pondering the choices presented.

"I pondered this for as long as my walk was, under the heat of a sun that shines brighter than years prior, and I could produce only an abstract." Spud looked around at his constituents and rubbed his hand gently, which was sore and red from prolonged exposure to the sun.

After an audible sip of his tea, Abdelfattah interjected as to make his presence known. "Conundrums of this type are better left to be resolved with time."

But Spud feared that time was the enemy of momentum, and if they were to fall for the allure of passivity, then his vision for the pre-mature WWRA would be a fruitless venture. He needed Solomon, an obstacle of great height but expansive scope, to provide legitimacy to its mission. Therefore, he blurted something, with little thought of the ever-growing consequences, just as he saw his company's muscles begin to decompress. "You speak only in avoidance to work?" His brows furrowed and his eyes pierced into the shadowy figure.

Abdelfattah smirked in turn, lowered his head in sarcastic apology, and allowed Spud to continue. "We must not be deceived by the difficulty of the matter. The truth is that our choices are ugly, but that is when conviction is needed most." It was as if he was holding himself back from saying the next couple sentences. "Either we find his family, dead or otherwise, and bring them back to him so that we might shine light through his oblivion, or we convince him of his own family's conclusion and thus push him from his past into the present."

Annabelle stood up and retreated a few steps back in appalment, while Abdelfattah, a man whose nature was curious until death, came forward once more. "Forgive the further interruption, but how do you suggest we achieve the latter?"

There were eyes darting back and forth scanning the faces around in a futile attempt to gauge each other's boundaries – how far would they go to help another in a bid to help themselves?

To the back of familiar grounds, the group found each other standing and glaring down at a patch in the soil that was a shade of colour different from the rest of the yard. They were led, all four of them, by the hesitant words of Abdelfattah two nights prior to this spot behind a brick building in which, once upon a time, their hands bled. The same man whose words led them there refused to participate or even attend this ritual of unholy exhumation in fear of spiritual punishment. Ulla, fearful not because of her beliefs but for her own mortality, was subjected to harsh words and consequently coerced into the activity. The first pair dug into the ground and soil lodged under their nails. "The ground is broken up." He looked up from his kneeling position at the three reluctant faces. "Please dig in before I leave another three graves to accompany this one." And so, they knelt, Ulla and Nick alongside Spud with their smaller shovels whereas Annabelle, who assumed command of the larger shovel, remained standing. Till the clock struck twelve, all through the night, piles of dirt formed behind each of the shovelers whose tears, apart from Spud, mixed with their sweat to roll down their faces and onto the field below.

"No more. No more!" cried out Ulla unexpectedly. Her usually tame presence as a subject of her stature and meek character lent her outburst more impact.

She paused for an onslaught of sniffles and weeps before adding, "Please sir do not subject me to more of this baseness. My morality banished, but I beg you to not send my mortality after."

There she was, with her dark hair and grey streaks and speckles of mud and her plump body supporting a black uniform and speckles of blood. Her round amber glasses lay beside her shattered, and her once adorable squirrel-like face collapsed into a disfigured pool of swelling, bruises, and blood. There she was, Ulla, laying on the ground and a man on top of her with a shovel in one hand. He was calm one moment and rabid the other with the mingling of guilt and desire like a starved man succumbing to cannibalising his recently deceased friend. There she was, an immortal in death, for how could Annabelle and Nick forget the sight they beheld.

"What say, you two?" Spud looked back in fury at the bystanders. "This a battle for the heart of this institution and if we do not weed out growing doubts, then our fate is no better than that of the building behind you," he pointed to the structure behind. "A remnant of lost potential and unrealised works of brilliance. Oh, if only you were to know what the likes of the Habers, the Oppenheimers, and the Schrödingers did, then you would shower me in praise for my sacrifice in this great pursuit."

Hours on and the wrapped skeletons alongside the unrecognisable Ulla were loaded into the back of a grey van. The white sheet covering Beatrice and her infant prevented the grave diggers from verifying the skeletons, not that they desired to do so. And even if they did, the skeletons provided no hints of the identity of its past owners beyond their height, the conditions of their bones, the clues of past trauma, and their dental assortment.

The two of them, one in the passenger seat and another in the back with the departed, sat in dreaded silence while the engine hummed on their way to save a man on the edge of a cliff. Annabelle, in the back, stared intently at the sheet that revealed the outline of the skeletons beneath. To her, in the days of WRITE infancy, C-1, Beatrice, was a student of Yan's before she ever was a writer. Solomon, an inspirator of the program, was fertiliser for the growth of a creative writing group into an institution of literary excellence. But there she was, C-1, buried by her publisher as Abdelfattah claimed, and there he was, C-14, a couple of miles away being buried by C-1 of the second draft.

Tortured by what she did and perhaps will do, an internal soliloquy ensued. *What did you think of me in life? I was an editor of yours, a responsibility I often neglected and a privilege I often exploited. Would you accept being the pain relief of another in death? Or am I adding to the brutality you were subjected to? If only right assumed the form of a human, for misguidance has assumed the form of two: Yan and Spud.*

Nick stared forward into the abyss of the night, and only in the finality of their journey discovered illumination by a singular light shown at the top of the Osroes house. He found it odd, for not once in his inspections did he notice that light. However, those were conducted during the day, and this would be the first sight of the house in the dark. Perhaps the light always remained on in hopes Solomon would see the shadow of his wife in their room.

The breathing sounds of a slumbering Solomon put the three archaeologists on edge, for every irregularity in his inhales and exhales warranted attention. Would he wake up to find the masters of his perception painting an illusion in his own backyard? Or would he be restrained by the images playing in his head – a sort of infatuation for the awful? Crunch after crunch of the soil beneath to leave a hole two metres long and only one deep. The bottom of their pants now a shade brown each side and the eyes of similar shade whipped them in stride. The guilt-ridden two were passengers of momentum, while the guilt-driven one was the fuel to an engine – a car accelerating with no steering.

The three dead lay adjacent to the shovelers as if to supervise their despicable act. They, the labourers, were grateful that a blanket of black dulled the details of the two skeletons and Ulla's corpse. Perhaps they were also grateful for Solomon's sounds, for not only were they audible indicators of his resting status but they possibly were spared the sounds of maggots scraping the tissue off their acquaintance.

Nick would have shrieked if his vocal cords afforded him the ability to shriek. Instead, as he stumbled backwards, the cracking of branches beneath his weight served as an alternative form of alarm. There was a tugging at the bottom of his pants, that could have only been construed in one manner: the dead had arisen as commanded by The Merchant as comeuppance for unscrupulous acts. Consequently, The Merchant having forgotten the severity of the dead's muscular atrophy, unleashed a benign group of crawling nuisances to execute his will.

Or was it a dog of brown and black fur, with patches of bald spots all over, with luminescent eyes of sorrow that commanded pity, with teeth askew and exposed as if they were escaping to a well-fed mouth, with the hills and troughs of its ribs exposed through skin?

Solomon did not neglect his companion of misery wilfully, but rather fed him as timely as he fed himself and in the same quantities. He believed the dog remained out of habit. It was the only place he had ever known and had Rugrub been presented with the option of a foster family then he would have run away and waved derisively at its previous owner. However, Sol was desperate for his dog to remain for he was a remnant of a nostalgically skewed past.

Having finally brought the whining guard to their attention, Nick was instructed to remain silent. For the first time, Nick saw the devil by Spud's shoulder, straddled to his back, whispering encouragement to him. Yet the devil assumed a palatable form, either because he loved his brother or because the actions Ulla was subjected to were of a larger devil.

The toe end of his boot lodged into the dog's abdomen and sent Rugrub crying into the Wandering Woods. Annabelle and Nick, children to an abusive parent, watched almost helplessly as the animal scurried away. Their sensitivities to his actions had dulled and they were left speechless as once before.

Claimants had proposed that Rugrub survived amidst the wilderness and years on fought off a couple of wolves to gain leadership over the pack. Revisionist squirrels, on the other hand, attested that they had witnessed the dog, which they named Bear Corpse, reside for the rest of its days in a shallow cave. Only one day, the furry animals claimed that a man of nature collected Bear's skeleton and walked off with it in his arms.

By dawn, as the sun broke the barrier of horizon, the proclaimers of Solomon's salvation had returned the dead to the mercy of their bed under a blanket of earth. At their extremities, the tips of their fingers to the edges of their memory, lay a reminder of their vile contributions to a night exhaustive on all fronts. When asked, years later, of the fateful night, each would recount it with varying degrees of detail with mentions of the devil, the sounds of whistling saints hiding in the woods, and attacks of a starved bear.

*   *   *

Three knocks in quick succession and one soon after – a hand against a tabletop, another against the floor, a knee that meets the ground beneath, and a head that follows them all. A clink of a cup was the last of what was heard before the eventual collapse. A wife impelled her husband to join her for a cup of tea, for which terms of reconciliation could be discussed. And had the husband not reacted with regretful aggression in their prior confrontation then hesitation would have defeated his simmering guilt. Nevertheless, Solomon found himself across from Luna losing sight of her as she morphed into a homogenous puddle of her past self and evaporated right before his eyes.

She rushed over to the fainting man and grabbed him by the abdomen and shoulder to support his fall. "I implore you to understand, not today but tomorrow, the maladies you have infected me with," Luna whispered agonisingly as she struggled to handle Solomon's weight.

"For the hell you have made me endure, I wish the same upon you. For your skin to burn and melt off you a thousand times over with no reprieve from the pain. And only after shall you be forgiven by God and embraced into the heavens above," she said vindictively before adding, "I prescribed nothing that you did not deserve. After you have answered for your misgivings, you may have an eternity of peace, Sol."

In response to his mumbles, of which not a coherent word was said, a singular clink of a teacup pried his fingertips off the edge of reality. He was in a room of absolute darkness, yet there was one source of light at its centre – his moon, Luna. Everything flashed, like the entire room was located inside the shutter of a camera, and Solomon found himself with his hands wrapped around her porcelain neck. He beseeched himself to halt the offensive, but his hands would not respond. Soon, he saw cracks emanating from her neck and the entirety of her head

285

shattered into an innumerable number of pieces. In that state, she resembled a broken Russian doll. From the rubble of his destruction, which appeared insurmountably larger than moments before, emerged Shams and Amar, prancing above the mound of their mother's shattered pieces. And Solomon called their name, pleading them to descend to his embrace. They agreed after much coaxing and when they approached their dishevelled father, he soon saw only Luna's face where theirs would be. "Please spare them!" he would yell into the infinite abyss. An echo would respond, "please spare them," yet it did not sound quite like Solomon. The father fell to his knees and sobbed uncontrollably. Another shutter flash, and he found, next to the remnants of his wife, two smaller mounds.

He awoke in his shed with the typewriter serving as a makeshift pillow for his head. Solomon traced his fingers against the imprint of several keys on the right side of his face. A migraine plagued his thoughts, and he could not determine life from death without cracking his own skull and surgically retrieving the information. His mouth dehydrated, eyes bloodshot, and generally fatigued, he found himself incapable of standing up for the first few minutes.

Only after a session marked by its brevity, he staggered across the canal from his island to the mainland with determination to build a bridge. And when he alighted his vessel on shore, he was bewildered by the lack of smoke dancing above the trees and music encouraging it. *Where are all the inhabitants?* At the top of his lungs and in no particular direction, he yelled, "Hello!"

When met with no response, he dashed through the jungle making an express journey towards the nearest town. Branches of nearby trees obstructed him, but he broke through them, sustaining minor scratches along the way.

When the swarm of trees ultimately opened to reveal a town, Solomon was taken aback by its state - abandoned. What better word could describe the huts whose eyes had no pupils. He scrutinised the pathways, the buildings, and any structure subject to human interference but found no evidence that the town was ever inhabited at all. Could he hear the whispers of hiding people? No, it was merely the rustling of leaves as the wind passed through.

Solomon ascended a tower a few stories high at the centre of the town, but as he rose up the winding staircase it appeared infinite. A window the size of his head appeared occasionally and every time he stood to note his progression, he would realise he was no higher than the trees. With every stop at the recurring window, his body would become revitalised as if spurring him on to continue. However long later, he was exhausted mentally by the game of restarts, and chose to give his ascension one final attempt. This time Solomon skipped a step with each push and avoided the allure of windows.

A flat roof greeted him through a window wider than any before. Ahead of him, Solomon could see stretches of desert beyond the jungle vast enough for his vision to betray him. Nonetheless, the signs of life were dim and the probability of existence of the mainlanders within his range waned. Upon turning, he could see the shoreline and in the distance the island of his origins. Its land formed a crescent – an invitation for a hug. Solomon's dejection was followed by descent and in little time he was back at his vessel pushing it off the beach.

As he sailed back to his shed, one push of the oar after the other, he stared back at the mainland with a yearning. Never before had Solomon felt this sensation. For as long as he had known the mainlanders, he desired solitary. Yet he was solaced by visions of smoke in the distance as a declaration of their everlasting presence and love for the hateful man. Oh, how he wished to see the smoke again, even if he were barred from seeing the fire. Solomon stared at the top bedroom window from the confines of his shed, hoping someday for a shadow to reappear.

Part 12: The First of Spring

O' what a sunny day beyond glass,
yet waking up was no little feat.
No matter how malnourished he was indoors,
he remained safe for another day.

Hair had found more growth than him,
yet it was not a necessity to shave.
No matter who would see him on display,
cavemen chose to reside in their caves.

How did he end up at the pinnacle of a mountain he refused to climb? He felt impotent against its incline. Ahead of him, on the flat peak, was a shed, much like his own except for weariness through time, for this structure appeared immaculate. A humanoid emerged from within its depth. It was hunched as a matter of its height against the shed's entrance, but when it ultimately straightened its posture, it was incomprehensible how such a creature would reside there to begin with. Skin of purple, hair of ginger, three eyes of cerulean blue, and an uncanny resemblance to Beatrice that forced Solomon to the ground and made him scurry backwards on all four.

"C-1?! What unholy demon had done this to you?" He yelled from far enough to avoid any physical altercation.

The humanoid's voice was soothing enough to elicit a compassionate stance from Solomon. "How the breeze caresses your skin up here. A hug from an angel, don't you think so?" Beatrice's clone looked off into the distance, shrouded by clouds masking the landscape. "What a dream it is for us to be up here, together, as we once claimed we would be."

What was there on the very top but them? He was suddenly flushed by a sense of loneliness that neglected everything around. Neither the sound of the rushing river, its value unknown to those that were forever there, nor the rhythmic drums of the people halfway up, who found comfort in the repetition, were present to rope him out of the drowning sensation. What treachery it is that success, by his definition, should make him yearn for the people halfway up.

Solomon found confidence in defiance to loneliness and approached the towering being. "What of us now?"

C-1 knelt to bring its height parallel to his. "The choice between two is simple enough that it fails logic." And then the humanoid began to sob. With every tear that made its way to the ground a sizzling sound of its corrosiveness was heard. Beneath Solomon, at the mountain's peak, was ground riddled with miniature craters the size of thumbs. Was he on the moon? For all the indents, the ground's greyness, the thinness of air, and the lightness of his feet mimicked the setting.

"Either we conceal ourselves from mortality up here or we succumb to it down there." And when Beatrice, or her likeness, noticed a consideration in Solomon it had not experienced, it detracted from the magnitude of the decision by adding, "Share with me this sight of the Sun – Oh, the glory – for otherwise, you accuse me of greed."

Solomon sat beside the humanoid on the cliff's edge for hours, which were not dictated by the movement of the sun; the orb remained a constant in its location. The clouds precipitated and new ones formed right before his observation. His eyes would track the droplets in their descent until eventually they combined in a haze that obscured the land below. But in that haze, Solomon would remember a purpose lost to him of his duty to the river people. *The clouds understand more than I,* he would think to himself.

"Are you not suffering?" Solomon was relieved to have finally asked the question. It was a rat burrowing itself out from within.

"A suffering I have known for so long, it's ambiguous to me. So shall it be the same for you, in time."

An impatience, and perhaps a stubbornness too, precluded Solomon from participating in yielding to time. The sharp nail of the humanoid clipped his right hand as he descended beneath the clouds and left the security of the pinnacle above. Although his thoughts danced to the songs of fear and regret, there was also a quality of peace – a slow dance by both emotions as submission to the harmonics of inevitability. He could hear, only faintly, the rhythmic beating of the halfway up people (halfway down from his perspective). Their repetitions synchronised with his heart, and with every slam of the drum, he would feel more alive. If he did not yield to time, it did to him; because he felt his journey was timeless, one with neither end nor beginning, as if he had always been falling.

Eventually, he met the ground next to the riverbank. The blood, which had been forced out of him, seeped its way into the river water. Solomon, his left side demolished by the impact, could see and hear, impaired, from his right. The sight, which was to many unsightly, was of a man whose left side abandoned him and whose right side combined with the earth to sustain him. He could hear the cries of the river people afar.

"The river runs red. What are we to do?!" One of the many spectators exclaimed.

There were murmurs around of divine punishment, others of the frailty of man, and some of neglected duty. Amongst them rose the chief's voice who bellowed, "Are my eyes any different than yours? This is the fruit that falls from a tree that had been planted. But our seed was rotten and, alas, so is the fruit."

"What are we to do?" The river people asked once more as though they had only been taught this one phrase and reared to repeat it collectively as a herd.

A pride of being called upon by the needy was contrasted by the chief's solemn expression. "Good people, great people even, pay no heed to the devil on your shoulders. The answer is good and therefore simple.

We must, as the good people we are, fast from both drink and food for as long as the river remains red, and not by colour alone. Moreover, if your hearts are as good as I believe, then further harvests are to be sent to me, a reflection of your goodness, to assess if the rot had spread to our roots. Gratitude to the Lord."

"Gratitude to the Lord," repeated the river people in unison. The crowd began dissipating.

Solomon saw two blurred figures walking side by side, one consoling the other. "We did not push him up the mountain and away from the Balikh. The boy looked up and never down," the man repeated with a sigh marked by a lack of belief in his own words and a grief he could not mask.

"Have we seeded this rot in him?" The woman cried in her counterpart's arms. "I hear it is silent up there, no river water to drown out the voice of the devil."

And Solomon, upon hearing the two, could do no more than mumble to himself, "Baba? Mama?"

*　　*　　*

To him this was a continuation of past events, and in death he had merely been resurrected back into his shed in the Wandering Woods. *Woes of which no one will ever know lie not in this life but the one preceding.* A thought that would have been dismissed as hyperbolic naivety if afforded the scrutiny of minds. From a slumber, which he was oblivious to, rose a sense of duty. But when his eyes shifted to search for a river beyond, he recollected his geographical tie to the Alienus. With that, his duty progressed onto tangible affairs with regards to an ever loyal and perhaps hungry Rugrub.

A visceral fear travelled down to his stomach. "Where could he have gone?" Anywhere that a dog could, but Solomon's judgement was clouded justifiably. Never, in all the months since his family's passing, had Rugrub left his guarding post just outside the shed. It was either an act of solidarity or cluelessness on his part, but where else would he go?

A combination of tobacco consumption and mouth breathing had left his throat dry, so when he attempted to call for his lost companion, his voice failed him. Harrowed by efforts of rescuing the dog from the wilderness of his imagination, Solomon stood aimlessly in the middle of the yard. Around him were overgrown foreign trees and a house no longer suitable as a home. It was as if the last string holding a veil in front of a canvas had been snipped and the perceived abstracts took definition. In the painting, wide enough to fill the sky, was a person and the Earth at its opposite pole split so that it may concave around them. Their view of the universe was obscured by the Earth because all they could see were the outstretched hands of people above and around. Yet one, even lacking the artistic credentials, would qualify the subject as alone. Contrarians would object, "They are not alone. This entire piece is an illusion of depth where there is none." But even critics could not deny, for they themselves are in a cluster of others at a scale miniscule to the universe, and still in this dense cluster, a concentration significant as far as all know, they feel singular.

The texture beneath his foot was different and struck him as peculiar for no reason other than his lack of direction. With every step, the soil gave way a little more than it did before. As he ran his fingers through the ground, he felt that it crumbled and was soft unlike the soil around, which had compressed with time into a cake of sorts. Solomon treaded a couple steps back assuming the form of a scientist unwilling to contaminate the subject of their study. He winced as a stray branch, amplified by the morning frost, caused a twinge in his barefoot.

When he finally regained his composure, Solomon could see a rectangular patch in the yard that was distinguishable from any other segment of ground. It was darker, not by colour alone, but due to the nefarious activities it hid. To him, there was a master at play, a dictator guiding his fate and they had placed this stray string protruding from a cloth. Solomon was under no illusion that this was the puppeteer's doing, therefore he resigned, with no resistance, to the will of the threads and pulled at a string unravelling a future that would in its eventuality lead to his demise.

Under his nails was a collection of soil and organisms unknown to the eye. His toes were dug into the ground and his knees were supporting the weight of a man turned dog shovelling all that they could behind them. Numbed by the cold soil, his fingers ached and were in danger of seceding their role into this endeavour of truth. No matter, he persevered, and only a couple feet down, perhaps shallower than he expected and had prepared to endure, a white island emerged.

Solomon's heart was a metronome – tick tock – a reminder of his greatest pleasure, his existence within the totality of humanity, his greatest achievement, his existence within the totality of humanity, his greatest ailment, his existence within the totality of humanity, and his greatest disappointment, his existence within the totality of humanity. But as a singularity, humanity concentrated itself into the island and such as an iceberg would, concealed more than it showed. What secrets would humanity keep from him? For, in his limited perspective, humanity in its entirety bore no significant secrets and that all which was right and wrong was clear to all.

Standing there, as white as the island that emerged, Solomon was met with a terrible truth: all of humanity lay beneath the soil he was digging. First, it was all but a cloth, a whiff of decay, and a trepidation about future discoveries. Then, it was a finger, and then two, and by the time Solomon managed to excavate the site, his mind had not yet caught up with his body. He felt a general weakness as though his whole immune system was exhausted from fighting off whatever despicable truth was overwhelming him.

"The river people," Solomon repeated, his voice trembling with every word. He choked to get the phrase out, but it was the only reasonable response to seeing two bodies covered in cloth, one of those an infant, and another body bloated and disfigured. There was comfort in the repetition, but alas, not enough.

The cloth, although protecting him from details, offered little protection because of its translucency and in the way of its outline. Valleys of death were visible as the cloth hung on the ribcage of the larger skeleton. And Solomon, try as he might, could not escape the hollow orbitals, which invited the gaze of spectators more than the most alluring eyes. And then beside the cavity where the chest was, he could deduce the outline of the immature skeleton. His eyes, eyes that the skeleton lacked, welled up. *A child whose scope of life itself is undefined? What – Why do our minds remind us of horrors we wish to forget?* he thought to himself. Then, the disfigured body, bearing the scars of atrocities committed that no garment could mask. One of its arms extended towards the other two figures – a plea for help for life or from it, for those final hours seemed an agonising end with which one may have chosen to escape altogether. The face was unrecognisable and smudged with enough dry blood to donate to another. Its skin was bloated and white like a porcelain doll apart from the few streaks of useless blood vessels.

The entire scene was a painting of tragedy with a symphonic melody playing in the background, and Solomon's heart a harp with plucked strings into palpitations; because although there was beauty in the perfection within convention, the irregularity in the beat reminded us all that there was something unusual about this. And in that irregularity, the way art contorts into a reflection of familiar emotions based on past experiences, the three bodies morphed in front of Osroes's very eyes into Luna, Shams, and Amar.

"Could it be – could it be them? No, I was told by sources of a reliable nature that my spouse and children, the very extension of my being, are missing, lost, and probably far away. Or is it them? Yes, three bodies, two of which are smaller. O heavens! No, it must not be them, for how could I, as a father, fail to find their scent when they were right beneath me? But who else could it be?" The scene contorted some more. "It is them – is it? Yes, it cannot be anyone but them." And then Solomon paused and every emotion within his range expressed itself on his face within those moments. "But who could do such a thing to them and for what reason? May the skies fall on them and the ground swallow them whole." There was a flock of birds that fluttered through the trees in unison as if migrating away from an upcoming disaster. When silence returned to him and the distractions were far enough to be considered negligible, a pain akin to a rubber band being placed around his brain ensued. From that, he could hear three consecutive knocks followed by one soon after. The images of Luna slammed against the wall repeated in his head and he could hear the wailing cries of his offspring. "Could it be – could it be me?"

At the riverbank, after rushing through a length of the Wandering Woods, he dropped to his knees ahead of the Alienus's water and washed both his hands and his face – cleansing himself of evil. As he raised his head from a puddle of water he had formed with both hands, Solomon saw a reflection of the devil in the river. None of its features were unhuman-like, yet the intensity of its pride in response to Osroes's tormented soul lent it a demonic origin. The water had turned dark and opaque and appeared still to the eye. A much more viscous liquid than moments ago yielded in it a quality of ink. *This is not the Balikh,* he remembered and set upon returning to his yard.

A rattling of branches jolted him out of contemplation while he trod back through the woods to the beginning of his end. Osroes's sight shot to the source in investigation. He could see a pair of large glossy white eyes. The figure, however. was veiled by the shadows of the thick trees. Almost in an instant, the eyes shut, and they disappeared seemingly forever. *To hell with it! The devil must have followed me from the river.* Solomon resigned back to his thoughts on his journey back to choice.

Months approaching years had passed since he had last seen his wife and children, but in that time, he had been denied the closure of guilt or innocence. For all those concerned around him, Solomon's family had simply ceased to exist and treated them as fundamentally deceased. Even if they were found, what life was there for them? Either they were dead, or they had left and had chosen not to be found, or they had been taken for so long that they were deceased by virtue of their soul - a most treacherous thought process. But no matter how long Solomon begged the investigators to search for evidence of their outcome, he was never charged or acquitted of any wrongdoing.

Osroes, dishevelled as he was, standing ahead of a grave, stared down with sorrow at a polaroid of the three bodies. He was not scrutinising the photograph as to assess whether his conclusion about the bodies' identity bore the burden of proof, but to lay a foundation of conviction whereby his conclusion was the truth and could be no other. This craving for clarity and resolution was born from the exhaustion of corrosive thoughts day by day, and the shame he held for subjecting his family to the burden of his unrecognised potential.

"What must have they felt everyday seeing their spouse and father unable to produce a single word? To keep them fed, to keep them quenched, to instil in them a belief of life beyond survival – I failed them." He had not uttered those words before, not to them and not to himself. "What must be done now? Beatrice would have known." And there, unbeknownst to him, lay Beatrice ahead of him.

There was a man who was all valued in the pursuit of betterment. A man Osroes himself admired long ago. He was the catalyst to the realisation of the obstacle ahead and how Solomon could overcome it. And no bigger obstacle lay ahead of Solomon now than the salvation of his own soul. Reduced to the essence of a child, he required the parental guidance of Yan. And perhaps not only was Dr. Eadful sought for guidance, but also punishment, for he could not possibly resurrect the dead and Solomon did not know if the damnation in an afterlife would be a severe enough penalty. Yet, that was only partly true, because Osroes himself, though he would not dare admit it, feared death profoundly. It was not only the death of his physicality, but a definitive end to his potential and the beginning of a challenge to his faith.

Forsaken to an expedition of therapeutic exploration, Solomon resolved to escape the self-determined confines in search of help. Nevertheless, he could not venture forth without completing a checklist akin to a pre-travel one, in addition to parading through familiar grounds and bidding adieu. He haphazardly returned the blanket of soil over the victims of his presumed crime. Afterwards, he entered a house he had refused to visit in a long time; he had only entered it before to retrieve a polaroid camera and to resupply on non-perishable goods. Solomon made his way to the top floor, finally turning off the bedroom light which plagued his every nightfall. He could lay the spirit of Luna to rest. When all was done and catharsis was achieved, he marched ahead to a dilapidated building he despised but whose occupant he needed.

*　　*　　*

"Buffoon!" he insulted his brother before adding, "Are you sure he did not see you?"

Nick shook his head nonchalantly with little care for what his brother had to say. He ran his hand over his face and closed his eyes, which Spud took to understand as "he was blind to me."

"We cannot compromise the fabrication of his closure. If he were to believe that the corpses were merely actors, then the fabric of this woven plot would unravel. And do you know what it would reveal beneath?"

The brothers were conversing in a hushed tone, well one of them was, but for no reason other than the preconceived notion that the walls themselves were spies. In their bedroom, laying on parallel single beds, in a household unoccupied by any but them and Annabelle, with her away retaining her bookkeeping duties at the publishing house, their caution levels remained heightened. In total contrast to Annabelle's delightful and tidy bedroom, which supported a bed befit for the

298

connoisseurs of slumber, the room of the Tatar brothers was dingy and deficient in both circulation and hygiene. The blankets on the bed, which lacked both covers and were unchanged for months, were a case study. However, to them, there was comfort in the filth, a sort of familiarity in the cosiness turned extreme, where the secretions of their bodies were forever collected in the room. It was a derivation of their childhood – a façade of trauma turned solace.

Nick shook his head once more, a repetition that would certainly cause his neck chronic strain in the long-term.

"Not a naked man, no," Spud shook his fist to hammer the point in. "Nothing, Solomon would see nothing. That nothing is everything, for the first question anyone and particularly Mr. Osroes would ask is 'what held the fabric up and gave it its structure?' A wound that partly healed yet still bled, would be gaping once more and the man would be lost to his questions."

*　　*　　*

"Would you believe such a thing?" Yan asked rhetorically as he extended the letter towards her.

Annabelle was lost in a train of thought that seemed to circle on itself to the extreme, and neither the end nor the beginning could be differentiated. For months she masqueraded as her senior's faithful bookkeeper to obtain knowledge for her principal benefit – a grout to growing cracks. Although the man, whom all her encapsulated anger had been internally directed towards, only displayed signs of jitteriness and had inexplicably aged a decade, there was no indication of his active role in the persistent disappearance of sought individuals. And her anger towards him began to falter, for Yan to her was akin to a father figure, whose actions perhaps at times represented an outdated ideology, but whose intentions could not be denied. Annabelle felt a modicum of sympathy for the head of the publishing house. *He tries to thread the needle with the least dexterous of hands, but one could*

299

not fault his willingness, she thought to herself.

Ms. Daffodil raised her head, which was nestled between crossed arms. With a blank expression and a scarcity of words, Annabelle grabbed the letter and read to herself.

'It is the least bit acceptable to insert oneself in another's affair, except to counteract a foreign interference. As you have decided to place your hands on mud, you have been requested to abstain entry from this house while we set it back to order. I ask you, gently at first and assertively if you persist, to respect yourself, as we once respected you, and leave this delicate matter behind. You are tampering with the same ideals you once spouted. How can therapeutic exploration be achieved when one is confined to the boundaries set by others? That cannot be! A writer that writes is a writer that is right.

Yours faithfully once but never again,

WWRA'

"The words of lunatics I tell you," Yan chuckled yet shook uncontrollably like he was excessively caffeinated.

Annabelle, the host of an apathetic heart jolted by fear, replied in the affirmative, "No doubt."

"I suspect it to be one of the smaller publishing houses seething from our continued success," Yan continued with enough bravado to shake Annabelle to her core.

What ignorance! I pity him, whose decisions were the subject of my hatred but whose intuition and resolve were once met with admiration. Why would Spud antagonise him in such a manner? While her thoughts were elaborate, she contrived to respond naturally as one unaware of outside players. "No better compliment to us than the grovelling of rivals," she responded with an air of naivety.

Later that evening – the most eventful since the night of exhumation – Annabelle sought to confront the schemer with a wrath she found to be justified upon reflection. It had been raining heavily, but not even the sound of the droplets pattering against the window could mask the slam of a door. She was panting deeply at the main door's entrance when Spud, in his worn nightgown, descended halfway down the staircase.

"Have some manners as to disturb yourself but not others," Spud addressed her crossly.

"Manners? You know nothing of the word," Annabelle replied with enough fervour to unsettle the elder of two brothers. "The fog has dissipated, and I can see clearly now that you derive much pleasure from toying with one who you perceive to be a competitor; to the extent that you would cause such distress to Solomon in the pursuit of this foul competition."

"Beware your accusations lest you lose your tongue," Spud yelled with involuntary spittle escaping the corners of his mouth.

"Your threats ar-"

"Not a threat but a promise," he interrupted her before continuing. "This is no wild west where you can set your guns alight upon entering a saloon, you wench."

Nickel, upon hearing the beginning of an argument, draped his head over the banister at the top of the staircase. His reaction was childlike and akin to the offspring of divorced parents, who were subjected to regular shouting matches. And what a sight to behold, for the child. Two titans of gigantic stature clashed before their eyes as they tried to evade the falling debris descending from the cracks in the sky. However, Nick's childhood was different. He heard his mother, frail as she was, exchange harsh words with one lover after the next. It was not the clash of two titans but the death of one, whose large body fell on top of him so that he was suffocated by his mother's carcass.

There was a prick in the balloon and a little tension managed to escape. Spud recollected himself patting down the nightgown, which had ridden up his legs and crinkled following his animated response. "Friend, Annabelle, have I not sacrificed my entire life for these principles which we now follow? Have I not acted when it was easiest to be passive?" He sighed heavily, assuming the tone of a disappointed headmaster. "It seems that the disease which overwhelmed Yan is infectious, your passion is misguided."

Annabelle would not tolerate his condescension. Although this was the same man that months prior, had brutalised a woman of close relations, she at that moment harboured nothing but resentment. Such was the way with Annabelle, she would fracture a person into different subparts; therefore, she could address each subpart on its own with no relation to the entity in its entirety. It was as if she would pick a section of the human out of a lineup and address them based on their categorised personality, while the remainder watched from afar on a subliminal bench. From Annabelle's perspective, there was: Spud the magnanimous, Spud the deceitful, Spud the brotherly... and many of which she herself could not recount.

"This shall not carry on any longer. Deceit and death are not the pillars of a writer, and I cannot stand here any longer while blood replaces ink." The door slammed once more, and she was out in the rain once more.

As she paced down the sidewalk in the darkness, she contemplated the grip around her heart. *Why do I feel such agony from him, for Solomon – a stranger to my heart?* she thought to herself. Perhaps it was a familiar guilt that strained her strings. Annabelle had tortured Osroes once under the instructions of Yan and now, she was torturing him all again under the instructions of another. It was that similarity she suspected, but could not know, that would drive her mad in pursuit of what was right. For as long as there had been air in her lungs, her decisions had been guided by predefined principles. Whether it was the faith she was brought up on by her orthodox parents, the anarchist manifesto she was allured by during her young and rebellious years, the writing principles introduced by Yan at WRITE, or the denomination of WWRA that brought her and the writing passionists together, Annabelle had operated within the boundaries set by those principles. Nonetheless, the excruciation of that long night would cause her to splinter from her core for the first time.

Presumably washed ashore at Solomon's door by a current she had no control over, Daffodil found herself standing in front of her sufferer's shed. Annabelle had seemingly found her way to his abode and back to painful recollections of Ulla's demise. Search as she could, frantic as she would, Annabelle could not find Solomon. The shed was empty with merely the remnants of smoked tobacco, scrapped writings, and canned food scattered all over a table. His backyard was no different in its dire state and the patch of soil that was once unique had begun to blend in after a period of rain. The house itself, which overlooked all else, was uninhabited and not a single light, top bedroom or otherwise, was on as indication of life.

"Solomon, Solomon," she called repeatedly. "I wish to speak to you. I bring light where you have none. I bring knowledge where you have been deprived of some," Annabelle cried out. Only the rustling of leaves following a gust replied. Her bones ached in the cold, such that her joints were stiff to respond to her erratic movements; her nose, no better, was a shade of red closer to her hair.

The Alienus's water glistened under the moon and was only visible to her in slivers of unobstructed paths through a section of the woods. *Follow the river to its sink, is the water clear enough for you to drink? Trace the river to its source, will the droplets fill you with remorse?* The nursery rhyme played in Annabelle's head and prompted her to visit a place only associated with the degeneration of morals and the inclination towards terror – WRITE. "If I were Osroes, then I would go there," she convinced herself.

Much like Solomon's residence, the hallways of WRITE told the tale of none, for not a single speck of dust was out of place. She refused to visit the yard out of fear of seeing Spud bludgeoning Ulla once more – it was a sight she shamefully curtained with blackout thoughts. Yet, with WRITE it was different. The images of her dancing through the hallways from behind the reception, prancing along the lunchroom, and into the leisure area, Annabelle felt a sense of nostalgia which painted WRITE in hues of gold. Even listening to herself, as an editor, call writers obscenities and subject them to painful exercises was manipulated to appear like a jolly walk through the park.

She collapsed near the vending machine in the leisure room, her black dress still wet from a night of rain. Her chest rose and sank with every breath as she succumbed to sobbing uncontrollably. How her own mind would lie to her, when she knew WRITE to be a house of horrors, confused her. She reminded herself how dreadful Yan was – from subjecting the program's participants to cruelty to defining their purpose and ripping it away. Had she gone out to the yard, Annabelle would have shared similar thoughts about Spud. But to her, there were only two of them, and now, there was only one.

As Annabelle rose to depart before the clock struck midnight, her shoulder clipped against the machine's door. The sharp pain was only noticeable for a moment before she was distracted by the sight of the open door. Only one selection remained in the vending machine 'Soul's Best Bar', which was predominantly disliked by the writers and editors alike. Although she ascribed to no superstitions, she was struck with the belief that the bar, which existed on its own amongst empty rows, bore significance.

"What am I to do with this disappointment of a confectionary?" She held up the bar to herself reading every word on the wrapper with unnecessary scrutiny.

To Annabelle, 'Soul' indicated redemption – an attempt of dragging her own out of a lake of fire. She rushed over to the reception, where she was familiar, from her days as an editor, and grabbed a pen. She did not know yet what to write but felt compelled to do so. *Only a fool would pass up such an opportunity*, she felt for no reason other than the series of coincidental, yet perhaps ethereal, events which brought her attention to the chocolate bar.

And with her body at the mercy of adrenaline, and her mind chained to subconscious superstitions, Annabelle wrote down the address of a figure divine in her eyes. Because, putting aside Glenda's towering figure, the nurse represented a definitively judgmental character whose every word fell blunt and true. That unfaltering belief in one's own words cut through a hedge of murk and represented to Annabelle and her gravitation towards principles a stem with which there was universal agreement.

"May you guide another soul," Annabelle whispered to the bar as she placed back in the same row.

Tears were still streaming down her face and the exhaustion was a secondary thought with this everlasting high. She ultimately returned to the conspirators' household with the same franticness she departed with. After a damp and cold night, Annabelle was sure to be subjected to the effects of hypothermia. But there was no time to consider her own maladies, and as soon as she put a foot through her door, she yelled, only interrupted by short rapid breaths, "Osroes is nowhere to be found. I fear for him."

In parallel to events earlier that evening, Spud was now halfway down the staircase again, however his younger brother had beaten him to the bottom. "You had me worried sick," he said initially with sarcasm before brushing aside his own comment and adding, "What do you mean 'nowhere to be found'? He has no place to be."

"Not the shed, not the house, not even WRITE....", she panted heavily. "The Earth opened up and swallowed him whole."

Nickel approached Daffodil and placed a reassuring arm around her. Once he felt her heart rate drop a level or two, he began gesturing with his hand: One - Man - Solomon - Looks - Up - To. Annabelle was not as proficient with the interpretation of sign language and felt calmer in Nickel's presence but could only stare puzzledly while he moved his fingers. Spud, on the other hand, immediately showed that he understood his brother and was quick to reply.

"The fool! Would he?" Spud pondered loudly, to others but mostly to himself. "Calamitous! We must prevent this exchange at all costs. For Solomon, there can all be madness in Yan's responses. 'My family is not dead? Who are those buried in my garden? Have I lost my mind? What is there to write when reality and fiction blend with no horizon?'"

*　　*　　*

In the small hours, those that exist after midnight and before sunrise, a fog descended on Osroes. This city, a house of his for a decade or so, grew more unfamiliar with every drop of the heel. The fog had only exacerbated this alienation of his surroundings. Fingers caressed the back of his neck – *Am I being followed?* he scanned the area around. Solomon could swear to himself, but not to any authority of his, that there were faces in the darkened windows. *To hell with the devil should he chase me to his own home,* he comforted himself. The sensation of being chased between looming buildings that whispered of his affairs heightened his excitement. Had he any confidence that the faces would not keep pace, he would have sprinted. Instead, Solomon shrivelled under the blanket he had wrapped around him and continued his nervous walk down one street and onto another. As he did, he prayed to God, not for mercy from damnation but to blind him from the face in every foreign window.

The faces became more absolute with each window until he encountered on a bench one with wrinkles deep like ravines of lived stories. Solomon paused to stare at the elderly woman lying on the wooden bench in the middle of a square connecting two streets. She was short and stout, with enough rags to shield her from the assault of

306

the coming winter. Nevertheless, he pitied the pathetic elder, whose situation distracted him from his own. *Only scoundrels would let their own mother sleep in the streets,* his thoughts of pity boiled into fury.

The woman, seemingly subjected to the same sensation Solomon experienced with the watchful faces, woke up to the horror of sympathetic eyes. She shrieked and scurried to the further end of the bench, pushing herself against the armrest. "What do you want? Leave me be!" she cried out.

"Pay no heed to me," Solomon extended his arms assuredly. "I merely came to offer my assistance. What despicable children you have," he let his tongue slip.

Her eyebrows dropped and her rotten teeth now shown, the woman replied, "You are blind sir. No yes, you must be. What assistance could you give me with that ball and chain you drag behind?" Tears had begun to fill the grooves in her face. "I pity you sir. Yes, you! My children neglect me, and I am the subject of their base actions, but still in their prayers I will always be." Her face, momentarily, reminded him of his own grandma and the music of childhood days played in the background. There they were on a veranda with the smells of jasmine and tea dancing on his nostrils. And then the gloom returned.

"But you, your children have no prayers for you. Your children are the very evidence of the rot in your soul," she cackled.

"What did you say?" In an instant, Solomon's blood boiled, and he lunged at the woman's neck.

And no sooner had he pounced than the elder screamed a song of murder. "I beg you, for anything I do not possess, leave me be and may God be merciful."

Osroes paused, unsure whether the woman had even said what he thought she said and continued walking down the other street. As he heard the sniffling of a fearful woman fade into the background, he reflected upon himself, a murderer on the brink of killing another. In a puddle, he saw a giant muskrat, himself, with sleepless red eyes and brown fur, the blanket, masking a filthy man covered in the dirt of his own victims. *How could I bring myself to kill an elderly woman?* Solomon was delirious and petrified yet seething all the same. For a second, he found peace in the jasmine and that second was stripped from him.

Keeping his head down to avoid images of the ungodly faces, his limbs swayed in and out of his view. Pale enough for a corpse and numb from the cold, they appeared foreign to him. Patches of his skin were dry terrains priming to flake. The hair covering his arms and legs were dark enough to appear drawn on, and if it were not for the unfounded determination to arrive at help, he would have scratched himself until every last hair follicle surrendered its role.

The quietude unsettled him and Osroes felt he was in a trance. A feeling unlike any other; only comparable with one WRITE task where the writers were unknowingly fed psychedelics. His cell's floor gave way to his weight and warped downwards till Solomon, young and ambitious, was stood across rows and rows of men and women in a space devoid of colour and dimension. In their natural state, as they were born, the structured rows of people began unharmoniously talking in a language he could not comprehend. Their words sparked a warmth in him - a tiny flame - that burnt from within as if all the blood pumped by his heart was replaced with acid. What was this gibberish that felt like the sun in both its harshness and kindness? And as he rushed between the columns of people with their endless sound, panicking at both his lack of comprehension and the burning sensation, he was halted by a man and a woman at the very last row who spoke in the same foreign tongue - his mother and father. As if a key to the cipher had presented itself, Solomon then recognised all the words.

The trance Solomon experienced during his walk was only similar to the WRITE one by definition. His, now, was an occurrence of senselessness. He felt beyond himself and yet within like a spectator of his own consciousness.

The key in the ignition was followed by rapid repetition. Not only could Spud not force the van to start in the foggiest conditions but also, he could not stop ideas of Solomon's trajectory from whirring in his head. *Where would he go? Where should I go?* His thoughts would pause for a second before circling back around. "Could this vehicle, for the Lord's sake, start?!" He slammed his hand on the steering wheel repeatedly both in agitation and in hope he could resuscitate the dying engine.

Annabelle and Nickel had chased after him, and now standing beside the van, responded in two different ways to his impetuous reaction. Nick had resigned to his brother's imposing momentum and watched from a distance, pleading inwardly, as Spud turned the key. Annabelle, on the other hand, whose spirit could not be confined by her delicate form, began slamming on the window with her open palm repeatedly.

"This is not the way!" she yelled and slammed again against the passenger seat window. "Let the man mourn a loss he does not know of. We have tangled his webs enough." But her cries were much like the suffocated engine sounds – background noise to a flood of thoughts.

Nickel's shouts were inward, although oddly he perceived them as being loud and clear. "Brother, have we not travelled down this path enough? Have we not seen the ruins at its very end? Let us return to our purpose of yesterday and write tales of our people, weary and weak. Let us forget of Solomon, of Yan, of WRITE and all. Let our words speak not to the deaf masses but to the conscious few. And although my words have no utterance to their ears, it may have so for their hearts."

Futile resistance to a man wholly consumed by desire, the engine gave way and started. It roared loud as if to say, "You persistent fool! I am trying to save you." However, by then, Spud was already on the cobblestone and halfway down the road. The fainting calls of Annabelle could be heard. "A beast of desire." And Nick, for his part, was overwhelmed with regret over directing the shooter's gun. He hoped, with no conviction, that the madness that had overcome his brother a few months prior was not a lingering virus in incubation.

*   *   *

Like a rabid dog, he had been breathing from his mouth. When he ultimately closed it at the thought, Solomon could taste the iron from his bleeding gums. His fingers fidgeted about, searching for a cigarette to substitute the flavour. There was none to be found and the realisation sent Osroes down a whirring path of anxiety. How he wished, for that moment, to watch the smoke escape his mouth and dance to the skies above. He would imagine part of his soul being stripped with the rising plume sneaking its way through the gates of heaven.

Having walked more than he had known, the shame that had drawn his eyes to the ground was countered by curiosity. Across the sidewalk was where both Yan's heart and head resigned. Solomon had tracked his mentor's progression in life hoping for his demise but fearing for his downfall. There was yet an admiration for him that loomed large; its essence sown into the very fibres of the once student's heart.

The windows of the building, like all-seeing eyes, caused in Osroes a state of dissociation – an extreme to the tobacco escapism. Verandas and behind them shutters of white and beige, plants that dove towards the ground as if to beg for water, washing lines that spanned across the street, music of a foreign tongue ('The breeze blew upon us from within the valley. O breeze, for the sake of love, take me home'), the smell of bittersweet marmalade being prepared on top of a stove, and the draping of intricate tablecloths from the verandas' railings – none of it notable to another onlooker, and yet it produced an effect within.

The fog created an effect akin to Eadful's ever-drooping brows, which seemed in a state of constant disappointment. Was there no building beside it? This structure of uninspired build and a fatigue of generational mediocrity, was there no more to it? Despite its blandness, Solomon felt its majesty. A house of stories, of morals, of guidance, of answers... of answers.

Although Solomon, sunken into his own self and separated from his own body, had no will to venture forth, the building, as if it had grown arms, dragged him through its main entrance. The smell of jasmine slammed him in his face. Seemingly delicately placed, there were Damask roses all around him in an arch. The entire hallway was bright and adorned with blue and white ceramic tiles displaying mosaic patterns. Through the bright hallway, towards the core of the building, was an open courtyard right out of his grandparents' dreams. In its middle was an octagonal fountain that ejected water at a low enough pressure that one could assume it needed a mechanic. There were trees of oranges and lemons, which held their fruit ripe. Between one tree and another was dark wooden furniture inlaid with enough mother-of-pearl to blind. And from a mezzanine right above, he could hear others speak in the same foreign language he heard in his trance. However, in this instance, the people speaking had a tone that travelled through his ears like droplets of olive oil – coating the entire canal and leaving a sense of warm pressure towards his drums.

Painting after painting, Solomon walked past women in various states of purpose, carrying jugs of water on their heads, kneading bread, and reading books in their traditional attire. He was in awe and after having felt like he had spent years exploring the glory of it all, he arrived at a door unlike the others before. It had brass hinges and a knob on a frame of varnished wood with its centre replaced by a slab of frosted glass. A pungent odour, one of death, crept from beneath and in the haziness of the door's window, he could see a macabre essence. Again, Solomon urged himself to resist the whispers of morbid curiosity, but such is the instinctiveness of Osroes, for he found his hand wrapped around the doorknob.

No sooner had his skin touched brass that Solomon's consciousness floated back to its rightful place. The entire paradise around him collapsed into a singularity, invisible to the naked eye, and was replaced by sorrowness of monotonous architecture. Rigid geometrical shapes, ones structural engineers wished for, defined each hallway. The colours of the walls and ceilings were bland to the extreme, such that hues of cigarette smoke and cracks of water damage evolved a character that the original artist themselves could not envisage. What tragedy it was to waste a canvas, the potential of it all, for the brutality of the mundane.

He rubbed his fingers again wishing for a cigarette to materialise, but instead he felt a file in one hand and the doorknob in the other. Osroes had been walking with the file tucked away beneath his arm under the blanket. *What is this thing, the object of my damnation, doing here?* And then his eyes shifted to the doorknob. *And what is my hand, the reason for my damnation, leading me to?* He was mortified by his thoughts, frozen by his own fear.

His hand, acting of its own accord, slid the file underneath the door. But Solomon dropped to his knees, cursed his own appendage, and began a panicked exercise of pushing his fingertips beneath the door. However, whilst attempting to retrieve the papers, a voice, only commanding due to its suddenness, enquired from the other side about his identity. Osroes stood up, hoping this was an extension of his periodic hallucinations. The voice again enquired, this time a little shakier.

An outline of a person appeared across the frosted glass. In reaction, Solomon jolted towards the exit he had been dragged through. He clipped the file cabinet and slammed into the bookkeeper's desk, but nothing would stop the staggering man from escaping the confines of his own actions. With his bare feet, he could feel the worn oak with each step. *What other rascals have escaped this same route?* he thought to himself. To Solomon, everything around was placed by a sadist for the purpose of suffocating him. His very breath, which he drew from excessively during his ascension to the ground floor, was dense and resisted the will of his lungs. Osroes's erratic climb was akin to a rag doll being pulled by its tip. He felt weak and would have gladly fallen to his back had it not been for his head.

Osroes, like a caged parakeet set free, was out and stood across the sidewalk where he once was. The fog was thicker now, and his own body was clouded by it. The building, barely visible, he had only just run out of, was nothing like it was when he first beheld it. There were no verandas or white shutters or music for that matter – just concrete. And the structure no longer looked down upon him in disappointment; there was an empathy to those windows, plain and square as they were.

This is the action of two minds, and I hope either is right. And if either is right, then which? I killed my family - No! Did I? Then, I come here to kiss a boot for a shred of salvation. Yet here I am retreating from the very possibility I might attain it. What cowardice! Am I ashamed? Less than a decade later and no novel to show for it. And better yet, no family to support me through it. I must have killed them because it would have been impossible to look them in their eyes every day and lie about the genius of my work. Did I? I cannot have. Perhaps I could have killed one. Perhaps Luna could have thrown the bricks I had been laying all around me in mockery and in a moment of psychotic rage, I threw one back at her head. Perhaps. But all three of them? Would guilt not have arisen after the first brick was thrown? Would my shame have been multiplied that I would kill Shams and Amar but to spare myself the pain of watching harboured hatred in their eyes? And here I am, at Yan's abode, proclaiming it with such confidence that it must be so – and I must be so – therefore it must be done. What hell is this? Have I underestimated the creativity of the devil? Moments ago, I could hear the angels speak in a foreign tongue. Was I in paradise? And willfully, I chose to touch brass and return to hell.

Hah! The comedy of it all.

In those moments, a figure emerged from the building's main entrance. It displayed the same erraticism driven by nervousness that, waning in Solomon now, was at its peak during his ascension. To the spectator across, the figure appeared to be a reflection of him, only staggered by time. Coup de grâce – a desire arose in Osroes to kill his own self, standing the width of the road away, to spare it the experience he had just gone and will go through.

Is this the road I have travelled? One with no other direction but to murder three times in quick succession and then to murder once more? I must not... Solomon thought to himself.

The figure took a couple of steps onto the cobblestone, standing in the middle of the road. It was frantically searching left and right for the file's owner. There were words uttered but were unintelligible to Solomon. He just stood there, in silence, camouflaged by the fog, spectating the actions of the figure. He knew, in certainty, that it would walk over in a few moments and assume the position he stood in currently. Osroes believed they would be merged in past and present, and their future trajectory would become clearer.

But all that was expected was interrupted by the bellowing of a bull. The beast's sound was constant and reverberated throughout the fog. Its eyes, yellow, bright, and round, penetrated through the thick haze. The figure was either stuck admiring its magnificence or shell shocked by fear. It was charging straight at the figure with full speed. And when the light of the bull's eyes fell onto the figure, Osroes cried out.

He recognised the man by his cerulean eyes. And before the bull could decimate Yan, Solomon ran ahead and grabbed him by his robe. Osroes pulled Dr. Eadful towards him with enough might. Although, for anyone around, the events transpired in mere moments, for Solomon and Yan, it felt long enough to write an entire novel about. The senior, in his robe and slippers, was mostly out of harm's way except for a trailing foot that was clipped by the charging bull. Both, former student and lecturer, fell to the ground, staring forward at the rear end of the beast. It was awfully metallic and appeared much like a van.

Once he regained a modicum of composure, Yan stared forward at his saviour. Sweat beads formed on his forehead and his heart was about to give out, but he felt compelled to extend a few words. However, he did not know which – words of gratitude for saving his life, words of query about the photographs he had just seen, words of reprimand for the murder of three others, words of apology for leading him up a false mountain and pushing him off, words of wisdom about how to adjust the course of his life, words of encouragement to complete his magnus opus, words of warmth for seeing an old friend, word of... words failed him, and he found himself incapable of uttering any except for these:

"O but many are the woes of Osroes." Both men wept side by side for the very beginning of the end.

www.ingramcontent.com/pod-product-compliance
Lightning Source LLC
Chambersburg PA
CBHW031323210726
48287CB00005B/1665